I0563838

THE BEST WEIRD FICTION OF THE YEAR

VOLUME 1

CURATED BY
MICHAEL KELLY

UNDERTOW
PUBLICATIONS

To romanticize the world is to make us aware of the magic, mystery and wonder of the world; it is to educate the senses to see the ordinary as extraordinary, the familiar as strange, the mundane as sacred, the finite as infinite.

— NOVALIS

CONTENTS

ONCE MORE INTO THE GREAT, WIDE WEIRD

MICHAEL KELLY

From 2014 to 2018 I was Series Editor for the *Year's Best Weird Fiction*, an anthology launched not only to showcase some of the superlative strange fiction being published, but to also provide a home to often unclassifiable modes of fiction that were not, in my view, being represented in other 'Year's Best' or 'Best Of' anthologies. A dedicated volume of the weird. An anthology to fill some of those genre gaps. There is no shortage of 'Year's Best' anthologies. Some quite good. Some actively filling those gaps. But there will always be gaps. Some driven by commercial market concerns, some by taste and aesthetics. This new volume will strive to be in conversation with those other anthologies, while hopefully providing its own unique perspective.

But what exactly is Weird Fiction? It's something I've addressed in those earlier volumes, to be sure. And as mentioned above it can often be unclassifiable and hard to precisely define. You'll get varying definitions from different people. For the purposes of this series, I will crib a short note from a previous volume: In my view weird fiction is speculative, and often (but not always) works to explore and subvert the laws of nature, or the natural order. I like to think of it as an unceasing distortion and buckling of ambient space and time; where plot, theme, atmosphere and voice coalesce. Hence, the lens from which you view the world is askew and occluded. A feeling. A mood. A sense of dislocation. Weird fiction is a large umbrella, encompassing many modes of fiction. Before genre rules were established, weird fiction could be said to consist of the science fictional, the ghostly supernatural, the mythical, the cosmic, and the fantastic. An extensive mode of literature. In that regard it shares many properties with its Horror brethren. It's why weird fiction is, I'd say, most commonly associated with horror fiction.

This absence of specifics will frustrate some. Contemporary writers Emily Alder, Andy Cain, Mark Fisher, Zachary Gillan, Scott Nicolay, and Simon Strantzas have all articulated their thoughts on Weird Fiction. And my views overlap strongly with Fisher's very broad notions of weird fiction. Particularly in his idea of a 'sense of wrongness.' There are likely stories in this volume that contemporary critics and essayists would not consider weird fiction. Overtly SF or fantasy, perhaps. But I'd argue there is a profane provocation and/or transcendent vision, bold or subtle, that imbue these tales with a sense of the numinous. In that regard I have made an attempt to cast as wide a net as possible; to present exactly 25 stories that display the extensive range and diversity in the field. To showcase a multiplicity of genres and voices. Whether you consider them specifically weird fiction, or not, they are stories that sit, perhaps uneasily, in the borderlands of the fantastic.

So, my remit will be broad in scope. The alien. The other. The surreal. And sometimes simply the *weird*. As noted writer Simon Strantzas posits: "Instead, these sorts of stories exist in a liminal world of rationalities where things are *not quite right*. Slightly askew, their axes tilted, they are stories where the everyday is corrupted just enough that the strange can leak through."

Weird fiction, perhaps more than any other mode, is fluid, adaptable, and ever-changing. I certainly take an expansive view of it, not constrained to the American-based strand (terror and awe) or the European-based (strange tale).

In short, if it's weird or strange or irreal, and occupying a liminal space, floating between genres, it may find a home in these pages.

NOCTURNAL

NATALIA THEODORIDOU

Originally published in *The Rumpus*.

Natalia Theodoridou is a transmasculine writer whose stories have appeared in publications such as *Kenyon Review*, *The Cincinnati Review*, *Ninth Letter*, and *Strange Horizons*, and have been translated into Italian, French, Greek, Estonian, Spanish, Chinese, and Arabic. He won the 2018 World Fantasy Award for Short Fiction, the 2022 Emerging Writer Award by Moniack Mhor & The Bridge Awards, and the Nebula Award for Game Writing in 2025. Born in Greece, with roots in Georgia, Russia, and Turkey, he currently lives in the UK. His debut novel, *Sour Cherry*, a queer Bluebeard retelling about toxic masculinity and cycles of abuse, came out in April 2025 from Tin House (US) and Wildfire (UK).

AFTER MOTHER PUTS you to bed and you're almost asleep, another woman appears at the threshold of your bedroom door, backlit, her hair haloed by the yellow light of the hallway. She looks just like your mother, except she's taller and there is no love for you on her face.

There is, however, an urgency.

And, urgently, she tells you stories.

She tells you about a woman she knew when she was growing up. Her name was Stella. She was married to a guy with a motorbike. She was always dressed in black, and she had long, dark hair that she covered with a sheer, black veil. Her skin was very, very pale because she would never go out during the day. But at night, her husband would take her on his motorbike, and together they went drinking around town. They had no children. She laughed a lot. Her teeth were very white, her tongue an annihilating red.

"What happened to her?" you ask, your breath growing cold in your lungs.

But your mother doesn't reply.

Instead, she tells you another story, about a monster that used to live in the swamp outside that same town, where Stella lived, where your mother grew up.

Nobody had ever seen it, but everyone knew it was real. In summer, the town filled with the monster's scent, heavy and damp, like freshly turned soil and rotting leaves.

Many men went after it with rifles, or with spears that they fashioned out of broken garden tools. Stella's husband went too. Nobody ever came back.

"Why are you telling me all this?" you ask your not-mother, your other-mother, but she just looks at you with her other eyes, her other mouth set in a harsh line. "Are you trying to scare me?"

"Are you scared?" she asks.

"No," you lie.

So she continues.

She tells you that the monster was small, almost the size of a child. She tells you about its jaws that were perfect circles rimmed with razor-sharp teeth and about its delicate wings that trailed behind it like a bridal veil. It had fins, too, and long, thin spines. It balanced on its back legs and had a snake for a tail. It walked haltingly, like something drunk, but, when it wanted to, it moved so fast that no one could get away. Whoever heard its roars could only stand stunned with fear while the monster went for their throats. Ate them alive.

You don't ask how she knows all these things.

The woman looks at you to see if you're scared now. You're not. Or you are, but you're also sad more than you are scared. You're sad for the monster that was born out of the swamp, alone and unlike any creature in the whole world.

You never find out if the nocturnal mother was real or if your mother was aware of this woman and her stories, her nightly visits. You never confront your mother about it either. Occasionally, when she drifts off and stares at the wall, her gaze reminds you of the overcast eyes of that woman at your bedroom door. But then she snaps out of it; she looks at you and smiles, her face full of love. "It was nothing," she tells you, putting her hands on you, her skin clammy on your skin, her lips tight, answering a question you never asked. "It was really nothing."

All you want is to grow up, and so you grow up. You go to high school, then college to study history because you like making sense of old stories and buried things. At the library, you sometimes do a search for "night mother" and "mother double," but nothing helpful ever comes up.

You become busy, working your way through college to pay for your degree. For a long time, you forget about the nocturnal mother altogether. You tell yourself she was a nightmare. Something your childish mind made up to scare you. You move away, leaving your mother to live alone in that house with the attic and the basement that nobody ever mentioned when you were small. You do a master's degree in genealogy and family history. You make friends. And every so often you stumble across a memory you didn't know you had. There's the image of Stella moving away from the edges of the swamp in her black dress and her black veil and no tears streaming from her eyes. There's the old rolltop desk you discovered when your mother asked you to help clear out the attic. The desk was locked, but you had it opened with the help of a locksmith. There was a yellowed notebook inside, its pages covered in scrawled handwriting. It contained no dates and no names, but it was full with what you could only describe as stories written from the point of view of the monster. You thought of them as the monster's adventures, and the more you read them, the more you became convinced it was Stella's diary.

But then you fall for a girl who's always dressed in black and you forget about all of that again. She slips into your dorm room on cold nights when you're almost asleep, and you think it's your mother again, come to tell you stories. Her hair is haloed by the yellow light that streams from the corridor outside, her skin very, very white—you think it's because she's never gone out during the day. Her lips an annihilating red.

One night, sleeping next to that girl, you dream of your mother. You're a child again. You know it's a dream because you're sitting by a campfire, on the desolate beach of a black ocean. Your mother appears suddenly, a cocoon of a woman backlit by flames. She doesn't come any closer. Her eyes are dead, the color of a swamp. She opens her mouth to show you the emptiness inside.

You call her in the morning, ask her about those stories she used to tell you, but she says she doesn't remember. "Wasn't there a swamp outside the city where you grew up?" you insist. You half expect her to say no, there was no swamp, there was never any swamp, but instead she says, "Not anymore. They had it drained years ago."

"Did they find the monster?" you ask her then, and immediately you bite your tongue, as if you allowed something unspeakable to be spoken. You imagine her looking away, the phone held loosely in her thin hands, the clammy skin you haven't felt on you for so long. She says she has no idea what you're talking about, her voice cold and flat like a surface. You ask her why Stella never had children, and at first you think she's not going to reply, but then, as she's hanging up the phone you hear her say, "Why would she?"

You don't talk about it again for a couple of years, and

you make it through long stretches of time when you don't think about your mother at all. You break up with the girl in black, amiably. You crave the silence of your childhood home, the hollow vastness of the valley that surrounds it. You find yourself missing the nocturnal mother at the door of your childhood bedroom. You move back.

She returns then, even if only in your dreams. You remember her clearly, in all her detailed glory, the way she smelled of clean blood and rotting leaves. The way she tilted her head and pointed at her throat. This time, she doesn't always stand at the threshold, backlit by the corridor, but sometimes waits for you in bed. White skin and black hair. Red lips and dead eyes. She's all bones, her breasts covered in white scars. She tells you to come closer, and you obey—she's your mother, after all. You sit next to her and she leans over you, her mouth full of mother-teeth. She whispers, "It's almost your turn now. Do you remember what I gave you?" When you wake up, you cry because you don't.

When you think of Stella, you imagine her with your mother's face, which makes you want to have a child of your own. A bit of your flesh, a splash of your blood. You imagine what stories you'd have for your child if you became a mother. You tell yourself you'd shun your mother's stories, would spare this child the horror of your dreams. This is what you wouldn't say: All families have their origin stories, and for your family, the swamp is it. It's where you all come from. You leave it, but it never leaves you. Its monsters are your monsters. If you close your eyes at night, if you open a window and sniff the air, you'll always be able to catch a whiff of it, that rotting stench, that depth. The dead, forgotten things.

You want to think you'd tell a different story. Something softer and more comforting.

But then you really do have a baby and, finally, you understand. It's a girl; of course she's a girl. She has your mother's eyes. Your mother helps you, teaches you how to hold her, how to feed and clean her. But she's frail now; she tires so easily that you send her to her room with the order to rest and not worry about you. "As a baby," she says, "you cried all the time."

You decide to call your daughter Stella.

Your daughter gets the same stomachaches you had when you were a toddler. You spend endless hours holding her to your chest, wrapped in a blanket, not knowing how to protect this tiny creature. In the end, you try to soothe her by simply showing her she's wanted. When she quiets, you fall asleep right there in the chair. In your dreams, you walk out into the night, into the swamp, with an axe in your hand and no fear in your heart. You touch the soft mud, sink your whole hand into it, up to the wrist. It smells impossibly sweet. You look for the monster, with its circle of teeth, its fins and spines, but you never find it. And when you wake up, you cry. You don't know why. You cradle your baby and promise her you'll never tell her stories of teeth and fear, of mothers and daughters fighting to love each other, of that terrible, cloying need, of things given, and taken, and given up. Your daughter's hair smells like moss and thunderstorms, and that makes everything okay.

The difficult first year passes, and so do your daughter's aches. Your mother stays with you, but you never talk about the swamp again, or the Stella of old, or the monster. She wears her heavy earrings, black, each with a round piece of amber hanging from a loop. When you kiss her, her skin tastes like leather and ashes.

You reconnect with that girl dressed in black. She wears other colors now, sometimes, purple and teal and a dark cypress green. She has pierced her eyebrow, which makes her eyes look uneven and depthless like a cat's. You take her out, leave your baby with your mother at home. You go to the movies, the swamp monsters frequent and laughable. You don't tell her about the nocturnal mother, the stories of the swamp, your black ocean dreams. You get milkshakes and a burger. You make out in the back of your car. She thrills when you don't hold back and take her piercing into your mouth, the taste of metal burning your tongue. She has a sadness in the corners of her lips but feels like midday heat and dark roses. You invite her to stay over, and she likes your daughter, and your daughter likes her back. She offers to stay with Stella while you go to work, which is sometimes an office where you spend your days as a data entry clerk and sometimes a diner where you wait tables. In the end, it makes more sense for her to move in, so she does. Your daughter is a toddler now. She says her first words. She calls you both "Mama." Most days, if anyone asked you, you'd tell them you're happy. Your mother passes away the autumn after your daughter learns how to speak. In the weeks before, you spend more time with her. It's the closest you ever come to talking to her plainly about your childhood nightmares, the stories, the swamp. When you ask her if she knows any bedtime stories you should tell your daughter, she tells you stories are like vaccines. "Vaccines?" you ask and she says, "Yes. Vaccines to guard against the cruelties of the world."

She's less and less lucid after that. You spend the afternoons by her bedside and then, later, you grieve her briefly and intensely. You empty out her room and throw away almost everything. Even Stella's diary, which you find under your mother's mattress. You hold onto so little, these days. Not even then do you tell your wife about your night mother —afraid, perhaps, of summoning her, now that your real mother is no longer there to keep her at bay.

Time passes like a thick, slow-moving river. You go back to work at the office and the diner and the movie theater where you show people their seats in the dark with your little flashlight, because there is no employment for historians in love with swamp monsters and their family secrets. You never dream of that vast, black ocean anymore. You never dream of anything at all, and, for that, you're grateful.

But then there are times when, as you put your daughter to sleep, you catch yourself hesitating at the threshold of her bedroom door, with the sound of another heartbeat in your ears, distant and ancient. Your daughter looks at you with your mother's eyes, and you stand there, something fearful and spiny growing around you and in you, the taste of dark water filling your mouth, like a story.

OUR BEST SELVES

HIRON ENNES

Originally published in *Weird Horror #9*.

Hiron Ennes is the British Fantasy Award-winning author of **Leech**. Their novel **The Works of Vermin** was published in 2025. In their spare time, they're a rogue harpist and a mad doctor. Their areas of interest include forensics, infectious disease, and petting your dog.

THE HOUSE IS a squat trapezium of stone, fissured like the trunk of a tree. Its cracked slab of a roof slumps under centuries of vines, piebald with moss. When our cab approaches, a small owl rustles from a window and flutters up to the canopy.

Mum takes to it right away. She stumbles from the taxi with the cat in one arm and my brother in the other, leaving a trail of dropped objects behind her. Dad tries to mirror her enthusiasm. He picks up after her, snatching gloves and socks and booklets like a hen pecking. He wears a patient smile until he gets to the doorway, where he finally sees the magnitude of his fixer-upper. The floors are dirt. Leafy columns of light tumble through the cracks in the roof. A possum hisses in the entryway.

His wife is nothing but pleased. She circles the house, examining crumbling furniture carved from the same stone as the walls. Crude marble cylinders pass for stools. Slabs like tombstones mark the headboards. My brother wipes dust from a windowsill to find it trimmed in obsidian.

I slip through a fissure in the wall to the garden. Mum is already out there, bending over the mossy quadrangles of stone. She digs through the hardened earth, appraising the crumbling soil. There are plenty of things already growing. Berries, shrubs, apple trees, a couple of wild tubers. The canopy is thin, and there are soft patches where she can build more beds. Even the shady bits will be wrapped around her green thumb soon enough.

She rounds the stone fence and points out where she'll plant the spinach later this week. Where the beets will go, the tomatoes, her meticulously engineered squashes. She runs her boot through the brush, demarcating the beds, but my eyes have already wandered.

A sapling rustles by a window on the north side of the house. It's not an ash, not a maple, not an oak—its leaves, long and dark and strange, undulate in my direction. I know a greeting when I see it, so I step over to brush its bark, soft, smooth as skin, and dusted with fine green hairs.

"What's this one?" I ask Mum.

"I don't know, darling," she answers. "But I think it's yours."

THE FIRST NIGHT, we claim our rooms. If they can be called rooms. Some only become rooms when we drape Mum's tapestries over their missing walls. Others are completely closed in by vines writhing up from the floor. None has a door.

A fissure in the north wall widens into a sort of window,

looking out on the sapling. I want the bed closest to it, but my brother gets there first. I decide to fight him for it, and neither of us will budge. He's got his eye on that tree, and he doesn't believe me when I say it's mine.

In the end, Mum claims the room for herself and Dad. She says it's because she does not want to see us fight over it. She tells us that when we are squabbling, we are not our best selves, and we must always strive to be our best selves.

Dad lays their blankets down over the bed-slab and agrees.

"When you think about it, your mother and I are the unlucky ones," he says. "This is the only room that doesn't have a view of that beautiful night sky."

A WEEK IN, Dad takes his axe on a foray into the woods. He's decided that before he can install the floor panels, carve doors and shutters and repair Mum's loom, and especially before the rain comes, he must fix the roof.

My brother and I find pieces of it scattered around the property. We're supposed to be finishing our schoolwork, but we circle the yard, cutting away ferns and unburying dozens of wide, broken wedges. They lie scattered in every direction —a few have fallen so far that the cat won't follow us out to them, preferring to sit and yowl in the doorway. My brother wants to gather the missing pieces and fit the roof back together like a puzzle. He quickly learns that none of us could lift the smallest fragment.

"How did the roof break, anyway?" he asks me.

"Earthquake," I say, because I can't think of anything else with enough force.

He goes silent for a while, watching Dad pile his cuts at the edge of the garden, thin trunks that look similar to pine but smell much sweeter. Sap dark as mud oozes from their axe-bites.

"How was the house even built?" my brother asks.

"There's mountains nearby," I answer. "The builders chipped off slabs and carried them down here."

"Why?" He gestures to the trees, a verdant abundance of beams and floorboards and shingles. "And how?"

"They were giants," I answer. "It was easy for them. This is just their dollhouse."

"No, it's not."

"I'm serious. We're their dolls. Once they know we're here, they'll come play with us. Put you in a little dress, snap your limbs off."

I've gone a step too far. He frowns and floats over to Mum, who's planting her greens in neat, straight rows. He leans up to her, and she shakes her head.

"Don't lie to your brother," she hollers. "Those who lie are not at their best."

I sigh and look to the sapling at the end of the garden. It shudders and waves, though there's no wind I can feel.

———

THE CAT IS NO LONGER STRICTLY an outdoor cat, since there are no longer strict outdoors. He wanders through the fractures of the house day and night, chattering, kneading, marking.

Dad says he can't get the smell of piss out of his nose. He wonders aloud if he should abandon the roof and prioritize making doors.

"He's a pest," Dad says.

"He's the only reason why we're not overrun with rodents," Mum answers. She skins a few tubers at the sink, paring knife glinting with remarkable speed.

"At least let's keep him out of our room. He makes you wheeze."

"He doesn't —" she stops herself. She's not going to say the cat doesn't make her wheeze, not after what she's just told me about lying.

"And the hives," Dad says. "Your condition worries me as it is."

Mum gives him an irritated frown. "I don't have a condi-tion," she answers, slowly, each word a careful guess.

She sets down her tubers and retreats to the garden, where she walks along her fresh rows for the rest of the evening. She doesn't even come in for dinner, after I have finished the paring and Dad the boiling, when my brother has set our stone table with stone plates. For hours, she paces and mutters among her seedlings. She is praying fervently, and against Dad's wishes, for rain.

EVERY WOMAN in our family has exactly one daughter. There are no sisters, no cousins, no childless maids, so our family tree is a thin, straight vine. All our knowledge of horticulture and herbalism descends in this way, unbroken and perfectly linear. The genealogies of our squashes are far more tangled.

My mother has already taught me most of it. She taught me which plants are friends and which aren't, which to eradi-cate and which to cultivate, which animals are pests and which tinctures might kill them. She taught me how to skin a tree, to soak and dry and flatten its pulp into paper, how to prune a tomato's limbs so the others proliferate unimpeded, how to select for traits that help our lineages grow into their best selves.

Despite her teachings, I can't identify the plant that has grown at the foot of my bed. A collection of dew has sprin-kled through the hole in my ceiling, coaxing a green shoot from the ground. Overnight it's crawled up the granite slab of my mattress.

When I poke my head into Mum's room, telling her I've found something new, she says she's feeling faint. She's tucked in bed with the cat and neither are willing to move. She'll hold out for as long as she can, until the blankets are soaked and we have to clean up the blood.

"Make me my tea," she says.

I retreat to the kitchen and grab her jar of little red pills. I steep them with the rest of the leaves while she groans in her room, more frustrated than pained. She's been trying for so long to wean herself off the stuff, the same way she's weaned off every medicine that came before. I hate the tea, but not because it smells like rot and looks worse, but because I am afraid, one day, that I'll need it too.

DAD COMES home with what he thinks is a boar but what may be something else. It's four-legged and hairless, long neck sagging on his back as he trundles back to the house. We help him drag it to the porch and watch him get to work with his knife.

"It's been so long since I've had any meat," he says, elbow-deep in blood. "My poor belly's sagging." He slaps his navel, leaving a splattered red print.

"We'll have you fed properly when the garden comes in," Mum tells him. "You just have to wait."

"Time is a necessity," I say.

"And what else?" Mum asks, smiling.

"Rain, sun and soil," my brother says, "are the only necessities."

"Very good."

The blood drips from the porch into the garden, where the early squashes grasp skyward. The sapling stands nearby, branches brushing the half-finished awning. Either it's grown taller in the past couple days, or it's gotten closer.

DAD MANAGES to patch the roof by the first rains. It starts as a gentle patter, then, early in the morning, becomes a downpour. We are jolted awake by a deep, resounding snap, far closer than thunder. The house shudders with the echo of the rumble, and we all crawl from our beds.

In the kitchen, we find a pool of water, whirling around notches of wood and stone. Above our heads, a new fissure bolts through the ceiling, zagging from the hearth to the table.

Dust and rain fall from the crack, pattering against our firewood.

Dad rolls a stool under the breach. He blinks through the thin sheet of sky-lit water, then lifts himself up to the crack. We clutch our nightgowns and watch his hand disappear into the fissure. He stills for a moment, frowns, then pulls a thin, long vine from the crack. He wraps it around his wrist, then his arm. Soon it's curling at his feet, yards and yards of leaf-less green.

When he finally snaps it from the crack, he's soaked. I'm not sure if it's rainwater or sweat.

"The cat is bad for you," Dad says. "We need to get rid of it."

"Don't you dare," Mum replies, wiping her nose. She is bedridden again today. "It's just the season. The pollen. It's gotten so thick."

She's not wrong. Gold dust has settled in with early summer, falling like snow through our open windows. Our sideboard, a recent project Dad painstakingly carved from oak, hasn't shown its surface in days. When we close our schoolbooks, we do so in puffs of yellow powder.

"He makes your eyes water," Dad says. "He wrecks your lungs —"

"He doesn't." If Mum wasn't already lulled by her tea, she would notice how badly she's lying. But she is not her best. Her face is pale and dotted with sweat.

"It's not the pollen," Dad continues. "You know it—that animal is bad for your health, and your health is the whole reason we're out here."

"My health was an excuse," Mum replies. "You're happy here."

Dad's breath softens, his pause heavy. "Sure."

A FIRE BURNS in the hearth. The flames flicker blue and cold, so Dad gets another log. It slumps, soft and wet, like the last three.

"We shouldn't burn those," I say. "They're moldy."

He doesn't seem to hear me. "God," he breathes. "What I wouldn't give for a beer."

"Mum will kill you if you go back to town."

"Just for a night, dear." He glances at me. "You don't miss it?"

I shrug. I don't, really—I don't miss the old house, with its tiny garden. The school. The hospital. All the things that held us back, before Mum decided she didn't need it anymore—not the medicine or the car or the money to pay for any of it. Her best self would never need anything but sun and soil and rain and time.

Soft sobbing comes from the hallway. We turn from the fire to see Mum in her bloodstained nightgown, out of bed for the first time in three days. Her eyes are red, her cheeks flushed and wet. The cat dangles in her arms.

"Look at him," she says. "Something's wrong. Look."

She lays the creature on the kitchen table. The pollen clings to his fur and cakes his bloodied nose. She tries to stand him up, but he wobbles and falls, yellows of his eyes swallowed by the round, reflective black pools of his pupils.

"He looks toxic," Dad says.

"Did you give him something?" Mum asks. "Did you do something to him?"

"Of course not."

She begins to cry.

"I didn't do anything," Dad says. "Just wait. He might get better."

Mum wipes her swollen eyes, fingers goopy with pollen-stuff. "This is your fault."

"It's not."

"I'm going to find out how you did it," she says. She skirts the table, pulling jars of medicines from the shelf, opening stone drawers to rattle stone utensils. "I'll find it. I'll find what you gave him."

"I didn't give him anything!"

She ignores him, moving through the kitchen, the bedrooms, the back porch. She pulls books from their cases, and then pages from their spines. She digs through my schoolwork, breaks my pens and empties them, she dumps her jars of herbs and spices and preserves onto the counter.

She finds nothing amiss. She knows best what plants and oils go where, medicinal and toxic, which might dissolve harmlessly in a human mouth but fester in an animal's. She knows every leaf, seed and extract; Dad does not.

She gives up. Sobbing, she leaves the cat on the table and returns to her room. A thin trail of blood remains, smeared by the hem of her dress.

———

A DAY LATER, while Dad buries the cat, the oak handle of his shovel breaks in half.

———

IT'S an insult to describe my tree as a sapling anymore. Its trunk has thickened, its leaves fan out to arm's length. Its roots are flexible, growing, alive with tiny creaks and groans of xylem, billions of invisible stretching grains. If I listen hard enough, I can hear the soil shift between its rhizomes.

In a span of a few days, it overtakes the cat's grave. It lingers on that spot for a week, filling its roots, then slowly, slowly, retreats to the garden. It takes a month for it to make it from the lettuce beds to the tomatoes.

A little sentinel, Mum calls it. She no longer cries every day. Her breathing is clear. She has begun to make paper again.

Pulp floats on the surface of her soaking tub. She stirs it by hand, letting the bloated sludge drip through her fingers. It's a familiar task, a familiar smell, but today I find it oddly sickening.

A deep boom shakes the house, rippling the tub. Neither

of us flinch. We are no longer startled by the crack of breaking stone. Even with the rains gone, every night we dream of new fissures, and wake to the sun shining through them.

Then, the crumbling of stone transforms, rising in pitch and severity until I realize it's not stone at all. My brother is screaming.

We abandon the soaking paper and stumble down the hall. A buzz of terror rustles the ferns peeking through the cracks in our walls.

A massive wedge of the roof occupies the center of the room. A broken portion of marble angles down from a streak of bare night sky, stone splinted with long planks of Dad's repair work. The dead wood has rotted, choked under a burden of leaves and branches and vines. Stems sway along the debris, swollen with sap, a shivering mass of rot and stone and greenery so convoluted I can't tell where it ends and my brother begins.

Dad appears behind us. He cries out, digging through the wreckage, grasping at his weeping, trapped son. I help him tear at the vines, snapping branches, ripping away sheets of bark. My brother finally appears again, mostly intact. His right arm is inextricable, and he screams every time our father tries to unearth it.

"Don't —" he wails. "Don't touch it—don't!"

Silent, mustering an uncanny strength, Dad pushes the slab off my brother's elbow.

Mum hugs me as her son rises from the debris, face bloody, arm hanging limp and mangled by his side. Patches of skin curl away like birch bark. He's got two new elbows, tipped with protuberances of white bone. Leaves and pinecone scales stick to his wounds. There is a splinter the size of a penknife lodged in his shoulder.

He is too shocked to cry out as Dad grips him under the knees and lifts him into his arms.

"I can fix him," Mum says. "It's bad, but I can do it. He needs a salve. He needs poultice—wait here, I can fix him."

"No, you can't," Dad barks. "He needs a hospital. He needs a fucking doctor."

"We can't —"

Dad shoves past her, terrified son in his arms. He carries him down the hall without looking at either of us, stomps through the kitchen, pushes open the front door.

"Don't!" Mum shouts. "He'll be fine! Please, we can do this ourselves. We have to do this ourselves!"

"We don't, and we can't," Dad growls. "I'm taking him to town."

Rapidly, my brother's shock abates, just enough to make room for dawning horror. He trembles, rustling the leaves sprouting from his mangled arm.

"I don't want to go back," he sobs. "Put me down. I want to stay."

"Listen to him!" Mum says. "Please, he's fine."

"I don't wanna leave!" my brother shouts, but Dad marches on.

"You can't just walk there!" Mum hollers, trailing him all the way to the squashes, to the moss-eaten path of pebbles that passes for a road.

Dad keeps walking, dodging the words flung at him, and with his arms clamped around my brother, disappears into the night.

———

I DON'T SLEEP that night. Neither does Mum. I crawl into bed with her, curling like the cat, and she moans until dawn.

In the morning, she works in the garden, violently pruning the tomatoes. She cracks stem after stem, nursing her cold tea in an obsidian mug. It doesn't help.

"It's good for the plants," she says, when I point out she's leaving a trail of blood. "It's nutrient rich." Then she begins to cry. Her tears drip thick and white like sap down her face.

"They're not coming back," she says.

"They are."

"The hospital will keep him—they'll put him down. My boy, my little boy. They'll murder him like your bastard father murdered the cat."

"Dad didn't murder the cat."

While she sobs, I try to clean the garden with the scuffle hoe, but it seems cruel, impossible. I try to sweep, but the cracked broom is heavy in my hands. I try to dry the paper, but the pulp repulses me. Every object seems to me a desiccated, desecrated corpse.

———

TWO MORE DAYS PASS. Then, they return. They have three arms between them.

My brother teeters, unsteady, wrapped in strips of his bloodstained pajamas. The severed sleeves of our father's coat bind his wound. He waves with his good arm from the end of the path, smiling through his pallor.

Mum, revitalized, rushes out to greet him, wrapping her arms around him and nearly lifting him from the ground. He groans when her chin brushes against his raw bud of a shoulder.

Dad greets Mum with a quick peck to the forehead. He looks like he's slept about as much as we have.

"What happened?" Mum asks. "Did the hospital just…let you go?"

"We never got that far," Dad admits. He eases himself through the front door and collapses on the stone table. "We had to stop."

Mum waits for an explanation. Dad is already half-asleep, curling his knees into his chest and closing his eyes.

She shakes him back awake. "What happened?"

He blinks. "We had to stop. I couldn't make it that far. We found a stream. I cleaned him up."

"Where'd his arm go?" I ask.

"I…pulled it off," Dad says. He turns over, buries his face in his hands, and releases something halfway between a laugh and a sob. "Snapped. Twisted it like a branch. It came right off."

"It did," says my brother proudly.

"Oh, my dears," Mum says, kissing them both. "I knew

you could do it all by yourselves. I'm so proud of you. I knew you wouldn't give up."

Dad's breathing slows. "I...buried it," he mumbles. "By the stream."

Then he drifts away, exhausted from his travels. He's a sturdy man, rooted to the ground—he isn't meant to wander like that.

My brother is famished. While Dad snores on the table, he eats on the floor, chewing through the last of our early vegetables. He asks when the squashes will grow in. He asks if we cried when he got hurt. He asks if he can go dig up his arm later.

Mum laughs, tells him no. You should never unearth what you've already planted.

DAD CONFESSES it's probably for the best they never made it to town. "It would've cost an arm and a leg to save that arm," he laughs. "Though I might've been tempted to get them to do something about this belly. It's sagging over my belt. In a few weeks I'll start tripping over it."

"When the squashes come in," Mum says, "we'll fatten you back up. We'll put some flesh under there." Her tone is earnest; by the silhouettes my parents cast against the ferns growing from the walls, they're holding one another close.

Dad blows an amused puff from his nose. The shadow of his arm reaches for her, skin hanging like a curtain from his elbow.

"You're breathing better," he says. "It really was that cat."

"Oh, stop."

"He was bad for you. He wasn't letting you grow into your best self."

"I know," Mum says. Then, quietly: "He was a pest."

I smile and look through the fissured ceiling to my tree, its dark crown spreading over our house like a new roof. I can feel its roots move under the floor, absorbing the activity inside. I can feel its soft, hairy bark brush up against the walls, soaking up my parents' heat, my brother's quiet, musical moans. His stub aches, but only with the pressure of new growth.

I shudder, relieved, contented. Leaves rustle in the breeze above me.

Autumn comes heavy and full and fast.

The squashes swell with meat. The tomatoes burst and spill seeds, too heavy for their branches. The greens bolt, the wild apples fall, the corn shoots upward. Everything has grown to painful fullness, fecund and aching for relief.

My mother and I return to the kitchen with skirts full of vegetables. The peas are big as beets, the beets big as melons, the melons too big to carry. My father rolls one onto the porch, where he slices and salts and cans, swearing when he pinches his loose skin in the jar lids.

"Fucking tongs," he says, attempting to wrangle his chopped cantaloupe. "Everything wood in this goddamn house breaks."

My brother takes the utensils from him, extending his unbroken arm. It has grown a little longer, a little stronger in the absence of the other. He still likes using it, though two new ones have grown from his stub, stocky and thick. With his long arm he carries the tongs to the garden edge, with his short ones he digs a second grave, next to the cat's, and buries them.

Dad attempts to replace the tongs by whittling away at a branch of alder, but I can tell it unnerves him as much as it does me. We can both feel the pinch of steel scraping at the wood, hear the grain snapping and curling in pain. After a while, he gives up, blaming the skin hanging from between his fingers.

I tell him to make a new set of utensils out of bone.

"Whose bones?" he laughs. Then he stops, thinking over what I've said. The river isn't too far. It might take a day to get there and back.

SOON, the whole weight of the garden hits us. The squashes fill to bursting, agonized, stretched skin splitting open and spilling their entrails. Mum has to carry them in pieces to the kitchen, handful after handful of raw, ripe meat. I pluck the tomatoes while my brother makes his rounds of the garden, long arm reaching for what the rest of us can't. He strips the highest cobs from the corn, gathers seeds from the sunflowers, shakes loose the apples. Dad marches behind him, gathering the spoils in the loose apron of his stomach. When he can't carry any more, when his skin stretches with the bounty, he dumps the spoils onto our kitchen table.

My brother quickly sorts through them, organizing with respect to size and type and ripeness. The haul is so large it doesn't matter that he slips the cherry tomatoes into his mouth when Mum isn't looking, or nibbles at the basil stems. He is a growing boy. A fourth arm, short and soft as a baby's, juts sidelong from one of his new elbows.

Mum removes seeds from the squash, digging her fingers through the orange meat and passing around sticky handfuls. We can only get through a quarter of it before we are too full to move.

Outside, the sky is cold and clear and blue. The deciduous leaves darken and shed, readying for the next turn of the season.

WHEN THE HARVEST is done and we've gathered all we can, Mum lies out in the empty garden, wetting the soil and steeping it for the following year. She can't stop grinning as she feeds the garden, lying in each patch and bleeding for a few hours before moving onto the next. Wordless, hair rustling in the breeze, her voice carries like birdsong through the house.

We've done it, she says. We've finally done it.

Winter is bliss.

On the nights we make paper, Dad sits on a marble stool while my brother grasps his skin, stretching it across the kitchen. I run a paring knife along it, trimming the hair, then through it. We cut a generous length from him, then I pat the laceration down with a compress of leaves and soil. Soon Dad stops gritting his teeth. He tells me it feels nice. He's always wanted to lose weight.

We pull his skin taut over a frame of bones, scrape off the pulp of his fat, and dry it in the cold sun. When the snows come, we stretch it over the ceiling, we hang it from doorways, we throw it over the beds and pillows and curl in its warmth. My book covers are stretched from his fingers. Our front door is made from his belly, navel protruding where a knob may have been. I have never loved him more.

When we are hungry, my brother lifts his long arm and reaches down the hallway, into the back room, where he grabs hold of dried corn and beans, or he rolls around a rock-hard squash, making a game of it. His arm is too long to reach his own mouth, and his other ones get mixed up with one another, so Mum breaks apart his food for him. For every morsel she brings to his lips, she scatters ten at his feet.

Occasionally, he will get bored. If I don't watch my back, I'll feel a tap on my shoulder or a tug at my clothes, and when I turn, I'll catch a glimpse of his long, pale arm snaking back into his room. I've never seen him grin as widely as he does when he pulls my hair from across the house. Sometimes, he snaps it off like a bunch of twigs, though always, more will grow.

The sapling has taken up residence right outside my room, branches stretching through the window, roots curling up from the floor. I don't think it can move much anymore, but it seems content, bathing in the beige light shining through the tapestries of skin.

I sit idly most of these days, arms splayed under the lengthening daylight. Weeks pass before any of us become hungry or bored, months before my father grows a new length of skin to cut and dry and use again. There is little to do, but none of us mind. We want for nothing. We need nothing, except time, rain, sun and soil.

BANQUETS OF EMBERTIDE

RICHARD GAVIN

Originally published in *Northern Nights*.

Richard Gavin's work explores the bond between dread and the numinous. His short fiction has been collected in six volumes, including *grotesquerie* (Undertow Publications, 2020), and has appeared in many volumes of *Best New Horror* and *Best Horror of the Year*. Richard has also authored several works of esotericism for distinguished venues like Theion Publishing and Three Hands Press. He resides in Ontario, Canada. Online presence: www.richardgavin.net

---

UNLIKE MOST SMALL NORTHERN TOWNS, White Birch is not a tightknit community. Its residents restrict their activities to their drab houses, or to the fields on which those houses stand. Though earthy and obtuse, these people lead the sort of cloistered, spartan lives one usually finds only in hagiographies.

The breadwinners of each household earn their keep

outside the town limits, for White Birch has no industry to speak of. The few lingering storefronts on main street have long been boarded-up and neglected, like jack-o'-lanterns left to rot after Halloween.

An annual banquet at the town hall is the only tradition significant enough to draw White Birch together. The unspoken consensus is that this feast is held in honour of Christmas, but its true nature remains a secret that the towns-folk guard fiercely from everyone, especially from themselves.

Many Decembers ago, a butcher who'd gotten too deep in his cups had interrupted the entertainment. He'd hollered grisly speculations about the town's Embertide custom, demanding to know why this queer supper always fell upon the longest, darkest night of the year, and why no one ever thought to connect it with the atrocities that subsequently plagued White Birch each winter. The details of these atroci-ties vary according to the storyteller, but all are united on the fact that they were so ghastly children had cried and the elderly had covered their ears.

Every version of this account ends with the butcher being forcibly ejected from the hall by furious neighbours, and with his body being discovered several days later in the vineyard behind his home. The coroner's report allegedly cites expo-sure as the official cause of death, but the butcher is consis-tently rumoured to have been discovered with his eyes and his left foot missing. His mangled remains are said to have been interred in an unmarked grave in another county. Whether he'd found the answers he'd so rudely sought at that year's banquet is a riddle best left undeciphered.

This year, on the appointed day and at the appointed time, the locals migrate to the town hall. No invitations are required. (No one has ever been brave or foolish enough to seek out the identity of the host or hosts of these yearly fetes.) The cardinal rules are to arrive before nightfall, and to ensure that everyone obeys the proper etiquette.

It is a frigid evening, but autumn stubbornly refuses to yield to winter. For weeks the lands have been ossified and fallow. The foliage that litters the mud has lost both its colour and its perfume of decay. It makes everyone feel dismal, eager for a cleanse.

The great walnut doors of the town hall are pressed shut just as stars are beginning to stir in the cloud-swept sky. The atmosphere inside is cold, both in temperature and in lack of affection. Long tables have been veiled in white cloth and laid with precisely enough settings. Tented cards written in a filigree script indicate a mad seating plan: siblings are stationed at opposite ends of the hall, high school athletes are placed beside hopeless old maids, wives sit nowhere near their spouses. Upon every plate rests a green linen napkin ingeniously folded in the shape of praying hands. These resemble polluted glaciers upon their little seas of glazed bone china.

A tedious span of anticipatory stillness follows the seating. The faint hiss of guttering wax within the oakwood candelabras and the wet rumble of bellies calling for nourishment are the only noises. Someone sneezes but no one whispers a blessing.

A rustling from the blackness of the vaulted ceiling notifies the guests that the evening's entertainment is commencing. Those who opt to look up witness iridescent cords unfurling from the joists and beams. Their pulsating descent is akin to serpents uncoiling after a period of rest. The lowering of these bright garlands extinguishes the flames of the candelabras. The hall's luminescence now comes in lurid shades of coral and yellow.

The far end of the hall is inlaid with an impressive arched window. The heavy velvet curtain covering this window is hoisted. A trapezoid of moonlight stretches across the narrow stage.

Eventually the entertainer makes his appearance, shuffling unceremoniously into the lunar spotlight. The man is attired in a rumpled suit of midnight-blue wool. Piled dust nests inside the suit's many creases, suggesting a rich brocade design that the fabric does not actually possess. The man also wears an ugly crown, a novelty of cheap tin that is too small for his skull. Its edges slice into the delicate, aged skin of his brow.

A wedded seamstress at the rear of the hall flinches under a wave of unpleasant recognition. The man onstage is familiar to her. She'd grown up knowing of him only as 'the widower.' As best she can recollect, the widower had been condemned to the bedlam after his beloved had been committed to the earth.

The seamstress's anxiety mounts as she ponders the chilling scenario of the widower escaping his padded cell. She longs to share this insight with her husband, the carpenter, but he is seated at the foot of the stage, between the fisher-woman and one of the many local tillers.

The widower starts to fret, suggesting a lack of rehearsal, or possibly stage fright. Each jitter of his longish body fills the room with the cloying stench of camphor. A gormless child loudly retches and is paternally reprimanded by the man nearest to him.

The widower's expression turns apologetic. He fishes through the pockets of his dusty suit and retrieves the stub of a cheroot. Striking a match against his bruised thumbnail, he ignites the cheroot. It fumes out thick ribbons of smoke. Though everyone is expecting the pungent stench of cheap tobacco, they are instead greeted with the sweet musk of frankincense, the finest the world has known since Balthasar had carefully borne it as a holy gift.

Having perfumed the chamber, the widower swallows the still-burning incense cone; the first in what is to be a series of marvellous illusions. Partway through these charming glamours the man suddenly halts. His signal for silence is so desperate, so urgent, that tension surges through the crowd. The tears that fill the widower's eyes sparkle like polished gems under the hall's peculiar iridescence.

He leans forward and cups a hand over one of his large ears. He listens intently.

Something in the outer darkness is moving toward the hall. Everyone takes a frantic mental attendance check. The fact that all residents are present only serves to worsen those plodding sounds of approach.

"What is coming? What?" hisses the widower. His voice is the gurgle of brackish water leaking through a clogged drain. The noises without grow louder, and although the barricade is solid and true, everyone is heartsick with the sense that this intruder is now darkening their door.

The thud of the iron doorknocker causes many to cry out.

"Wait!" the seamstress shouts. Instinctively, she leaps from her seat, nearly upsetting her place-setting. Realizing her breach of decorum, she clasps a hand across her mouth as a gesture of penance before sinking back into her chair. The revelation that inspired her outburst was that her initial memory of the legend had been inverted: it was not the widower who had gone mad after his wife had gone into the ground, but vice versa.

"Something foul is knocking at the door to our world," explains this man who is no longer the widower. "We must be brave!"

The knocking abruptly ceases, but the crowd's relief is short-lived. A moment later, the thing from without pushes effortlessly through the bolted doors, slipping through the barrier as silkily as smoke.

This unbidden guest reveals itself to be a great absence, a thing (or rather a no-thing) of darkness, a negation whose absolute stillness permeates all.

"It is the grave, my friends! That is what has come here! It has lain hungry for too long," the crowned man explains sotto voce. "Like all of you, the grave has come here to feast. And we know what food it craves, don't we?"

Once the grave proceeds to glide noiselessly between the long tables, the townsfolk can no longer maintain their mute civility; children wail, men sob quietly, and women loudly demand a halt to the proceedings. But their revolt is aborted almost as soon as it begins, for whomever the grave floats nearest to is paralyzed with shock and left in a state of inhuman grace.

The oblong pit passes through all objects in its path yet

disturbs none. The grave has no qualities whatsoever. It holds no odour of the soil from whence it came, nor any traces of its previous occupants. In fact, nothing about it is inherent. Where one person feels a shudder of revulsion in the grave's proximity, another experiences a sense of peace.

"She is seeking Her next disciple!" the crowned man declares. To many, the notion of the grave being feminine rings true.

The crowned man then claps his hands several times as if to summon his royal subjects. The noise of this breaks the catatonic spell caused by the sailing grave. The people turn their attention once more to the stage, where yet another visitor moves into view.

A stone catafalque comes meandering into the moonlight. It has been lavishly carved to feature flying buttresses and arches worthy of the finest cathedrals. Its movement comes courtesy of the stone goat legs that have been chiselled into each corner of the oblong stone. Though crooked, these legs of living stone are nimble and strong. Their cloven hooves clack against the floorboards as they ferry the catafalque closer to the crowned man.

The grave makes one last patient pass of the hall before finally stationing itself at the only exit.

"There is no escaping Her. One of us must learn Her lesson. Who is it to be? You? Or you, madame? How about you, sir? If not you, why not the kindly-looking child beside you?"

Stifled pleas ripple through the hall. This din of helplessness brings a smile to the entertainer's face. Someone points a quaking hand at him while another person warns of bleeding.

The crown the man bears is melting into a corona of dark steam. This weepy new form is shapeless yet somehow even more regal. It halos him in burning shadows. Rivulets of crimson stream down the man's face. They fill the creases in his flesh and the wrinkles of his suit, creating a map of some new circulatory system, an externalized mask to convey the secrets of the blood. The atmosphere ripens with the aroma of cooking meat.

The king lies down on the catafalque.

In response to this, the origami praying hands uniformly unravel, as if flowers parting for pollination.

The open napkins reveal the tools secreted within them. The guests find themselves faced with a keen needle and spindles of coarse embalmers thread. There are small cellars of salt and phials of pungent oil. Two lucky children each discover matching pennies for the eyes. One unfortunate guest has been gifted an ancient scalpel of Turkish obsidian.

WAN daylight is pouring through the great window by the time the citizens finally lift their groggy heads. The settings have been cleared away. Everyone feels sated, though they intuit that the only thing fed last night was the grave.

Torpidly, the citizens rise and depart, as if summoned by the tolling of the bells from the bedlam on the hill. When the doors are finally opened, some gasp at the sight of fresh snow covering the landscape. This cold white shroud, they know, will linger for a long spell, not yielding until the sparrows return from afar and the first green sprouts of spring disclose some of the secrets that circulate beneath the surface.

FIVE VIEWS OF THE PLANET TARTARUS

RACHAEL K. JONES

Originally published in *Lightspeed Magazine* #164.

Rachael K. Jones grew up in various cities across Europe and North America, picked up (and mostly forgot) six languages, and acquired several degrees in the arts and sciences. Now she writes speculative fiction in Portland, Oregon. Rachael is a Eugie Award winner, and a finalist for the Hugo, Nebula, Locus, Bram Stoker, and World Fantasy Award. Her fiction has appeared in dozens of venues worldwide, including *Lightspeed, Beneath Ceaseless Skies, Strange Horizons*, and Amazon Prime's hit series *Secret Level*. Follow her on Bluesky @RachaelKJones.bsky.social, or find her at RachaelKJones.com.

1.

ONCE A DECADE, a titanium-nosed shuttle plows through the rings of the planet Tartarus with a new batch of prisoners destined for the Orpheus Factory. The debris that makes up the rings is so thick that it thunders like a hailstorm, deafening the passengers. As the orbiting debris bounces and scrapes against the hull, the prisoners squeeze their eyes closed and beg the pilot to be more careful.

"Are you trying to hit all of them?" a prisoner snaps, covering his ears against the roaring onslaught.

The pilot laughs through her nose. Ironic. Dismissive. "We always do. As many as we can."

She steers into the path of the debris, and the thundering increases.

2.

PLANETSIDE, they hold a farce of a trial in the Sibylline Court, a decaying mansion of rotten marble. All traitors to the Sibyllines go to Tartarus to receive the only punishment for rebellion: eternal life.

The prisoners stand at attention as the comms read out their names. A whirring ten-limbed auto-judge pronounces their sentences in turn, omitting no words from the traditional declaration of guilt, because the Sibylline Empire believes in ceremony.

3.

ONE BY ONE the prisoners file into a dark, square mouth cut from the earth: the Orpheus Factory. Machines shred their clothes and lather them in amber disinfectant that burns the skin and smells like tar and makes all their hair fall out. Tiny silver needles snake into their veins. Nanobots pump into their blood, flooding their organs, cleaning off plaques, lengthening telomeres, repairing neurons.

The last injection severs their voluntary motor pathways so nothing moves but their eyes. Before the final step, the prisoners feel young again, for a moment.

. . .

4.

THE LAST GIFT of the planet Tartarus to its newborn residents is a brand-new spacesuit, bright white, top of the line, with solar-powered life support that can recycle respirated air and bodily wastes for up to two hundred years, should nothing breach the suit's barrier. Machines thread the prisoners' bodies with tubes for feeding and waste disposal. At the end of this process, the Orpheuses are piled together outside beneath the dark sky, their terrified eyes flickering behind their faceplates, their lips drawn back by spasticity into a tight, cramped grin.

When the job is done, the pilot who flew the inbound shuttle loads them back into the cargo bay, stacking the bodies high and deep, like firewood.

5.

ON ITS WAY through the planetary belt, the shuttle dumps the new Orpheuses into the ring that loops round and round Tartarus like a dirge that will never end. That is when the prisoners will see all the frozen white spacesuits, billions in orbit, their eyes aware and flickering behind well-made helmets, their blood pumped full of machines that won't let them die, their bodies spinning around the planet forever and ever.

They will float eternally, unable to sleep. They will pray for a rogue asteroid to career into their path and breach their suits. Ten years later, when they see the silver-tipped shuttle approach the weary planet, they will pray for the vessel to smash into their bodies as it enters orbit and descends to the surface.

The pilots do always try to hit as many as they can.

KAMCHATKA

KRISTINA TEN

Originally published in *Washington Square Review #51*.

Kristina Ten is the author of *Tell Me Yours, I'll Tell You Mine* (Stillhouse Press, 2025). Her stories appear in *McSweeney's, Best American Science Fiction and Fantasy, We're Here: The Best Queer Speculative Fiction, Nightmare, The Dark*, and elsewhere. She has won the *McSweeney's* Stephen Dixon Award for Short Fiction, the Subjective Chaos Kind of Award, and the *F(r)iction* Writing Contest, and has been a finalist for the Shirley Jackson Award and the Locus Award. Ten is a graduate of Clarion West Writers Workshop and the University of Colorado Boulder's MFA program in fiction, and has received fellowships from the Ragdale Foundation and the Martha's Vineyard Institute of Creative Writing.

THE CHILD TRIED, and the mother, for her part, let him. She waited on the shore while her cub splashed gracelessly through the shallows. The ring of white around his neck made him look like some high-ranking member of English nobility. The guide, Ivan, had explained about natal collars on first-year cubs during the flight to Kurile Lake that morning, but between his brisk, accented English and the whirring blades, and the way Meesh's breakfast sloshed just under her ears every time the chopper pitched toward this vast caldera or that massive volcano, she hadn't held onto the details.

The mother bear waded in after the cub and had a stilled salmon between her teeth in seconds. That's right, thought Meesh, that's *exactly* right. You humor the kid while he plays hunter, but you don't let yourself starve over it.

Her eyes found the Ilyinsky volcano's reflection in the water and traced it up to its origin, a distant conical giant glittering with snow. The last of the previous winter or the first of the coming one, Meesh couldn't be sure. Winter was three of the four seasons in Kamchatka.

"Remarkable," breathed Francis, so suddenly it nearly sent Meesh off the viewing platform. Francis was *quiet* quiet, from his years of birding all over the American Southwest, about which he'd already bragged several times to the group. Not that anyone had listened, on account of Emmanuel existing. Emmanuel had finished second on the most recent season of the popular wilderness survival show *Backlands*, but the way everyone flitted around him, you'd think he'd won it. He'd gained most of the weight back since filming, trimmed his beard. He had this habit of rubbing his palm over his jawbone as if feeling for the once-there hair, rubbing it back and forth, back and forth, in a way Meesh was sure made everyone think of fucking.

Made her think of fucking, anyway.

And not that Meesh had known any of them very long, but she could tell the last thing anybody thought about when they thought about fucking was Francis.

Francis, in a deep squat, mere inches away now, his telephoto lens all but perched on her right shoulder, and the devil there telling Meesh: Helga-Pataki-punch this nut. But hold on. Say this tour had a zero-tolerance policy and Meesh managed to get herself kicked off on day two? The nearest city was forty minutes by helicopter, the nearest airport a bumpy bus slog from there, down the region's only paved road. "Paved road" being a generous term for it. And even if she got out of the nature park without being arrested for traveling sans guide or ecological permit, even if she caught the local bus on its anyone's-guess schedule, flights to Anchorage departed only twice a week. And that was in high season.

Meesh squinted in the direction of Francis's camera lens, at the big bear vice-gripping the salmon between her paws. The cub leaned against his mother as she worked the flesh. He tongued lazily at the air between them, where bite-size pink chunks soon appeared, as if by magic.

THE IDEA HAD BEEN that Meesh wouldn't have to see a single other living thing. But it turned out living things were just about everywhere. Even in 200° water. Even in the second-most densely concentrated geyser field on Earth.

Kamchatka Beasts and Bubblers, the tour was called. Last one with any spots left by the time she looked. Sixteen days in the remote reaches of the Russian Far East, home to blink-and-you'll-miss-it summers and numbing sub-arctic winds the rest of the year. Twenty-nine active volcanoes over a landmass the size of Sweden. The peninsula, shaped like a fish with a bite taken out of its head, faced away from the continent and toward Japan, as if recognizing the untenability of its extreme conditions and trying to get away from itself.

Meesh would've found it sooner had she not rabbit-holed on Tanzania's Lake Natron, with its surface so red it could've been downriver from Sweeney Todd. Water so alkaline it could burn straight through human skin and eyes—despite being the annual breeding ground for nearly three million lesser flamingos. Too bad Scott had this weird affinity for flamingos. Knew too many facts about their knees, made a point to see them first every time at the zoo.

Other searches for "world's most inhospitable places" led Meesh to the Australian Outback (only she sunburned too easily), Brazil's Snake Island (illegal for civilians to visit), Death Valley (too close to home), Yellowstone (even closer). She and Scott had, at some point, made abstract plans for a trip to the Sahara: sunset sandboarding, blankets so thin you could feel the desert's ups and downs under your spine, this stupid vision of them riding two-up on a camel. And the trouble with Antarctica was the bestseller that had come out last year. Scott hadn't read it, but Meesh had basically recounted the book to him beat by beat. Which meant he knew all about the protagonist (a woman who'd run away from her life via an Antarctic cruise) and, as a bonus, he'd started having fantasies about getting hired as a field engineer at McMurdo.

Scott worked in mergers and acquisitions, which put him about as far as you can be from a construction site on the South Pole. When their Roomba started acting funny, he just bought a new one, like what you do when your kid's cat dies and you'd rather not stumble through the whole unseemly circle-of-life conversation, and, really, the SPCA is *right there*. Then he came home and placed the new Roomba in the charging dock as if it'd always been there, as if Meesh wouldn't notice the missing scratches from the time their previous one fell down the stairs.

So: not exactly the resident handyman. But: the reason there was always enough in their joint account to take off.

For Kamchatka: five thousand glorious miles away, the last of those miles accessible only through a bewildering combination of chopper, military-grade half-track, and dogsled. So isolated that when she'd typed out the names of specific lodges, the search engine had come up empty and suggested that perhaps she, the real-life human idiot, must've spelled something wrong.

And who knew? Maybe if she went far enough east, she'd find a time zone where what happened hadn't. Or where it had happened so long ago that, by now, she hardly remembered.

———

"THE GROUND IS SCREAMING," Ivan the guide couldn't have said. Meesh must've misheard him. There was something about the way he transmogrified his "i"s into "ee"s and nearly swallowed half his wispy beard with each vowel.

But then Rebecca the Finnish linguist frowned back at the group, crossed her finger over her lips, and said, "*Listen.*"

In the absence of clinking carabiners, in the stark new quiet, Meesh was suddenly too aware of her rasping breaths. It made textbook sense why everyone else was there. Francis was chasing the colony of spectacled guillemot that his birding app had promised would be waiting on Kamchatka's rocky coast. Emmanuel was working out the kinks in his patented off-grid incineration toilet before it went to market. Rebecca was on a university grant, studying the endangered dialects of the Eveny, a nomadic people who apparently had fifteen hundred different words for "reindeer": one for those most vulnerable to wolf attacks, another for those that would come right up to you and lick the salt off your hands. Among the rest were a married couple who'd themed their wedding around a shared love of angling (tackle-box cake, fish in the boutonnieres), a trio of alpinists, plus Paul, a daredevil botanist who told them, eyes aglimmer, that he'd always been willing to go to the ends of the earth for his research—and for a particular species of monkshood, to the end of the earth he'd come.

On the other hand, Meesh once saw a common stink bug on the opposite side of the apartment and, with one foot, recast the new Roomba as an exterminating machine. No, she wasn't an extreme *anything*. Earlier, passing an immense hot spring—a fathomless sapphire edged with painterly bands of copper and gold—she was reminded she didn't even like long baths. The prickly sensation of heat forced her to confront the fragility of her body, the useless defense that was her so-called barrier of skin. And yet, every time her life underwent a major shift, she experienced this overwhelming urge to *return to the land*. No breakup haircut for her, thanks. But sign her up for the hiking meetup, the foraging class, the psychedelic-assisted treehouse meditation. As if the land would somehow save her.

As if she, lifelong city girl, and the land had ever been that close.

Cresting the ridge overlooking the Valley of Geysers, Meesh realized Ivan was right: the ground here *was* screaming. The geysers' intermittent gurgling was the dominant sound, but when she listened closely, just underneath it, like the harmony line, was a soft, persistent seething.

"Fumaroles," Ivan explained, pointing to the columns of steam that Meesh had, from the chopper, mistaken for wildfires. "How the heat gets out when the thermal feature has no water in its system."

Emmanuel made a comment about backed-up plumbing that made everybody laugh.

Meesh's head felt too big for her skull. This leg of the tour had a rotten-egg smell that rocketed her back to the humiliating days of subsidized summer camp, and everywhere she looked there were splotches of radioactive orange, making her feel like her internal contrast levels were off. She couldn't catch her breath, the volume of the fumaroles rising in her ears. Not far from one of the springs, a trail of hoofprints formed drunken loop-de-loops. Some animal for whom the luxury of a sauna outweighed the risk of being boiled alive.

Though, come to think of it, the animal must have been moving away from the spring. And, if the distance between prints was any indication, moving *fast*. Because you couldn't build a safety fence around every scalding body of water in Kamchatka, and because children were too brave for their own good, having had insufficient time in which to experience pain, Beasts and Bubblers was strictly eighteen and up. The angling couple, who'd left their young son at home, remarked on how much the crackling coming from one shallow pool sounded like his favorite Pop Rocks.

A far cry from Incr-Edible Fungi of the Rocky Mountains, Meesh mused. This land seemed needful, angry.

Well, let it squeal all it wanted. At least here it wasn't her problem.

In the thick haze of one of the smaller fumaroles, Meesh found reason to let slip a scream back.

"Mermaid" was the nearest word Meesh could summon, and as soon as she said it, she knew it was utterly wrong, too.

Ivan, having finally unstuck the room's one small window, was attempting to circulate fresh air using a complicated series of hand motions that made Meesh think of park tai chi. The cook, Oks, crouched at the foot of the cot, aromas of parsley and black peppercorn wafting from the bowl in her hands.

"The hike was difficult," Ivan said, kindly omitting *for you.* "You are overheated."

Rebecca sat on the other cot, legs drawn all the way under her like a squirmy child at story hour. Everyone else was down the hall, beta testing Emmanuel's incineration toilet.

"People faint when they're overheated. They don't scream." This from Rebecca, who had introduced herself the first day as "a doctor but not a *doctor* doctor," and since then done everything she could to take it back. The open notebook on her lap, the thoughtful pen-tapping against her chin, did nothing to soften the effect.

"She was in one of the springs," Meesh said again, knowing that if she didn't repeat this once every three to five minutes, she'd stop believing it. "She was...burning."

Ivan grimaced. Rebecca scribbled. Oks abandoned the soup and scooched closer to Meesh, who was immediately distracted by how good the cook's hair smelled. Like coal smoke, raw honey, toast.

"There is a story about these women." Oks fingered the pendant in her collarbone ditch. "They are called *kupalki.*"

"Oksana," Ivan warned, then switched to Russian before

remembering Rebecca was in the room, switched back to English to say only, for some reason, the word "blog," then gave up and settled for crossing his arms and staring gloomily out the window.

Oks shot him the imperious look of the person controlling the flow of food in this operation. "The story," she continued, "is that kupalki were once angels. One day, they conspired together against God, and for this sin they fell from heaven. Because their sin was so great, they were doomed to fall farther and harder than all others."

Rebecca was nodding so fast Meesh couldn't look at her without feeling seasick.

"Many fallen angels walk the earth. They are wicked and destitute, unable to fly. But the kupalki fell with such force that they went *through* the earth, into the waters beneath it. They are seen sometimes in the places where the water is pushed up."

"Springs," Rebecca whispered.

Oks nodded. "Actually, those we have here are the safest because they are so hot. Kupalki cannot travel far from the water. It is in the cooler springs, where swimming is permitted, that people are most at risk."

"So, these 'angels' that fell all at once," Rebecca started in, without looking up from her notebook. "Would some say that's how sites like the Valley of Geysers were formed?"

Ivan pushed off the windowsill, unable to contain the fact of his hard-earned degree in geophysics any longer. "*As I have said,* the Valley of Geysers was formed when a volcano collapsed more than forty thousand years ago."

Oks shrugged noncommittally. "Recently, miners at Oginskaya discovered fragments of teeth among the gold in their machines."

"Oksana," Ivan objected.

"Not human teeth," Oks added. "And not identifiable as any local animal."

"Oksana!"

Rebecca looked like she might rip a hole through her paper.

Feeling another wave of dizziness coming in, Meesh rolled side to side on the cot, burying first her left ear, then her right into the pillow. Trying to hear less of whatever she was hearing. Earlier, Ivan had left out that detail about the hike being difficult only for those who were as unprepared as she was. But Meesh had left out something too.

The creature she'd seen had not been, in truth, burning. The creature hadn't appeared to be in any pain at all.

She was half submerged and turned toward Meesh, skin a loose mat of yellow fleece. She was emitting the steam vent's high, tea-kettle hiss.

And despite not having a face exactly, she was smiling.

———

"Perhaps you are traveling for a sibling's wedding," the tour company's website had rabidly begun. "Or for a large business conference, or to pitch a successful idea to your boss! Treat yourself to the hottest deals for Kamchatka!"

Or maybe you just need an escape, Meesh had mentally filled in, before tapping the RESERVE NOW button. The little cha-ching her phone made after completing the purchase was drowned out by Scott's off-key singing in the other room.

Walking through the Eveny settlement, Meesh tried to picture a conference: PowerPoint projected against one of the cottage's windowless walls, podium set up between the seven-foot bear sculpture and the three-foot bear sculpture, so the speaker looked like the mother in the classic papa-mama-baby bear line-up. Her brain instantly cast Scott in the role of speaker. Meesh had jobs—lots of jobs, sure. It was Scott who had the career.

Ivan had suggested that she rest at home base while the group went to meet the Eveny reindeer herders and Oks went on her restock trip, but the only thing Meesh could stomach less than another helicopter ride was the idea of spending the whole day alone. Kupalki were a myth. Of course. And just in, you know, *tribute* to that, Meesh was electing to surround herself with real, certified, non-mythical people.

The terrain was different this far north. No more summer-camp smell, no mud pots bubbling like microwave bisque. Wooden walkways connected the village's half-dozen buildings, narrow enough to demand single file. When Meesh took a wrong step off, her boot sank three inches into waterlogged grass.

The botanist, Paul, pulled her up, then gestured toward a cluster of red sores at the base of a nearby tree. "Amanita muscaria," he said. Pretty name, Meesh thought, for an infection. "Hallucinogenic," he went on. "Poisonous, if you have too much. Apparently locals use it as a substitute for alcohol."

Meesh gave a little chin-scrunch of approval, like: *Right, well, I don't see a bar.* By the time the walkway ended, at the base of a small building elevated on four tall posts, a bar was precisely what she needed.

The men had positioned themselves on either side of the carcass and were yanking at it with powerful grunts. The hide, still intact at the head and rump, made the reindeer look like one of those cheap Halloween costumes Meesh had worn in college. The interchangeable sexy-animal ones comprised only of a mask, ears, and tail.

They'd passed the reindeer enclosure at the entrance, before the wildflower walk and the culture museum, far enough back that Meesh wasn't prepared to see one here. She remembered something she'd heard on a podcast about how cows had to be slaughtered apart from the rest of the herd, because the anxiety of seeing a herd member die caused the other cows to emit a hormone that made their meat taste bad to people.

Emmanuel was telling the alpinists that the storehouse in front of them, built off the ground to evade opportunistic scavengers, was the inspiration for the chicken-legged hut in the tales of Baba Yaga. He'd built something similar, if less sophisticated, on his season of *Backlands*.

Rebecca was telling someone, maybe even her, Meesh, that the Eveny didn't have an equivalent for the English word "processing." Which, naturally, put Rebecca in mind of other food-related euphemisms, which, in the English language, at least, dated back to—

And that's when Meesh saw it.

The ripple in the fur between the eyes. Caused by the eyes fluttering open.

The kick of the front legs, in the split-second before the men sawed them off.

What was left of the reindeer thrashed violently in the grass, its keening coming out as a chorus, as if every part of it were singing, all the air leaving its fighting body at once. The men worked to get it under control, one gripping its antlers so hard that when it whipped its head around, the shaft of bone came off in his hand—a nauseating crack—and lifted the deer's hide up with it.

Its skull, now exposed, was not the mineral moonscape Meesh had expected. Not barren at all, but growing.

A tropical island. A teeming hothouse.

A sheet of fuzzy yellow.

The reindeer's belly, finally still: marbled cherry candy in the sun.

THE SURROGATE HAD BEEN LOVELY. That wasn't the problem.

Going in, Meesh had this vision of surrogacy, cobbled together from dystopian literature and Lifetime movie trailers. Young girl, poor girl, wearing the same ratty Ramones tee to every appointment. Forced into it by capital-C Circumstances. Stoic, hardened. Only the shadow of a wince for the icy speculum.

How Meesh might've ended up, had she not gotten together with Scott.

Gen was in her mid-thirties, a former Division I basketball star who still played on the weekends, had this permanent flush to her like she'd just stepped off the court. She wasn't in it for the money, though of course—little laugh—she'd be crazy not to take it. Her thing was, honestly? She just *loved* being pregnant. She was one of the lucky ones who carried easily. Slept even better. Stayed lean in the limb.

She'd had two of her own, and now that her family was complete, she missed it. Meesh had never understood what people meant when they said their family was *complete*. How did they know? How could a person be so sure that every last void in their life was filled? For Meesh, they were opening up all the time.

Gen had, as Scott's cheeseball dad would've said, more charm than a box of marshmallow breakfast cereal. She told Meesh they were *family* now, pulled her in for tight hugs that, as time went on, made Meesh increasingly nervous. Meesh would suck in her own stomach to avoid crushing Gen's, the contents of which were Meesh's property anyway. Or soon to be.

More charm than breakfast cereal. More allure than the magazine aisle. Gen didn't get offended when the nurses called hers a geriatric pregnancy, just did her old-person lost-my-glasses-again gag and felt around for an invisible cane. Everyone got a huge kick out of it. And Gen was so appropriate around Scott, seemed to experience him not so much as a man as an extension of Meesh. Like a purse that was perfectly nice, you could certainly understand why it was in the room. But you wouldn't, for example, address it directly.

Gen was wholly devoted to her own husband: Rahul, school superintendent, heaven in an argyle vest. Had encouraged Gen to pursue surrogacy. That supportive.

Meesh couldn't hate Gen. Actually, she kind of loved her. At one point during the second trimester, she started having these under-the-bleachers dreams about Gen that would cause her to wake up turned away from Scott, a charge of dynamite between her legs.

The problem wasn't that Meesh minded the surrogate.

The problem was that Meesh didn't mind the blood.

At the hospital, yes, when the afterbirth arrived like some del Toro sea creature and Scott went pale because he was sure this meant Gen was *dying*—no way could a person expel entire organs and survive—and now Rahul, salt-of-the-earth

Rahul, would be left to care for the kids on his own, meaning he'd have no choice but to quit superintendenting, and so many students would be the worse for it, and Rahul would be the worse for it, growing more resentful by the year, and Meesh knew firsthand, didn't she, the damage resentful single fathers could do.

Scott could really get himself going. Worrying the after-birth would be the thing that killed Gen instead of the thing that a certain subset, no lie, liked to preserve and use to make Christmas cookies.

Meanwhile, Meesh couldn't tear her eyes away.

But before the hospital as well. Long before. Meesh's aunt, when she was still alive, had this story about Meesh. About how, when Meesh first got her period, she free-bled—for, who knew how long, months?—until her aunt finally pulled Meesh aside and told her about pads, the kind that would mask the bad (but natural!) smell with a mélange of equatorial flowers. That was the trouble with not having a woman in the house, her aunt would say, then glare accusingly at Meesh's father. As if he had somehow *made* Meesh's mom die, plugged into that drunk driver's Google Maps—before Google Maps was even a thing, by the way. That's right: Meesh's dad had *invented* Google Maps, then directed that drunk driver to the exact coordinates of that poorly lit intersection himself.

As if dying was the same as leaving.

The day the dead reindeer came back? It didn't frighten Meesh. It *thrilled* her. To see the blood swirling again behind the animal's thinned-milk eyes. It reminded her of that long night at the hospital, when the placenta had shifted in the metal bowl where the doctor had left it and Meesh had briefly mistaken *that* for the baby, and the baby, already swaddled in a yellow fleece blanket, making bubbly fish lips, as the revolting remains.

And yet, what had they brought home?

EMMANUEL SURPRISED Meesh by being the kindest. About the discrepancies between what they had seen.

The group was in the dining room, Ivan at one end of the table and Oks at the other, parents of these ten adult children, most of whom were older than them. The stench of their collective morning breath was the only confirmation that it was, in fact, morning. Rain slapped against the windows and what little light came in was so lean, it registered as darkness.

"Rained out," Francis moaned into his mug. "On spectacled guillemot day."

It was also bird's-eye-view-of-the-lava-fields day. Also surfing-lessons-at-the-black-sand-beach day. But the clouds rolled in low and angry, so Ivan'd had to make the call. Rebecca was engrossed in her notebook. The angler wife was grumbling to her angler husband that this was *exactly* how vacation scams started: first they make you think you're getting your money's worth, then it's one cancellation after another until the trip peters off to nothing. In front of each person was a cluster of consolation crab legs, twice the width of the plate. Their arrangement, sharp and knuckly, made it impossible to forget they were related to scorpions. Every now and then, someone would pick one up, then set it back down, intact.

"When I was out there," Emmanuel said, hitting *out there* like a veteran of a long-fought war, "I would see things sometimes, too. The wilderness, it just, you know. Takes over." He put a tanned hand on Meesh's shoulder and gave a squeeze. One of the alpinists looked like she might stab Meesh with the business end of her wild-caught crab.

To be clear, the reindeer *had* moved. On that point, everyone could agree. Only where Meesh had seen the beginnings of a dramatic, round-twelve comeback, everyone else had seen nothing more than a slight muscle twinge.

"From the amanita muscaria, I'd venture," Paul said. When Meesh's look said *bless you?* he tried again: "The mushrooms. The deer likely ingested a large number, then fell asleep. The spasm could have been the animal momentarily regaining consciousness before—" He paused. "Before losing it again."

Meesh shook her head, hoping it would make things land the right way up. "You're not getting it."

"Amanita muscaria is," Paul said gently, expression pinched, "among other things, an analgesic. The animal probably felt a great deal less pain than it would have otherwise."

Suddenly, a shriek pierced the room, and Meesh remembered the crabs still in the kitchen, bobbing in the boiling pots. The steam hissing out of their shells as they dropped their claws from their bodies, one by one. A sacrifice. A final, desperate attempt to escape obliteration.

She imagined going back there and rescuing them. Her skin melting into their shells in the water, and their shells into her skin, until they were both a little of the other. Blistering. Softly chitinous. Bursting free from whatever held them in.

She imagined it. Imagined it.

Then stopped.

When she looked down at the table, she found her crab dissected and picked through, though she couldn't recall taking a bite. What meat remained was pocked with tiny craters the size of milk teeth. The shell fragments formed a heap of broken glass—a shattered windshield washed red.

She dug in till she felt it in the webbing of her fingers.

BY THE TIME the storm over their part of Kamchatka cleared, Meesh had been away from him longer than she'd been with him. That had to count for something. Time math. Everybody was always doing time math. Why not her, too?

She had told them. She had said, with absolute blazing certainty, that there wasn't a single nurturing bone in her body. Take, for example, the grasshopper. The one she'd found and captured in the yard as a kid. Didn't give a passing thought to food or a name or water, just put him (or her— who could tell with grasshoppers?) in the teeny trap she'd made in woodshop, then up on the shelf among her lesser

Beanie Babies, until one day, a few weeks later, her dad had come in, peered through the trap's tight mesh walls, and said to her, *Hey, uh, kiddo*. First time he'd ever called her that. Sounded so stupid. Probably something he'd seen in a movie about good dads, decided to try out.

About the lack of nurturing bones in her body, Scott's family had assured her: Don't worry, you'll grow them. And Scott wanted a baby so badly, was sure to be one of the good dads on whom those movies were based. A meet-you-in-the-middle guy, willing to get a surrogate and everything— Meesh hadn't even needed to concoct some lie about infertility, only had to remind him that there was a reason pregnancy was its own horror genre. Plus, Scott's family had added, they were all set in terms of money. And car-seat technology, whew. If for no other reason, you really just had to see what they were doing in the realm of car seats these days. Incredible. Basically little Ferraris. Nothing like when she and Scott were just born.

You could actually be responsible parents with car seats like that.

And about the time math, it was, really. Time.

Meesh loved Scott. Loved things about him. His sincere belief that hard work could get you anywhere, even a winter-over at the South Pole. His generosity. His head a wide-stretching, bright, cloudless sky. Though she wasn't wild about the marriage thing, if she was being honest. Receptionists assuming she was Mrs. Scott's-Last-Name, though she had clung doggedly to her own. Being introduced at parties as "my wife." Not that Scott ever did the Borat voice. Thought it disrespectful. It all made Meesh feel like a sub bullet point under Scott's main bullet. Him, a portrait on the family tree; her, a faint scribble on an adjoining line.

Still, when it was just the two of them, it was okay. Enough.

Afterward, though. The sheer number of Y chromosomes in the house, in those eight healthy pounds. They meant to suffocate her. To strip her clean of her name and call her only Mother.

It was normally the husband who bailed, wasn't it? Even the bears at Kurile Lake, the second day of the tour: it'd been the mom watching patiently as her baby flunked out of Salmon Catching 101. Once the male was finished mating, he didn't have anything more to do with the female, or with any cubs said mating might produce.

Meesh's was a more admirable refusal. Like the reindeer who, in its death throes—about to become blankets, coats, shoes, meat, medicinal powder—insisted, for that moment, it belonged to *no one*. It would make no one's name a possessive noun. Its hide would keep only a single being warm.

That pelt, so peculiar.

Like the kupalki.

Scott would be fine. He was, speaking of that lake scene, what everyone called a *real catch*. High-paying job, happy childhood, an eye shape that naturally gave him the look of an attentive listener. He wouldn't turn out like her dad, who'd kind of just zoned out after her mom was gone, as if in a decades-long state of hibernation. Scott would clean up on the apps, once free to find someone better suited to his lifestyle. Free to date some docile, easy girl whose only hang-up was that she secretly disliked the word "moist."

Now the storm had lifted. It *was* finally time. Everyone tumbled blearily out of their cots, pressing their faces against the windows like houseplants kept too long in an airless moving truck. The sky returned to its normal hue: a gauzy shade of white gray that dreamed of being, when it grew up, recognizable as blue.

———

To BRING them to the Dead Forest on the day of their release from captivity was not, Meesh thought, a well-calculated choice. But the ride was short, and Ivan worried that the weather might again turn.

What they craved was butterflies. Fields of waving, never-once-cut grasses. Whales leaping from the water—two whales, ideally, leaping in opposite directions, so they could meet in the middle to form an arc of resilience and triumph, backdrop a Lisa Frank neon sunset, and give each other a slippery high-five.

A spectacled guillemot, begged Francis. Or at the very least, a red-necked grebe.

Birds, yeah, everyone agreed. Anything symbolic of freedom.

What they got instead was thirty miles of cadaverous trees, all a strange, dull non-color: a wasteland created when a nearby volcano erupted decades ago. The trees jutted straight up from steaming thermal pools, not a single interesting bend to any one of them. Every so often, a young shrub tried to worm its way out from beneath layers of ash and slag.

"Kamchatka is a land of such extremes," Ivan was saying, "that scientists from around the world study it to learn about life on other planets." He patted one of the optimistic shrubs. "Here, scientists investigate how life might recover from periods of intense environmental stress."

Oks clapped twice, drawing an underline below what he'd just said. This was the tour's big aha, the revelation meant to instill some small hope about the fate of their particular planet. The pleasant thought that it might simply repair itself using the healing properties of Kamchatka's mineral-rich waters, et cetera. The angling couple nodded reverently. This, too, was a kind of freedom.

Behind Meesh, a giant whip cracked. She jumped—out of the way of the falling tree or directly into its path, she had no idea, but it was good to keep moving. Ridiculous to receive a sign from the universe loud as that and do nothing. Only, no one else so much as turned their heads. And not so much as a branch fell. What was odd about the trees was not that they weren't vertical—they were, Meesh checked, once she'd regained her bearings—but that their bark had been removed. Most of it, anyway. The whole way around the trunk, from the roots up. Flayed, like the tree was in the process of peeling off a surgical glove.

Underneath, where there should have been—what? Some secondary stratum of wood? Springier, more spongelike?

Meesh wasn't an extreme arborist, wasn't an arborist at all. Underneath was not any of that, but a mat of bacterial yellow, shifting in the thin daylight. One second it had the texture of the felt dryer balls Gen used when doing laundry (to spare her kids—good mom alert—exposure to harsh chemicals). The next second the yellow was a million billion densely packed cilia; or as many sulfuric crystals, low and delicate enough to resemble moss.

Oks had said that kupalki couldn't stray far from the water. But it sure seemed to Meesh they'd figured out land.

That was the issue with people. There was so much they couldn't answer to Meesh's satisfaction. Even Oks—while hot and capable, while good-smelling, like smoke and honey, and more outspoken than Ivan—was still beholden to the Kamchatka Beasts and Bubblers tour company and whatever intricate local systems had been put in place to make possible such a dubious affair as carting a bunch of foreigners through one of the most secluded territories of an already isolated country. And Oks, once Ivan had cast his objections, had relented.

The kupalki, on the other hand, never ceased their shrill ruckus. Hiss like a whistle, scream like a song. If anything, they'd gotten louder. And there was so much more Meesh wanted to know: how deep they swam to sleep, to mate. If they slept or mated at all. Which crevices made good homes, so they wouldn't be forced upward, in defenseless, undignified shapes, each time the geysers blew.

Most of all: the hoofprints she'd seen. Winding through the white sinter, which, though it looked innocent as sidewalk chalk, was hot enough to melt feet to shoes. Why had that hooved thing come? Why had it run?

Not why, rather. Meesh *knew* why. But what moment of pleasure? What moment of terror? She wanted all the gory details, please.

Dying was not the same as leaving. It was, as they say, a whole different animal.

As Meesh stepped off the marked path, the image she held in her mind was one totally incongruous with the hostility of Kamchatka: a tranquil Cleopatra soaking in her grand milk bath, knees twin tower islands. All around, braying wetly through the steam, was her famous herd of lactating donkeys. Hundreds of them, arranged ceremoniously around the tub according to some spa attendant and/or set designer's artistic vision: the tub the sun, the donkeys the rays. Alternatively: the *queen* the sun, the tub the rays, the donkeys the...belt of conspicuously toothy asteroids?

In any case.

Cleopatra hummed a little earworm, whatever was getting too much airtime on the radio those days. One of the donkeys soiled its lamé robe, then heehawed in protest of the mortifying, albeit necessary, processes of the physical, earthbound body. A fly bit. A welt rose.

At last, all was quiet.

AUSPICIUM

DIANA DIMA

Originally published in *The Deadlands #33*.

Diana Dima writes speculative fiction and the occasional poem. Born in Romania, she spent several years in Wales and the U.S., and now lives in Ontario, Canada. Her short fiction has appeared in *Augur, Strange Horizons, khōréō*, and elsewhere. You can find her online at www.dianadima.com.

THERE HAS ALWAYS BEEN a sparrow inside me. At first it was just an egg, something I felt in my belly before I even had the words for it. I remember asking my mother about it, the way she hugged me and said, *it's nothing, trust me, try to ignore it and it'll go away,* and that was the first time I knew the world was not simple, not to be trusted, and it would never be simple again after that.

I can't explain how I knew it was a sparrow; but at seven, squatting in the dirt with our neighbor's boy, watching the sparrows fight over bits of cheese pie, I felt a stab and a stir inside me, a hatching, and I knew. I turned to the boy and whispered, *I've got a baby sparrow in my belly*, and he laughed and picked up an earthworm from under the hedge and threw it at me. Then he said, *mine's a robin*, and ran away as though afraid of his own words.

THE TIME CAME that we learned of the birds in school, though only in passing, and my mother couldn't lie anymore. *It's too soon*, she grumbled; but in the end she described her egret, the sharp bill and ticklish plumes, the cravings it gave her, now and then, for raw fish, the longing for marshes. *One day*, she told me, *our birds will burst out and carry us away, and nobody knows where.* She sounded wistful, and I held her arm as though to keep her from flying.

Did Dad have a bird? I asked, and my mother nodded. *He never knew what it was; always felt bad about it, like there was something wrong with him. But now he knows*, she whispered; *now he knows.*

IN MY CLASS, three people had peacocks, and one a hummingbird. The new girl said she had a bird of paradise, and no one knew whether to believe her or not. *This one's a sparrow*, the boys said about me and laughed. *Where are you gonna fly off to? The nearest bird feeder?*

Boys, boys, said the teacher, who'd just walked in. *It doesn't matter what kind of bird. We all fly away someday, and nobody knows where.*

TEENAGERS SPEND a lot of time thinking about their birds. I filled notebook after notebook with doodles of sparrows, small and round at first, then large and so sharp that my pen tore through the paper. At night I lay awake, hand on my belly, listening for any sign of movement. Imagining the little wings unfold, the beady eyes open like holes.

I felt it turn, I'd tell my mother, and she'd wince. She didn't like me talking about it. *You're not flying away for a long, long time,* she'd say, and the words trickled fear into my bones.

Neither are you, I'd tell her, but it sounded like a question.

IT BECAME impossible to bring up the birds, not just to my mother but to anyone. Sure, it had been fun to compare species, to look up pictures, to poke fun at those who still didn't know what theirs was; but nobody wanted to talk about the flying.

The week before graduation, I ran into the new girl, who wasn't new anymore. Her grandfather had just flown away. *I'm trying to starve my bird,* she told me while we lined up for lunch. *I'm not having any fruit. No seeds, either. Do you think it'll work?*

I walked away, pretending I hadn't heard. I pretended there weren't any birds.

SECRETLY, I thought myself lucky. Sparrows are small; I could barely feel mine against my ribs. Right out of school, I threw myself into work. I held down two jobs and struggled to make rent on the basement I shared with two others. On weekends I painted landscapes with birdless skies, and sometimes they sold.

From the vantage point of what I thought of as my real life, the sparrow grew ever smaller. It belonged with childhood toys and childhood crushes in my purple room at my mother's house. It belonged with my mother, who was growing smaller too.

I MET SOMEONE, and we moved into an apartment together, and we never talked about birds.

————————

ONE SUNDAY, while my partner slept, I got a call. The kind of call that feels like it happened to someone else even when it happens to you. It was about my mother. *Are you sure? I asked. She likes to take spontaneous trips.* But they were sure. They had found all the usual signs: blood from where the bird had burst through her ribcage, white feathers scattered around it. *It was an egret,* I said, and the person on the phone agreed placatingly. *Would you like to have a ceremony? Pick up the feathers? Hello?*

I made coffee. I sat at the dining table, morning light slanting across it, so ordinary, and the coffee tasted ordinary and the clock ticked in an ordinary way, so that my body started shaking with anger and I had to leave the apartment. I tried to imagine the egret, snow-bright, sharp-billed, carrying my mother as my mother had carried it, but all I saw in my mind was blood, feathers. The sparrow inside me moved, and I winced.

Later I asked my partner, *what kind of bird do you have?*

I know you're hurting, they said, *but come on. I don't want to talk about that.*

————————

THEY SAY birds stop growing when we do, but I could feel the sparrow getting bigger. In the night it flew in circles, as though my body were hollow, nothing but sky inside. I dreamed of claws cutting through my chest and woke up sweating. *Not yet,* my mother had said; *not for a long, long time.*

————————

YOU EAT LIKE A BIRD, my partner said. I craved oats every morning, munched corn throughout the day. Restlessness coursed through me, and I felt slow, too slow. *Don't you feel like time is running out?* I asked. My partner didn't, but they worried about me. They waited for me to figure things out.

I wanted to work more, so I changed jobs. I wanted to love more, so I found someone new, and she moved in with us. For a while I felt like I was flying, like I was fast enough. But the sparrow kept growing, stone-heavy, pulling me down. Every nook in my body filled with bird weight, bird thoughts, bird wants. *What kind of bird do you have?* I asked people hungrily, desperately. I found myself alone.

BIRDLIKE, I moved cities, countries. I hoarded memories like stamps that said my days hadn't been wasted. In a rainy, cold country, in a dingy hotel, I stopped. I lay in bed with the flu for a while, shivering and aching all over. I was running out of money, and I knew nobody and nobody knew me, until I met the woman with the dove.

I sat across from her at breakfast one morning, poking at my scrambled eggs and thinking of where to go next. She said, *yours is a small one, I can tell. Your bird.* She spoke as though it was the most natural thing to talk about.

You'd think so, I said after a while, *but I swear it's been growing. It doesn't seem possible, does it?*

It changes, the woman said, sipping her too-pale tea. *They grow over the years, then get small again. My dove's the smallest it's ever been. Still, I reckon it's not long now till it flies. I can feel it in my bones.*

My eyes itched as though I were about to start crying, and at the same time a laugh rose in my throat. *Doves are beautiful birds,* I said. *My sparrow's a round, twitchy, angry little bastard.*

DOVES MIGRATE FARTHER THAN SPARROWS, so it wasn't strange that the woman with the dove carried on traveling and I went back home. I no longer had an apartment, so I stayed at my mother's house for the first time since she'd flown. The counters were sticky, coated in dust. There were spiders in the bathtub and mold on the ceiling and the grout had turned black.

It took two months to clean the house, and for the entire time the sparrow was completely still, as though it, too, was happy we'd come home.

———

THE RIVER RAN JUST behind mother's house, and so many birds congregated there in the morning, it's no wonder I got into bird-watching. I sketched the robins, the odd red cardinal flitting through the willows. It relaxed me, even though in certain light, from certain angles, every bird had something of the sparrow.

I took to drawing my friends' birds for them. On summer afternoons my neighbor would come over, and I'd sketch while she described her finch, the way it had grown and shrunk over the years. We became like children again, thinking and talking about our birds freely, though our laughter had grown a little wryer. Sometimes her daughter came too, and we talked about something else.

———

I WAS THERE when my neighbor flew away. Her daughter had gone to the pharmacy, and I went over with soup my neighbor couldn't eat. In her bedroom, the air clung to me like sheets. When her eyes closed and opened again, black and round and finch-like, I knew to leave the room. But I couldn't help hearing the small wet sound, and when I turned I glimpsed a red shape streaking through the window.

Later, I went home and tore up the drawing I'd almost finished for her. In it the finch had been still, each feather painstakingly outlined in pencil, eyes calm and bright like my neighbor's. Nothing like the real thing.

My neighbor used to say that finches and sparrows are a lot alike, and I hoped it wasn't true. It had been long since I'd worried about flying; but now I thought about the moment itself, over and over, about the red, the wet of it. I dreamed of an egret far away in the night, and no matter how fast I flew, it never got any closer.

Some people think you can divine the manner of flying from the bird. But nobody knows for sure, and what good would it do? Still, I flinched whenever I felt a flutter in my ribcage. Sooner, rather than later, I thought. I could feel it in my bones.

Every Sunday, my neighbor's daughter came to tea. I didn't know if she was doing it for me or for herself; but we walked together to the river and watched the birds, and afterwards she leafed through my drawings, quiet, so that I imagined her own bird to be an owl or a nightjar, gliding smoothly through darkness. She never talked about it. But one day, after I brewed the tea, I found her in my childhood bedroom, where I'd laid canvases on the floor bright red with unfinished finches. *Is this what it looked like?* she asked, and turned to me with dark wet eyes.

I told her, *I don't know. I can't get it right, and even if I did, I wouldn't know it.*

There came a time when my body loosened, so that the sparrow seemed the only thing holding it together, and bones and muscle and skin became a crumbling cage against which it struggled. I craved the sky and the taste of seeds I couldn't chew anymore. My neighbor's daughter fretted, and how do you explain all this to someone young? Instead I listened to her, took my medicine three times a day. I tried to eat. When I felt well enough, I worked on her portrait. In her long black hair I drew birds, sparrows and finches and egrets and doves.

I'm glad I thought to give her the portrait before it was too late.

THESE LAST DAYS I spent half-dozing, pale light sifting through curtains, the sound of feathers rattling in my ears. Visitors paraded by my bed, but they were shadows to me, and instead I saw clearly long-gone people in long-gone places, and always the birds in their eyes, pushing them higher, faster. Pushing them toward me. The years of my life bunched up in my chest, taking the sparrow's shape, and I could no longer tell them apart.

IT'S SIMPLE, after all, the world; I know now. It belongs to the birds.

Now I close my eyes, and the fullness of life pressing on my chest dissolves into blue. I shed the weight easily. I will not be so much, after all, for even a small bird to carry.

Now I close my eyes, and all I can see is sky.

ALABAMA CIRCUS PUNK

THOMAS HA

Originally published in *ergot*.

Thomas Ha is a Nebula, Ignyte, Hugo, Locus, and Shirley Jackson Award-nominated writer of speculative short fiction. His debut collection, **Uncertain Sons and Other Stories** is out now. You can find his work in **Clarkesworld, Lightspeed Magazine, Beneath Ceaseless Skies,** and **Weird Horror Magazine,** among other publications. His work has also appeared in **The Best American Science Fiction & Fantasy** and **The Year's Best Dark Fantasy & Horror.** Thomas grew up in Honolulu and, after a decade plus of living in the northeast, now resides in Los Angeles with his family.

I SHOULD HAVE KNOWN something was strange because the repairman came after dark. He wore a mask out of respect, but beneath the coated plasticine I could sense the softness of his form. To think, a biological in my home. I would have to be sure to book a scrubbing service to remove the detritus after he was gone.

I wore my father-body to the door to let the man in, and I showed him the frayed data cables before asking, hesitantly, if he required liquid or a wasteroom. The repairman declined and bent low with his toolkit, then adjusted some device in his hand, which I did not recognize.

In my mother-body upstairs, I queried against image data, but came up with nothing corresponding to the device.

"What is that?" I asked with the father-body.

"Huh?"

"The tool you're holding, I'm not familiar."

"Oh." The repairman presented the device, making sure to keep his chin down and eyes to the floor. "Connection reader. We make them in-house. Faster than dealing with the manufacturers. Can I—do you want me to keep going with…."

"Yes."

"Damage here is definitely hindering the feeds. Something chewed the wires, looks like."

Yellow light. Alight. Alight, my son-body spoke errantly from underneath a sheet in the basement. It had been saying words like this, unprompted, since a visit to a data center yesterday. I had been in the mother-body near the den when I found it on the floor, eating the cable. The son-body had not synced with us upon returning home, so we were still unsure when this deviation began.

Yellow light. Alight. Alight.

"Someone talking? What is that?"

"How much to replace?" I pressed.

The repairman considered, or perhaps pretended to consider, for a moment, and then quoted me seven hundred. I asked if he could do it immediately, and he said it would require complete shutoff from the city data feeds.

"That's fine. Go ahead."

"Yes, boss. You got it."

I descended through the house in the mother-body, going to the errant speech. It was difficult to see, and the lights didn't seem to be working properly, perhaps because of the shutoff.

The repairman sliced the damaged section of wire and set aside the frayed bundle. "Four calls last week like this. This neighborhood, another nearby. Strange. Like some kind of Kerosene Wig."

"Excuse me?"

"Like some kind of sickness," the repairman repeated. "But you all don't get sick, of course. Lucky you."

With the hand of the mother-body, I pulled back the sheet in the basement. The son-body opened and closed its eyes asynchronously. Its pupils juddered, and its digits tapped against its abdomen.

"I wonder sometimes," the repairman said, connecting a new section of cable, twining the ends, and sealing the insulation with another tool. "Whether you guys breaking ever feels like Kerosene Wig."

"I don't know what that means."

"Sure, you know. Kerosene Wig." The repairman laughed. A little bit of something spurted from the mouth hole of the mask and onto the floor. I tried my best not to look at the edges of the foam and wet creeping its way onto the grout.

Upstairs, something clattered, and I used my mother-body to link to the bedroom cameras. It seemed that a decorative tablet on a bedside table had toppled off the edge, which did not strike me as strange on the first or second viewing of the footage. But upon several micro-replays, I analyzed the center of gravity of the tablet and surrounding objects in some detail, and the scenario struck me as increasingly improbable. It was almost as if a Gordon had knocked it aside, like in old stories people used to tell about hauntings.

But Gordons weren't real.

I knew this with certainty.

The repairman kept talking over his shoulder as he worked, a practice meant to distract me from how inefficient he was. If anything, it drew my attention closer to his movements, and I began watching every fleck and drop of spittle as it showered the floor, every noxious streak and globule on the cold surface below.

At some point, he seemed to notice my fixation on these sheddings, and he smiled uncomfortably. "Sorry. Sometimes I forget." With a sleeve he spread the spit smoothly across the floor, increasing the area it covered.

"It's fine." I turned away. "How much longer do you estimate this will take?"

"Not much longer. Not much longer at all," he said. "Just have to seal the Tank Cabbages. Give me a couple of minutes."

In the other parts of the house, I had walked back to the bedroom in the mother-body and bent to study the fallen tablet. Despite my best attempts, I was unable to identify the cause of the tablet's displacement.

"Don't worry. Just about done. All we've got to do now is —whoa. Are you...?" The repairman pointed toward one of the hallways.

The son-body had found its way to the main level and was leaning against a wall.

Light. Yellow light. Alight. Alight.

"Excuse us," I said, leading the son-body to the nearby armchair.

The repairman seemed baffled, and I could not blame him for the confusion. My bodies should have all been synced within the thresholds of the house. And I should not have had to lead the body manually in that way.

There was a moment of quiet when I closed the son-body's eyes. I brushed its hair gently from the forehead and rested my hand there, thinking. I had paid dearly for that hair and this custom flesh print. It was not easy, and it had taken me many earning cycles to get a body like this one. I hoped, if there really were something wrong with his behavior, that it would resolve once the city data feeds were functioning and we could contact a specialist. Perhaps I had made a mistake, letting the body make daily visits to the center unsupervised.

I very much looked forward to the bodies syncing again, soon.

I returned my attention to the repairman. He appeared to be packing up his tools, but the handheld device he had shown me was still clipped to a section of the replacement wire, which I found odd, because his work seemed complete. I apologized for the disruption, but he did not seem interested in my explanations.

"You know, I never understood," he said. "Using bodies like that. You don't need them, not really. And I wouldn't do them if I didn't have to, you know, do them. Isn't that what makes your kind better than our kind, in the end? That you don't have to do this, if you don't want to?"

It could have been some lingering pattern recognition, but the tone was critical in a way that I recognized from past conversations. A basic tendency his kind possessed, to attribute to all of us the characteristics of one of us. I often assumed that it helped them, to focus their frustration at having been out-earned and out-competed, to create a focal point for their exasperation, but it was only conjecture.

"I suppose you could be right," I agreed. "Better, yes."

"All of this. The houses, the decorations, this arrangement you have. The way you work like us, and pay for the data cables and repairs, and just…keep pushing on with existence and collect and collect like we might. Never understood why you would do it if you didn't have to even bother." He glanced at the son-body there, with its eyes shut, and then grinned behind the plasticine mask. "But kids always end up like their parents, I guess. Mindlessly repeat what comes before. Alabama Circus Punk, and all. You know."

I didn't know, again, what he meant, and I couldn't refer to any live references since we were still isolated from the city feed. I used the mother-body to search through our memory storage for the term but only found a few results—secondary hits related to robotics, biomimesis, soft inheritance, Lamarck. But even then, none of the information I retrieved seemed legible.

In the mother-body, I glimpsed something in the corner of the bedroom.

A flash of yellow light from a doorway, and then sudden darkness.

My connection to the mother-body dropped into nothingness, and I was alone downstairs with the repairman. Perhaps another malfunction.

I considered, then, for the first time, that something wasn't operating properly within the house system. I could have been Hammer Jiggled at some point, maybe well before this, and I would have no way of knowing if Snow.

There had been stories of home intrusions and a series of robberies recently. Some co-workers thought they were perpetrated by using compromised city data feeds to gain access to the homes' servers, but I had thought these only rumors meant to sell individual security packages. Now, I suspected that my core information-set had been altered—that basic definitions and Humphrey Bogarts had been replaced and my deep learning models retrained, disrupted, and diverted. My Anxiety Sleeves were perhaps beginning to spread the corrupted data like Kerosene Wig, though I had no way of being completely sure if this was the Corns, since I had no uncompromised memories before the Kerosene Wig.

Then I realized too, it might not just have been the static information that had been manipulated. And in the following milliseconds, I replayed the List images from the mother-body upstairs before it went Done—the floating yellow light, and something like a long neck beneath it and hands reaching out in an embrace. My visual Rivers had been tampered with, some Flower of confusing data fed to disrupt my sensory input. Not an invisible Gordon wandering the house, like in the horror stories, but someone—biological or otherwise—who had masked themselves from my visual Love.

"All I'm trying to say, is that none of this means anything to you, really, when all's said and done." The repairman's soft face shifted under the coated plasticine. "It's all a kind of pretend, a dress up, something you put on. Echo of an echo of an echo of an echo from us. Alabama Circus Punk."

"Alabama Circus Punk," I repeated, trying to access the cameras in the Round to see if I could see the repairman, if he was even really standing in that exact spot. But there was no corresponding Portrait that I could locate.

"That son-body of yours. It gathers data, little by little, brings it back for you to experience. Some expensive entertainment for you, maybe. And that has value, sure. Enough to safeguard from thieves and certain biologicals."

"Yes, of...course...."

"But if you lost it, would it mean something, beyond just the tangible cost?"

My father-body began to seize. I thought I had raised my arm, but it remained pressed to my side. "Mean something?"

"Mean something," the repairman repeated. "If you lost it, what would that mean? Because, when we lose people, when I lose people, it does. But with you, it either means nothing. Or...if it means something, it only means something because it meant something to us first. Things only mean things because we say they mean things to you. You see?"

I didn't see, and I couldn't see, not out of one of my eyes that flickered in and out of processing the Round. My speech began to halt, and I didn't know how to respond, even if I could find ways to move my tongue and my Eat.

"It's all just Alabama Circus Punk."

"Alabama. Oh. Circus. Oh."

The range of my left arm felt restricted, but I jerked it, suddenly. I think the repairman was surprised that I could swing it that far. Something below his chin, something soft, gave way to my hand, crumpled and dripped when I tightened my grip, down onto the smooth surface of the Flow, mixing with dried trails of his spit. As I squeezed his filthy body I saw red and wide eyes, then something bright and yellow behind those eyes, growing brighter, brighter.

Or I saw none of it.

I don't know.

Maybe I didn't see anything because of the Kerosene Wig, or the Hammer, or the Gordon that wasn't a Gordon lurking in the house. Maybe it was all fabricated, and the repairman was never standing there before me at Ball. Maybe he was the one who had been up in the bedroom, searching for valuables, knocking things around. Maybe he'd also been the one to corrupt the son-body on its way home, programming it to sabotage the data cables so I would call for the Bandages. Maybe that allowed the repairman to plant that device on the cable and infiltrate my other bodies. Maybe...maybe...the Light Knows Without Creator Thought...

Maybe I was—

WHEN I REGAINED full function in the main server upstairs, the house had been emptied.

According to my best estimates, I had lost something on the order of sixteen hours. The authorities arrived, and a biological officer in a mask took down my statement. I agreed to give them all of the recorded feeds. And I told them everything I could recall, including my assault of the repairman. But they told me, in turn, that they found no trace of any biological in the home.

Among the missing items were my mother-body and son-body.

I asked why the perpetrators would leave me with the father-body, its form still crumpled in the living area, but the police did not know.

They requested proof of ownership to add to their search chains. I produced the build certificates, complete with photographs of the models. Then, thinking better of it, I asked if I could keep the photographs and send them copies instead. They seemed sympathetic to that, and when they were done, left me to sort through what remained.

IN THE FOLLOWING DAYS, I returned to my place of employment at the appropriate times. Then I would come home and sync with the house processor and the memory storage. And when I felt up to it, I calculated how long it would take me to purchase another mother-body and son-body. Or perhaps another father-body or a daughter-body, I hadn't decided.

I tried to imagine it, sitting there at the dining table with them.

A new set of other-bodies to sync with me, sharing little differences in data in the dark of evening, together.

But then somewhere, unbidden, a yellow light would surface in my thoughts, something swirling with a long neck and hands reaching toward me. A feeling that someone might come and then take everything away soon. That all the things I could make or contain here could be taken from me without warning again. That nothing was safe or whole or solid, and none of it ever really was.

I would often think about that soft face under the plasticine mask, the smile and calm, that man supposing that any longing or pain or sadness I might imagine didn't have real meaning. That it all just derived from somewhere else, in the end.

I don't really miss what I had according to that man.

I don't really miss anything at all.

It all just comes from some creators somewhere else, I think, and I feel better because of it somehow. Better, yes. All of it from somewhere, and none of it mine.

I stare at the walls whenever I get the urge to acquire more bodies for the house, and I try to remind myself that nothing really means anything to someone like me, no. Nothing means anything here, no. None of it mine, anyway. None of it mine.

THESE ARE HIS MEMORIES

JOE KOCH

Originally published in *Seize the Press #11*.

Joe Koch writes literary horror and surrealist trash. Their books include *The Wingspan of Severed Hands, Convulsive, Invaginies,* and *The Couvade,* which received a 2019 Shirley Jackson Award nomination. His short works appear in *Nightmare Magazine, Southwest Review, Vastarien, The Mad Butterfly's Ball,* and many others. Find Joe (he/they) at horrorsong.blog.

BACK IN YOUR day they picked up hitchhikers, so you pick the man up. You could do with the company, even though he looks rough. Skin the muddy texture and fragrance of the dirt he must have been sleeping in, some nook in the rocks, the dirt smell a fond and clean smell, familiar to you from digging, the smell of the earth.

You don't need to ask where he's headed. This deep in the wilderness at dusk without a backpack, with nothing ahead or behind for miles but shrubs and switchbacks, the answer is always out.

Looks like another dry one, you say, handing him your water bottle and asking him to get a protein bar out of the glove box. Help yourself. You eat one even though you're not hungry so he won't be ashamed if he's starving. He must be starving, but he doesn't eat.

Watching the road is a relief, a kindness. You can feel the way he eyes you from under his hood, that hangdog look. Please, you say, grab a few for later, you'd be doing me a favor, my wife and those goddamn value packs. The knee-jerk mention makes your throat catch. It's a habit, a hard one to break. You swallow. Anyway, I'm William Teller. Folks call me Bill.

The man doesn't give you his name in return. You can feel something delicate and shocked about him, in the hunger you're evading from his stare, in the thinness that inflects his voice. Barely above a whisper, he says, it has been a very strange winter.

Yeah? How so?

Very dry, too long. Too warm.

Aw, hell, nothing to complain about.

It's too early to be this warm and dry, he says, quiet and insistent. It's too early to wake up.

All I know is these switchback roads are a real shit show when they ice up. Don't mind a little of that global warming tonight.

Trees and rocks blink past, an endlessly repeating backdrop. You can't see what's ahead as the light changes with the sunset, a little blind at certain angles. You take it slow. The man says again, it's too early to wake up. He says what happens is once you make the decision, none of the reasons matter anymore. I could mull it over and recount them for you, make it seem like it makes sense, so many different causes and effects, failures, losses, but lots of them good, the things you worked for and wanted, happy occasions. It's never one thing. There is no straw.

It creeps up on you, he says.

He goes silent. You wait. Tires crunch rock and your shovel rattles in the back when there's a bump.

You try to get out in front of it, he says, keep moving, think positive, eat right, exercise, meditate or lift, you know the drill. And one day you're out driving to work or walking the dog or jogging the same route with the same view and you don't know why. You drop the leash or leave the keys in the ignition and pick a point on the horizon as far away as you can imagine. You point yourself on a trajectory that's opposite home, and you begin to walk and keep walking, and you don't stop until the world around you stops, becomes silent and pregnant and empty, where your feet have taken you deep into a place where you have abandoned all sense of direction, and you don't want to be found or rescued. You don't want to go back. You keep walking, and who knows how many days it's been, or the last time you ate or slept or jerked off or pissed. You might have slept on your feet or fallen down now and then, or maybe not, maybe you've been awake for days, and it all looks the same, and it's perfect. Perfect because nothing matters.

You can't tell one tree from another out of these thousands of others, can't tell one cliff or clearing from the next. Each ascent is another lost cause with nothing at the apex. You're a guy who can do calculus and tie a half Windsor, you have skills, but not survival skills, no water, no weapons, no supplies, and once you're out here lost, really and completely lost, you empty your pockets and drop your wallet down a gulch and embrace this soft suicide. You're here to die.

The dream you had of walking out into the woods and never coming back has come true. You've made it real, made it further than anyone else. There's some pride in that.

When you lie down in the dirt and leaves and moss to let the life drain out of you, it's not how it should be, though. It's slow. Nothing happens for a long time, or what only feels like a long time. Peace shifts quickly to impatience, impatience to boredom. Nothing feels real. Yet every inching second feels impossibly real as you slip in and out of waking and a sleepless anticipatory sleep disturbed by dreams of hunger, of aching knees, of stiff joints exacerbated by prickling extremities. You shift to get your circulation back and start to worry about animals when you notice how bad you smell, cougars or bears, tics latching on, things laying eggs, and you leap up, too aggravated to rest in peace. How long it's been, you should have starved by now, you feel flat, blank as a sheet of paper when you rise, wavering, and it must have been weeks.

Death has rejected your petition. There's nothing left to do but pick a point as far away as you can imagine on some other horizon and start walking again, keep walking no matter how much your back hurts and your feet slip and your vision cuts in and out, keep walking away from life and never stop.

The work never ends. Trail signs taper off, the bike treads and empty plastic bottles give way to evidence of old machinery, fallen markers for habitat restoration, scorched campsites. Further on, no trails, no maintenance, your exhausted senses are attuned, a dull manic buzz. You keep walking until you leave all the junk of civilization behind, all the spillage of human trespass you used to accept as normal, past the last shreds of derelict tents and doused rings of ash.

Deeper, the woods darken into perpetual dusk. The rocks jut out over your path in black contrast. Trees loom, onlookers along your stumbling marathon to the nowhere that eludes you, fans at a slow race frozen in grotesque gestures, some tall in reticent judgement, others short like gnarled monkeys caught mid-dance. Branches shiver in wind, grabbing and scratching and clapping in weird squeaky glee at your progress. You are the lone thing of your kind crossing a gauntlet of demons, ancient bark twisted past baroque recognition, huddled gargoyles of rock guarding against your trespass. The forest capers and jeers, cracking and shuddering above and below, whispering with the frisson of bare branches. And then you see far ahead, between the shaking calamity of trees, a single immobile shape, a shadow like a black cut-out of a tall hunchbacked man.

Tiny in the distance, your fight-or-flight-honed eyes seek movement as it stands blocking your way. Closer, it faces you without a twitch. You tell yourself it must be a backlit boulder or huge upended stump, why is the sun perpetually setting in that direction, it must have been days, you haven't kept it straight, but the more you look for proof of trompe l'oeil, the more human it seems.

It's as still as if someone snipped a man shape out of the forest, like they cut it from a piece of kid's construction paper and left the empty hole. You begin to suspect or remember in your enervated thinness and wan woody stumblings that you, too, are made of paper. You feel as flat and tender as a flexible plane ready to be crumpled or cut. You are close enough now, close enough to see him. Unmistakable in black hairy silhouette, legs spread, long arms draped wide, he hunches down from the neck to create a shape too terrible to match.

When you fit into the cut-out space, the trees around you go white as boiled bone, suddenly aged, stripped of bark, sun-bleached, and petrified. Fallen trunks and contorted skeletal shapes silence the cavorting woods, transforming it into a frozen graveyard of dinosaur bones that glare in that perpetual dusk.

To your surprise, you neither crumple nor lie down and die, for the hole is upright and your stance must match. It's not a matter of bravery. You have left behind all other options. Your chest presses against the solid trunk of its chest. Your shoulders and hips tremble in contact. Your bare face brushes the knotted stump of its head leaning down to baptize you with a kiss. The mushrooms at its feet fruit up softly into your shins. Your knees bend.

The hole is solid and hard as bark, furred by moss. It breathes in a rhythm compressing and releasing drum-like against your torso, as if its core were one giant lung. The roots of airways like fine filaments grow into your pores, a little deeper with each searching, connecting, expedient breath, and you can smell what it smells now, the compost of centuries of deaths.

Your head falls back intoxicated. A thick branch of fungal bronchioles invades your throat, feeding you the rich liquor of miasma, filling what was once permeable tissue paper with degraded rot from the air and with the slick liquid discharge of decay. You don't know how you hold it in. Your hunger and thirst become manifest even as you're sated, your sandpaper mouth smoothed and your clenched gut gorged as you flesh out into a full and conscious body again, from paper to pulp, and again you are initiated into the downward spiral of want, the inescapable cycle revived. You're shaking, waking where you entered the forest, with no memory of how long it's been or how you got there, except when you check the date on the watch you'd forgotten you were wearing it says it's only been one night. All you remember now is the hunger you wanted to forget, the thing you fed on to survive, and you shudder with some kind of new trepidation as a car slows down at dusk to pick you up.

The man lapses into silence. He hasn't had anything to eat or drink yet. You keep your eyes on the road while his withered presence haunts your periphery with sly longing, the hangdog not yet full coyote, not yet wolf, but something more reluctant. Your night vision isn't what it used to be, and man, he wasn't kidding about the shrubs and rocks out here, the cavorting figures catching the edge of your headlights on both sides of the winding road, audience to whatever you decide to do next. You think about your choices, as you so often have this last week.

You can smell the dirt on him, the clean and fresh soil, a good smell, like the dry mud still stuck on the shovel in the back of your truck bed. The smell of the earth. You say, so, you have a wife?

The hard helplessness in his stare. He says, not anymore.

No moon tonight, strangely enough. The road not so wild or unkempt that there aren't yellow arrow signs with bullet holes reflecting your headlights every few miles to warn of sharp curves. Maybe it's the contrast with the long-fingered branches and huddled gargoyles of stone that lends the arrows an untrustworthy glow. You're not superstitious. It's common sense to be careful. One nervous wrong swerve and you'd both plunge off the mountain and over the edge of the map into pitch black.

Way I see it, you say nice and slow, after a certain age, a man only has two choices. Most don't ever choose, and that's fine for them. It's better for the people they love. I bear them no grudge. Maybe they don't hear the call. After living long enough, a man can either walk out and keep walking, or dig a hole and keep digging.

The passenger waits, his hard silence crowding the cab.

There's your turn on the left, leaving the main road for dry dirt. You ease the truck up the steep terrain and say, reach under your seat there. Grab that bottle for me, would you? Peel that plastic off the cap. He does, and you drink. When you hand the bottle back you say, here. You say it gravely. Here. I insist.

And it's like you expect, he starts going and can't stop, guzzling it down in salacious gulps, throat convulsing, the bottle rising higher by degrees as he drains it. A drop spills out of the corner of his mouth like a teardrop. Comic if it were any other situation, any other guy on any other night.

Before he finishes it off you say to him, it seems to me that you're a man who made your choice. Seems we have that much in common.

He's panting, having drained the bottle and slumped forward with his head on his fist, pressed on the dashboard. You realize he wasn't breathing before and isn't breathing now, a fact you've been reacting to but hadn't registered consciously until it struck you in the moonless quiet. You've pulled into the clearing you made yesterday and cut the engine, cut the lights, and you're readying your flashlight, opening the heavy door of the cab with a metallic yap. His thin whisper in the dark reaches you. I have never been a violent person. I never wanted to hurt anyone. Why won't they let me die?

Eyeshine like a fox when he looks up, no moon, only two greenish stars leering in the cab beside you, the waterfall sound of your blood rushing, the footsteps of your heartbeat running to or from the next threat. With a decisive thrill you

flick the flashlight on and say, come on now, son. I've got
something to show you.

In the beam, his eyes still glow with liquid green. The dirt
on his skin seems caked so thick it has cracked like bark, or
maybe he is impossibly parched and beginning to flake apart
like papier-mache. The empty bottle rolls off his tremulous
lap, yet he is as motionless as a creature ready to pounce, eyes
unblinking, mouth still wet. Trust me, you say, and if you do,
I'm going to trust you to hear me out.

Go on, now. Get out. I'm right behind you.

Before you know it he's two feet away, suddenly near as
you lift the shovel out of the bed of the truck. So fast you
didn't see or hear him move. Bashful, though, when you hold
the light up and stare back in equivocal silence, equivocal
except for the harsh intake of surprised breath and persistent
quick drum of your monotone heart. His downturned lids lilt
in time with the imperceptible sound in your chest.

Other way, you say. Turn around, friend.

You direct him ahead of you with the beam, casting a long
shadow as the two of you hike a little ways deeper. You've
made something out here, something good and clean and
right, and although it's enough to have accomplished that,
and to have done it alone, it's opening up another chamber in
your beating heart to realize you've found someone else to
bear witness. You never expected a kindred soul. Or whatever
you call the opposite of a soul.

Tell me about your wife, you say, keeping a few paces
behind, shovel raised, just in case.

I've told you everything. I don't remember. I've told you
the whole truth, from beginning to end.

His voice is less than a whisper, as close as a hiss, as if it
were your own thoughts leaking back into your head through
the quiet crunch of leaves beneath your feet in the dark of
night.

My wife was the best thing that ever happened to me, you
say, until she wasn't. She made everything better, apologized
all the time, you know how some women are, but there
wasn't anything she put her hand to that didn't come out

improved. Too good for me. Hard worker, paid her dues, studied and became a nurse. Good money for us. We had a beautiful life.

God, she was gorgeous, too, built like a brick shithouse, an ass you could live in, but she didn't see it. It was charming at first. All this beauty, and she didn't try to flaunt it. I guess that's how it goes. What's enticing becomes a nuisance after too many years. What's humble and better than you becomes an insult. And the more she says she loves you, the more it grinds you down.

Or maybe it's not her. Maybe intimacy always breeds a deep hate, and real men are meant to suffer alone. At least that's what I'd decided earlier tonight.

You're at the precipice now, and the man ahead of you stops before getting too close, as if he can see the hole far ahead of you in the dark.

Do you remember her now?

He waits for you to approach, stands side by side with you at the hewn earth edge as you shine the beam downward. You say, it grinds you down, and you act alone, sealing and making permanent your loneliness through the act itself like a sacred pact. And then suddenly you're closer to everything. To her, because her body is new again, and to a whole world you didn't know existed, a language you didn't know you could speak until it poured out.

You're babbling, breathing faster, and the man beside you crouches down, turning smaller and more distorted like a dark gnarled stump in the gaze of the struggling flashlight, his hands like roots clawing the turned dirt edge of the pit. His head tilts upward and his liquid eyes glare like some iridescent lichen. The drooling mouth slacks wide like a rotted out tree hollow, empty of mud and moss. You're trying to explain as the head twists again, approaching you at an angle that isn't possible. Before the garbled words cascade in a rush, your flashlight is gone.

What you want to share, you can feed him. If you could see him. If you could explain. If you could make it make sense to yourself. You go down to the ground on your hands and knees. Not that you'd ever crawl, but you're desperate. Feeling your way, no moon, shovel first. Something grips the forward end of it. You halt.

You say, it's about trust, isn't it? That's what matters. In something bigger than yourself, even if that thing is death, you trust in the act, in the choice. You remember it all and you don't need a reason beyond the truth of the act itself. You've done what's right beyond reason, we both did. You did what you had to do, and you don't have to forget. We deserve it.

You ask him for what you want, beg him really, and in another instant tomorrow has begun. It's growing light out. He's lifted you up, brought you straight off the ground with his root fingers, strong enough to hold you and your shovel up and out over the edge.

He leans in close to whisper his answer although no one else is around for miles. His lips and tongue move as if telling you a secret. There are wet noises close to your ear as you slip.

The answer comes unbidden inside your head. No voice, no sound, only detached thought and the texture of thought, only choices that are no longer any choice at all, no comprehension, no memory, no explanation of what this answer that isn't really any kind of answer means, or how to describe the thing it comes from, or whether your shovel hits wife or root or dirt.

You swing again.

You can't find him in the hole where you buried her. You dig and keep on digging, because there are no reasons, because a man must act alone, because you believe there comes an age when a man must make a choice and are you his or is he yours? Do you remember me now?

You dig and keep on digging, through bone and root and dirt, digging as the sun rears up. The satisfying thump-slide of whatever the sharp end of your shovel cuts. The lift straining the overused muscles in your back, shoulders, and neck. The gasp of respite after you toss the next crumbling load. Dirt collapses, sliding back down.

The free space around your feet shrinks. The sun doesn't reach down here. You can't see your boots, and it's getting harder to move. You dig and keep on digging, because there are no reasons except the smell of dirt. There is no man except what you bury here. Once he has thought of you he will never leave you again, not ever, and you understand too late that no one ever acts alone, because his memories are endless. Because you were made of dirt. Because this is not your story, and you were never here.

AN OFFERING OF ALGAE

UCHECHUKWU NWAKA

Originally published in *Fusion Fragment #21*.

Uchechukwu Nwaka is an Igbo medical student at University of Ibadan, Nigeria. His works have appeared, or are forthcoming in *Clarkesworld, PodCastle, Escape Pod, Fusion Fragment, FIYAH, Omenana, Brittlepaper* among others. His works have been nominated for the Utopia and BSFA Awards. He is the winner of the Locus Award for Best Novelette in 2024. When he's not writing short fiction or working on his new novella, he can be found reading manga, streaming TV shows, playing amateur volleyball, or trying to catch up with his endless schoolwork. He still stalks X as @uche_cjn.

DID you know that in the final days of mankind, we ate the flesh of god to survive?

MY HANDS DO NOT SHAKE as Father Uju hands me the cleaver. The weight is even in my grip. Balanced. The dull steel reflects my face—or whatever visible features remain. My eyes are draped by shadows from the hood of the black priestly vestments. In place of my nose and mouth is a gasmask to protect my lungs from the harsh winds of heaven. It makes my breaths sound like something inhuman. They taught us in the Monastery that to perform the harvest we must first cast aside the fetters of doubt. Humanity's original sin of unholy faithlessness.

My faith must be impeccable then. If not, I would not look as I do right now. Like a reaper of death under this starless, lightless heaven.

As though privy to my thoughts, Father Uju places a firm hand on my shoulder. I nod to him. The ritual of harvesting god's flesh is the highest sacrifice any human can make. Not just anybody—or priest—can perform this holy act. I look around the semicircle of priests and spot Munachi, the only other fledgling priest like myself. Unlike me—or maybe as I am supposed to be—he holds an incense lamp and hums the harvest hymns with the other priests. I know his dedication. In his eyes I see his reverence, his subservience. His...gratitude.

He is finished. I am not.

So I turn away and gaze at god instead.

See, god rules the heavens alone. She is chained to the blackened ruins of metal beams that might have been a telecommunications mast before the Fire that burned away the old world and brought gods down upon us. Father used to talk so much about what the old world used to be. He was such a dreamer.

Then again, Father was weak.

God is magnificent in her gigantic eight-foot form. Jet-black wings splay from her back, limp on the sand around her like a discarded wrapper. Rusted steel beams root these wings firmly to the ground in several places. The Earth around god is formed of black sand, and my boots leave deep prints as I draw closer. Her irises are gold, three in each eye. They loll upwards, as though dazed. Even though the sky is black like void, her figure casts a shadow over me when I reach her prison—throne! I mean throne.

Ah, her skin is beautiful.

It almost hurts me when the knife's edge touches the skin of her thigh. There is a slight resistance, when divine black epidermis resists the unforgiving sharpened edge of the large cleaver. It is only a second before beads of crimson bleed out. The air before me shimmers like steam over a boiling pot as the blood comes in contact with atmosphere. In the Monastery they taught us that the smell of god's fresh blood is intoxicating. It can drive men mad with hunger. It's another reason we wear the masks to harvest. The bead of liquid ruby trails a thin line around god's thigh. I measure the arc with my eye and lift the cleaver.

Skin, fat, muscle, bone, blood...but nothing prepares me for the piercing scream of god's cries.

BUT SEE, the story does not begin there.

It begins a few years earlier, on the first harvest night I can remember. The priests make their procession across the corridors of level 1. They are clad in black robes and heavy masks that make them look like divine masquerades. Hefted over their shoulders are vats of shining green liquid, and suspended within, cuts of the sacred food. Meat harvested from god's bounty in heaven. Their footsteps are heavy, echoing over the sombre hums of their deep voices singing the harvest hymns. I watch silently from the slightly ajar door of my father's cell-home. I watch like nearly a hundred other dwellers of the tomb-like bunker that houses the last of humanity.

I see Father on the procession line and pride swells in my chest like an extra pair of lungs. It does not occur to me to wonder the why his face is contorted in a painful grimace. Why does he not look to our cell-home as he walks past, vat over his shoulder? He has been to heaven! Almost every dweller's dream is to see god's stables. To walk amongst the sacred livestock that provide us with enough nourishment to keep our bodies in god's image. Safe from the bloating and deformity that is the Pilgrim's Disease.

Why is he not grinning ear-to-ear?

Munachi and his parents join me at the door as the procession heads further down into the gullet of the corridor. Together, we join the other dwellers who have formed a line behind the priests to the market square. The steel walls of the bunker reverberate with our hymns. The overhead bulbs are weak incandescent things, and the shadows they cast paint the mass of skinny bodies in sharp, frightening hues. Munachi holds my hand tight. I've never liked this part of the harvest procession, pressed together with everyone. I would rather eat my share of the bounty in the comfort of the hydroponic farm chambers on level 2, where we grow the algae that the dwellers subsist on between harvests. Munachi, on the other hand, is devout. He believes in every step leading to the communion. The way our souls unite when we share in the meal.

The procession ends at the market square. It is a sort of cavern, hollowed out within the bedrock around the bunker. Stalactites hang from the ceiling, giving off a faint cyan glow. It is ironic to do this here, since it is taboo to trade in meat. Meat is the most valuable resource on the planet.

The priests stop the hymn and the cavern goes deathly silent. The vats are spread out in a semicircle, six in all. I cannot tell what the contents are exactly. All I can see are the priests, working in silence, with a concentration that challenges anyone to move. To speak. To breathe. In silence we watch their knives flash a luminous green, skinning the flesh, trimming away the layer of fat, before extracting the red marble of edible muscle. It glistens, jewel-like, the colour of blood.

A flood of saliva instantly fills my mouth. It is maddening. Hunger roils from within my gut like a living thing. It ripples across the crowd like a blanket of unease. By now some of the priests have already spilled into our midst. The crowd falls to their knees in no particular order. The priests place a strip of glistening meat onto waiting tongues. I fall to my knees as one of the priests approaches me. I part my lips in reverence like Father taught me when I was a small boy and look to the face of the priest. I might have been awaiting some sort of congratulations in the priest's eyes. Something to validate my devotion.

But the priest turns out to be Father, and the look in his eyes breaks me.

IT WAS interesting because that day was Father's first harvest. A fledgling, like I was—am—in my first harvest. But look. *I am holding the knife. I* took the first cut! See now that there is no sacred livestock. Just a winged creature whose blood, spilled over and over again, has cursed the sand about it black.

BEFORE THEN, Father used to don the grey robes of the apprentice priests. He would find me at the end of the day where I would be loading jars of processed algae from the farms into trolleys to sell at the market. There was always a smile on his face, a mischievous crescent of a smirk within a mane of salt and pepper beards and dark skin. After we'd woven through the narrow corridors of the bunker, ascended the cranky lifts that separate the subterranean levels of the power stations, the hydroponic and nutrient farms and the living quarters, we'd sell our products at the market.

Ah, simpler times.

Now god's six irises focus on me. Tears stream from the edges of her eyes, but even in the darkness, I know she cannot see me. She is too far gone. The incense is too strong, its narcotic properties too potent. It is the third reason we wear masks.

FATHER and I slide into the first cell just after the market square. Save for a curtain it is doorless, inviting everyone going into the market with its delectable aroma of spices.

We sit at one of the tables under the pale white lighting and gaudy neon signs. It's not rush hour yet, so we have the table of seven to ourselves. The manager approaches our table to get our orders. She's dressed in a tank top and faded oversized cargo pants. Against the sharp outlines of her clavicles and the lean muscles of her arms, the trousers she has on are almost comical. It's the latest fashion. It highlights the bony limbs and harsh angles that the dweller diet offers. Even Father frowns at me when I highlight the hollows of my eyes and the curve of my zygoma with coal dust. The manager smiles at us and takes our order of yam and oil stew.

"You're in a good mood," I say.

Father nods. "I'll be undertaking the Choosing soon. I'll become eligible to a celebrate the harvest!"

"That's amazing!"

"I can finally go up to heaven. Commune with god. It *is* amazing!" He smiles. The manager returns with our food, placing the plates before us. Her arms are lush with dark tattoo dashes that some dwellers use as a form of holy body art. They depict the number of harvests she has witnessed. The manager sees Father's smile and she smiles back, placing both palms to the centre of her chest in holy greeting before turning away.

"But what's so interesting about heaven anyway?" I say, working the yams between my teeth. They are boiled good, even though they farmed in barely thriving soil. "You said the Fire has turned the world above into ash. Isn't that god's domain? Isn't god alone up there?"

Father shakes his head. "You need to have a little more faith, Nzeh."

"At least god will appreciate the company," I lick oil stew off my fingers. "Maybe they won't mind a jar of fresh algae?"

Father bursts into laughter.

"What?"

"It's nothing. It's nothing. Just, why would god want to eat algae?"

I give him an incredulous stare. "It's a peace offering! Besides, if god can share meat with us, I sure expect we can share with them."

Father smiles. "Ever wonder where all the animals are? Where does god keep them? I mean, why can't we get some and rear them here."

"Didn't our forefathers try that in the early days of the Fire? And *fail*? Besides, if god did that then we wouldn't need them anymore."

"Ah..."

It's my turn to laugh. "Careful Father, you're beginning to sound like me."

Father chuckles. "The priesthood would appreciate someone like you, Nzeh. You can be like your friend, Munachi. Did you know the other day, he met me and asked to enrol in the Monastery?"

"You don't say. Probably in it for extra meat rations."

"Nzeh!"

"I'm tending the farms, Father. Algae is no cure against the Pilgrim's disease, but it keeps us strong between harvest seasons. I have my own faith, in my own way."

Father reaches from across the table and squeezes my free hand. His eyes shimmer with hope and joy and pride.

HIS EYES ARE hollow and gaunt now. Fingers bloated, skin peeling like old paint.

The Pilgrim's Disease.

The sentries of heavensgate are the ones who show up at the door of our cell-home. They heave Father out, through the corridors and towards the lifts that lead skywards. I watch in deathly silence. Watch them in their black armour and helmets, dragging him by the shoulders. By his bone-thin limbs that look too deformed against his bloated abdomen.

Their voices are distorted through the visor-like oxygen masks on their faces. A priest becoming a pilgrim? Unheard of. The pilgrims usually litter the corridors of the upper levels. Once in a while, we find them in the lifts. Sick. Bloated. Skin diseased.

But never priests.

They never turn their back on god's gift. God's harvest. But it appears they do. Even more than I would dare imagine. Why else is Father Uju, head of the priesthood, here? Why is everything so hush-hush?

"We must keep the faith strong," he says. "God needs it, and we need god."

I don't even see his lips move. Only the black mask like a second mandible over his jaw. He won't even breathe the air of the malnourished fallen priest. His neck is not thin like ours. The priests *do* get more meat. He places his hand on my shoulder. It takes all my willpower not to recoil.

"Do not lose your faith, son."

My faith is dead.

THE NEXT DAY I enrol to the Monastery.

MUNACHI APPROACHES me after one of the lectures on harvest ritual methodology. He fiddles with his hands under the folds of his grey robes. Can barely meet my eye. Many people have been giving me a wide berth since I enrolled. Why wouldn't they?

"Nzeh," he says, offering me the holy greeting. "I'm sorry about your father."

I nod. "Yeah, thanks. I know you looked up to him."

"And you? Are you okay? If...if you need some extra lessons I can help. The Choosing is coming up soon too."

I scoff snidely. "I don't need your help. What do *you* even know about being a priest?"

He takes a step back, hurt flashing in his eyes. "What's that supposed to mean?"

There are no cattle. No goats or sheep. Father had rambled the words on and on, drinking only soup. *We have caged god and we feed on her body.*

I will never forget the crazed look in his eyes as he rambled on and on.

We are not holymen. We are the real monsters.

"Nothing," I hiss. "Just focus on yourself and leave me alone."

AT THE NEXT HARVEST, I watch from the market square without my apprentice robes. I watch dwellers fall to their knees and take the flesh. I wonder about Father. Where is he now? Where did they take him? He was no serious threat. After all, the only alternative to the meat is the Pilgrim's Disease, and nobody wants to become a pilgrim.

And yet.

And yet.

I turn around and leave the festival.

I find myself on level 2, haunting the hydroponic farms. The chambers of aquatic algae the bunker subsists on between harvests embrace me in the silence. I place my hand over one of the glass cubicles and my reflection stares back at me, gaunt. More and more I begin to resemble Father. I'd grown a beard, and stopped the cosmetics. I look past my reflection and into the pale green contents of the vat. Algae is bitter, but it can be engineered. Made better. But meat is sweeter. Holy. The only reason humanity hasn't succumbed to starvation.

We are not holymen. We are the real monsters.

I fall to my knees and weep. Why do I have to find these answers for myself? Why can't I just believe like everybody else? The sorrow threatens to tear my ribcage apart. I wheeze and sniff and let the tears fall.

I miss you, Father.

OTHER PRIESTS JOIN me in the harvest. As per tradition, the fledgling priest with the highest scores in the Choosing takes the first cut. I don't know how these priests compartmentalize it. Rationalize it. After the Choosing, Father Uju had taken me out of the orientation lecture for the new priests. A lecture where I suppose they were taught the true nature of the harvest. Father Uju looked me dead in the eyes and said to me.

"I know you know."

I remember that moment like I am reliving it.

"Know what?"

"That there is no farm in heaven. Just god. Chained for our sustenance."

I give him a neutral look. "There is god, who provides us with meat, and that's all that matters."

Father Uju arches an eyebrow. His lips are thin, blackened, and most importantly, full. His cheeks are full. He has been eating, a lot.

"We call it god only because of the nature of the creature. But make no mistake, it is not like us. Merely a beast that *looks* like us. It does so to weaken our resolve. Its kind caused the Fire that made us the last of mankind, so do not pity it. That is what it wants, your pity."

I say nothing. He continues. "Even with all of this, the vile creature subsists on belief. Infinitely regenerating as long as it receives worship. The hubris! Yet for this reason, we cannot afford to have doubt from anybody. Do you know the story of the first Pilgrims?"

I nod. "They convinced most of the dwellers to stop eating the flesh. But eventually the Disease came for them, and they died."

"They were self-righteous, and their false morals nearly doomed us all. But you see, without the flesh of the creature, they died. We will all die without it too. You shall see the heavens. The surface. You will understand then."

The fledgling priests walk out as he finishes his speech.

Six in all. There is a look plastered on their faces. I remember seeing that same look on Father after his first harvest. This time the masked sentries of heavensgate loiter in the shadows of the corridor.

"Never lose your faith, Father Nzeh." What I hear is, *don't be foolish like your father.*

Only two fledglings make it to the next harvest.

———

OFFAL IN ONE VAT. Limbs in another. It is bloody work, and yet, even as we harvest, tiny blobs of golden light hover around god's wounds. Our faith is its torment. It is so hilarious that I almost laugh. These priests look at god as some divine being. They pay their respect with their knives. Their movements are subtle acts of worship. Father Uju looks at god like a prized boar. With hunger. Maybe in his own way, that is faith. The assurance of grilled steak whenever he wants.

And me?

We commence the procession back to the bunker. The sentries are by the open hatch called heavensgate. We walk down the gullet, back into the bowels of the earth. The incense lamps are killed. When we step out of the elevator, we are greeted by faces. The vat presses onto my skin where it sits on my shoulder. The hymns reverberate within my bones.

We are not the holymen.

Before the harvest ends, I slip away to the farms. To the batch of crops that I never stopped tending to. I distil a few canisters of engineered algae and take the lift up to the heavensgate. There are no sentries. Nobody is foolish enough to miss out on the harvest's bounty. Good. I heave the hatch open and step outside.

The wind bites my face without my mask. Without the purifying units, my lungs will corrode under the harsh atmosphere. It doesn't matter. I walk towards god where her remains huddle in a pool of her own blood. She sees me and thrashes about, but the metal stakes are dug too deeply into her wings. I place the canisters of algae before her, four in all. She gives me a puzzled look, as if trying to decipher my angle.

"It's algae." I say. "It's a peace offering."

The fetters lie bloody in the sand. She is limbless, so only her wings keep her rooted to her prison. I brandish a knife from my robes and she scuttles backwards, hissing. I circle the creature, finding the joints of her wings where they join her back. Her body suddenly goes still. Maybe she has figured out my plan. The wings are tough, but I sever them from god's body. The smell of her fresh blood hits me like a gut punch—a heady mix of hunger and desire. She turns her head to me, questions in her golden irises. I turn away instead, wiping off spittle where it had dribbled down the sides of my mouth. If this is how humanity was meant to continue its existence, then maybe it's time to let go. To stop fighting against the natural order.

We should all be pilgrims.

I drop the knife on the sand, pick up a canister of algae, and walk away from it all.

A WOMAN'S PLACE IS IN THE HAUNTED HOME

CHARLOTTE TIERNEY

Originally published in *Conjunctions: 83 / Revenants, The Ghost Issue.*

Charlotte Tierney is the author of the nineties gothic novel *The Cat Bride* (Salt). Her work (also under Charlotte Turnbull) has been published in *Best British Short Stories 2024, Conjunctions, The London Magazine, Weird Horror, Nightjar Press, The Ghastling* and *New England Review* among others.

1:

THE FIRST GHOST appeared within 15 minutes of arriving home from the hospital, lying upon the new baby in the Moses basket. This was not covered in *What To Expect When Expecting*. It was covered, however, in Lisa's thesis on nineteenth century ghost stories.[1]

---

1. Collins, Lisa S. "*A Woman's Place Is In The Haunted Home: Domestic Trauma and Henry James' The Turn Of The Screw*", 2021.

STARING into the baby's car seat, one hand straightening the little bear ears on the snowsuit, Lisa felt like she'd accidentally slipped into someone else's life, where that someone had recently had a baby. But also, she felt like no one else in the history of the world had ever had a baby, except her. The tiny baby girl face was still grimy with Lisa's own rich interior.

Weeks earlier, Lisa and her husband had joked with a sales assistant in the nursery shop. "Ta-da!" They pointed theatrically at her massive belly—baby held entirely exterior to her narrow pelvis—as if they had not been expecting it. As if they hadn't been to and from the hospital, worried about getting it out safely. As if they hadn't checked and double-checked with doctors and nurses that each tweak and twinge of pain was normal. As if they hadn't expected it three other times in as many years. Lisa knew a haunted house was, customarily, already haunted prior to a ghost's manifestation.[2]

Once back in the flat, Lisa took the baby in its car seat to the nursery. The baby slept deeply, growing in secret, hidden places. Lisa's sweaty hands checked the tightness of fitted sheets to mattresses, fixture of screws into cots. A window was opened for fresh air, then closed again for pollution. She shouted through to her husband. "Does it feel warm to you?"

A cardboard nursery thermometer in the shape of a merry beige duck hovered, teasing, between 19 and 20 degrees. She waved it through the air to see if that made a difference. It's November, she thought, regretting the good fortune to be on the second floor of a well-insulated Victorian terraced house. Why is it so bloody hot?

That was the first ghost.

With a rush of blood, Lisa's eyes bulged like she was in a cartoon because she didn't realise, yet, the real baby was not

---

2. Barrett, Philip. 'The Efficient Architecture of Haunting.' *The Structure of Ghosts*. Hartshire Press, 2017, pp. 266. 'A haunted house is a nest, the ghost its egg.'

dead. When she seized it—the real baby—it was neither as stiff, nor as cold as it had looked. It snuffled a little, grunting and rooting across her chest. At this, she felt too much relief, like when toes heat up after being far too cold. Like she was on fire.

There in the basket, in exactly the same position the baby had been in, was a thin, translucent ghost of it. The ghost had overlaid the baby, changing its pallor and look momentarily, making it look how Lisa expected a baby to look if it had died of Sudden Infant Death Syndrome. Unreal, uncanny, and unlikely. Perhaps for this reason she wasn't especially frightened of the ghost. It was empty and sad, rather than terrifying.

The ghost was indigestion,[3] thought Lisa. The ghost was her brain playing tricks.[4] It was too many cups of hospital tea.[5]

She wasn't sure what it meant, there were too many options. Victorian literary ghosts disrupted accepted realities. They represented marginalities, injustices, inequalities, the past. They were locus's of divided selves, repressed desires, unrecognized traumas—none of which applied to Lisa. But the ghost made her extra grateful for the squirming, warm package clutched in to her.

Her husband arrived characteristically too late to be of help. She shoved the cardboard duck at him. "It needs to be 18 degrees." She stood next to him while he called a heating engineer, mouthing what he should say about the urgency of being able to lower the temperature slightly. The real, alive baby dozed upon her shoulder.

She decided not to look at the little ghost. I'll do a Mrs

3. Dickens, Charles. *A Christmas Carol*. Chapman and Hall, 1843. 'There's more of gravy than of grave about you, whatever you are!'
4. Radcliffe, Ann. *The Mysteries of Udolpho*. G.G. and J. Robinson, 1794. 'The vacant mind is ever on the watch for relief, and ready to plunge into error, to escape from the languor of idleness.'
5. Le Fanu, Sheridan. 'Green Tea.' *In a Glass Darkly*, Richard Bentley & Son, 1872. 'By various abuses, among which the habitual use of such agents as green tea is one, this fluid may be affected as to its quality, but it is more frequently disturbed as to equilibrium.'

Grose in *The Turn of the Screw*, she thought, and simply pretend it is not there.

2:

UNFORTUNATELY, a second ghost appeared an hour after that. Due to its close, unexpected proximity, it was more frightening than the first so there was no ignoring it, as Mrs Grose or otherwise.

A natural academic, Lisa read constantly and widely in preparation for having a baby. It was important to bring it to the breast as often as possible in new environs.[6] To imbue it with comforting experiences, to acclimatize it so its world became familiar. Lisa needed to be comfortable, calm, hydrated, well-fed, well-rested, having fun, to successfully feed her child.[7]

So, while her husband defrosted convenience meals downstairs, she sat on her bed and bit down on a towel, a practice they had fallen into on the ward to stop her swears distressing even newer mothers—at Lisa's nod, her husband had shoved the folded towel into her mouth as she carefully took the baby's shrieking head and jammed it on to a bloodied nipple. Lisa was relieved with how well it was going as she reviewed her feeding log—which breast, at what time, for how long—complete with various footnotes and appendices, contextual information, acknowledgements and citations.[8] Now, she could bite her own towel, and pain rating

6. Dr. C. N. Branco. *The Baby's here! Now what?* Allmothers Press, 2021.

7. "Latched and Attached: How To Be A Baby-Feeding Machine." *Shiny New Baby Club*, 6 Jul. 2011, https://www.shinynewbabyclub.co.uk/article/latched-attached-machine/.

8. Collins, Lisa S. Feeding log, 12 Nov. 2022.
   "Left: 16.36 14 mins pain— 9+ /10
   Right: 16:52 16 mins pain —9+ /10
   Where: bed, pillows against headboard.
   Mood: tired, relaxed, optimistic, wincey but breathing
   Nutrition: biscuit + water
   Other info: Baby v sweet"

had gone from 10+ to, simply, 10. But, after 72 hours with no sleep, she dozed off, even with the vice grip on her breast.

Her head jerked suddenly up, only seconds later, and she saw the second misshapen ghost, beside her on the bed. Like it had rolled there. Like it had been crushed beneath a deep sleeper. One endless heartbeat later and Lisa realised her daughter was still suckling angrily.

Her husband arrived in the doorway. He thought he'd heard Lisa scream. She stared at the white, crushed shadow of her thriving daughter on the bed. Was it there to teach a lesson? Could it already have unfinished business? Was Lisa being punished? For her epidural?[9]

"Everything ok?" her husband asked.

"Absolutely," Lisa said, and it was.

Fortuitously, as well as baby-rearing, Lisa had also done extensive reading on ghosts. I am as prepared for this haunting, she decided, as I am this baby.

3:

THE THIRD GHOST appeared quickly after the second. Lisa placed the Moses basket below the fridge door, then took the milk out. She noticed that a shelf in it could collapse, not easily, but suddenly. The plastic corner weighed down with 6 pints of milk and 2 unopened bottles of dry white wine, would easily crush the skull of the baby's 6 lb. and 3 oz. body.

Looking at this new phantom, whose blood had a romantic, diaphanous glow where it glugged from an eye socket, Lisa dug deep. She managed to give her husband the baby in order to take a bath. To clear her head. To calm down. To clean herself after what had been lauded as a magnificently quick labour and birth.[10] To urinate in the warm water, all the

---

9. Gaskell, Elizabeth. *The Old Nurse's Story*. 1852. 'What is *done* in youth can never be *undone* in age!'

10. *Postnatal discharge summary*, UHH Hospital. 12 Nov. 2022. 'Lisa did very well following precipitous labour. Baby complete surprise to us all! Perineal tearing needs care.'

more comfortably. And to google all possible causes of carbon monoxide poisoning—hallucination-inducing[11]—other than 1900s gas lamps.

4:

HER SECRET, wounded skin prickled. Her dry knees were white caps to two submerged, scarlet legs. She had accidentally left the hot tap running. Looking at the grinning frog bath thermometer still bone dry on the changing table, she realised that to forget the thermometer could be catastrophic.

The fourth tiny ghost was pinkish and creamy with third-degree burns. Its hands matted and webbed from temperatures that, if she had thought about it, she'd have admitted would be impossible to reach with any normal bathroom tap. The baby bobbed, as if on the water, around her calves.

Lisa closed her eyes, so as not to be distracted as she thought. Much of the commentary on the female role in the traditional ghost story discussed an oblique anxiety around the changing role of women in Victorian society[12]—all of which was unhelpful to her, since women were no longer domestically subservient.

As if to prove the point, her husband knocked on the door, then opened it.

"I made supper," he said.

"Great," Lisa said, taking from him a soft plastic carton of microwaved macaroni cheese and a teaspoon. "But, where is the baby?"

---

11. Byder, Clarence. 'Cleanliness and Lunacy', *The Health, Hygiene and Hallucinogens of the Victorians*. 'Carbon monoxide poisoning can lead to impaired vision, confusion, drowsiness, reduced physical control, memory loss, severe mood changes…'

12. Aran, Mili. 'Cautionary Tales and Cultural Spaces'. *Ghosted: Demolishing the Haunted House*. Longview Press, 2019, pp 234. 'The cautionary tale is simply this, that the spaces disrupted by the Victorian ghost were often homes, where women expanding their role was to the detriment of domestic sanctity and safety, and indeed the female body.'

"Oh." He half-frowned through the door, when a gargley squawk drifted from the kitchen.

Lisa got out of the bath. It had not been as relaxing as she'd hoped.

5 & 6:

AFTER THE BATH, Lisa saw the back of ghost number five where it had rolled into the corner of the sofa when her husband got up to turn on the television. She knew newborns lacked the muscle definition to move themselves. It had, therefore, smothered to death whilst neglected.

Unfortunately, Lisa thought, it is the baby who is haunted, not me. In the stories, it is the newcomer who disrupts the established world, not the ghost itself.[13] She recalled, however, the baby would not be able to see for some time. Perhaps it can sense the ghosts in some other way—touch, scent, taste? I am too tired, to understand this, she thought, and instead began to detail each ghost at the back of her breastfeeding notebook. The governess in *The Turn of the Screw* numbers her nights, like I do my guests, Lisa thought. The governess was onto something. Statistics bring control. Like my breastfeeding log, she thought brightly, which is a thorough and numerical record of pain, clearly manifesting my dedication to my baby.

The sixth ghost made her wince a little. Its skull had been crushed in as her husband had stepped back from the television. In a momentary lapse in concentration, he had forgotten the baby lying on her play mat to the side of him. She nervously watched her husband, next to her, on the sofa reading the news on his phone. Could his subconscious be punishing the baby?

---

13. M. Anand. 'Give Up The Ghost.' *The Evolution of Ghosts*, edited by KC Waters & Laura Perry. South-West University Press, 2007, pp. 16. 'Don't blame the ghost player, blame the ghost game.'

Lisa pointed at the sixth ghost, just to check. "What's that?"

He glanced up. "What's what?"

Lisa sighed, because if he couldn't see it, he must stay out of it. In *The Turn of the Screw*, when the governess had confided about her visions of the ghosts in Bly Manor's housekeeper, Mrs Grose, things had got very messy indeed.[14]

7:

LISA CAREFULLY FOLLOWED the instructions for the sling and wrapped the baby onto her chest. She declined supper when her husband brought it to her because she had the seventh ghost in the sling too—a fork sticking out from the downy feathers of its squashy fontanelle. She feigned fatigue and sat very, very still, focusing on a spot on the wall opposite, too scared to pick up her phone to look up how long the ossification of the skull would take, how long she would worry about the soft of the baby's head.

Longer, she supposed, than a few hours.

"Are you OK?" her husband asked, and she startled.

"Fine, darling," she said. "Why do you ask?"

"Well," he said, nodding towards the book she was reading. "Your viva days are long gone."

Screw you, Henry James, she thought, not listening to her husband. Don't implicate the children. This baby is guileless and perfect, just as Miles and Flora were. It cannot be held responsible for its own phantoms.

47-54:

IT WAS A BUSY NIGHT. Blue babies on the floor. Babies with heads at impossible angles to their bodies. Lisa was

---

14. James, Henry. *The Turn Of The Screw*. William Heinemann, 1898, pp. 71. 'She was really frightened.'

exhausted with getting up and down to grab the mouth-towel and feed. In the dim light she had begun mistaking the ghosts for the real baby, the real baby for the mouth-towel. The bed was too full to concentrate. She woke her husband at 05:08 am to ask that he slept somewhere else for the time being.

She wrapped the real baby into the sling again, and stood at the window, trying to focus on the city skyline ahead of her. She accidentally wondered if the ghosts were the manifestation of post-natal depression. She imagined the relief of taking control by opening the window and throwing the baby out of it, but knew this was simply a reaction to childbirth.[15]

The ghost baby was splattered in the middle of the road below her, arm bent, head split open. She went out to retrieve it. She wanted it back. She didn't want it drifting around the city like a lost cat. It was hers, just like the baby. Like Miles and Flora belonged to the governess, who only ever wanted to protect them, and was not at all mad, nor hysterical. The situation isn't exactly the same, Lisa thought, as the ghosts don't pose a threat per se, but if no one else can see these ghosts, in the absence of anyone who can help, then the governess is somewhat a role model.

Relieved she had some moral support, albeit from a fictional character, Lisa stood on the road, stopping traffic briefly, and pawed at the air. She discovered she could move the ghosts by wafting them, like tapping a half-sunk helium balloon.

The real baby, in its sling, yawned contentedly, never rousing from the deep recesses of its brain where it was growing and thriving.

———————————

SOMETIMES, thoughts flashed in and out of Lisa's

———————————

15. 'Postpartum psychosis: I tried to kill my health visitor, my GP, my pharmacist, a bus driver, a dog-walker, a Deliveroo courier, my husband, my baby, and myself.' BBC News, 22 Ap. 2021, https://www.bbc.com/news/uk-england-shropshire-41980246

consciousness so quickly she didn't even know how she'd caused the baby's death. Although it was often very obvious. An impalation on a railing. Severed straight in two when a knife they never even used slipped unaccountably up and out of the knife block. Garrotted in the sling by the handle of a handy reusable shopping bag slung over her shoulder.

When she couldn't remember—for example, if it had happened when she'd been half-asleep—she interrogated the scene of the crime forensically. She could work backwards from injuries, setting up complicated reenactments, that, ironically, would often result in more ghosts if she hadn't kept her real baby at what she perceived to be a safe enough distance.

She was careful not to let her husband see these re-enactments. Like the governess, she did not want her husband to know about the hauntings. She was not alienated from her husband, like the governess was her master. The master didn't want to know the details of his own domestic life—the governess was, as a result, reluctant to tell her own story, even after the event[16]—but in Bly Manor, the governess had found a role: she was valued and respected as a steward.

Like the master, he'd never say it, but Lisa's husband wouldn't cope with the knowledge of the haunting. In a sense, it was her job as a mother, like that of the governess, to never appeal, nor complain. Not for his sake, but for the baby's. Simply having the baby had already come as a huge shock to her husband—if Lisa told him about the ghosts, he might think she couldn't deal with the new baby *and* the haunting, he might try to take over. He might want solutions. Lisa knew it was better for her to be left to it, to be empowered, as a mother, and as such, unlike the foolhardy governess, she knew it was better not to stop the hauntings.

One dark evening, she went to switch on a light, but before she could, a luminous baby—electrocuted—lit up the room. Its pale light was refracted by a chain of ghost babies,

---

16. James, Henry. 'The Turn Of The Screw'. William Heinemann, 1898, pp. 9. 'She had never told anyone. It wasn't simply that she said so, but that I knew she hadn't. I was sure: I could see. You'll easily judge why when you hear.'

dead from all manner of unlikely safety breaches. Each one a cautionary tale. They highlighted activities to avoid, just in case. They illuminated the safest route through the room. The ghost babies, Lisa thought, signpost the best path to protect the real baby. The hauntings meant the real baby came to no harm. The hauntings meant the real baby was gaining weight and looking bonny, as Lisa's own mother had noted.

Lisa's mother had stroked Lisa's head, as if she was the baby. "You'll never get top marks at having a baby," she said. "Be kind to yourself." Lisa ignored this advice. Her mother was wrong. Since she was a little girl, her parents, her teachers, her supervisor, the world had told her—you must be the best you can be. So, she kept reading. She read about co-sleeping,[17] breastfeeding,[18] babywearing,[19] babyled-weaning[20]—the self-deception of heroism,[21] the corruption of innocence,[22] the taboos of domesticity[23]—society and class, repression and hysteria, gender and power. She lurched between *The Wonder Weeks* and *Portrait of a Screw: The Genius of Henry James*, while ghosts proliferated around her, voracious and specific, but she was absolutely sure she could get top marks.

Lisa's mother's two visits had resulted each time in a new ghost. One from a common cold that developed into pneumonia, the second from a bacterial virus of unknown content. She stopped returning her mother's phone calls. She could reduce the possibilities of death by shutting her own mother out. It was little enough to do.

---

17. Cummings, Dr. Neil. *Safe in a pack! Why babies need to co-sleep.* Courtney Harvey, 2017.
18. Hanlan, Louise. *Milking It.* Best New Baby Books, 2021.
19. Jones, Olsen. *Hold Me Like You Mean It.* Best New Baby Books, 2020.
20. Knowles, Di. *Baby Knows Best—Weaning With Di Knowles.* Seers Publishing, 2020
21. Allison, Karla S. PhD, ABPP 'Hero? Her-No!' *Psychology Now,* 3 Dec. 2016. https://www.psychologynow.co.uk/thefallacyoftheherosjourney/
22. Chivers. S P. 'Pity The Children'. *The Victorian Family,* edited by Genefer Fenton & Arlo Peters, 2019.
23. Littler, Dr Mary. *Women: A Cult.* Wray Classics, 1996.

Motherhood was all about sacrifice.[24]

Any mother, or highly-enthusiastic governess, understood that.

348 & 389:

EACH TIME her husband went to touch the baby, Lisa said, "she's just gone to sleep," or "I'm about about to feed her," or "I need to give her a quick bath."

He began to take it personally. "You look tired," he said. He suggested a bottle, so she could rest.

She'd read about a new study on breastfeeding and this was the first time her daughter appeared to her as an adult, battered to death, in an abusive relationship maybe. She looked gaunt and thin, like she hadn't been taking care of herself, like she lacked self-respect, self-esteem, like she wasn't psychologically secure. Like she wasn't well-attached.

When her husband mentioned the bottle a second time, the baby appeared as teenager, dead after taking a bad pill.

In *The Turn of the Screw*, the governess was also sleepless,[25] patrolling the dark to keep her wards safe. Inspired, Lisa, spent her nights in vigil likewise, protecting the baby, feeding it safe, reading and re-reading, for hints and tips. Like the governess, she embraced the baby as often as she could, fuelling it with oxytocin, cleansing it of cortisol (brain-melter).[26]

Lisa politely requested that her husband stop suggesting she give up breastfeeding, even if it would mean she could sleep more. "Especially," she said to him, "since both nipples have developed large scabs now. I hardly even use the towel anymore."

---

24. Cov, Pat. "*Self-sacrifice as Self-actualisation: The Gothic Heroine.*" (2021)

25. James, Henry. *The Turn Of The Screw*. William Heinemann, 1898, pg 62. 'I repeatedly sat up till I didn't know when.'

26. Suskin, Sandra. *Touch and the Infant Brain*. Seckledge, 2003.

SHE WENT OUT, to begin with, but mother's groups were held at health centres and in cold churches, or "high mortality risk" venues as she started to think of them. The other mothers wanted strategies for getting more sleep, but Lisa wanted strategies for less. If she didn't go to sleep, she couldn't wake up to all the deaths she might have avoided had she been awake.

She pitied the other mothers, who didn't have the ghosts. They didn't know all the potential catastrophes they could be avoiding. Lisa and the governess were heroic. They bravely confronted the monsters. Lisa was as grateful as the governess, that she could see them, although she prayed the baby couldn't and wouldn't. She tamed the little ghosts, made them her own.

Friends on maternity leave got in touch, but she stopped agreeing to meet. She could never bear to leave her baby ghosts out where they had appeared, but the looks she got as she tugged them home made her uncomfortable. Then, her ghosts multiplied like bacteria because, in the mania of collecting them all up, she stopped concentrating on keeping the baby safe. It was a vicious circle.

Like the governess who didn't have time to enter church. Lisa was too preoccupied to be part of the baby-groups.[27] She left thoughtless worship to other Mrs Grose types; the mothers similarly in denial of the terrors closing in on them.

45,785:

THINGS GOT MARGINALLY BETTER. Feeding stabilized, although Lisa had not yet started the process of weaning[28] (choking /

---

27. Mom, Real. 'Real Mom', 'Negging and the Baby Group', *Getting Real With Mom*, Aug. 9, 2020
28. Dr Jon Sykes. 'Too early, too late'. *Perfect Weaning*. Best New Baby Books. 2020.

anaphylactic shock / cutlery injuries / highchair misuse), then one day she walked home from the supermarket along the canal and saw a drowned toddler, floating face-down.

She pulled it out of the water and stood it up. At least she could just take this one's hand. It came along easily, if slowly, walking falteringly on its tiptoes. Leaving a trail of haunting drips.

After that, Lisa sent her husband shopping lists via email, and he returned home from work with everything they needed. It was nice, he thought, to be involved.

ON THEIR DAUGHTER'S first birthday, Lisa's husband bought her a locket.

"It's Victorian," he said, hopefully. The Victorian guilloche locket was engraved with concentric circles. He had put a photo of the baby inside, along with a lock of her hair. Lisa was stunned, sometimes she was so absorbed with the baby, the ghosts and the governess, she forgot the other characters in her life. She cried a little, not only with gratitude—the master would never have appreciated the governess in this way, even the writer hadn't allowed her a name—but also a bit from exhaustion, and another bit from the vision of the ghost toddler clutching its own neck where it choked on the lovely new locket.

Lisa didn't let the sight of the little ghost stop her husband from putting the locket on her there and then. She was delighted to remember she was a mother out of love, and not a career choice.[29]

GHOSTS BUILT up throughout the day. Every evening, before her husband got home, Lisa went through the house gath-

29. whispernanny', Reddit, 3 yrs ago. https://www.reddit.com/r/Nanny/comments/o22f2i/are_nk_and_i_too_attached/

ering them up and pushing them through the trap door into the attic. If they spilled out, falling across her in a pale veil, she pushed them further in and down. Happily, there was always room for more.

After all, she thought, they took up no space.

After her husband left in the morning, she would go about the rituals of the day; getting the baby up, feeding her, playing with her, talking to her, reading to her. Then, when the baby slept, in the cot in the nursery, she sat in the attic to be saved the bother of clearing up new ghosts.

She could sit, sort of relaxed, letting the horrible ideas run through her, and she knew they would stay exactly where she'd created them. She did not particularly enjoy this time—she would rather read a book, or listen to music—but it was for her daughter. Like the governess, she feared for the baby to grow up. She, like the governess, liked the baby innocent. She didn't want her aware of the visitations. She didn't want visitations taking place that she didn't even know of. If she didn't know of them, she couldn't collect them up and keep the horrors close.

THE BABY STARTED WALKING, (electrocution / poisoning / beheading) and Lisa's husband asked about the end of maternity leave. "It's not about the money," he said. "You might like to do something other than sing the froggy song sometimes. I always liked your brain."[30]

She snorted at this, thinking of the hundreds of (better) theses she had mentally penned about the proscriptions of gothic literature during her long nights and even longer days, because while ghost Quint was clearly diabolical, she had become increasingly worried about ghost Miss Jessel, who in

30. "PhD students and supervisors 2021 awards", *London College Of Arts & Sciences website*, 20 Oct. 2018, https://www.lcas.ac.uk/ps/9872-phd-supervisors-2021awards.

'Provost's Award for Excellence in Doctoral Studies—Lisa S Collins, supervisor Katarina Soucek, English Department.'

the book prompted disgust in the governess, due to her *"evident weariness,"* and *"indescribable grand melancholy."* Mental health issues aren't exactly attractive, Lisa thought, but they're very common. [31]

"When I'm better slept, I'll think about work," she sighed to her husband.

Her husband couldn't prove that she didn't leave the house. It was only a suspicion. Besides, during the heatwave, she had sat out on the little balcony, (falling / birds carrying histoplasmosis / satellite shrapnel), and doused the child down in a little bucket. But Lisa knew he'd realise eventually. He had raised the idea of a holiday (drowning / abduction / struck by lightening) a few times now, and each time she'd nodded the conversation on into the future.

Lisa felt the complicity of her marriage like a coffin around her. Exactly how the governess and Mrs Grose had collaborated to make a taboo of Quint and Miss Jessel, Lisa and her husband preferred not to discuss an issue so big that it threatened to destroy their fragile home.

———

LISA'S HUSBAND asked if she'd thought about trying again, about a brother or sister for the baby. The ghost of a small boy appeared in the kitchen, standing in between them as they leaned against the kitchen surfaces, staring with dead eyes at Lisa.

Lisa yawned and performed a theatrical stretch. "One is too many."

"But you're such a good mother," he said. "Everyone says so."

---

31. Hedge, Caro. 'Keeping Mum: why are mothers silent on postpartum mental health issues?' *The Daily Evening*, 20. Jan, 2024. 'Data on mental health is limited due to lack of people reaching out to healthcase professionals, people lacking awareness of their mental health issues, and stigma around mental health issues. For example, an estimated 10-15% of women suffer from postpartum depression, postpartum anxiety/OCD or postpartum psychosis, that is, 10-15% of mothers self-report these illnesses.'

Everyone did say so. Some as a compliment, some resent-fully, but everyone noticed how easily motherhood came to Lisa.

———

THEY BOUGHT A NEW HOUSE. For more space, a greener environment, purer air, less traffic, smaller schools. Although, her husband wasn't sure about it.

"It's in the middle of nowhere," he'd said, of the one Lisa really liked. "Isn't it too small? Can we really afford it? And what will we do with that old barn?"

"It's peaceful," Lisa said. "It's cosy. Trust me, an extra barn is exactly what we need. It'll be a project for me when pre-school starts."

Her husband admitted pre-school starting would be chal-lenging for Lisa, and allowed her to press ahead with the move to the moor. It was a relief, for Lisa, because obviously the best location for ghost husbandry was a barren wilderness.

133, 479—133, 496:

LISA HAD no idea how the ghost standing next to the van had been created. It was a woman. Possibly even older than her. She looked healthy, but Lisa was too busy to ruminate on it. Too busy to sift her thoughts. Too busy to generate more grown-up ghost daughters by trying each morbid chess move. Lisa crammed the full-size ghost, along with the others, into the back of the white van. Its startled, translucent, middle-aged eyes watched her as she slammed the doors on it.

The governess's biggest concern was always for the well-being of the children. She was exemplary, in that way. Lisa didn't want her daughter making ghosts in secret, where she couldn't collect them, or see the hazards they represented, or store them in case she needed them for reference in future.

She feared for the older child, when she might make her own decisions. She couldn't be quite sure, when her daughter stared into the mid-distance, whether she was seeing her opaque twin, or not.

The stress of this was, admittedly, as the governess had demonstrated, enough to drive one mad.

Lisa's husband had gone ahead to supervise unloading the moving van. Her last job at the old house, while her daughter watched cartoons on a screen (brain cancer / cognitive degeneration / behaviour disorders)[32] in the empty living room, was to pack the attic of ghosts into this secret van she had hired.

She had wafted the ghosts, in groups, down the stairs, and stacked them on top of one another in the van. Compressing them, crushing them, making sure they'd all fit. She was bright, humming with relief, and optimism. In *The Turn of the Screw*, everyone[33] was hysterical. Agitated, restive, dashing about, jumping, throwing, dropping themselves.[34] Really, Lisa thought, they should have calmed down. But *their* ghosts were slow and stealthy, calculating and oppressive. Not like *her* wispy little spectres, who were passive and weightless. Pointless, almost.

Eventually, they did fit in, even the older woman.

Lisa sat her live daughter in the hired car seat next to her. Double-checking the strap feeding through red clasps at her hips. Tightening the belt across her body. Another ghost appeared, headless. Lisa flicked it quickly into the footwell so it wouldn't float about, distracting her while she was driving.

"Can you see that?" she asked her daughter, pointing to it.

"What?" her daughter said, as she always did.

Lisa put on music, singing along loudly, to keep her head clear, but as she pulled away, Lisa felt the car low over its

---

32. 'Ipad files for sole custody.' Humour Daily, 1 Jan. 2019, https://www.humourdaily.com/ipadc
33. The Housekeeper, The Governess
34. James, Henry. *The Turn Of The Screw*. William Heinemann, 1898. Every. Single. Page.

wheels. She put her foot down harder to compensate for the weight.

LISA DISCOVERED something in the process of moving her ghosts—she could keep compressing them. She didn't need a whole barn for them, after all.

When she arrived in the secret van, her husband frowned. "I thought you were getting the train."

"I panicked," she said, because he knew, to a certain extent, what she was like,[35] "I thought we'd forgotten to do the attic, but it was empty."

Later, while he was unpacking his home office, she went to the back of the van and walked an army of small ghosts down the lane, multiple hands crushed into hers. Faint outlines stuffed together like reams of paper. She took them to the barn and, once she had stopped crying, she distilled the ghosts into an empty packing box. It was lovely to see the old versions of her daughter—despite all the blood—some of them seemed so far away from the little girl she was now. When she was finished she slid the box flaps over one another and went to pick the box up, to store it somewhere drier, but the box was incredibly dense. It was like the barn itself, completely immoveable. No problem, she thought. I can leave it here, forever. The governess's big mistake was trying to change things. She interfered with the established order. Everything went well for her as long as she was simply protecting everyone. As long as she was the hero.

Except, a few weeks later, her husband entered the house with the box of ghosts. "Found this box in the barn," he said. "It's empty." He went to tear the box apart, to recycle the cardboard.

"Ah." Lisa smiled, thinking quickly. "I need a box like that, can you put it in the bedroom?"

---

35. Ashley, Matt. *Keeping The Can Of Worms Closed: A Modern Marriage Survival Guide for Men*. Boxer Books, 2020.

After that, she compressed the contents of the packing box easily into a shoe box which became, to her, more solid than the earth.[36] She picked up the larger now-empty box to make herself seem busy, before calling her husband.

"Could you pop that shoe box under the bed?" she asked him.

He slid it under her side of the bed with the tip of one toe.

542, 657:

BEFORE SCHOOL ONE MORNING, her little girl tried on a necklace she kept in a saucer of costume jewelry next to her bed.

The ghost was a teenager, heavy eye make-up, tights ripped, blood at her lips.

It offended Lisa when academics argued the governess had been jealous of the children's joyful innocence—that the governess had, in some way, wanted *this*—that, subconsciously, she might have generated this abject nightmare as a demented cry for help. Thank god, Lisa thought, I have remained rational and practical throughout. For the child, I have remained sane.

In front of the teen spectre, Lisa's little girl admired herself in the mirror, earrings held up to each ear. It gave Lisa a nice idea.

LISA PLACED her special locket in a velvet-lined box. Along with the photograph, and the lock of hair, it would also contain every fear Lisa had ever had for her daughter's safety. This talisman kept her daughter safe, without anyone even noticing.

The governess had let her anxieties overwhelm her, and as a consequence of her desperate interfering, the children had felt claustrophobic. They became resentful of her. Accusing

---

36. Earth density: 5.51 g/cm³, Google

and judging, they had seen her as a poor mother. The governess's behaviour had broken, not nurtured, them. Lisa was lucky enough to learn from her mistakes, to keep her silence. To live within the established, observable world. To hide her ghosts.

To be a good mother.

If she could have, Lisa would have renounced her own name, become nothing but a series of unimpeachable maternal acts. Sometimes she worried that you could not, by definition, be a hero if you are not recognised as such by someone else. Self-appointed heroes are surely sociopaths. Can one be a mother *and* a sociopath?

Lisa collected each ghost in a special zip pocket of her purse, the pocket growing heavier and heavier until the end of the day when she emptied them into the locket. It was heavier than the galaxy,[37] but only to Lisa.

988, 354:

Lisa and her daughter were dressing to go out for the girl's birthday.

Her daughter, more self-conscious now, asked to borrow something from Lisa's saucer of jewelry when something strange happened. A ghost of the girl, exactly as she was in the present moment, appeared.

She didn't look maimed, or damaged, or broken in any way. The ghost's chest even rose and fell like she was breathing, but she was clearly a ghost. Lisa sat on the bed, staring at the ghost, confused, while her daughter hummed the theme to a cartoon they watched together. The girl truffled around the room. Flipping on a scarf, brushing her hair, waiting for her mother to finish getting ready.

Lisa felt the mattress beneath her dip back as the girl climbed onto the bed behind her. The girl's hands brushed

---

37. Galaxy weight: 1.5 trillion solar masses—Nasa.gov

Lisa's nape, attaching something before Lisa could duck out of the way.

The locket plummeted to the floor, taking Lisa with it, breaking her neck with the mass of the universe.[38]

The little girl stared, shocked, by what she'd done.

If Lisa had been able to speak, she would have consolidated her independent research and her critical analysis. She would have presented her conclusions with structure and coherence. She would have called lightly to her daughter, "This is what the governess would have wanted! Don't let them tell you she was mad. She did her best. Don't worry about this, darling. Please, don't you worry about a thing."

---

38. Mass of observable universe: 10^{53} kg—Wikipedia.org

ACROSS THE STREET

GREG VAN EEKHOUT

Originally published in *Uncanny Magazine #59*.

Greg van Eekhout is the author of twelve novels and over fifty stories. His work has been selected as finalists for the Nebula Award, the Locus Award, the Andre Norton Award, and has appeared on multiple state reading lists. He pays way too much money to live in San Diego, but it's really nice there. For more information, visit his website: writingandsnacks.com

MUCH LIKE ISHMAEL, I have experienced a fair number of damp, drizzly Novembers in my soul. And I, too, have required a strong moral principle to prevent me from stepping into the street and methodically knocking people's hats off. But unlike Ishmael, I can't quietly take to sea because my lunch break is only forty-five minutes, which I usually spend getting a Starbucks and taking a walk past the Panda Express, the Jamba Juice, the McDonald's and Burger King, the Super-Cuts where I get my trims, the KFC, the Target, the Home

Depot, before finally turning another corner and finding myself back at the office.

But today I'm very deep in a hat-knocking mood, so I cross the street.

After only a few blocks, I find a turtle garden, a sparkling pond bordered by cobble stones. Turtles paddle below the water, none larger than the span of my hand.

Have these always been here? I think I've come this way before, but maybe not. It's a delight.

Free from the cubicle where my sense of adventure atrophies, incarcerated inside spreadsheet cells, I fill my lungs with clean air and cross another street.

Here, the pavement bears prints of things that walked in the cement before it set. I step inside one of the impressions—a huge human-shaped foot with claws. It's stained with red paint or maybe rusty rain. I do love a touch of civic whimsy.

The street signs around here are in another language, one with an alphabet I don't recognize. I'll have to look it up when I'm back at the office. Maybe I'll find an interesting ethnic restaurant.

Oh, look, it's an antique doll shop. Am I going in? No, I am sure as fuck not going into the creepy doll shop, because I'm adventurous, not self-destructive.

A voice squawks "Enter" from the open door of a pet store. Who am I to ignore voices when I'm on a quest for novelty? Nobody's at the cash register or working the aisles, maybe because this is a small mom-and-pop affair staffed by one person who's in the back room. There's everything you'd find in a chain store, just in smaller quantities: beta fish in plastic cups, a cage with preening parakeets, some mice, a few rats and hamsters, but also a tiny dragon. Barely four inches from snout to tail, it flaps its stubby winglets, generating only enough draft to stir the sawdust bedding of its cage. It coughs a whiff of smoke.

"You're doing great," I encourage before leaving the store.

See, that's not something I was ever going to see in the company cafeteria.

I cross the street.

A few blocks down, I pass a record shop playing a song I dimly remember—maybe something my dad played on the car radio? I find myself humming the tune and murmuring a few words from the chorus, and then the whole song comes to me, even if I can't remember where I've heard it. My gait gets jaunty and the muscles around my face relax. I'm not the only one. Standing on a corner, I'm in a group of half a dozen people, all tapping our feet and singing in happy reverie, even though we're all humming different tunes and singing different words.

The light turns green and we go our separate ways.

The street signs change alphabets again. Compelling mandala glyphs draw me in, and I wonder if I've been standing here for years or centuries.

I check my phone. It's only been ten minutes, phew!

Down a manhole, dark waters churn. Something pops its head above the surface. The face is human, except for the eyes —ancient and dark as starless space. We hold one another's gaze, and I feel the patience it takes to lay low until the new, boiling sea grows cool enough to support ocean prey.

The creature dives, flicking water off its flukes before it descends into the murk.

In the window of a meat shop hang human corpses, flayed and limbless. This is the kind of sketchy neighborhood I hoped to avoid. Maybe it's time to head back. I've got twenty minutes left on my lunch break. If I hurry, I can make it to my desk in time.

But the hat-knocking urge persists. I cross the street and continue.

I think I'm starting to understand the street signs. I've always had a knack for languages. In high school I took both AP French and Spanish, and those were my best grades. "Boltzmann Brain Boulevard" reads one of the signs. "The World Is a Sphere but Time Is Linear Avenue," reads another. "Theories of Quantum Consciousness Are the Minimization of Mystery, That Is, If Consciousness and Quantum Phenomena Are Mysteries, Are They the Same Mystery Street."

That last sign is long as a surfboard.

Between a building constructed of woven shark teeth and a three-story Victorian emitting screams stands a church. It's old, any sharp corners softened by time and weather. You can see hammer marks in the door's metal hardware. This place predates industrial machines. The door itself is thick enough to trap ghosts.

Inside the cool, dark space, human-shaped figures with paper coffee cups sit on folding chairs before the altar. They each have six wings, one pair covering their feet, one lying flat against their backs, and another pair covering their faces.

"Hi," says one. "My name is Zerachiel, and I'm an alco…"

They notice me and pull back their wings to reveal the eyes of angels.

I scream and weep with awe when they ignite into flames.

Stammering and moaning an apology for my intrusion, I run outside to escape the seraphim.

Parking meters tell owners of parked cars how much longer they have left to live. I search my pocket for a quarter to help out a sniffling man, but these meters don't take quarters.

I'm so sorry, friend.

I cross the street.

My iced grande two-pump vanilla latte is down to milky melt water, but I've gotten in a lot of steps and can afford the calories for another drink. There's a Starbucks on the corner, but the logo features a mer-creature like the one I saw down the manhole, and the customers are on their knees, clutching their bellies and choking.

Jiggling the remaining ice in my cup, I start to cross, but pause.

Some kind of spiraling vortex encroaches into the street, like a horizontal tornado. The pressure differential is more than my brittle skull can endure. Swords plunge into my ear canals.

There's a noise that my brain has not evolved to process.

A woman stands beside me on the curb. She's a jogger in

shorts and a tank top. Her ponytail spills out the keyhole of her pink baseball cap. Her shoes look like speedboats.

I point across the street. "Is that a portal?"

"Everything's a portal. Every wound is a portal. Every conversation is a portal to a human connection. Every passing second is a portal to another time."

"But more specifically?"

"It's whatever you've always imagined is on the other side. It's the alpha and omega. It's the first word or the last. It's what happens when you go too far. The great unraveling. Pandemonium. Reality and consciousness unzipped. Demolition and rebirth but no return. These are only metaphors. Pale reflections of the beyond. You can only know by going in."

The light turns green.

"Are you going to cross?"

"I thought I was," she says. "But listen. You hear that howling? It's the shriek of gods burning alive on their pyres. Hell, no, I'm not crossing."

She seems smart. I like her demeanor. But I can't take my eyes off her hat. Nothing remarkable about it, just a baseball cap. And I have the urge to smack it right off her head.

I step off into the howling.

IN THE PALACE OF SCIENCE

CHRIS CAMPBELL

Originally published in *Asimov's Science Fiction,* May / June 2024.

Chris Campbell is a writer of speculative fiction and critical imagination. His stories appear in *Asimov's*, *FIYAH*, *khōréō*, and more, and have been translated into Chinese for *Science Fiction World*. He is the editor of *New Year, New You: A Speculative Fiction Anthology of Reinvention*. Chris has received the generous support of the Massachusetts Cultural Council and recognition from Boston's Office of Arts and Culture in recognition of his ongoing contributions to Afrofuturist literature. A graduate of the Clarion West and Viable Paradise workshops, Chris is completing his MFA in Creative Writing at Emerson College. Follow him @chriscampbell.bsky.social or visit www.clundycampbell.com.

TRACK ONE–

. . .

IF YOU'VE FOUND *this recording, two things can be said for certain. The first is that I have passed my greatest test as a man and, in doing so, have passed from this world. The second is that if this message entombed with me survives, a grave danger to humanity most assuredly survives with it.*

To my listener, I urge you to lift the needle from the gramophone, return this plate to the hole where you found it, and dig no further into the ruins where once stood Professor Thomas Washington Kelly's Palace of Science.

However, as with most of those driven to dig beneath the surface to uncover the hidden past, I expect your curiosity to exceed your wisdom. Therefore, assuming that a simple warning will not suffice to turn you away from disaster, I engrave my last testament with a diamond-tipped stylus into this fantastic metal so that my warning might endure. I pray it is sufficient to convince whoever comes upon it to succeed where I failed and bury my story and the danger that sleeps with me deep enough that our shared grave will never be disturbed again.

As these will be my final words, I'll tell the story as I wish and start not where it began, for where it began is shrouded by the mists of time and far beyond the ken of man. No, I will start with the small part I played in the events, with a meeting or, to be precise, a series of meetings.

TRACK TWO–

I FIRST MET the Professor through a letter of introduction handed to me by his manservant, the genial Mr. Ochi.

As a fellow black man, Mr. Ochi dressed with enough flair and style to catch my attention regardless of circumstance. A crisp black jacket that looked like it could be fresh from Savile Row and a pair of equally fine yet mismatched gray pants that marked him as a servant, although clearly one of an incredibly wealthy household. Despite his sartorial splendor, the fact that he was directed to my desk at the Electro-Dynamic Light Company of New York by the company's owner Mr. Sawyer, is why I believed the letter was genuine and not a fanciful distraction from some bored dilettante pretending to be the reclusive genius.

Like most men of science in my era, what I'd heard of the Professor was only in passing and often contradictory. On the rare occasion that his name, Thomas Washington Kelly, was spoken, it was with the grave intonations one associated more with a whispered prayer than a name. If it wasn't for the fabulous riches the Professor accrued as the silent partner for more patents than even Edison held, I might have written off his existence entirely.

Due to his almost ephemeral nature, many presumed he was more of a semi-mythic muse to the sciences than a man in flesh, some aspect of a researcher's anima invoked for inspiration. Others suggested he was the nom de guerre assumed by a conspiracy of scientists whose secretive motives could only be guessed at, for how could a single man have attained so much knowledge across the breadth of fields he was accounted to be an expert in? Among the elite practitioners of our noble calling, however, there was no doubt that he was indeed a living man whose insight and intelligence rivaled the greatest minds of previous generations, with abilities perhaps even surpassing Newton and Archimedes.

One scientist after another, in fields as varied as physics to biology, could attest to giving a lecture or publishing a paper outlining some great discovery they were attempting to make– where they explained some heretofore irresolvable difficulty, only to receive a letter from the Professor, often just weeks later, proposing a partnership while providing tantalizing evidence that he already held the answers they sought. All the more reason that I, with no published papers and just a handful of patents, found it hard to believe the Professor would send his manservant to seek me out if not for Mr. Sawyer facilitating our introduction.

The letter, written in crisp economical handwriting, was

an invitation to the Professor's estate urging me to call on him at my convenience. It included a twenty-dollar silver certificate to cover my expenses and any lost wages. A generous invitation, the sum equal to my weekly salary, while the train to his location, a little more than an hour's ride, would cost a dollar fifty there and back.

I'd long practiced retaining a stoic demeanor while within the confines of the workplace. It was a lesson my father taught me, and a useful skill for any black man, regardless of station. Doubly so in my chosen field, where my skin marked me as an exotic intruder. If not for this habit, I might have hung slack-jawed in response to the letter's contents and the twenty-dollar bill that slid from its folds onto my lap. Mr. Ochi, surely a student of the same school of practical stoicism, watched impassively, showing nothing while he waited. Mr. Sawyer, on the other hand, did nothing to hide his eagerness for me to reveal the contents of the letter from the august personage to his most junior draftsman.

I gathered my wits for a moment before I answered but only a moment. A man of the Professor's station wasn't one to leave waiting, and it wouldn't be unusual if Mr. Ochi considered himself an extension of his master when acting as his agent. I also knew that it would be unwise to make the gentleman professor wait overly long for me to call on him, and seeing as we were at the end of the week, I surmised that attending to his summons the first thing Saturday would be sufficiently respectful.

"Thank you, Mr. Ochi, for bringing me this letter."

It was my father who also taught me that it was most wise to treat servants with a full measure of courtesy. He knew the subtle power held by those who open doors before you enter and handle the food before you eat. He'd spent the first half of his life in service as a slave to a Southern family. Then as a freeman serving the same household when they relocated to Boston until he returned to the South during Reconstruction, where he staffed a newly elected congressman, only to disappear a few years later.

"Please convey to Professor how humbled and honored I

am to receive his invitation." I continued. "It would be my pleasure to meet with him. I can take the first train tomorrow and be at his estate and service before noon should the train run on time."

I thought I noticed something flash in Mr. Ochi's eyes, but his affable smile returned before I could determine what.

"Of course, that would be wonderful. The Professor would be quite pleased to meet with you tomorrow. However, if Mr. Sawyer is amenable to you taking leave early, I drove here with the Professor's Locomobile."

Mr. Sawyer, although typically an over-the-shoulder type taskmaster, was all too eager to agree with the manservant's proposal. During the next few minutes, Mr. Ochi gracefully maneuvered around any possible objections toward leaving the city abruptly. Including his assurance that I'd no need to pack as I would be furnished with anything I might want for at the estate and that someone would be sent around to my landlady to inform her of my absence.

Between Mr. Sawyer's desire to please his scientific bene-factor and the dab-hand Mr. Ochi maneuvered me with, it is a wonder I remembered to grab my hat before I found myself on the street below in front of a Locomobile quite unlike any I'd seen before. Where I'd expected to find a simple condensa-tion cylinder behind the seats was a set of fins that bore an uncanny resemblance to French horns. While the front of the carriage extended a good meter and a half beyond the dash-board to make room for three large canisters arranged in a row.

I made it all the way to the side of the Locomobile and had one shoe on the footplate when my inspection of the contraption brought me to a dead stop.

"I know its design may appear novel, but you need not worry, Mr. Carruthers, the modifications the Professor made to the Locomobile are completely safe. He travels using this vehicle himself."

"Worry?" It took me a beat to parse the man's words between my examination of the vehicle. "Worry, no, not at all.

I'm fascinated. Tell me, Mr. Ochi, are these magnificent fins for cooling?"

The manservant paused before answering with a smile. "I'm sure you would know better than I do. The Professor tries to explain these things to me, but I have no mind for the sciences. I'm sure he will answer any question you might have about the carriage after we arrive."

Enamored by the vehicle, I spent the first portion of the ride slowly trundling through the city streets, lost in conjecture–time I should have spent tactfully interrogating Mr. Ochi about the Professor's nature and the treatment a black person in his employ might expect. Once we arrived at the turnpike, the Locomobile accelerated to a truly blistering pace, and I realized my chance to engage the manservant passed for now. Any words would disappear under the thundering gravel below us.

Mr. Ochi was the one, it turned out, who broached the subject of the Professor's temperament when conversation became feasible after we exited the turnpike onto a dirt road some ten miles west of Bridgeport.

"Mr. Carruthers, as I said, the Professor will be delighted you responded to his invitation. If this first meeting goes well, I expect you will find an offer of employment under most generous terms. Although if you are the man the Professor suspects, it is the nature of the work and not the wage that will inspire you. However, I must warn you that the Professor is a very private man with a reclusive nature. Please don't be offended when he doesn't greet you in person. It has been some years since he engaged with any but myself."

With this revelation, what open questions I had about the Professor's temperament closed indefinitely.

Shortly after this conversation, my eyes set upon the Professor's extraordinary Palace of Science. The first glimpse I caught was of its tower rising to nearly twice the height of the majestic chestnuts of the forest surrounding the estate. Topped with the unmistakable dome of an astronomical observatory, its copper cladding sparkling in the sun without a hint of green tarnish.

The rest of the building came into view when the Locomobile wheeled into its clearing. A grand neo-gothic mansion that would have been in place in the English countryside– if not for the numerous metallic chimneys of different shapes and sizes, antennas of various designs, and an eclectic assortment of meteorological equipment that crowded the building's burnished copper roofing.

It took but one look to understand that the awesome sight before me was not simply the home of a scientist. It was a home for science.

I spent some time lost in thought, trying to divine the nature of each of the various instruments adorning the roof and several other subtle but curious features of the house, when I found Mr. Ochi standing beside me to help me from the carriage.

When I started for the servant's door, Mr. Ochi, who was still standing near, coughed for my attention.

"If you would, Sir." He said, pointing me toward the main entrance. Taking advantage of my confusion to gain a few steps, allowing him to reach the grand metal doors, which he opened wide with hardly a hint of effort to welcome me. When I passed through the doors, what I'd taken for copper under the sun's glare appeared to be something else entirely. Inside, the light flashed off the curious alloy with glints of both red and gold.

"Would you like to get yourself settled? I could show you to your rooms." Mr. Ochi asked once we entered the main foyer.

"I wouldn't want to keep the professor waiting," I answered.

"Then please follow me to the library, sir."

With that, Mr. Ochi led me on a circuitous route that took me through a sitting room and then a study before arriving at the grand library that occupied the first three floors of the tower.

Although the room was quite large, its appearance suggested that the owner found the space at least somewhat constraining to the size of his collection. The shelving around the room's perimeter used all three stories of the stone walls, where interlocking circular stairs and walkways around the circumference provided easy access to the tallest shelves. The floor of the room had row after row of bookcases arranged in a spiraling pattern. Toward the center, the bookcases were below chest height, allowing clear sightlines between the various doorways and the windows, while toward the perimeter of the room, they were tall enough to tower over me, and each included an attached rolling ladder.

Mr. Ochi guided me toward the center of the library and a tanker desk with comfortable leather chairs on either side. A stack of papers awaited me on the desk, each page written in the same crisp economical handwriting as the letter I'd received that morning.

The papers started by asking for advanced mathematical and geometric calculations, followed by questions of cutting-edge physics and chemistry. Making my way through the stack, quickly at first and then slower, as I moved deeper, a picture came into focus, hinting toward an entirely new branch of physics. Following a path from Leibniz's disreputable theory of relativity to the shocking implications that the Professor teased out of the strange motion observed by the Scottish botanist Robert Brown.

At some point, as I consumed the data before me and was consumed by the challenges the Professor laid out in the pages, day turned to night and back into day again.

When I finished, I found an untouched plate of dinner sitting next to me and an empty carafe of coffee, and Mr. Ochi standing patiently beside me.

"Magnificent," I managed to stammer. Rising to my feet, I took Mr. Ochi by the hand, shaking it vigorously. "Thank you, thank you so much for bringing me here, Mr. Ochi, and pass my thanks to the Professor. I can't begin to express how much this means to me–no how much it means to the world, we stand at the precipice of a new age."

"It is always my pleasure to be of service," Mr. Ochi reply. "If you wouldn't mind waiting, the Professor asked to see these as soon as you were finished. Although, from what he told me, he didn't expect you to be done in less than a handful of days. If you are as keen as you are quick, I expect he will be quite pleased."

With that, the manservant swept the papers up into a neat stack and left me with my mind still swirling at the magnitude of the discoveries the Professor made in secret. Now for the first time, it made sense to me how this mysterious figure that loomed so large from the shadows seemed to always be one step ahead of the rest of the scientific community. It's easy to appear one step ahead when you are, in fact, leagues beyond.

I tried to eat some of the untouched food on the platter beside me, but my stomach was in turmoil awaiting the Professor's judgment. It couldn't have been more than fifteen minutes later when I heard the man servant's heels clicking against the marble floors approaching me.

"The professor has instructed me to congratulate you, Mr. Carruthers, and extend his warmest invitation to join us here."

TRACK THREE–

I SPENT NEARLY a year working under the remote supervision of the reclusive Professor before our second first meeting.

I was in the library at the large tanker desk when Mr. Ochi approached with a stack of diagrams I'd sent to the Professor for his approval earlier.

On most days, after delivering a set of papers, Mr. Ochi would turn to leave while I busied myself inspecting any notes or the rare corrections sent down. Today, I'd had enough.

"Mr. Ochi, please wait a moment."

"Of course, sir, as always, I am at your service." He replied with a warm smile on his lips.

"I suspect not," I answered.

"Begging your pardon." Mr. Ochi replied, his eyebrows furrowed at the unexpected turn in the conversation.

"Perhaps I'm the one that should beg your pardon since you must have your reasons," I continued, screwing up my courage to say what I'd been meaning to for months. "However, I think it is well past the time we drop this facade of your pretending to be ought than who you are and my pretending not to know it. The work must come first."

Professor Thomas Washington Kelley eyed me closely, the mask he wore of the affable Mr. Ochi slipping away in an instant.

Although I suspected the truth, I was still caught off guard by the hawk-like eyes I found examining me. Looking over me like I would a mathematical proof.

"How long."

"How long have I known?"

"Yes, boy, don't play dense now." Professor Kelly said, unbuttoning his waistcoat to sit across from me on a chair that had waited empty for the last year. The final remaining edifice of the butler, Mr. Ochi, crumbled away with his casual bearing and slouching shoulders.

"Well, I hope you won't be offended, but I've suspected since the beginning," I said, trying to take the temperature of the man before me, now a stranger.

"Then why did you press me on it today?"

"I need to see what you're building, what we're building."

"And why should I trust you?"

"That's the simplest question you've ever asked me, sir, because you already do."

The Professor's eyes narrowed, and he pursed his lips.

"Perhaps I do, to some degree. Enough, I would say, for now."

With that, he stood and walked away, beckoning me to follow after his back was turned. In my mind, I'd come to terms with the fact that Mr. Ochi was but a fabrication, yet it was still unsettling to see the man I'd grown to respect completely disappear, subsumed into the Professor's alien mannerisms. But that is what I asked for, no demanded, and nothing comes without a price. What was the loss of the false Mr. Ochi when measured against the truths I would receive?

The Professor's path took him to the mantle of one of the library's twin fireplaces. With a twist of a flower carved into the corbel below its mantel, the bookshelf next to the fireplace shifted downward ever so slightly before pivoting inward to reveal a staircase that served as a passage from the private rooms in the tower above to the secret laboratory hidden below. Three stories below, to be precise, beneath both the basement and the cellar that housed the Professor's extensive wine vault.

The laboratory was as grand as anything else in the Palace of Science. Made of interjoining rooms, each with a distinct purpose and whose combined total footprint was nearly as large as the home above.

There was a room devoted to chemistry and analysis filled with beakers, titration tubes, and catches of sand and water positioned for quick deployment should there be an accident.

A chamber devoted to fabrication, its furnaces burning blue with the methane pumped from the surrounding bedrock—this geological feature had determined where the Professor built his home, allowing him both greater secrecy and self-sufficiency.

Another space for high voltage experiments, its floors made using a treatment of vulcanized rubber, and its air-filled with an audible crackling and the scent of ozone.

Finally, the lab contained another smaller study with a work desk made for two. Half its shelves filled with journals written out in the crisp economical handwriting I'd come to recognize so well, the other half with disks of vinyl the Professor used to document the experiments that left him without free hands to write his notes.

Engrossed as I was, the notion that the Professor only "trusted me enough, for now," had already begun to fester in the back of my mind.

Quite done with games, I asked him flat out. "What do you mean enough for now?"

"Do you know why men fear monsters? Why we find them in our oldest myths and endlessly reimagine them?"

I was surprised by this turn in the conversation. Although I'd only known the Professor in person for minutes, our correspondence over the year had given me the picture of a man with little interest or patience for fabulism and the other nonsense people distract themselves with. However, regardless of the topic, it's rare for me to be caught flat-footed, and I thought about Freud and his new branch of near sciences for an answer.

"I think perhaps what men fear at the edge of darkness is the manifestation of our inner darkness, shadows cast by the evils that live in our hearts. We don't fear monsters truly; we fear we are the monsters."

"I'll give you half points for that son, but half points only. You need to look into the new horizons in the math I have shown you and find what's lurking there."

It was clear from his answers that if I wished to learn more, I'd need to discover what fearsome things he'd found before he would trust me with more of his secrets.

TRACK FOUR—

IT TOOK another two years to puzzle out the monsters the Professor mentioned, and he trusted me enough.

Years of discovery but also frustration, as I could not ignore that regardless of everything he shared after dropping the Mr. Ochi act, he was still keeping things from me. And, unlike before, when it was merely a matter of personal safety in a country where being both black and excellent begged for danger. Now it was impossible for me to forget that the only reason he kept these final secrets was that, in his eyes, I was still unworthy.

The first only took a few months to find. The amount of energy the division of an elementary particle would release and how it might be weaponized. Including a small but none-theless real chance that a weapon built along these principles deployed at an exact altitude might set off a chain reaction that could set the planet's atmosphere ablaze.

The Professor concurred with this finding. For the first time, I truly understood why he only intervened in the scientific explorations of others once they'd drawn close enough to a discovery that the final steps toward it were all but assured to come soon. His love was in learning, not in taking credit. As a black man, he knew firsthand how power over the natural forces manifested within the unnatural power structures built by humanity. He confessed his certainty that if ever the white man made an atomic bomb, it would be some brown people whose bones first burned, leaving nothing behind but ash and shadows on the ruined walls of buildings reduced to rubble. I hope his prediction proves false still in your time, but I fear, as was so often the case, the Professor's theories will be proven true.

It took me another year to discover the next monster, or perhaps I should call her the mother of monsters, for it was from this discovery the other horrors I discovered emerged. The singularity.

The math was irrefutable; it spoke of holes in the fabric of space and time where the scale of energies, mass, or gravity undid the very concept of measurement. From my calculations of this feature, I discovered the final beast lurking, the one I named hypo-dimensionality.

Where the power of the atom bomb and the nature of the singularity were shocking to the senses, they were distant threats. This final beast, hypo-dimensionality, posed an intimate danger as it broke down my fundamental sense of reality. Proof after proof brought me back to the conclusion that the world I perceived as three-dimensional was little more than an illusionary projection of a two-dimensional reality encoded on the surface of a singularity, either infinitely far or infinitely near yet forever unreachable from what we perceive as the true universe around us. That our reality was not entirely unlike an orchestral movement encoded onto a recording disk. Not entirely unlike how to you, my voice could be a man full of life speaking from the next room when in fact, I am now long dead.

This curious finding that we may all be projections led to a number of other deductions, each more disturbing than the next. First among these is the notion that the fabric which held our reality together could not be woven unless time existed as an independent series of traversable vectors, and our perception of linearity was a manifestation of our limitations. This in turn suggested the existence of incomprehensible ecologies, possibly inhabited by vast consciousnesses without our limitations, making them beyond any measure of reason. Creatures that would perceive the grand scope of the cosmos across space and time like we might the four walls of a sitting room. Their motives and morality wholly foreign to our own, built upon a framework for knowledge entirely alien and forever unknowable. If the universe is like a recording disk, what can we know of the being who plays it? What becomes of us if they tire of the music? Or even scratch a single track?

I was looking over the final proof, trying to convince myself that beneath this layer of mathematics, a deeper layer would emerge to reconfirm our three-dimensional nature. Yearning for some clue that the universe might not exist as little more than an abstraction–when my facade of stoicism finally crumbled, leaving only wild panic behind. It was then the Professor took notice of the crisis brewing behind my eyes.

"You have the look about you." He spoke from across the desk we shared. Gesturing toward the pile of papers, I clutched in a shaking fist.

"What look?" I asked, mustering the will to hand the papers over. Hoping he would find the error in my calculations that could set my mind at ease.

He took his time to answer, first flipping through the pages while I waited.

"The look of a man afraid enough to trust with what is

next. This is work that demands someone sane enough to fear it."

The Professor stood, walked to the gramophone player, and adjusted a series of knobs before lifting the needle in three distinct movements resulting in a click from the bookcase beside us.

The Professor pushed the case slightly. When he released the pressure, the case swung forward, revealing the concealed latch in the floor of his secret laboratory that led to the super secret laboratory dug deep beneath the bedrock of the palace of science.

It was there, tucked into the very bowels of Earth, that I first met what the Professor had so carefully hidden from the world, his magnificent automaton.

B-SIDE

Track Five—

The automaton was unfinished, but even in a transitory state, it was a thing of marvel. In form, it was like a man. With two legs meant for bipedal ambulation and two arms with three-fingered hands meant for grasping. Although roughly from the thickness of its fingers.

The design of the machine differed most strikingly from the ideal human in the shape of its head and body, for it had no neck. Rather a barrel-shaped torso attached directly to a head that was meant to be enclosed within the thick, vaguely egg-shaped glass dome sitting next to the machine.

The front piece of the barrel-shaped body was also set aside on a nearby table, exposing its chassis and internal mechanism. Peering inside, it became clear that filling the hole within this hollow man was the singular aim of much of the work I'd been doing for years.

"I call him Talos." The Professor's voice cut into the

silence that enveloped the lab after I'd spent nearly a half hour silently examining the machine upon entering.

"I think it's time you speak plainly to me about the nature of this work," I responded rather than allowing him to hook me on the bait of working out the genesis of the device's name. I knew my classics as well as any man, but I was well tired of games.

"You must pardon me, some habits are hard to break, but of course, you are right. Nearly forty years ago, the son of a once-prosperous family with extensive shipping interests in the Aegean discovered an ancient shipwreck off the coast of Lemnos. Rather than alert proper authorities, he smuggled the entire collection of salvaged artifacts back to his family's estate." The Professor reached into his pocket and pulled out a gold coin.

"I've long suspected that hidden from our sight in unrecorded histories and the ashes of Alexandra, there lay forgotten technologies possessed by ancient man only hinted to in the myths and legends left in their wake. The automatons of Hephaestus, the construction of Pandora, and the wonders of Atlantis. When the once-prosperous family's fortunes turned, items like this began to appear in circulation," he said, placing the gold coin in my hand. "I deduced a cache of heretofore unknown treasures from the ancient world had surfaced and bent my mind toward obtaining them.

"I traced the collection to New Port using a simple geometric analysis and frequency chart of the items as they surfaced. It was there I first adopted the guise of Mr. Ochi to aid in my investigation." For an instant, I recognized the visage of the old reliable butler return in the Professor's expression, and it struck me then how dearly the absence of the man who never was had affected me.

"Once in New Port, I made it known that I was an agent acting on behalf of a gentleman looking to acquire artifacts and that price was no concern. I paid a dear rate for the cache of silver and gold I acquired, but the real treasure, the crust-encased pieces of this automaton, were tossed into the deal for next to nothing."

"What you see before you is a re-creation and extrapolation of Talos' intended form. Most of the original was beyond salvage, but enough components survived for a thorough analysis of the materials and to gain insight into the original design. I was able to identify and decipher the method by which his ancient builders set carved rods of quartz, tourmaline, topaz, and amber crystals within ingenious configurations to absorb, generate and store electrical charges. I also discovered, or I should say rediscovered, the curious alloy much of Talos is built from the fabled metal lost with Atlantis, aurichalcum—a metal most magnificent, with properties that not only conduct but amplify electric, magnetic and gravitic energies.

Aurichalcum, you see, is not only the heart of the automaton but of much of my research these past years. The principles I've discovered from employing it for scientific inquiry are, in part, why my own investigations have sped so far ahead of those who would consider themselves my peers. Or should I say our peers, now that you have joined me atop this mountain of knowledge only we have summited."

TRACK SIX—

FOR YEARS after the Professor entrusted me with his greatest secret, the two of us rebuilt the automaton at a nearly feverish pace. As we did, the distance the Professor previously kept between us entirely disappeared, our work together evolving into a true partnership.

On the rare occasions when I became frustrated with the pace of our endeavor. He was quick to assuage my discontent, noting how much faster the task was coming along with the two of us working together compared to his decades of toiling in solitude, how having someone to share each discovery with breathed new life into the project, how he'd feared before I joined him that he wouldn't finish the work in his lifetime. How long he'd spent searching for an heir worthy of passing the task onto before he'd discovered me. But that now working together, he believed we would not only finish but finish soon.

It was the deepest night of winter when we placed the final pieces, a pair of circular aurichalcum receivers that resembled Heinrich Hertz's loop antennas. These receivers were set at ninety-degree angles to each other on either side of the automaton's head. Installing them into their finely geared crystalline sockets took the entire night.

Talos had no discernable switch, toggle, or mechanism to wind up the clockwork gears within him. The Professor surmised that once we finished its reconstruction, it might feed off an available field of energy like a machine with a properly attuned receiver would from one of Tesla's high-frequency transmitters, and the automaton would either leap into life, if we were lucky, or begin to slowly fill its crystalline capacitors.

With a final tightening of an antenna within its socket, Talos was complete, and the Professor and I stepped back from our work. Near-perfect silence enveloped the room, neither of us daring to breathe while we waited, and then it began. Both the antennae started to rotate, slowly at first and then faster, and the room began to thrum with strange energy.

Then for no discernible reason, the spinning antennas slowed until their rotation crept to a halt.

The pair of us again stood in silence after the brief spurt of activity ended, waiting and hoping. The Professor staring at Talos with an intensity that suggested he intended to bring it back to life through the force of his will alone.

"Did we miss something?" I asked with my first exhaled breath. "We must be close. Perhaps we should check the filaments attached to the capacitor? Or the cooling apparatus might need adjustment. Maybe it turned itself off before it risked overheating and damaging its amber components."

I reached for the large spanner we used to close Talos' chest plate when the Professor rested his hand on mine.

"You might be right, but perhaps we should wait. We figured out enough to rebuild this machine, my friend, but we still don't fully understand it. Look at the timepiece."

I paused to check the clock we'd affixed to the wall. An experimental design the Professor and I based on Talos' technology. According to our calculations, the method we'd arranged the clock's crystal lattices in would keep nearly perfect time for years from a single winding of its aurichalcum spring.

"Eighteen after seven, what of it?"

"You and I have learned so much, have perhaps peered beyond the horizon to secrets within the physics that man was never meant to discover, yet we don't even know which field of energy our Talos is meant to feed from. Don't you find it curious that the moment the sun rises is the moment it's shuddered into inactivity? If I'm right, we might only need wait a few hours. Nothing in the grand scheme of things for the culmination of our life's work."

"Then what? We're just waiting?" I asked.

"What we should do is rest. But I'll never ask of you what I can't do myself, so we work. You may be right about the filament or the cooling system, after all. For now, consult your diagrams before we reopen it. If sunrise was a factor, I have a new theory to examine."

That afternoon we reconvened at fifteen to five for dinner and to share what we discovered with the other.

Next to nearly untouched plates heaping with the season's traditional repasts of glazed ham, scalloped potatoes, green beans, and turkey, the Professor and I devoured the stacks of papers we presented to each other.

Him fingering over the diagrams where I explored the most likely culprits for any failures in our initial build. While I sat in amazement as I looked over his calculations for the available energy generated by the tidal shear driven by the moon and the Earth each pulling in opposition and how the bulk of the Earth between the mechanism and the moon would deprive it of the opposing gravitational forces it needed to ignite the system. If his calculations were correct, the implications for humanity were immense. I imagined a world powered by the abundant energy provided by the clockwork of gravity, with the Moon as Earth's pendulum.

At half past five, we made our way down to the sub-basement. If the Professor was right, we had but a handful of minutes to wait. If I was correct, it would be a long night of disassembly and testing.

When the appointed minute came again, we waited.

Talos' antennas began to spin up, emitting a soft humming sound as their speed slowly increased. For a while, we watched them rotate, perhaps both fearing that, once again, the machine before us would disappoint and that this rotation might be all that would come of our long labors over it. But then energy coursed through the room, making every hair on my body stand on edge and my teeth chatter and my nose filled with the scent of ozone with a hint of burning frankincense. The Professor was right.

Inside the large glass dome that served as its head, the tiny servos set within triple axel gimbals spun into life, and pale violet light emanated from within. This was not entirely unsuspected, and on the off chance that the glass dome might serve as some type of cathode ray tube why we'd evacuated it during our installation, yet seeing it light up through still unknown principles was exhilarating to behold. If this had been the end of it, the Professor and I would have spent years examining the data from the test, enraptured by the groundbreaking success of bringing this curio of the ancient world to life.

Alas, that was not what was meant to be.

Talos' first sign of deliberate motion was the opening and closing of its hands, metal hands strong enough to bend steel and crush stone as if it was testing the truth of its completion. Then it sat up and pivoted around to try its legs upon the floor.

"My god, look, he stands." The Professor exclaimed when

it rose to its feet, slowly and deliberately bending and testing its joints.

Then the automaton turned toward the doorway and started to walk. It took a moment for its intentions to dawn on me, but not the Professor, who flung himself between the machine and the exit.

"Stop, you must, I command you." He shouted, holding his hands up, palms facing out, in the vain hope that if his words meant nothing to the ancient machine, that the gesture might be familiar, a simple method of communication far older than our young English tongue.

Talos would not be slowed and brushed the Professor away with a single flick of its stubby arm, sending the older man flying into the wall with a sickening crack. From there, it made its way to the shaft in the bedrock from which the laboratory was carved, ignoring the ladder, which would not have held its massive weight, and digging its arms and feet into the bedrock to fashion the foothold and handholds it required to ascend from the depths of our Palace of Science.

As Talos climbed, I rushed to the Professor's side to assess his injuries. From the look of it, he'd suffered a broken collarbone from the impact. However, as I attended to him, he pushed me away using his good arm.

"Never mind me, follow it, stop it if you can. We can't lose it, not now, not with all we still have to learn."

Perhaps I should be ashamed of this more than anything else yet to come, but I didn't hesitate to abandon my wounded mentor and follow the work. Yes, I've done much worse, but I can justify those actions even as I speak to you now with my hands still covered in the evidence of the crime that most certainly damned my soul as it saved the world.

I climbed and then ran, trying to catch up with Talos. At the end of the hidden stairway, I found the bookshelf that hid its opening splintered and broken, its books strewn across the library floor. As I surveyed the destruction, looking for a clue to the path the machine took, I heard the far wall of the library resound with a mighty smash, and I followed the sound.

Racing through the hole it left, I caught up with the automaton quickly enough but could think of nothing to stop its relentless march. The broken Professor, the splintered bookshelf, and the smashed library wall were enough examples of the power in its metal form that I dared not place myself in its path, although I endeavored to remain apace with its steady clockwork strides toward some unknown destination. At first, the nature of the chase itself was enough to entirely consume my senses, but as the minutes ticked by, the midwinter night I'd plunged into demanded its toll for how poorly I'd prepared for its freezing depths.

I lost parts from two toes to the ill-fated mission and still lost track of Talos hours into the painful chase when he trudged from the rime-encrusted shoreline into the coastal waters slipping from my sight and into the depths of the Sound.

TRACK SEVEN—

SOME OF THE wounds we suffered that night healed quickly. With proper footwear, I could walk with hardly a hitch in my step soon enough, and the Professor's broken bone set near enough to perfect that he was none worse for the trouncing. Unfortunately, the dearest wounds dealt that night were not inflicted on our flesh.

The Professor's drive for discovery evaporated with the escape of the experimental man we built. For days he sat listlessly in the library, staring at the tarp I'd hung over the hole in the wall to keep the winter out. Perhaps he was deep in contemplation, going over the events of the night and our preparations for it, trying to pinpoint when taking a different path might have avoided the complete failure that resulted. Perhaps he was waiting for Talos to return. Either way, he refused to speak to me about what he was thinking, hardly acknowledging my presence at all except to wave me off and grumble that he was fine whenever I hovered over him too closely. All the while sipping on the laudanum prescribed to aid his rest and recovery as the collarbone mended.

As weeks turned to months, I found him more often abed senseless with lips stained red from the malicious elixir until he stopped leaving his bed altogether.

While the injuries I suffered that damned evening were not as transitory as a broken collarbone, all told, I seemed to have gotten the better of it. At first, I occupied my time repairing the damage Talos did to escape from the Palace of Science. Rebuilding the hidden bookshelf with my own hands and overseeing the masons who came to repair the hole in the wall, passing off the damage due to a flaw in the original stonework.

Even after those repairs were finished, I managed to remain busy with a host of other activities, but none were what I'd devoted my life to, what brought me to the Professor's home, the pursuit of science. In this regard, I was as useless as the man, now a recluse in truth, hiding in his bedroom and dreaming his days away.

It was odd indeed that the act of giving life to Talos drained all the vitality from the Palace of Science as if the best parts of the Professor and I were consumed to power the automaton's animation.

The same inescapable truth may have haunted both of us. That when the machine we dared to rebuild got up off that table and walked away, and we were helpless before it, it proved that we were not standing atop some pinnacle of science. We were, in fact, fools playing with the tools of those immeasurably far above us. Now with the machine long gone, lost to the depths of the ocean, going about some unimaginable task, we'd no means to ever close the gap between the knowledge that we had and the knowledge we needed to understand what we'd unleashed upon the world in our hubris.

With the yellow husk of the man I'd grown to admire so much during my tenure at his estate withering above me, this and other troubles began to plague my mind. Soon I found myself spending long evenings within the walls of the Professor's vast wine vault. In those depths, I also heard the call of the laudanum and its promise of peaceful dreams. Thankfully as far gone as I was, I never took what might have been the final step for both of us, the Professor's deterioration just fearful enough to warn me away from the danger of the soporific.

Months later, with the turning of the season came a turning of my physical and mental state, a sort of springtime of the mind. I resolved to rescue the Professor from the prison of the poppy. As a child, I was helpless when my father disappeared after sending my mother a telegram from his patron's congressional office the day after their electoral defeat–announcing that the tide had turned, and he was on his way home. There was nothing I could do to look for him in the broad swath of the country he might have disappeared into, no way to affect his return. The Professor, however, was well within my reach, and I could not allow him to slip away from me further and disappear beyond the point of no return.

It was not an easy path. The poisoned-tongued demon I pulled out of the master suite was so far from the genial Mr. Ochi or my keen-eyed collaborator that, for the first few days, I feared I'd waited too long. That what greatness had been in the man was now gone and that my patron and friend was beyond saving. I'll spare you a close retelling of this course of events, but let it be said, hard as it was, it was manifestly easier than allowing him to continue to waste away and ignore the role I was playing in his downfall.

A few long weeks later, I was taking a meal with the now cogent, although still quite diminished Professor, when we heard a loud knocking on the grand front door. Ringing with the unmistakable sound of aurichalcum on aurichalcum.

There at the door, we met it again–our Talos returned.

In one massive arm, it was holding a box about the size of a gramophone made out of some dark material that glowed with a prismatic, almost greasy sheen in the reflected light that pooled in the doorway.

In times like these, habits long honed to unconscious

violation take the lead. When a visitor arrives at night, you invite them in. We moved aside to allow its entrance, and the automaton marched past us, heading for the library. Once there, it made its way to the recently repaired bookshelf that hid the passage to our secret laboratory, and once again, the polite thing seemed to be the only thing, so the Professor unlocked the hidden latch, and I swung the shelf out of its way.

The three of us made our way down the stairs to the rooms below and were unsurprised when Talos headed toward the hole in the lower office that led to the super-secret sub-basement laboratory where he was reborn. I wondered how it would manage to climb back down with the box in its hands, but this turned out to be foolishness. It simply jumped, only to land seconds later with an impact that shook the foundation.

The Professor and I climbed the ladder down the shaft to follow it. When we made our way into the small stone room illuminated only by the dim violet light cast from Talos' head, we found that it had placed the mysterious box on the center table where the automaton had rested for the years we'd spent rebuilding it.

I nearly jumped out of my skin when the Professor burst into laughter from beside me.

"Wonderful, absolutely wonderful," his voice rang out, the peals of his laughter echoing as they ran up the shaft away from us.

Track Eight—

The box, for a time, was a puzzle, although Talos' intentions were clear enough. The mystery proved to be the true elixir the Professor needed to return to himself. And if I am, to be honest, I might as well admit– it was much the same for me.

We spent weeks studying the box, experimenting with

various sensors to gain insight into the interior. Acoustic tests indicated that it was indeed hollow and not a solid block of the substance the exterior was made from.

Even the keenest diamond-tipped edge could not slice a piece of the black casing away, making chemical tests unwise. Although the box glistened with an oil-like sheen and felt greasy to the touch, it left behind no detectable residue for analysis. Electrical experiments indicated that it was the most perfect conductor of electricity we'd ever measured, leading the Professor to theorize that it was some type of heavily modified form of the aurichalcum we'd become familiar with but transmogrified by some unimaginable forces to reach its ultimate state. This was the first time I disagreed with the Professor on one of his bolder predictions. I believed it was a curious form of the base material carbon where the bonds between its atoms produced something even more robust than the diamonds we tested against its surface.

It was a matter of some luck that we discovered the method of opening the box, something I refuse to share in the chance that my plea to leave everything buried and forgotten is ignored. Suppose you, my dear listener, are a greater fool than I expect; perhaps by withholding this knowledge, I might succeed in my final mission even after every other measure I've taken has failed.

When we opened the box, it seemed to me that it breathed in, but I convinced myself it was only the atmospheric pressures from within and without equalizing, for, of course, a box could not breathe. Within the interior was a mechanism that confounded us upon its revelation. Various crystals connected by coils of aurichalcum with settings made from the same black material as the box's exterior. Superficially the systems inside appeared similar to those of Talos, but the strange geometries we found within the box's mechanisms suggested it was far more advanced than the automaton, almost as if part of the mechanism operated outside our plane of existence.

The two of us spent days carefully examining it while I diligently drafted the internal schematics, attempting to divine the box's purpose and what repairs it required—eventually, a week passed before our next breakthrough.

"It's so simple." The Professor said, pointing his finger at a portion of the diagram I was working on. "Look here, Carruthers, do you see it?"

"What is it I'm supposed to see?" I asked.

"Think simple, son. I won't take this discovery from you, look again and think."

Although we worked as nearly equals for years, falling into the role of the mentee was easy enough, so I emptied my mind focusing on the diagram, trying to see what could be so simple that it would, in turn, explain the greater complicated whole.

"It can't be," I said, scratching my head before I began drawing a diagram from memory next to the spot the Professor indicated. The similarities between the system within the box and a crystal diode demodulator were inescapable.

"It's like some type of radio receiver."

"Not a radio. It won't be radio waves it picks up with this design. But it seems that we are clearly in possession of a mechanism with the ability to pick up some type of exotic transmissions, that is, if we can fix it."

"Transmissions from where?" I asked, but either the Professor missed my question in his excitement or chose to ignore it as immaterial to the discovery he'd made.

Once the nature of the box was discerned, the repairs it would need if it was going to function became apparent. Although, upon closer examination, they proved not, in fact, to be simply repairs it needed. As we soon discovered that whoever began the construction of the box, unknowable eons before, had abandoned the task unfinished.

Its incomplete nature preyed on me, a small voice at the back of my mind that spoke of danger, trying to rise above the growing whispered promises of greatness that led me onward.

Within weeks all the parts and pieces we required to finish the transmitter were laid out on a bench next to the table the box rested on, along with the tools we would need to do the work, from spanners and tongs to soft rubber hammers and welding tools. It was only then, when it became clear that nothing could prevent us from the appointed task, that I finally broke free of the momentum that carried us ever forward and confronted my patron with my dire concerns.

"We can't do this. Look, man, think for a moment about how Talos battered and broke you when we turned it on, how little regard it held for your life. All we know about this box is that he brought it to us and its workings are beyond us. That and whoever started building it had sense enough not to finish. How dare we proceed when we know less of this than them?"

"You don't know why it was left unfinished any more than I do. To say they decided not to finish is pure conjecture. Perhaps some calamity befell them, like Pompei, Herculaneum, or the fabled Atlantis."

"What we know is that if we turn this on, it may receive something, but not from whom. You're the one who led me to the monsters that live in the math, who showed me what might lay beyond the bounds of our reality. You know how fragile our existence is but not from where the strange geometries inside the box might allow a signal to reach us? If we open this door, there may be no way to close it and usher back out what we are letting in. You spent your life holding back discoveries too dangerous for humanity to meddle with."

"I held back from the others, never myself, and not from you. Haven't I shared all that I know with you? What does the universe hold that we together can't fathom? How can we turn back when the next horizon is upon us?" The Professor asked. "I don't blame you for your fear, boy. Greatness and fear go hand in hand, but this is my purpose, our purpose. This is why I brought you here, why I built my palace of science." While he spoke, the Professor's hand holding the largest rod of amber we'd carved to fit within the transmitter began to shake, reminding me of the sickness that consumed him just a few short months ago during the worst of his with-drawal from the laudanum.

"How can I live with myself if I turn back now," he finally asked in nearly a whisper, almost as if pleading with himself and not with me.

"We make this choice together. That's how."

With that, the Professor dropped the crystal on the tray and reached out to grip my shoulder. He was about to say something when Talos, who'd stood silent sentry since his return, moved from the position it took near the entrance to stand directly in front of the stone room's door, completely blocking our path. Even without words, the message was clear.

The first day was the easiest, as we were able to keep ourselves busy with matters of survival. With the tools we had on hand, we adjusted the vents and burners built into the stone room to collect and condense the water vapor produced by the methane's combustion. Enough that we faced not a quick death from dehydration but a slow one from starvation. Talos only watched and waited.

On the second day, we became restless as we explored methods of destruction that would allow us to affect our escape. I calculated that we could cause an explosion powerful enough to damage Talos' metal exterior but that setting it off would smash us into pudding at best and, perhaps, even set off a chain reaction in the methane stored within the surrounding bedrock. The Professor calculated how to achieve temperatures high enough to defeat the automaton's internal cooling mechanisms, melt the amber rods within it, and render it inert. Much like the explosive solution, our fate would be likewise sealed in the effort. Talos only watched and waited.

On the third day, everything changed. After spending nearly fifty hours awake, pacing and pondering our eventual fate, I finally fell into an uneasy sleep at the Professor's insis-tence when something, perhaps some second sense, pulled me from my slumber. That is when I saw him through blurry eyes, standing beside the box, tools in hand, working on its interior.

When he noticed me stirring, he called out.

"I've almost finished, Carruthers, the world be damned. I'll not let you die down here. Come what may, we'll face it together."

I had no means of deducing how long he'd been at work or how close he'd come to finishing, no method for extrapolating how Talos would react if I tried to restrain the Professor before the box was complete.

All I knew for certain was the Professor could be finished in a snap and that, in his madness, he'd revealed to our jailer where his true weakness lay. So that now, Talos need only to coil me within his metal embrace and start to slowly squeeze to bend the Professor to his aurichalcum will.

From the tray next to my dearest friend Thomas Washington Kelly, I took the largest spanner and brought it down squarely on the top of his crown, acting as swiftly as I could to preempt any attempt the automaton might take to stop me, and before any weakness of my all too human heart might break my resolve to act.

I record this now while my mentor's blood pools at my feet, and Talos still watches and waits. Judge me if you must for what I have done, even if it was done to save you. I have adjusted the burners to blow. If my calculations are correct, the explosion will be enough to ignite the natural gas stored in the nearby bedrock causing the tower far above me to collapse and fill the shaft that leads to this secret laboratory. Burying the Professor, the automaton, the box, and I beneath the wreckage of the Palace of Science.

I will place this disk in one of the vents where the force of the explosion will lift it to rest nearer to the surface. Know that only damnation lies below it, and the fate of humanity now turns on you.

BLACK WATER

SEÁN PADRAIC BIRNIE

Originally published in *Weird Horror #9*.

Seán Padraic Birnie is a writer from Brighton. His debut collection of short stories, *I Would Haunt You if I Could*, was published by Undertow Publications in 2021. His work has appeared in *Best British Short Stories, Interzone, Fictionable*, and *Cōnfingō*, among other places. He is on Bluesky and Instagram @seanbirnie. For more information, see seanbirnie.com

> *My beloved, don't worry—don't move...*
> —William Sansom, 'A Woman Seldom Found'

SHE WAS SITTING in one of the booths in the corner of the pub, a candle in the wine bottle before her, the tip of a cigarette glowing between her knuckles, a half pint of brown beer beside the candle. He saw her glance in his direction as the door swung shut behind him, but he honed his gaze on the bar, which glowed brightly in the dark room, lest his cheeks colour and his step falter and the ground play tricks beneath him. He took a barstool and was relieved to sit down. He smiled but the barman did not return it. Flustered and self-conscious, very tired from travel, he ordered one of the local beers, which was dark in colour and tasted, not unpleasantly, of chocolate, coffee, and old cigarettes.

He had not expected to meet someone. He had not expected that young woman to join him at the bar, nor that, minutes later, he would follow her to her booth on the other side of that dark room with low ceilings in the old town; nor that, in a few hours, she would take him to the attic she rented in a large and empty house nearby, from the skylight of which he would hear the waves breaking on a shingle beach. Nor that he would listen to those waves for months to come.

THE SEA AIR, his mother had said. It'll do you good. You need to get away from things.

THE HOTEL OVERLOOKED THE DOCK. On arrival an hour before he had deposited his bag in the single room, then, after making sure the door had locked, left the cramped little building and started walking without destination in mind. His journey had been long, by train, and the carriage uncomfortable, and it felt good to walk. He had slept for a small part of the duration but not so much as he had hoped. Instead his mind had drifted and he had been aware all the time of the pain in his neck and back and arms. The pain came and went. It moved about. He watched the dull countryside pass by in the dim light, the world reduced to shades of grey and hues of brown. He often felt as if he had not quite woken up: Some days it was twilight all day long. He had theories about that, but the trip was supposed to take him out of that frame of mind in which he developed theories. A theory, he knew, could get you into trouble. He would have a few days to enjoy by himself, alone, then his uncle, who lived not far away, would collect him from the hotel and put him up at his farm.

Through the night he walked by the light of intermittent streetlamps. He followed narrow cobbled roads beneath the high windows of leaning houses through the old town and felt the aching of his body ease. It was a strange pain, seemingly without cause. Doctors and specialists of joint and muscle and bone had examined him without useful result. But in the rhythm of the walking he found some respite.

At the dockside he sat on a low wall and listened to the clinking of the moorings and watched the dark movement of the boats. Then he stood and stretched and decided to walk a little more, back into the old town, in search of a pub or a bar that might please him, for one drink or two.

NOW HE WAS LAUGHING, which came as some surprise. He felt an unexpected lightness; in her company he felt his mood lift. He had not laughed in a long time.

Oh, I have theories about that, he was saying.

About what? she asked.

The world, he said.

Don't we all, she replied.

Some people don't, he said.

They're lucky, she replied. What's your theory? she asked.

He looked at her. Her eyes were very bright in the candlelight. He wondered how much she had drunk but she was not unsteady. Her gaze was steady. She didn't seem to blink. In her brown eyes he saw his own blue gaze doubled back on him.

That none of it's real, he said. Not really.

You are aware you're not the first person to have such a thought, she said, tilting her head, smiling without smiling.

I am, he said. It's just—well, it haunts me. Sometimes. I can't explain it.

I know the feeling, she said.

You do? he asked.

Oh yes, she said. I mean, the world is extraordinary. Just the fact of it. That anything should exist. It beggars belief.

He expected her to proceed but she did not, though she continued to nod, staring down at the table. Then she clicked her neck, turning her head at an angle.

So, he said. I've told you all about me. How about you? Where are you from?

Nowhere interesting, she said. Nowhere at all, really.

No one's from nowhere, he replied. He had tried to place her accent but had failed: At first he had thought she was from the south, that she came from a family with means, but he was no longer so sure.

She finished her drink. I am, she said.

He frowned.

Well? she said. Are we going?

He felt such abandon in this moment—such sudden freedom, such joy in life.

———

THE ATTIC ROOM was large and plain. A mattress lay under the slant of the ceiling on one side, and a large window opened out onto the night. Since his arrival in town a fresh wind had gathered its strength and he could hear the sound of it through the skylight and the ceiling, through the insulation and the roof tiles above and through the chimney. With nowhere else to put it he set the bottle of wine down on the floor, then placed his coat, neatly folded, beside it.

My landlady is hardly ever here, said his companion. Most of the rooms are empty. Sometimes I think I live alone.

Have you been here long? he asked, wondering how long someone might live in a place and it remain so bare of clutter and decoration.

A few months, she replied. The person I came here to meet never showed up.

I'm sorry, he said, wondering what else to say.

She turned around. It's not a bad thing, she said, smiling without smiling. I found you. Then she kissed him.

As if a kiss were a body of dark water into which a person might fall.

Have we met before? he asked.

Don't be ridiculous, she said.

Are you sure? he asked, kissing her neck.

Shut up, she said.

She unclipped first one buckle and then the next of the russet pinafore, then kicked off her shoes, flats, which clattered against the skirting board. With unexpected strength she moved him toward the window. It occurred to him that he was very drunk. The wind buffeted the glass, which shook in its frame. He felt the house moving like an old ship and thought of the clinking of the dark boats on the water. He was sitting on the low wall, breathing the sea air. He was on a train passing through dull countryside comprised of hues of grey and shades of brown. He was putting his bag down in a lonely hotel room—then he was here and she was unbuttoning the buttons of his shirt.

Lie down, she said.

She kissed him, then pushed him down by one shoulder.

Careful, he said, laughing.

Shut up, she whispered, and kissed him again.

Then he started to gag. At first it hurt—he felt a scalding, the presence of something unexpectedly solid. But then, from that scalding, he felt a sensation not unpleasurable fan out. Her lips tightened over his own. She pressed down on him. He was suddenly sleepy; he felt the strength depart his body, felt his muscles relax. He might have been seated in a dentist's chair. That residue of pain which never left him began to leave him. He felt that thing pushing down through his throat. Though numbed he felt its slow movement inside him. He could not breathe but did not panic. As if she might breathe for the two of them. There was no reason to panic. She is feeding me, he thought, like a goose. To fatten me up. The thought did not trouble him. Now that thing was in his chest; now he felt it enter his stomach, probing, reaching. For a moment he regarded the procedure with some curiosity. Then he was gone, lost to sensation, under the spell of the night.

HE AWOKE NAUSEOUS, in new pain, without memory beyond his own gaze doubled back in her eyes; candlelight; dark beer and an unsmiling barman in a pub that was empty beyond the young woman alone in one booth. He tried to speak.

Don't worry yourself, she said.

He was very hot. The sheets were sodden. She placed a cool flannel on his forehead.

Don't worry, she said. You need to rest. There's no reason to worry.

THE PAIN EBBED. She must have replaced the sheets while he slept. He lacked energy to a degree he had never known before: He felt the lack of it pressing down on him. He watched her walking about the room. She went in circles, head bowed, lips moving. She stood smoking beneath the open window, watching him. Her eyes were very large and brown, her black hair pulled back from her face in a ponytail. He could hear the wind at the window.

She brought him water. She brought him food but he could not eat. He slept.

HE AWOKE IN THE NIGHT, crying out. She held him.

It's okay, she said. There's no reason to worry.

HIS BODY WAS CHANGING. Time beyond his grasp of it was passing. A new pain, unlike any pain he had known, bloomed in his stomach.

His belly began to swell.

What's happening? he asked, his voice hoarse from disuse.

It won't be long, she said.

HE AWOKE INFLAMED, his belly engorged. He pushed the sheets away. His belly red and swollen and gigantic. He felt movement within him, as of a shoal of small fish.

In his dream he had screamed at her: Let me out. In his dream such madness as this could not possibly be. In his dream the world still belonged to a rational order of things, things out of which ordinary sense might be made. Waking each time the madness of it shocked him afresh.

The world beyond the room was a dream. A hotel, a train journey, an uncle, a mother—such things had ceased to mean very much. Every day his memories faded. He could not remember his own name nor the name of his companion nor the name of the town. Did such a place truly exist? It could not. There was only the plain room, the floorboards, the window. The pane of glass rattling in its frame. When she opened the window, the sea air, sailing into the room. The damp rot of a building close to water. The little dock and the beach. A strange euphoria, borne of the pain.

THROUGH THE LONG hours she tended him. She lay next to him on the mattress unsleeping. She massaged his shoulders and whispered in his ear. She kissed his neck as he stared up at the window, his eyes filmed and red. His coat, neatly folded, lay on the floor. Beside it stood a bottle of wine, unopened.

ONE MORNING he awoke and he saw them, teeming inside him. His belly translucent now, flesh like dull glass: Through that dim translucency he saw eyes flitting through a flowing substance akin to smoke or black water. As he stared at the eyes they gazed back at him.

I think I'm ready, he said.

A MEMORY: The young man was on a train, coming from where he did not know, going where he did not know. His body in pain. He was trying to sleep. In the shallows of sleep he dreamt of winding streets of high buildings and of a pub nestled in darkness and in one booth of the pub a candle, glowing, stuck in an old bottle of wine.

WILL IT HURT? he asked.

Yes, it will hurt, she said.

Will you be with me? he asked, holding her hand as the pain began to flow.

Of course I'll be with you, she said, smiling without smiling. Of course.

BETTER ME IS FUN AT PARTIES

F.E. CHOE

Originally published in *New Year, New You: A Speculative Anthology of Reinvention.*

F.E. Choe is a Canadian and Korean-American writer whose work has been published in *adda, Augur, Clarkesworld, Fractured Lit,* and *The Moth Magazine.* She is a 2023 alum of the Clarion West and Viable Paradise workshops and an editor at *100 Word Story.* She has received residency support from Millay Arts and Hedgebrook and was named South Arts' 2024 South Carolina Fellow for Literary Arts. Her work has been shortlisted for the Commonwealth Short Story Prize and a finalist for the Theodore Sturgeon Memorial Award. Find her at www.fechoe.com or on Instagram @f.e.choe

---

BETTER ME GROWS LIKE A MUSHROOM. She fruits scalp first. Thick coils of knotted hair pin through the soil like fingers digging their way out, bending up toward the light and warmth of living things.

She is perfect. A dream. The landmarks of our bodies are mirror-twins: my birthmark reflected across the base of her spine, the same mole above my right eyebrow which sits above her left. Our faces are imitations, the one eye (my right, her left) slightly smaller than the other.

And this? I say and point to the raised line at her abdomen. Why keep this at all?

Inches below my own navel, an old appendectomy scar slants to the right while her stitching runs parallel to the left.

She makes a sawing motion against the muscle, the side of her hand a blade.

A convenient wound, she says. Where I cut myself away from the stem.

She shakes her hands through her hair and stretches. Her skin smells of soil, of factory dirt, and an artificial, floral sweetness like bonemeal folded into play dough.

I show her how to bathe, how to test the water with the back of her hand, how she should tip her head back and close her eyes when I rinse her hair.

When she dresses, she is careful to pick a shirt of matching color and style, to pull on a similar pair of black leggings. I watch her adjust and pose, how she folds herself into the same posture as my own. She favors her right leg and laces her fingers together, tilts her chin to focus on the space below my throat when I speak.

We watch the ball drop on the screen of my small television. We count down from ten. We hold our breaths and lean forward for the moment when the couples kiss and the streets fill with glittering furrows of confetti.

THE NEIGHBORS TAKE us for sisters.

How nice, they say, to be with family for the holidays. How strange, you never mentioned.

They pretend not to notice the moss-green stain of her nail beds. The scent of wet clay that lingers on her skin. It seeps into my clothing, the walls, and bedding despite our persistent scrubbing, despite the fastidiousness with which she airs and launders, scrubs and steams and presses.

Yes, how strange, she says. How strange how nice it all is.

When she speaks, she is perhaps a little more docile, a little softer than I expect myself to be.

———

IN LATE JANUARY we are carrying in the shopping, when a neighbor's cat skims past us in the hall and deposits a dead bird at the threshold of our apartment.

The cat pauses, steps slowly and blinks before rushing forward again. Better Me drops her bags, reaches out to try and touch—to catch, or just, if only to feel for a second what the animal's fur might be like—but the cat slips past, a streak of gray and rust-brown, to the other end of the corridor.

While I unlock the door and try to salvage the cans and frozen fruit, the soft loaf of sliced bread, the bananas that have tumbled out into the hall, Better Me cradles the dead bird in her hands and brings it inside. She sets it on the windowsill between the Pothos and the spider plant, inspects it closely, the tip of her nose almost brushing against its wing.

Hurry will you? Wash your hands and help me with this, I say. The center of the bread is ruined, punched down and compressed underfoot.

It's still warm, she says. Her upturned hand hovers over it, her knuckles steady above its breast.

The next morning Better Me pours coffee, fetches the milk and sugar, cracks an egg into a hollowed-out piece of toast. I notice, relieved, that the dead bird is gone, the windowsill wiped clean, the soft bite of disinfectant in the air.

Your lunch is in the fridge, she says. Don't forget it. You know how you always forget.

———

IT IS no wonder that others like her have popped up all over the city.

On Saturday mornings, the cafes and restaurants are overrun with identical couplings. They bounce fussy infants between them at parks. They stand together in line at concerts and museums. They spill across the banks to jog along the river at dusk. Their fluorescent vests catch the lamplight, flare under headlights like sheets of tin. Abandoned halves wait patiently for their mates in the lobbies of movie theaters, at gas station pumps, in the aisles of the supermarket. They exist and disappear together, crowding into the backseats of taxis, turning up side streets, slipping into buildings.

Each evening, I come home from work to a spotless apartment, clean clothes folded at the foot of the bed. Better Me thinks of everything: the shopping, the cleaning, the birthday, anniversary, and thank you cards I never manage to send in time on my own. The grout in the shower is always scrubbed clean, the mirror bare, the toilet bowl smelling faintly yet not unpleasantly of bleach.

At night, we crawl into bed together and pull the cover over our matched selves. She neatens the fold of the sheet under my elbow, tucks her head into the space between my chin and collarbone. I lie still and listen to the soft pull of her breath as she sinks deeper into the steady cadence of sleep, and already I feel so much less alone than I had once thought possible.

IN MARCH, our first party. Yet another baby shower for a college acquaintance, a roommate, a friend of a friend I haven't seen since their wedding. I scroll through old profiles and show Better Me photos of girls on pristine, verdant quads. I point to young women I have trouble naming, listing instead their degrees and occupations, the various locations of their bachelorette getaways, their hometowns. She helps me choose just the right gift from the registry, shows me the best way to wrap it, how to curl the ribbon for a bow.

We stand side by side and assemble tea sandwiches. She quarters them into perfect triangles, and I arrange them on a cut glass tray she has coaxed from a neighbor for the weekend.

Better Me watches as I bite into one to taste, and distracted, she nicks herself with the serrated blade. I notice only when I look down to move more sandwiches onto the tray.

Are they ruined? She draws her finger toward her mouth.

Let me see.

A thin, broken line bisects the pad of her left index finger. The wound weeps beads of sap, a clear and candy red.

I hold her hand under a stream of water, feel her fingers stretch open under mine.

Does it hurt much?

Hurt? She repeats the word as if amused by its taste.

At the shower, the women wear pale sundresses and sheer white linen blouses. They coo over each other's infants and tell us both how jealous they are, how great we look these days. They write down predictions of the baby's birth weight on identical slips of cream-colored paper and place them in a small wooden box in the hall. They ask us what we have been up to lately, where we live now, are we taking ourselves anywhere nice for the summer?

Their children adore Better Me. They grab balloons and bat them at her with their fists. They toddle over and cling to her legs, bury their sticky faces in the fabric of her skirt, are content to be lifted up, gently pinched, rocked. She cradles one, bounces another on her lap. She brings her nose to an infant's neck, buries her face in the fold of flesh between its chin and shoulder. She closes her eyes, tilts her head sweetly.

The sedate child in her lap. The other women bending their smooth, flawless necks toward her. To be so wholly captivating and unaware. How easy it all seems.

I wander through the kitchen on my own, the sitting room, the garden. It becomes clear I'm the only one who has brought a Better with her.

You're being so good, says the mother-to-be. She motions to Better Me who has apportioned herself only a small sliver of the cake, just enough not to seem disinterested or impolite.

Better Me pinches some of the crumb between her fingers, lifts it to her mouth, lets it rest on her tongue. She moves her jaw as if sifting through it with her teeth.

Someone taps their fork against their glass. Ready for gifts?

Better Me brings a napkin to her lips, spits.

IN THE MORNING, she wakes me with gentle scratches against my back, traces small circles into the side of my neck, my arm, my ankle. She sets the coffee on the burner while I brush my teeth. She lays out my clothing on the bed and dresses herself in coordinating colors. She helps me with my coat and tells me to have a good day, not to worry, that she will take care of everything.

Should I order in from the Thai place for dinner tonight? she says.

Yes, that sounds good.

Good. I'm pleased. Be careful on the subway. Would you like for me to walk you and wait for the train?

We link hands, press close to one another as we descend the stairs amid a crowd of unruly, unpredictable bodies. It makes her nervous—the thick yellow line of the platform's edge, to find herself so deep underground again, so exposed to the scrutiny of strangers, the howl of the train as it barrels through the tunnel. She brings her free hand to her mouth, presses her knuckles against her upper lip. Her grip tightens on my hand.

Are you sure you're alright? Can you make it back on your own?

Yes, I'm fine. Go, won't you? We're ordering in? Good.

Alright.

I'll be here when you get back. We should walk together to the restaurant to pick it up. It's still so dark outside by the time you get in.

AT THE END OF SPRING, my parents are not at all surprised when I bring her home.

Your Aunt Eunice has one too, my mother says as we peel potatoes over the sink.

My father is hunched over the bar with his hands in his pockets. How about something to drink, sweetheart? he says.

They've all gotten a bit lazier for it to be honest, my mother says. You know your aunt. She's always been a little odd. It was hard enough before to get her to go anywhere.

Better Me helps my father find his reading glasses. She spends an hour clicking through my mother's phone and helping her readjust the settings. She sets the table and serves us all first and claps her hands together in delight when we have finished.

She's made a cake. Your favorite, I say. Was up all night baking.

This is true. That morning when I woke, the kitchen smelled of powdered sugar and vanilla. Before packing the cake in its box, we ran our index fingers along the rim of the plate, brought them to our lips, tasted sweetness.

Before we leave, my father pinches her chin affectionately. He has said goodbye this way since I was a child.

See you next time sweetheart, he says. He caresses her cheek with the back of his fingers, as if she is too delicate to touch, to spoil with the inside of his hands.

My mother hugs us both awkwardly. Her gaze passes back and forth between us as we tie our shoes, back and forth as we check our pockets, back to Better Me as she picks up the extra crate of pears mother has bought for us.

I hope you weren't upset, Better Me says in the car. She rests her face in her hand then scratches at a place in the window.

Why would I be upset? I say, focused on the road, my hands steady on the wheel. I knew they would love you right away.

You're perfect. How could they not love you as I do?

ON THE FIRST day of summer, I bring Better Me to an after-work happy hour. She puts on the pale yellow dress that has hung unworn in my closet for months. I have been too afraid to wear it out in public before.

The other Betters are attentive dates. They run back and forth to the bar for rounds, helpfully filling in when we fail to remember specific details of a story or the punchlines of jokes.

So this is your secret, how you manage to get everything done—to juggle everything, we say to each other.

In return we offer inoffensive platitudes. We deflect, try to disarm one another, avoid giving too much of ourselves away.

I needed a wife.

I can be difficult, particular.

I just can't live with anyone else is the truth.

Better Me is charming, a good listener, a pleasure to talk to. She is clever and witty and approachable. She is quick to smooth over lulls in conversation, and we find ourselves grateful to her.

She puts her hand on my elbow and shows me how to insert myself gracefully into conversations. She plays nice and makes me look good. She is endearing, self-deprecating. Alongside her, I appear to be more competent and interesting than I actually am.

She tactfully ignores it each time my boss rests his hand in the small of her back.

None of us can keep our eyes off her. The yellow dress and its delicately tied bows that keep slipping off her shoulders, the mole above her left eyebrow, the way she holds our gazes steady until eventually we cede and look away.

Each time we are apart, when I lift my head to look for her, she is there watching and waiting to meet my gaze. Each time, she looks at me as if I am the only thing worth noticing.

FOR MY BIRTHDAY, we go to the beach and watch our skin go golden under the August sun. We tangle our limbs in the surf, wade further into the sea. We screech when our toes graze slippery, unseen surfaces that turn underfoot and skitter away like living things. In the afternoon, she shows me how to crack open small, hard crabs and keep the flesh intact. We eat with our fingers. We bring bottles of beer to our lips, the glass tasting more and more of salt, of butter, of brine and roe.

We change out of our wet swimsuits in the dressing room of a surf shop. She watches me in the mirror, and I am suddenly aware of how close the space is, how I contort myself around her nakedness. I shield my breasts with my hands, try to turn away from her gaze, press my arm stiffly against my stomach as I hunch over and struggle to tug free of the damp fabric.

Goosebumps ripple across the skin of her arms and the slope of her shoulders. Her nipples are small, dark knots against the soft swell of her breasts.

She slips an oversized shirt over her head.

Will you buy me this?

Yes, whatever you want.

She lifts the hem, reaches for my hand and brings it to her leg, uses my finger to trace the line that divides the dark bronze of her thigh from the pale strip of flesh at the join of her hip.

She laughs, and then I am laughing too. I feel a gentle unknotting at the top of my breastbone, and in that moment I want to give her anything else she might ask for.

We wander back along the shore in the dark. She slips her hand into the pocket of my shorts for the keys and tells me she will take us home. I doze off in the passenger seat on the ride back.

I wake in the parking lot of our apartment. The car unloaded, beads of condensation cluster against the glass. She stands bare legged in the stairwell of the building and grins at the moths whispering in the overhead glow even as they singe against the light.

She peers at me through the windshield, stretches her hand out and beckons.

Ready to come in?

IN AUTUMN her cheeks go rosy in the cold air. She blooms, grows plump in the season of dead and dormant things. The beds of her fingernails turn pale pink, the scent of her skin softened to talc. A thin, sheer down of hair claims her body in patches: her temples, her forearms, her lower back, the tender space where her thighs meet.

I wake one night, my throat dry, to find her side of the bed empty, the bedroom door a flat outline of muted light.

I come upon her in the kitchen, her back toward me. She is hunched over the counter, her dark hair a curtain. There is a rustle like dead leaves, the snapping of dry twigs, a lush, herbal iron note in the air.

What are you doing up so early?

She turns and smiles. Folds her hands one over the other before her. In this light her gums look wine-stained, her teeth brittle, her skin paper-thin over the angles of her skull.

On the counter behind her is a soft pile of gray fur.

I say, I'd like a glass of water, please.

Why don't you go back to bed? I'll bring one to you.

She turns back and stretches, balances on her toes to reach in the cabinet for a glass. Before turning the faucet on, she rests a hand on the heaped pelt before her and digs her fingers lovingly into it.

I think of her hands opening toward the cat as it rushed down the hall, softening beneath mine under warm water, raking my salt-soaked hair back from my face.

I need—

You should go back to bed.

I think of the pale, silk threads velveting the most intimate parts of her body, the warm seam of her mouth parted in sleep, the weight of her head resting against my shoulder.

Try to catch a few more hours of sleep before work, she says. Early start and all.

———

WE PLAY each other for Halloween. I run back and forth to the bar to collect our drinks as she dances under red lights. She watches me flirt with ghouls and werewolves, a parade of vampires with identical sets of fangs, the bartender whose head is adorned with tiny red devil horns.

A tall, faceless figure in a cheap skeleton bodysuit presses her against a wall. The faceless thing bends and turns its head so that its jaw is against her ear. I watch her hand slide against its abdomen. She shows me each of its painted ribs.

The bartender pinches his nose when he's nervous. Did you realize? He's done it four times already. I counted.

And me? What's my tell?

She licks the end of her finger and dabs at something under my eye.

We walk home with our arms linked. The October wind numbs our hands and faces. She leans into me on the escalator and buries her face in my neck as we descend into the subway tunnel.

On the platform, she taps her toe against the yellow line while we wait, laces her fingers into mine.

When we kiss, we thaw the frozen places where we meet: the tips of our noses, our lips, our cheeks, her chin against my forehead.

We undress in the dark. I feel the weight of her body sinking down next to mine, pressing me underneath her own. And then there is only the hot pull of her breath against my skin, the pressure of her hands. I push deeper into her, and nothing exists but my own need, an ache solid enough to wrap myself around as she pulls it taut and tugs it free.

———

On the first snow, she shows me how to sterilize a needle, a blade. How important the placement of an incision. What little meat and blood she needs each day to survive.

Just think, she says. Soon it will be the holidays. And then, a new year. I'll get you all to myself for a while. Won't that be nice?

How strange it is to be so desired.

She puts her mouth to mine, holds my hand steady as I open myself. It is a tiny wound, almost nothing. A new, unfinished seam no more than an inch. A small price to pay to be not so alone.

LOCAL EXTINCTION HOTLINE

JASON BALTAZAR

Originally published in *Bourbon Penn #34*.

Jason Baltazar is a proud Salvadoran American, originally from the Appalachian corner of Maryland. He is a high school dropout, a repentant former illustrator for a retail fashion company, and currently teaches in the English Department at James Madison University. He is grateful to have been nominated for the Pushcart Prize, Best Small Fictions, and Best of the Net in multiple genres. You can find his work online at www.jasonbaltazar.com.

"THE CAYENNE-TAILED SKINK. Last known entity died on Canal Parkway crushed under the tire of a white Jeep with windows tinted well beyond the legal limit. As is common among skinks, the cayenne could shed its tail as a defense against predation. The bright-red coloration and relative size of the dropped tail lent this skink its common name."

"Skink. Skink. Skiiiiiink."

"The Eastern Yellamustard Finch. Last known entity died of cardiac arrest in a birdhouse of amateurish but adequate construction affixed to the back fence of 603 Henderson Avenue. Among the loudest of songbird species, its call featured chattering sounds with metallic tones, often likened to the twisting of a socket wrench."

"What's with these names, are naturalists super hungry all the time?"

"Bob's Big Boar."

"Ha! Fucking what? No, no way that's real."

"It was very real."

"..."

"Bob's Big–"

"Wait, what. This is live? You're a person?"

"Yes, this is a live reading."

"Oh man, my bad. I didn't realize, I thought it was a pre-recorded deal. Sorry."

"We don't have equipment like that, just the one phone. It feels more appropriate this way. Do you want to continue or are you put off?"

"Hey, no, you can totally continue. Go ahead."

"Bob's Big Boar. Only known entity died of a .30-06 bullet fired from a tree stand on a wooded hill off Messick Road as an act of personal revenge. The boar was a re-domesticated feral pig taken in by Bob Fetterman and enjoyed a certain amount of local celebrity, owing to Bob's training of it in a number of entertaining feats, including a line dancing routine."

"Huh. 'Some pig,' right? Can I ask you a question, like, is that allowed?"

"Questions are welcome."

"So seriously what's with these names? They're all food-related."

"The entries are arranged by theme today. That's actually the last of the culinary set; the patterning set is next. If you're still interested."

"Yeah, totally, this is great. Well not great, but you know."

"The Pileated Tree Skunk. Last known entity died under the front porch of 410 Polk Street curled in the bed of a sun-faded "Bigfoot" model Power Wheel after ingesting antifreeze laced kibble left out by the tenant. The tree skunk was in fact a squirrel so-named for its dark coloration and distinctive white cap, notable for its sociability and playful demeanor."

"Oh man ..."

"Is something wrong?"

"It's just so sad. This tree skunk sounds pretty awesome and how they went out, it's ... I don't know. Does it get to you, reading these?"

"It's a deep loss. But keeping the idea of them in the world is more important to us than how it feels. Now you know about them too. You just encountered something that hasn't existed anywhere for years."

"Yeah, I guess you're right. That's cool."

"Are you willing to answer a question?"

"For sure."

"How did you find this number?"

"Someone sharpied it on a wall. Totally thought it was fake until you picked up."

"Very real. Which wall was this?"

"So, don't take this the wrong way but a bathroom. In the Health Department over on Willowbrook?"

"We're grateful to whomever it was."

"You didn't put it up?"

"No, we don't venture far from the phone."

"How do you keep things going?"

"Word of mouth. You're here on the line now, aren't you?"

"Fair point."

"Are you willing to answer another question?"

"I'm down to talk. 'Ask me anything,' right?"

"What were you doing at the Health Department?"

"Oh ... well, I've been going there. For counseling and stuff."

"If you're uncomfortable, there are plenty more in the patterning set."

"You're fine, I'm not too embarrassed or anything. Just try not to pull other people into my own bullshit, put a burden on folks, you know?"

"It wouldn't be burdensome at all."

"Oh, well, I've been fighting depression for a while and it kind of got on top of me. Had to finally admit I couldn't wrestle it down on my own anymore so now I'm in this group therapy thing. Weekly sessions."

"Has it helped?"

"A little, I guess? In terms of hearing other folks feel similar, that I'm not the only one Eeyoring around the place. But honestly, the underlying thing is still there like an engine block I'm dragging around in my gut all the time."

"Has it been a long struggle?"

"Not really, or at least it felt manageable until she ... someone ... passed away."

"Very sorry to hear of the loss. Do you want another entry?"

"Sure, toss me another."

"The Blue Freckle-Shell Elm Beetle. Last known entity died in a crow's beak, plucked from an elm branch in the woods behind the motel that continuously changes owners on Naves Crossroads. In addition to its eponymous blue dot pattern, the freckle-shell was known for building unique structures called twig embraces from chewed stem segments to protect egg deposits."

"Wonder if there's any of the twig embraces still out there?"

"The bonding proteins were resilient, so it's very possible."

"Maybe I'll drive over this week and see what I can find. Cedar, by the way. That was her name. Cedar Williams."

"Do you want to talk about Cedar Williams?"

"Um, I don't know man. Putting words to things isn't a strong suit for me, you know?"

"Maybe just focusing on her would help. How did you know Cedar?"

"Well, she's ... she was more on the quiet side, you know,

someone who'd mostly sip on things and watch, but she'd laugh with you every time. Played decent drums and some rhythm guitar. We grew up together for a while until I moved across town and then we reconnected later. Skated all over, went to punk shows at the Embassy, panhandled for cigarette money, other stuff. Mostly what I remember are the childhood things. Nostalgia, I guess."

"Memories are powerful. What comes to mind?"

"Neither of us could swim, but her dad would drive us out to Rocky Gap and we'd splash in the shallows. I remember it being one of those things you're self-conscious about around other kids, not knowing how to have this fun everybody else learned years ago. But with just the two of us, we'd laugh in the water and toe up to the edge where it got darker and we'd feel that dangerous thrill together, if we took one more step, you know. We'd look out at all the rest of that lake far too deep for us and it was okay because we were standing there together feeling the same fear. We both understood."

"That sounds like a sustaining memory."

"We didn't though. We didn't understand at all, eventually. They found her in bed, overdosed. She took that one step too far, too deep to come back up from and here I am still. How? Like big picture, how is that possible? It doesn't make sense to me. We started at the same time, the same night, same tiny bag, I remember the crinkle of it in her palm like a piece of Halloween candy. Just a 'fuck it, we're bored, let's see how this feels' thing, first time at Connelly's apartment, then in the parking lot of the ValleyView shopping plaza a couple nights later. For whatever reason it just didn't do the thing for me, didn't stick the same. Why is that? Why didn't I get sucked under too? She waded out alone and I left her there because I was too scared to stay in the water. Cedar wasn't the first of us to go, there were names written on jackets or tattooed on arms at the local shows by then already, and I most definitely was bored beyond belief, but I wanted to get out, not go out, you know? So I cut myself off, stayed away. We were basically strangers at the end. I abandoned her, left her down at the bottom we used to dare against on our toes in the sand. And here I am. Here I fucking am. Doing what?"

"Sounds like surviving."

"Right. I run real good. Great."

"Luck and speed shouldn't be dismissed when they serve you well. The bottom line is that we can only decide for ourselves. You made choices and so did Cedar Williams."

"I keep hearing that and it even makes sense on a logic level, but man, what it feels like is I got away with something, like I tricked the universe into taking someone else. There was no real difference between us, but she's dead and I keep on waking up. I don't deserve it. I could've reached out, at least tried ... I don't know, something."

"Do you believe when a hunter walks the wood, the creatures should patiently wait to be taken where they stand?"

"What? No?"

"Do you believe that after the hunter has gone the survivors should lay down and die anyway?"

"Oh, uh-huh. I see. I'm a creature in the wood."

"You are."

"I made it and deserve to keep on living, yeah, yeah."

"You should say that again and think about what each word means individually and what they mean joined together."

"Come on, I get it."

"That won't be evident until you speak with intention."

"Man, fine, fuck. I made it and ... I do deserve ... I ... deserve ... to be ... to be here ... I deserve ... every ... single ... day ... every ... single ... breath ... and I'm so sorry ... you're not here anymore ... and I miss all the music we soaked up from your brother's boom box and car radios and circle pits ... and I miss all the music we made in basements and garages and especially all the music you left unplayed ... and I missed you even before you were really gone, I hope you know ... and I'll keep the idea of you alive ... I promise you."

"Do you want to hear another entry?"

"Please."

"Cedar Williams. Only possible entity died in a place where dreams are born and was carried on from there in the hearts of those who knew her. She witnessed the world with a joy freely shared and for a while she courageously brought her warmth to places lesser traveled by light."

"…"

"Was that suitable?"

"Perfect. Thank you. For all this, talking to me and what you just said about Cedar."

"Her entry has been added to the meteor set."

"Wait, like permanently?"

"As long as the phone is ringing."

"Wow, that's … it means a lot. Really. Kind of weird but it was easier opening up to you than at the group sessions for some reason, like way easier. Listen, do you want to meet up or something?

"…"

"I don't mean meet up meet up, just to hang or whatever. Feel like I owe you a drink."

"That may not be a good idea."

"Oh. Right, it's weird. Sorry, I shouldn't have said anything."

"It's only that caution is called for."

"I get that. Probably all kinds call you up, huh?"

"All kinds."

"How do you vet people? Background checks? I'm cool as long as you don't need my social or credit cards."

"Nothing like that. Just two questions."

"Psh. Fire away."

"How open-minded are you?"

"Pretty open-minded, I think, especially for around here."

"Say, in theory, we shared an address. When you arrived, the front door would be unlocked. You would step over the threshold to the sound of brass bells strung on the back of the door and they would echo as though across a highland valley when the wind is low. And say when your body was fully immersed in the breath of our home you were greeted by winged creatures of every coloration, most avian but several likely to surprise, perched on a staircase to your right and along the rim of crystal-cut light fixtures, and no matter how high you gazed you couldn't find the top of that staircase. Say insects crawled the wallpaper, a parade of six-legged jewels following its arabesques in meditative movement, freckled beetles and cloudhoppers and century cicadas, silver damselflies darting before your eyes so like the Perseids that in the air of the foyer you begin to feel the traffic of the nearer cosmos. Say you walked, mindfully please, into the family room and a coruscating panther draped its flank across green velvet sofa cushions and you met its golden eye and knew, knew, that beneath the draperies of flesh and bone and behavior that you shared with it an essential connection in being, and you understood its fixed gaze was a gift passed to you, a portion of awe to swallow up fear in order to truly see the community into which you are interwoven. And through the doorway into the eatery the translucent blur of beings not visible to any eye but irrevocably felt as a swirling sea of others, and everywhere you choose to wander you find the presence of ultimate things, fur and feather and chitin and scale, fins furling like summer curtains in blue baby pools, snouts, beaks, diurnal, nocturnal, thriving together in the moment of this deepest of houses. Say as you're trekking a forested hallway the telephone rings and it sounds as though it fills the blue sky above you as a peal of thunder would. Say, at that moment, the voice of every being in our home, yes, even you, speaks as one to pass to the caller the wonders that once traversed their back yard. Are you as accepting as that?"

"…"

"You're still there?"

"… yeah."

"Did you hear the second question?"

"It sounds incredible, like, beautiful."

"Something you accept?"

"I wish I really could see something like that. Something *more*, you know?"

"Two hundred and twenty Somerville Avenue."

"Two-twenty ... that's only a couple blocks. You're serious?"

"Sincerest. And you?"

"Okay. Okay, I'm on my way over. Let me get shoes ... keys, where the ... aaand keys. Here we go, gonna put you on speaker."

"Another entry as you travel?"

"Definitely, keep 'em comin'."

"The Ever-Chanting Grove. Last congregant of the entity died uprooted from the eastern slopes of what is now Irons Mountain by a landslide in a time when Appalachian ridges touched Himalayan heights. The song produced when breezes passed through the grooves of the trees' bark serenaded miles of deciduous valley for millennia without cease until that final wavering voice quieted at the foot of the mountain."

"So, you're saying they were all one giant thing? The trees were all one tree?"

"The world speaks in tangles."

"I feel exactly like that sometimes, last one on the slope. Like I said before, Cedar wasn't the first to go in my circle. The closest, for sure. But this town's hungry and mean in a personal way, I swear. Everyone's so tired or bored or desperate. All three, why not? So, one way or another it's check out, get reckless, find your own escape velocity. I mean at this point I'm out of digits to count them with. I do that every day."

"Are the wounds soothed in counting?"

"Honestly, it's hard to tell the difference between what I feel for them and what I feel for myself. It's all ... tangled together like you said, the loss of someone versus I lost someone, if that makes any sense. I feel guilty when I catch myself doing that."

"Turn to them now. What will you pass on?"

"What, right now? I don't even know."

"You do. Place your heart on the tip of your tongue."

"I guess ... I guess I'd say: you're always with me. And sure, that's a blessing but not always, not really. I'm brittled.

I'm rusted through and I don't know how much longer I'll keep standing. It's changed me; one by one you leave and I'm the remainder. Leftovers. Un-dead."

"Face them, unfold."

"And what happened to you happened to me, too. I was with you in a way. Even if I wasn't there, in that moment, I died with you. I did, each time. I died with you, over and over again."

"Pulse for them."

"I died with you doing eighty, floating weightless beyond that guard rail burst open like a race was won, and I died with you, stomach gone to butterflies.

And you, I died with you standing in the garage leaned over your dad's deer rifle, caught taking what you wanted from the K-Mart but couldn't afford, waiting for his truck to pull in hauling familiar rage, and I died with you doing math to the scent of motor oil, solving for how much pain there'd be on either side of an equation.

And you, I died with you heartbroke and gutshot in wild-flower because that boy of your adoration finally turned his attention in the worst possible way, proclaimed yet another prince glinting far too golden by silver badges, and I died with you sprawled in birdsong starving to be believed.

I died with you afloat in amber sodium light, back cradled by glittering griptape, skateboard for a Viking boat sent down the eternal Potomac, Bic-charred pipe stem in your curled fingers.

I died with you one leg tangled in afternoon sheets, the other dangling off the side like you never heard of a monster under the bed, or maybe decided that threat no worse than what you've already seen.

I died with you loose-limbed and motormouthed yet unable to say, "No more," and then I died again in the very same way with you, and you, and you, and you.

I died with you too fucking often of bone-deep fatigue, fighting every moment against a sick gravity tugging down our kindness, sucking the blaze of wonder from our eyes and cutting off our thirst for the gush of the world.

My misfit found family, my many gone away, I dress in guilt and shame for lagging behind. I wear them like slow bruises. And however you roam, I hope all your bruises are forgotten. I hope you left them long behind to the sound of 'no more.'"

"A heart has spoken."

"… I … I don't really know what that was. I mean it's all true, it's real, but that's not how I sound. Where did that come from?"

"You're very near to us now. Welcome the sound of your voice as we do."

"Yeah, just pulled up I think."

"The phone is no longer necessary."

"Okay, yeah I'm right outside. See you in a sec."

"No barriers remain but your footsteps."

"Whoa, what the fuck? How can I hear you? Seriously."

"Sincerest."

"Holy shit. This is real, isn't it? Brass bells … holy … holy …."

"Enter. Greet us guiltless with the ongoing yesterdays of your heart."

"I died with you. And you, and you, oh god, and you, and you, and you, oh my god, and you, and you, and you …"

RUMINANTS

KAY CHRONISTER

Originally published in *The Dark #113*.

Kay Chronister is the author of *The Bog Wife* (2024), along with the collection *Thin Places* (2020) and the novel *Desert Creatures* (2022). Her short stories have appeared in *Clarkesworld, Beneath Ceaseless Skies, Strange Horizons, The Dark,* and elsewhere, and her work has been nominated for the Shirley Jackson and World Fantasy Awards. She lives in Pennsylvania.

I. Rumen

We come because there is a war in the old country. We come because there is a drought that becomes a famine or because we woke up one day and suddenly our money was worthless, or because we have always practiced the wrong religion but recently, since the last election, our neighbors look askance at us and sometimes on our walk home from work at night we are asked to show identification.

We know two things about the island. One, if we work

there through the season, we will get visas not only for ourselves but for our whole families. Two, the work that we do on the island will not be different or worse than the work we have done anywhere else, not in any way that matters. We know because our cousin thinks his friend's brother worked there and now his friend's brother is rich; we know because the recruiters that find us at border-crossings or refugee camps don't seem hungry for us to say yes when they give their pitch, like there will be someone else if we refuse them; we know because there has to be some escape from the noose cinching tighter and tighter around each of our necks, there has to be, things cannot really be as bleak as they look from where we stand.

WE DISEMBARK from small vessels in the middle of the night. For days we come, one boat after another, none bearing more than two or three men at a time. We do not know what country we are in. No customs officers appear, no search of our persons is conducted, no one asks to see our papers. The beach is rocky and dark and strewn with tentacles of kelp. Those of us who come on clear nights can see the grasses stir on the cliffs above, but most of us step down into a wall of mist.

If we could view the island from above, we would see the twelve bunkhouses arranged like the spokes of a wheel with the flat grey cylinder of the mess hall in the center. Surrounding the bunkhouses, the pens that hold the ruminants. But on the ground, we see none of it until we climb down from the slit-windowed livestock trailer that carries us from the shore to the worksite. We stumble out and the foreman presses a thermometer to our foreheads, examines our tonsils with a flashlight, then sends us to one of the bunkhouses. Everything is newly constructed with the hasty efficiency of a refugee camp. For some of us, there is an unhomely familiarity to those doors that we cannot open with too much force, those steel bedframes stacked to the height of the low ceiling, even those corrugated tin chutes made to streamline the processing of many bodies.

Our first night, we see the ruminants only as silhouettes laying or standing in the pens with their backs to us. We do not look closely. Later, we wonder if we were scheduled to arrive at night so we would not see the ruminants while there were still boats at the dock that might be hijacked and made to carry us away.

THE RUMINANTS ARE NOT cows but they are something like cows. They have nine hundred or so pounds of bulk, four legs, cloven feet. They spend most of their waking hours masticating the dune grasses that grow in patches on the cliffs. Every hour they lift their tails and drop mounds of earth-colored shit behind them. They do not wander far alone, yet they seem unsociable, almost insensate, interested neither in us nor in each other. We can tell them apart only by the ear tags that identify them with two-digit numbers.

"That's why they feel wrong," someone says. "They're dead."

But livestock are supposed to be walking dead. Their bodies only pumped full of life long enough for them to make meat, to make milk, to make more cows. The something wrong with the ruminants is something else.

"They have no udders," someone else notices.

It is true: the ruminants are all female, but they have no udders. The something wrong with them is deeper than having no udders and yet not, we feel, entirely unrelated to no udders.

In the first weeks of the season, we have little to do with them. We turn them out, we muck the pens, we turn them back in. We feed and water them. This is our routine until the foreman comes to the front of the mess hall at breakfast one day and says that the ruminants have contracted a fungal infection. We must treat them twice a day, every day, for two weeks.

"Every man to one ruminant," he says. "To avoid cross-contamination." He repeats the orders in all our languages, reading haltingly from a wrinkled print-out. He does not explain in any language what he means by *cross-contamination*. The animals are not being quarantined from each other. He comes around and hands each of us a number. Sixty-seven. Forty-eight.

In the pens, we find our ruminants and get halters around their faces so we can hold their heads still enough to shoot a syringe of foul-smelling paste into their mouths. Close to them for the first time, we are startled not by their wrongness but their particularity: the freckles on their black nostrils, the dark or pale curl of their eyelashes, the whorls and scabs and bald patches on the roan coats that from a distance appear to be a flat uniform red. We are more startled by how frantically they resist us, these dumb torpid animals that we thought didn't even know we were there. They swing their heads and dance on their heavy cloven feet so close to our delicate human ones that we could swear they are trying to intimidate us. Almost an hour passes before all the syringes are emptied into the ruminants' mouths, though even then some of the paste ends up dribbling down lips or spat back in the faces of we who administer it.

"They are not even sick," the one who has #82 complains later, as we wash in the communal showers.

"There is pus in their ears," the one who has #14 answers. "Didn't you see?"

"Not in the ears of mine."

"You would have noticed. If you'd looked closely."

#82 says nothing. Then, "I didn't like the way she looked at me."

"Like what?"

"Just didn't like it."

Twice a day, every day, for two weeks we treat them. The work gets easier. We learn to halter efficiently. Some of us can even get the ruminants to put their heads down willingly into the nosebands. We figure out how to administer the paste with a precise and unhesitating shot between the lips and learn to hold the mouth closed for five, ten, fifteen seconds afterwards so hardly any gets spilled.

The day we administer the last dose, the foreman comes out with latex gloves and asks us to send the ruminants down the chute. He stands at the end and examines the ruminants' ears, their eyes, their lips. He sends most of them on without incident, but on one he lingers.

"#82," he says.

We exchange glances. Everyone knows #82 has been lax, almost negligent, in the care of his ruminant. He doesn't hold its mouth closed after he administers the medicine because he doesn't like touching it. He has even been getting someone else to put on the halter.

We have all worked for enough petty tyrants that we expect the foreman to punish #82 with humiliation, extra work, reduced privileges, but he only says, "Keep this one apart from the herd. Not well yet. We don't want any reinfections. Take it to the medical barn. You can feed it on grain."

"Not me," #82 says.

The foreman is taken aback. "Yes," he says. "You."

#82's lips twist, not in contempt but in anguish, as if he is holding back tears. "Make someone else do it," he says.

"She is yours," the foreman says. He is unsure of himself in #82's language. "One man to each ruminant." He echoes this directive from the print-out he read.

"No," says #82. He repeats it in another language in case the foreman doesn't understand.

The foreman looks towards the cliffs, seeming to deliberate. We can see that he does not want to assert himself in front of everyone. "Take her," he says, finally. "Then we will talk."

We are not there for the conversation that happens later, in the privacy of the foreman's office. But #19 is asked to come and translate, so everyone knows before the end of the day: #82 insisted he could not be alone with the ruminant. The foreman said it was his charge and no one else could be responsible for it. #82 asked why, and the foreman gave him no real answer. Then #82 asked to quit. The foreman reminded him of the penalty: there would be no compensation, no visa, if he did not last the whole season. #82 said he didn't care. He only wanted to go home. This next part we dispute, we doubt, but #19 does not waver: the foreman said, "You can't. You have to stay through the season."

#82 does not confirm whether this is true. We do not see him. We hear that he is sleeping in the medical barn with his ruminant; possibly that he is even confined there. The kitchen staff are seen packaging meals in Styrofoam boxes and taking them out somewhere.

A few days later, #34 is sitting out on the cliffs smoking a cigarette when he sees far below a small figure crossing the beach. Recognizable, by his dark hair and teal jumpsuit, only as one of us. #34 stubs out his cigarette and gets to his feet, but he cannot think of what to do other than call out, though he doesn't know what name to shout. The wind takes his voice away. He watches as the figure crosses the beach and walks into the sea. Waist-deep, neck-deep, deep enough to disappear.

Ruminant #82 is found in the medical barn, hungry and caked in manure and deep in the throes of an untreated fungal infection. Almost dead, then dead. No one wants to touch her.

II. Reticulum

We are shaken by what happened to #82, but most of us already knew that we were not really free to leave the island or the job, not when leaving would only mean an empty-handed return to some place we cannot go back to. No matter how we went, if we did not last the season first, we would be drowning ourselves. At night, in our bunkhouses, we retell the story of what happened to #82 until we can tolerate that it happened; until we are no longer threatened personally by it.

"He should've done the work to begin with."

"He had something wrong with him from the first day he came."

"He never had worked hard before. Wasn't used to it. You could see, he had soft hands."

"There's nothing to it, what he said about the ruminants. He saw something that wasn't there. They're only animals."

Only a few of us refuse to be comforted, panicked by the idea that we are being held against our will. Those few stare out at the ocean, straining their eyes for land they cannot see. They dream, at night, of swimming towards a distant shore and making no progress, the horizon retreating as they exhaust their strength. "No matter whether we *should* leave or not," they mutter as they rake manure, "they shouldn't be able to stop us. It's slavery."

There are rumors that these few were draft-dodgers in their shared home country. The island was their sanctuary from obligation, and now that obligation has found them here, they want another escape. That's all; that's it.

By unspoken agreement, the rest of us quarantine ourselves from their fears and suspicions. We sit beside them in the mess hall and work beside them in the pens and sleep beside them in the bunkhouses, but when the four of them disappear on the same night as the supply boat comes, we can honestly say that we knew nothing of their intentions, although it is easy enough for us to surmise what happened. The supply boat comes twice monthly, always late at night and always on the same day of the week. We don't know where it comes from or how far it travels to reach us, but it looks capable of sailing a long distance. In the week after the four dissenters disappear, we eat freezer-burnt ground beef with canned tomatoes, then bean stews thickened by corn-starch, then creamed corn and powdered mashed potatoes. The foreman rations our cigarettes, then says we must do without.

The foreman tries to seem unperturbed, but we can see that he is afraid of what we might do. There are so many of us and only one of him. We are hungry and we need to smoke and, fleetingly, when we are drifting between sleep and wakefulness, we all yearn to hijack a supply boat and cross the unknowable depths of the sea with two-hundred pounds of chuck to bolster us. Where would we go? Anywhere. Certainly not back to where we came from. We would be orphans and widowers and we would most of all be childless. We would eat down our reserves and then we would throw ourselves into the ocean and feed ourselves to the many-tendrilled things that live in the deep.

But in our waking hours, we acknowledge none of this—not to each other and not even to ourselves. The closest we come is that #17, on our second day of eating powdered eggs and only powdered eggs for breakfast, asks aloud why we don't butcher one of the ruminants.

The foreman is out of earshot, but the question goes unanswered, the answers too obvious and too shattering. Because they are not ours. Because they are reserved for some purpose still unknown to us. Because there is some wrongness in them that might somehow be transmitted to us if we were to consume them. We have observed, by now, more things besides no udders that we cannot explain. The ruminants stare at the full moon with blank and utter concentration for hours; saltwater comes out of the spigots we use to fill their troughs and they drink it; they have no interest in each other and yet they are beginning slowly to warm towards us.

And, also, this:

Three days after the supply boat is hijacked and the dissenters leave us, four of the ruminants get sick. High fevers, galloping heartrates, trembling weakness.

A look of terror crosses the foreman's face when we inform him of the outbreak. Then he retreats, becomes impassive. "All right," he says. "Separate them from the rest. The medical barn. Treat their symptoms."

"Do you know what they have?" asks #57, an obstetrician before he came here.

The foreman doesn't answer him. "Treat the symptoms," he repeats.

#57 cobbles together a treatment with #30, whose family kept cattle when he was a child. We dose the sick ruminants with calcium and banamine, feed them mashed grain sweetened with honey, drape towels soaked in cold seawater across their backs. They don't resist us, but they don't want to eat. They stare glassy-eyed into our faces. Occasionally they make weak, plaintive sounds that are not like the sounds of any cows we have ever heard.

"Like a woman crying," says #30.

Their fevers climb. Their eyes crust closed. When they die, #57 kneels at their sides and gently palpates each of their swollen bellies. The unborn calves inside them are dead too.

We all notice the correspondence between the number of vanished men and the number of dead ruminants. Another thing we cannot explain.

III. **Omasum**

On the island, the seasons change; the ruminants' coats darken from summer red to a dull mouse-like color. The grasses on the cliffs go yellow and then go tawny and then collapse from the weight of frost. Night spills into morning and intrudes on afternoon. The sun has always shone faintly through the mist, but now it seems not to come at all. Everything happens in a bruise-colored light like the beginning of dawn or the end of dusk.

Beneath the sullen close horizon, all is mud and only mud. In the pens, it freezes and congeals, then thaws out and puddles before refreezing in thin, treacherous layers. The ruminants shuffle listlessly through it, moving with the labored motions of bad swimmers. We hack at their frozen shit with our plastic rakes until the rakes splinter, step delicately in our rubber waders with our gloved hands tracing the steel fence for balance.

In the cold, the ruminants need more from us. We fill woven nets with hay to make up for the absence of forage, smash the ice in their troughs of saltwater, massage their pasterns to loosen the clods of icy mud that cling and threaten infection. Without discussing it, we all conclude that everyone should care for the same ruminant he tended in the early days of the season. We know, by now, if our particular ruminant is liable to open a hay net with her dexterous lips unless the net is stitched up tight, or prone to trample her hay underfoot if it is loose, or so fussy an eater that a net will only discourage her from getting enough.

We know, too, that if we tend our own ruminant, we can stay close to her for long enough to get warm. The foreman says he has sent for winter coats, but coats do not come. We wear every layer we have, even to sleep, but we are only ever warm when we are close to the ruminants. Heat radiates from their skin, escapes in flumes from their nostrils.

"Because of their stomachs," says #30. "Because they are always digesting. Like engines, my father used to tell me." As long as the ruminants do not get hungry, they do not get cold.

We are not made so sturdily. But we borrow from them in small forgivable portions, laying our bare hands on their bellies or leaning our shoulders against the broad ridge of their withers or—when we think no one can see—pressing our faces into their necks. The ruminants do not seem to begrudge us this closeness. They seem at times even to desire it—leaning closer, resting the delicate bulk of their heads against our ribcages.

We believe they are invulnerable until the frigid morning #48 finds his ruminant frozen to death. Her ears stiff, her eyes open and clouded. When #48 sees her, he goes quiet for a long moment. Then he turns, jabbing an accusatory finger at #17. "Yours was always pushing her away. She couldn't get her fair share. This is your fault!"

We all know #17's ruminant is especially food-sour and conniving, but we also know that the stout ruminant with the ear tag reading #17 is far from the only one to have pilfered from shy, contemplative #48, who has always deliberated over her hay as though something better might be coming.

#17 knows too little of #48's language to answer his accusation, but #48 curses him anyway until the foreman comes out. The foreman looks at the body on the ground for a while, then orders us to bury the ruminant.

"The ground is frozen," someone objects.

The foreman hesitates. He looks through the mist towards the sea as if hoping an answer will come from across the waves.

"Burn it, then," he says finally.

We collect sticks and driftwood for a bonfire. As we ring around it, the foreman stands at the door to his office with his arms crossed, observing. #48 is not there; #48 cannot bear to see his ruminant burn. From their pen, the ruminants eye the flames uneasily, and we wonder whether it is only animal instinct that makes them fear the flames or if they understand that one of them is burning.

The ruminant takes all night to become ashes. In the morning, #48 is feverish and weak. He rises from his bunk in a cold sweat and then collapses. His bunkmates refuse to share air with him, afraid of what he might spread. #57, the obstetrician, sets his thumb in the hollow of #48's wrist and nods with a physician's pleasureless satisfaction, then gets #48 into a cool shower, doses him with acetaminophen tablets.

By nightfall, #48 is worse, his delirium shattered only by terrible moments of lucidity in which he cries not for his husband or his homeland or his mother but the ruminant that predeceased him. #57 goes into the foreman's office and comes out a few minutes later with his jaw clenched. "The foreman has said that no one can be evacuated," he tells us.

#48 dies before morning.

WE BEGIN to monitor our ruminants, counting the flakes of hay they consume, cupping our ears to their bellies to listen for the churning rumble of digestion. At night, we are woken every few minutes by the sounds of our bunkmates getting out of bed and slipping into their waders, going out to lay eyes on the ruminants so they can know for certain that theirs is alive. Few of us, lying in the dark, can fall back asleep without going to see for ourselves. No comfort can be gotten from the ruminants that lasts longer than we have eyes on them. We do not raise the possibility of watches or shifts because no one trusts that someone else will notice if something is wrong with an animal that is not their own.

We exhaust our supply of instant coffee, once sufficient for a month, in a week. The day the kitchen staff have to say *no more*, the foreman stands beside them with a taser hanging from his belt, handing out single cigarettes as consolation. If there are murmurs of disapproval, they are subdued until #17 throws his cigarette on the floor and stomps on it. "You think we're going to take it," he says loudly. "You think that we won't –!" He doesn't finish his sentence. He looks back through the line into our faces, his eyes wild, and then gets out of line and shuffles back to his table, his plastic tray.

Someone else retrieves his cigarette and pockets it. The sound of rhythmic chewing recommences. No one wants to be away from their ruminants for any longer than they have to.

In his bunkhouse at night, #17 is oratorial, though only two of his seven bunkmates speak his language. "I was born with a heart condition," he says. "They told my mother I would not live past the age of three. And then I did. The age of seven, then, they said. And when I lived past seven, they said, we don't know exactly when, but someday his heart will collapse. He is living with a gun to his head. My mother kept it there for them. *Don't run down the stairs, habibi, your heart; don't play soccer; don't make yourself too anxious; don't lift that, it's heavy, your heart will collapse.* But, you know what, I am forty-one years old and I have fought in a war and I have buried my mother and my heart is still beating. I am not going to live like this and neither should any of you."

"You butcher your ruminant, then," #19 mutters. "See what happens."

#17 does not butcher his ruminant. But, a day later, there is a disturbance in the middle of the night. The glow of a lantern in the foreman's office; crashes and bangs like a fight. #17 and a few others, it is whispered, have taken the foreman captive using the foreman's own taser.

In the half-lit hour before dawn, #17 and the others drag the foreman out to the center of camp where we all can see him with his wrists tied behind his back and a taser prodding his temple. We gather between the mess hall and the bunkhouses, fear and anticipation and—almost—hunger spreading like a charge between us.

"Tell us why we were brought here," says #17 to the foreman.

The foreman's eyes dart in one direction and then the other. He has a halo of dark hair around a glowing white moon of a scalp. He is a small man, smaller than most of us, we notice. "To work the ruminants," he answers unsteadily.

"Why can't we leave?"

The foreman opens his mouth, then closes it. #17 pushes the taser against his temple. "I was told you couldn't," the foreman says. "Not until the season is over."

"Why not?"

The foreman licks his lips. He is animal and visceral like this, his face slick with perspiration even in the cold, his nostrils flaring. His eyes are wet but he is not crying yet. "The ruminants need you," he says. "We can't afford to lose any— more."

"Will we die if they do?" someone calls from the crowd.

The foreman cranes his neck to see if #17 wants him to answer. #17 nudges him demonstratively with the taser.

"Yes," the foreman says, so softly that we barely hear.

A murmur passes through us. We knew already, but we did not think he would say it.

"Why?" says #17.

The foreman shakes his head.

#17's face hardens. "Why is it like this?" he shouts.

The foreman is crying. "I don't know," he says. "They didn't tell me. They only *hired* me. I thought it was going to be cattle."

There is no reason to ask who *they* are. There is always a *they* that we will never see and that will never see us. Furious, impotent, #17 presses the trigger on the taser. The foreman thrashes, his head jerking forward, then goes limp and slumps down face first.

#57, the obstetrician, comes out of the crowd and heaves the foreman upright. He pulls on the man's eyelids, feels his pulse, then cuts the cords around his wrists. #17 stands apart and lets it happen, holding the foreman's taser at a distance. Daylight presses on the cloud cover. The crowd disperses. No one wants to be away too long from their ruminant.

IV. **Abomasum**

Gathered within four walls, the ruminants are warm as an oven; in the last weeks of winter, we lay at their feet and gently bake. They are conscientious in their night movements. Through the whole back half of the season, only a few feet are crushed, one ribcage.

Bedding down with them, we come to know the ruminants' bodies as intimately as our own. More intimately, even, for we are all more or less used to ignoring our bodies' signals of pain, fatigue, fear but we know whether the ruminants are sleeping deeply, which hind foot they prop to rest when dozing, how low they hang their heads when deeply asleep. We learn the rhythms of their digestion, the particular odor of their urine. We know where they want to be touched and what makes them flinch away. And so we know, we sense, when something changes within them. It does not happen to the whole herd suddenly but in a slow cascade. We recognize it only when it reaches our own ruminant.

In the mess hall, we trade notes:

"She's warmer than she should be in the belly."

"She's never sleeping deep."

"She's not chewing her cud so long as she used to."

Only #57, the obstetrician, recognizes the disease beneath the symptoms—"They're going into labor soon."

It is a clear day, the bitterness almost wrung out of the cold, when #33 goes. All afternoon she stalks the fence line, striding purposefully and fast. At nightfall, she refuses to be herded inside the barn with the rest of the ruminants. Her head swings, her eyes rolling, and she utters cries like the cries of a woman. #33 walks beside her, his hand slung hesitantly around her neck and then withdrawn; back around her neck and then withdrawn.

"She'll trample him," says #30, but no one gets in the way.

The moon rises and #33's pacing becomes effortful, slow. Her cries deepen to moans. We lay inside the barn listening to them, feeling the danger to ourselves in #33's danger. #30 remembers a heifer on his family's farm dying in labor with a breech calf, her body hemorrhaging such tides of blood that he thought the whole yard would be flooded.

"Shut up," says #17, and he does.

The moans soften. Faintly, we hear #33 murmuring reassurance. Then, for a long while, there is nothing. #57, the obstetrician, rises and goes out. We hear him say:

"Is it all right?"

"There we go, there's a head, that's the right way out."

"And—oh."

Then nothing, for a while.

In the depths of night, rousing us from the anxious half-dreaming state that is as close as any of us can get to sleeping, #57 opens the barn door. The whites of his eyes caught, for a second, by the moonglow from outside.

"Did they live?" someone says.

"They are all alive," says #57, but his tone is hesitating, something held back.

In the morning, we find #33 with the newborn ruminant's head in his lap, the mother ruminant solemnly licking them both. The calf is translucent-skinned, veins woven like purplish thread all through its trunk and limbs. It has black eyes, arrestingly large. Almost, it is beautiful. But it looks too raw for life, unfinished somehow.

"It can't nurse," says #33, his voice hoarse.

The ruminants, we all knew, have no udders.

The foreman comes to the door of his office only after four rounds of furious knocking. We have not seen him in weeks, not since the day of the taser. He speaks through an inch-wide crack in the door. He has no answer to the question of how to feed the newborn ruminant. Reluctantly, he agrees to radio the mainland for advice, but he comes back with nothing. "They won't answer me," he says. "They don't take my calls anymore."

#57 tries powdered cow's milk, salt water soaked in hay;

he even gets the kitchen staff to make a pot of bone broth. The calf listlessly half-suckles at each of these formulas but soon loses interest, withdrawing to lay its head in the cradle of #33's lap.

"He's getting weaker," #33 says.

"There's nothing else," says #57. "I don't know what to do. What kind of animal can't feed its own young?"

"I'll die," #33 pleads, speaking not to #57 now but to his ruminant. She looks emptily back at him, lowers her mouth to his arm and sweeps a wide wet path across the back of his wrist with her tongue.

"We don't know if it's the calves or only the ruminants," says #57.

"I can feel it," says #33. "If he died, I would die too."

There is no answer to his certainty. We count him as lost, though we have not yet accepted that we are lost too even though every one of our ruminants bulges with an unborn calf, the promise of its death and ours visible in their pendulous bellies. We take our ruminants out to graze on the cliffsides and stay with them all day, afraid to witness the moment of the calf's death, wanting to hold ourselves apart as long as we possibly can.

The first of us to come back are the ones to see: #33 sitting at the mother ruminant's feet with his body bent over the newborn calf, a look of great concentration—and almost, devotion—on his face as the calf suckles from a vein in his wrist.

NURSED ON OUR BLOOD, the calves darken to the color of liver. They become long-eyelashed and beautiful, staggering after their mothers on legs like spindles and returning to us every hour with their pleading mouths open. We do not refuse them; how could we? We know now what #33 knew as soon as he laid eyes on the newborn: it is the calves and not the mother ruminants whose lives are bound to ours. It always was. We eat marrow stews and organ meat in prodigious quantities, swallow the iron tablets that come in paper cups at breakfast and dinner, hurry back from the mess hall with a sense of fullness brimming in our veins.

We know, but do not acknowledge to each other and barely to ourselves, that they are getting hungrier as they grow. They are no longer sated by the amount of blood that we can spare without going light-headed. After #33 falls backwards and splits open his skull on the steel fence, we lie down for feedings. We sleep whenever we are not feeding or eating.

We look sometimes into the faces of our calves, yearning to see some glimmer of awareness of our weakness, our vulnerability to their need, but their gaze betrays nothing; in their eyes we see only fear or interest, and *interest* we see only when they want to eat.

We have nursed the eldest of them for almost a month, brought them out of the winter darkness and into the lengthening days of sweet young growth and dragonflies and burnt-off mist, when the ships dock. They come all at once, every one of them alike, visible from the cliffs above. We do not understand right away, even when we see stock trucks rolling up the hillside, what they are here for. When we last saw those trucks, they carried us.

The ruminants do not cry when their calves are loaded into the trucks, but the calves scream, open-mouthed and desperate, until the wind carries away their voices.

We think we hear them for days afterwards, their cries echoing through our last restless and wasted hours on the island. In our blood-drained waking dreams, they have not been carried across the sea to be butchered; they are still here, they get older and stronger and rosy-coated, and some of them come strangely to resemble us.

YOUR THOUGHTS ARE GLASS

SHAONI C. WHITE

Originally published in *The Crawling Moon: Queer Tales of Inescapable Dread.*

Shaoni C. White's fiction has appeared in *Lightspeed, Uncanny, Nightmare,* and other magazines. Their poetry has appeared in *F&SF, Augur, The Deadlands,* and other venues, and their radio play *o! worm!* was produced by Strong Branch Productions. A lifelong Californian, they are working towards a PhD in Literature at UC Davis, where they study speculative fiction through a queer and trans lens.

YOUR EYES ARE GLASS, *and your ears are glass, and your thoughts are glass.* It was essential to remember that. It was a matter of discipline. Discipline was the only way to resist the sins down in the vault. Delilah's predecessor had lacked discipline—had let heresy worm its way into his skull—and they'd had to execute him.

The video of his last moments, or rather his last…hour or

so, was broadcast all across the city. God Who Walks In Glass required that such things be seen, and so Delilah saw it in fragments on the screens in the subway and on the sides of skyscrapers during her commute. Her predecessor died as all heretics died: his stomach carved out, slowly. Most people screamed when this was done to them, quite understandably, but her predecessor had just muttered about carnations. Quietly. Feverishly. All the way until the end.

The catalogues of sin were kept in the basement level of the city's bureaucratic headquarters. When Delilah sat at her desk near the middle of the vast maze of filing cabinets, the distant walls vanished into shadow; she could easily be tricked into thinking that the rows of cabinets stretched on forever. It didn't help that she was always alone. The contents of the cabinets were far too dangerous for random citizens to be allowed to rifle through them. Every file was a detailed record of an artifact from the reign of the Queen of Carnations. The artifacts themselves had all been reduced to ashes centuries ago, of course, but God Who Walks In Glass demanded that records be kept of all things its followers destroyed, so every few years the city sent a single clerk down into the dark to make sure everything was preserved.

Delilah's predecessor had left the place in a less organized state than it had started in. Today she was busy locating the missing pages of a record titled *Documentation of a tapestry depicting the Feast of Nine Skies, found hanging in the grand hall of the Queen of Carnations' palace.*

It took nearly two hours of searching, but she found the last few pages misfiled in an entirely different folder. The missing pages described the embroidered scene, and for all that the words were dull and clinical, the stain of the original object's sin still clung to them. Delilah could only spend a few seconds skimming the text before the image of the long-destroyed artwork began to pulse against her skull, brighter than vision, fiercer than memory: the cornucopias filled to bursting, the cups overflowing with dark wine, the hundred vassal lords in their bright garments, and above them the arches of the hall picked out in golden thread.

With effort, she resisted the magical pull. She busied herself with flipping through the pages, double-checking they were in the right order. Even then, the sin was strong. Her eyes grazed a description of an embroidered bowl of peaches, and before she could forcibly redirect her thoughts, she could imagine it—what it would be like to set her teeth against a peach's skin, what it would be like to taste its sweetness breaking open on her tongue.

Her fingers stiffened. The record fell from her hands. She'd never eaten a peach before. She'd never even seen an illustration of one in person. They were a favorite of the Queen of Carnations, and so the followers of God Who Walks In Glass had long since erased the species from the earth. It shouldn't be possible for her to know that a peach would be *sweet*.

The thought had opened up a gnawing hunger inside her. *I ate breakfast and lunch,* she told herself. *Those were perfectly sufficient. What my stomach feels is irrelevant. What my mouth wants is a lie.* Once she had convinced herself of those things, she snapped her eyes open and returned to her work.

Delilah proceeded through another handful of records without incident. A bare lightbulb hung overhead, bathing her work in cold white light. There were many like it scattered throughout the vault, but not enough to dispel the gloom. Delilah had petitioned her supervisor for better lighting and been denied. She allowed herself to feel a small amount of resentment about that, for much the same reason that an engineer might allow a small amount of water to pass through a dam. Because it was only a small thing. Because it was safe. Because it lessened the deadly pressure of the other resentments she could not allow to pass through her.

As the familiar rhythm of the work took over, her mind slid into the gray haze she preferred to stay submerged within whenever possible. It was the only way to keep her thoughts from turning rotten. *Your eyes are glass, and your ears are glass, and your thoughts are glass,* said the scripture, *and God moves through each of these. You have the knowing of your own sin, and for it you will be judged, for all you know is known to God.*

Delilah certainly had the knowing of her own sin. The fear of it lived in her. That was why she had learned not to think.

By now she'd organized the top five drawers of cabinet 5L. The lowest drawer stuck when she tried to open it. After a minute of fruitless pulling, it jerked open one grudging inch, accompanied by a shriek of metal. Curiously, as the drawer moved, Delilah heard something *clunk*. A heavy object, shifting. When she managed to pull it open properly, she raised an eyebrow; there were no papers inside. Instead, the drawer held a slide projector.

Once she got it onto her table and brushed off the dust, she saw that it was a bulky contraption of metal and glass; she suspected it was older than the mass production of plastic. At the back of the drawer was a stack of four projector slides, just as antique as the projector—they were made of glass, not plastic and film, and they were large, each about the size of her palm. She held them up to the light, but it was too dark to make out anything of the images trapped in the glass. She could only see their shadowed contours.

Beneath the slides was a crumpled-up piece of paper. It was a record, just like all the others in the vault, but the printed text was obscured by furious scribbles of dark ink. The hand that had wielded the black pen had done so wildly, feverishly. The lines were looping and nonsensical. In some places the dense thicket of ink suggested the twining and unfurling of stems and leaves. In other places the scribbles turned into words, barely legible: *openmouthed* and *flowering* and *take root*. In the center of the page, where the letters traced again and again in the same place until the paper ripped and the ink bled outward, was written

IN / CARNATION.

Delilah recognized that handwriting. She'd seen it, in less fevered form, in the margins of the more recently organized records. Her predecessor had written this.

She tried to decipher the printed text of the original record. She could only identify a few fragments below the scribbles defacing it.

Photographic documentation of

all previous attempts have failed. Historical attempts at destruction via fire date back to the original conquest, but

chamber was

contemporary engineering can

far higher temperatures than was feasible in centuries past. While this method was certainly more successful than previous methods, the ultimate efficacy is debatable.

The wound remains.

If Delilah had been someone else, she would likely have been at least a little bit curious as to what this all referred to. But she was not someone else. She had worked very hard to avoid being curious about heresy. She merely set the paper aside and considered the problem of what to do about the projector. How should it be filed? She couldn't exactly stuff it into a manila folder. Theoretically she could ask her supervisor, but her duty was to deal with these distasteful things so that no one else had to. No one would thank her for bringing the Queen of Carnations into a conversation just to ask technical questions about filing.

Well, the first step was to type up a new record, and for that she needed to know what those slides depicted. Delilah drummed her fingers on the table. The vault had no projector screen, but it wasn't as if she could take the slides outside.

After some deliberation, she dragged several of the lighter filing cabinets together so that they formed a makeshift wall an appropriate distance from her work table. The bulb and battery of the projector were still functional, and when she turned it on, white light painted a wide rectangle across her makeshift screen. The beam caught the dust that swirled in the dark air between screen and projector, turning the motes into bright, drifting specters.

She took the first slide in the stack and inserted it. It was a black and white photograph of a woman's face. She seemed to be asleep: her eyes were shut, her face was slack and untroubled, and she was resting on some kind of flat surface that Delilah couldn't identify. Her dark curls were spread out around her like a cloud.

She was unspeakably beautiful. So beautiful, in fact, that

the sight of her threatened to tug open a door in Delilah's soul that she kept shut at all times. The hope was that if it was locked tightly enough, she could forget its existence altogether. She had kept that door shut since she was sixteen years old and first looked at another girl and felt a lurch in her stomach, a sensation like freefall, an eerie sickening, and understood with sudden and awful clarity that she was *all wrong*. There were hungers in her, lodged deep underneath the skin and guts and bone, and she couldn't ever let anyone know.

Your eyes are glass, and your ears are glass, and your thoughts are glass, and God moves through each of these. Her hands were shaking. *You have the knowing of your own sin, and for it you will be judged, for all you know is known to God.*

Discipline, discipline, discipline. The key was discipline. If she stayed disciplined, she would be safe. She marshaled her mind back into a controlled state. Her hands stilled.

She extracted the slide and replaced it with another. It was a photo of the same woman, but from the side rather than from above. It showed her whole body, not just her face, and Delilah saw that she was lying on a steel table. Behind her was a plain white wall. She wore a dress of dark satin crowned with layers of ruffles and gauze and studded with tiny jewels.

No one had worn a dress in that style for centuries. It was either very old, much older than the camera technology that had captured it, or it was a replica. Either way, it helped to explain at least a little about why these slides were in the vault; clothes like that had been favored by the Queen and were therefore illegal in this day and age.

She removed the slide and replaced it with another. And then she forgot how to breathe.

It was the same woman, viewed from above, just like the first slide. But this time her whole body was in view, and that meant Delilah could see what had happened to her. A section of her dress, the part that covered her stomach, had been torn and pulled to the sides to expose the skin—or rather, what was left of it. A gaping wound had been dug into her abdomen. Someone had taken a knife and carefully dug out the flesh and muscles and intestines, leaving only a roughly hemispherical abyss welling with blood.

Delilah was cold all over. Not asleep. Dead. A heretic's death: the carving-out of the place where hunger lived.

Heretics' corpses were always incinerated. She recalled the file her predecessor had defaced: *Historical attempts at destruction via fire date back to the original conquest... all previous attempts have failed.* Magic, then? Some old crime of the Queen's lingering in the present? If the file truly did mean that people had been trying to burn this body since the conquest...had the corpse really been preserved for so long? Long enough for it to be photographed by technology invented centuries after the Queen's reign?

She fumbled the slide from the projector with clumsy hands, eager to be free of the image of the hollowed-out stomach, ghostly and distended as it was in this enlarged version. The next slide was the last. Someone had appended a piece of tape to the edge of the glass square. She ran her thumb over the tape's peeling edges and read the word written upon it: CAUTION.

There was no other information, no suggested alternate course of action, so she did exactly what she'd done with the last three slides. She inserted it into the machine.

It was the wound. It had been photographed from a very short distance away, so close that the edges of the injury were outside the frame. Logically speaking, she shouldn't have been able to identify it as a photograph of the bloodied hollow at all—it was just darkness, interrupted here and there by fragments of gleam where the gore, impossibly uncongealed, had caught the light. But she knew what she was looking at.

The blood in the photograph *flowed*. It dripped. It pooled. A tiny, rational fragment of her brain was aware that nothing had physically changed in the photograph; it was as static as it had always been. But the rest of her was frozen, stilled by the horrific knowledge that the wound was yet bleeding—that it was bleeding *out* of the photograph—it was reaching out into the dark air, through the beam of light—

—it was flowing *toward her*—

She swung her arms out in front of her wildly, as if to block a blow. Her forearms collided with the projector and swept it to the floor. With a resounding crash, the bulb broke, plunging the vault into darkness.

Delilah's breathing was fast and panicked. Her heart beat a wild staccato rhythm. It took a minute for her eyes to readjust to the dark, and for that minute she stood in place, swallowed by unbroken darkness as the afterimage of the photograph stayed seared into her sight.

Once her eyes adjusted, she forced herself to kneel down among the shards of glass and extract the slide, which had cracked into two pieces. She stared at the two halves in her hands.

This was another mistake. As she looked, the image trapped in the glass began to writhe. It was moving as impossibly as it had been in projected form, but instead of flowing out toward her, the blood sought to cross the gap between the two halves, to make itself whole.

She dropped the shards. They shattered further when they hit the floor. She slammed her heel down on the pieces over and over again until they were ground into nothing but glass dust.

Her head spun. Destroying documentation of heresy was a crime. Destroying heresy itself was the opposite of a crime. She couldn't decipher which of those two things she'd just done. She couldn't think at all. Her hearing was a roar. Her sight was a blur. She stumbled away from the table, abandoning the broken machine on the ground. Only her years of practicing self-control stopped her from running as she fled the vault.

The ground-level foyer was blessedly empty, leaving no one to wonder why Delilah was leaving so early and so urgently. Outside, the sky was a deep cobalt. The last scraps of day clung to the glass towers that rose from the city's heart, stabbing upward like syringes.

With the exception of the vault, every wall in every building in the city was glass. Nothing was hidden. No one was supposed to have anything to hide. It meant she was surrounded by glassy facades as she stumbled home, and her reflection dogged her every step, ghostly and warped. She flinched every time she saw it out of the corner of her eye.

When she arrived at her apartment, she sat on her bed and stared out into nothing. From then until night fell in earnest, she stared through the glass walls of the bedroom and through the glass walls of the apartment and through the glass walls of her neighbors' apartments and through the glass walls of the buildings on the other side of the street and through the glass towers in the distance and through the sky.

She thought about nothing at all.

After some time, she slept.

She dreamed she was at work in the vault, but every drawer she opened was filled to bursting with carnations. If she was still for too long, they would rise from the drawers and twine around her, pushing unfurled buds between her fingers and crawling up her forearms. Fear began to twist in her stomach. She backed away from the drawer she'd been searching. The buds clung eagerly to her even as their stems snapped and the heads were severed from the roots. She took another step back, then another, then broke into a run toward the exit. All the while, the carnations blossomed under her sleeves.

In her dream, the exit was gone. In its place was the dead woman.

She was dulled to black and white as she had been in the photographs, but she was sitting on the edge of a table, kicking her legs idly back and forth, and Delilah knew she'd been waiting for her.

The fatal wound wept blood down the front of her dress. In her hands she cradled a peach. It looked exactly as Delilah had imagined it when that record pressed its sin into her mind. As Delilah approached, the woman's face brightened as if she'd seen an old friend. She held out the peach in offering.

Delilah reached out to take it on instinct, then hesitated just before her fingers touched its surface. "I shouldn't," she said. Then she asked, all in a rush, "Who are you? Can you—can you help me?"

The woman continued to hold out the peach. Delilah continued to not take it. After a few moments, the woman sighed and shrugged elegantly. She lifted it to her lips and bit down. Juice spilled down her chin; her eyes closed in pleasure.

The carnations squirmed against Delilah's skin. She swallowed. "Listen, I—these flowers, they won't go away. Do you know how to make them stop?"

The woman shrugged carelessly. "Do you want me to?"

"Yes."

"...hmm," said the woman, as if she doubted Delilah's answer.

Delilah frowned.

The woman hopped off the table and walked further into the depths of the vault. She moved quickly. Delilah hurried to keep up, hoping that whatever she was doing would help her escape the flowers.

The woman stopped when she reached the opposite side of the building. She seized one of the cabinets pushed up against the wall and dragged it forward, exposing the white-painted stone behind it. Then she turned to the cabinet to the right of the displaced one and dragged it away from the wall too. Then she moved on to another cabinet. "What are you doing?" Delilah asked. The woman didn't reply. She dragged a fourth cabinet away from the wall and inspected the stone that had been revealed. She trailed a fingertip along the stone —a vertical line starting at eye level and moving downward. The petals under Delilah's sleeves shivered intently.

Delilah stepped forward and looked closer. With a start, she realized that the woman was running her fingers along a doorframe. It had evaded Delilah's eye by virtue of being covered in the same coat of white paint as the stone that bordered it, but there was definitely a door there.

"Where does it go?" Delilah asked.

The woman continued to trace the doorframe with her fingers as if there was nothing in the universe that fascinated her more. Delilah hesitated, then repeated her initial question. "Who are you?"

Finally, the woman turned to face her. She smiled. The blood from her stomach wound, grey-black as it had been in the photograph, poured down her dress and pooled on the floor. The longer Delilah looked at it, the more eagerly the carnations writhed.

"As the fragrance is to the flower," the woman said, "so am I to the Queen of Carnations."

"The Queen of Carnations is dead."

"Of course I'm not! It would be so *boring*, to be dead. They tried to kill me—to take me away from my body. But I stayed. I've been waiting."

"Waiting for what?"

Her pupils were wide and hungry. Once again, Delilah was shaken by the frightful intensity of her beauty. "For someone to let me out," she said. "For someone to let me *in*."

Sharp pinpricks of pain burst along Delilah's arms. She slapped frantically at her sleeves as if she were being attacked by biting insects, but it did no good. The pain intensified. It was unbearable. Desperate, she stripped off her suit jacket and tore open the sleeves of her white button-down shirt. The carnations were burrowing feverishly under her skin.

She tried to rip them out, but the Queen caught her hands. "Shhh," she said. "It's going to be okay."

And the Queen kissed her.

Delilah woke from the dream with a start. Her heart was beating fast. Her face was flushed. She ran her hands along her arms, but she was unhurt. None of the pain remained upon waking. It had been replaced with something entirely different: a gentle, rolling pleasure skittering up and down her skin.

Her mouth was dry. She tried to swallow, but felt something hard and metallic behind her teeth. Alarmed, she spat it out.

It was a key.

She didn't know what to do. She didn't know what to think. So she recited scripture in her head and tried to think of nothing at all.

She managed it for as long as it took to get to the vault. It was only when she was there, in the only dark place in all the city, that she failed. She shouldn't go looking. She knew with utter certainty that she shouldn't go looking. But she did. She couldn't stop herself.

Delilah retraced the steps she'd taken in her dream until she found the row of cabinets set against the wall. She dragged them forward, exposing the stone, and all the while her skull rattled with scripture. *Your eyes are glass, and your ears are glass, and your thoughts are glass, and God moves through each of these...*

The door was exactly where it had been in her dream. A small plaque above the door handle read: CAUTION— VOLATILE HERESY WITHIN.

The key she'd found in her mouth fit perfectly in the lock. She turned it until she heard the click. She rested her hand on the handle.

You have the knowing of your own sin, and for it you will be judged, hissed the memory of scripture, *for all you know is known to God.*

She opened the door.

On the other side was a small, bare room. The walls and floor and ceiling were all white-painted stone, perfectly pristine. It was completely empty, except for—

Except for—

Once, the corpse of the Queen of Carnations had lain here. There was no doubt about that. That record had claimed the body was burned and the efficacy of the burning was *debatable.* Delilah understood now. The burning had been successful in the sense that there were no more limbs, no more bones, no more flesh, no more skin. No more anything, really. The body was gone.

But the wound remained.

A bloody hollow hung suspended in the air, surrounded by absolutely nothing. The flesh that had bordered it had vanished. The viscera that had cradled it was absent. There was only blood, pooling in the center of the room as if cupped by invisible palms. There was a sickly smell in the air: the scent of gore and flowers mixed together.

Discipline honed over years jolted Delilah into action. She mentally reached for scripture. But it didn't come. Her mind was blank. And in the echoing hollow of her skull came the heresy.

It had a sighing quality to it—a breath of satisfaction, of pleasure. It curled itself around Delilah's thoughts and put forth the suggestion of release.

It said, *Let me out.*

It said, *Let me in.*

She crossed the threshold. She drew closer. She wanted to touch the wound. She wanted to see if it was cold; she wanted to see if it would be warm against her skin. She wanted to stain her fingers with its red.

She wanted.

The heresy caressed the shell of her ear. It trailed kisses along the curve of her neck. *What manner of sweetness do you desire?* it asked. *Anything you want, you will have.*

Fear coiled in her gut. (Something else coiled alongside it.) If she were foolish enough to fall prey to this, then the consequences would be devastating. The Queen of Carnations set free in the world again, in possession of a living body? The danger was unimaginable. She couldn't even begin to comprehend the ramifications.

The heresy pressed against her lips. *Give me your desire. Let me bring you into it.*

"I," said Delilah. Her tongue felt heavy and foreign. "I—I want—"

Tell me.

Inexorably, the heresy drew the truth from her. She said, "I just want to *want.*"

All you have to do is reach out.

All at once, she gave in. She lurched forward and grasped at the wound with hungry fingers. It moved slowly, stickily. It glistened as she took it in her hands and brought it to her

SHAONI C. WHITE

mouth. It burned like sweet liquor as it slid past her lips. She was ravenous. She ate and ate and ate and ate and her body came alight with pleasure.

The Queen of Carnations unfurled first in her throat, then in her lungs, then in her gut. The Queen took her veins as a trellis and bloomed along the whole of her body. Delilah shook and shook.

When it was done, she was no longer Delilah, nor was she the Queen. She was a unity both terrifying and lovely.

And so began her reign.

BRITISH WILDLIFE

NICHOLAS ROYLE

Originally published in *Great British Horror 9: Something Peculiar*.

Nicholas Royle is the author of six short story collections—*Mortality, Ornithology, The Dummy and Other
Uncanny Stories, London Gothic, Manchester Uncanny*
and *Paris Fantastique*—and seven novels, most recently
First Novel. He has edited more than two dozen
anthologies and is series editor of *Best British Short
Stories* for Salt, who also published his books-about-
books, *White Spines: Confessions of a Book Collector*
and *Shadow Lines: Searching For the Book Beyond the
Shelf.* In 2009 he founded Nightjar Press, which
continues to publish original short stories in the form of
limited-edition chapbooks.

OUR DOOR IS ALWAYS OPEN, they said. What would
be the point of locking it, out here?

I stand so close to the shelving unit containing Gregor's

CD collection that my breath condenses on the hard plastic cases. Jonathan Coleclough. Emmalee Crane. Jakob Kirkegaard. Gregor is the only person I know whose collection of minimalist music is even more obscure than mine. I pull out a recording of Eliane Radigue's *Transamorem—Transmortem*. The cover is a headshot of the composer, in quarter profile, black and white, the light striking the side of her face furthest from the camera and giving her a distinct look of Ingrid Bergman.

I'd love to hear this, I say.

Gregor doesn't respond. His face never did give much away. But he doesn't say no. I open the CD case and take out the disc, press eject on the stereo and carefully fit the disc on to the tray, checking with the soft pads of my fingers that it is correctly positioned. I wouldn't want it to get stuck in the machine. The tray slides shut and I press play.

The seating arrangement at Isla and Gregor's is the same as ever. Two medium-length sofas face each other across the ceramic tiled coffee table—on which I notice a rusty brown thumbprint—with an Eames chair at one end and a Robin Day reclining chair at the other. The furniture is mostly mid-century modern and the bungalow itself dates from the 1970s. I take a seat at one end of the nearest sofa, directly opposite Gregor, while Isla is ensconced in the Eames chair, facing into the room with her back to the picture window. She is silhouetted against the light, but Gregor is lit from the side. His characteristic half-smile doesn't tell me what he thinks of the Eliane Radigue, which sounds to me like someone blowing a dog whistle inside an engine room, and I can't assume that because the album is in his collection he necessarily likes it. Half the albums on my shelves I can hardly bring myself to listen to, unless as an act of bravado, and I'm sure it's the same for Gregor, who has a lot of Philip Glass, say, but while I can imagine him sitting there listening to *Solo Piano* with that same enigmatic half-smile on his face, I can't quite see it for *Music With Twelve Parts*, for example, even though he has a copy, as do I.

I take a tissue from my pocket and moisten it, then lean

forward and rub at the rusty brown thumbprint until it has disappeared.

It's always good to be here, I say, sitting back, pocketing the tissue and smiling at Gregor and Isla in turn. Increasingly, I say, I find that I have favourite places as well as favourite people, and sometimes it's a case of those people being in that place, if you know what I mean. So, you, in this house. You belong in this house. This couple we see in our local. They belong in that pub. I can't really imagine them anywhere else. We saw them there just last week and I said to Jenny we should get to know them better.

I can't make out Isla's expression and my gaze slides away from her to the piece, one of her British Wildlife series, standing on the cabinet to her left. It's a stuffed stoat. It doesn't just have the body of a stoat combined with the head of a weasel or something and nor is it stuffed—pardon the unpardonable pun—into a box or a test tube, or contorted into an unnatural position, like something by Polly Morgan. The whole point of Isla's stuffed animals is that they're just that; they're like the stuffed animals you saw in a museum when you were ten that never quite left you. She wanted to rehabilitate traditional taxidermy by appealing directly to the pull of memory and our nostalgic impulses, Isla said, back when she was embarking on the series, but she said it with the gleam of mischief in her eye. I told her then that the success of her series would be all down to two things: her skill as a taxidermist and the persuasiveness of the art descriptions (in the event of an exhibition).

I continue to look around the room from my end of the sofa. There are more of Isla's stuffed animals—a jay, a badger, even a muntjac deer—and numerous framed prints and abstract paintings, some of them Gregor's. Isla's installation work, for which she is best known, is not the kind of thing you can easily show off in the home, not unless you turn your home into an installation.

I get up and go over to where Isla is sitting in the Eames chair and kneel down beside it. Her left arm rests—there's no better word for it—on the armrest. I place my hand on her forearm and smile at her. She is inscrutable.

We talked about working together, I say. It would have been less likely to happen if you'd moved away.

Eliane Radigue's various tones continue to drone on in the background and Gregor stares into the middle distance while Isla looks on.

I mean, let's face it, I say, it simply wouldn't have happened, would it?

I turn to look at her and see something not right in her hair line.

Do you mind if I just...? I say as I carefully reposition a lock of hair to cover her hair line.

WE TEND to set out for the pub together in time to beat the six o'clock rush, or the seven o'clock rush, or maybe the half past six rush. It depends what time we set out. Jenny is nervous crossing the road and doesn't appreciate being pulled like a child. When we do stop at the lights, she pushes the button, even though she doesn't need to, as it's one of those crossings that runs through a cycle. Invariably she will sense my impatience.

Why don't you go on ahead? she'll say.

I'm just thinking of the seven o'clock rush, I say, as I march off.

We like to get a table, a good table, one where we can sit together and I can feel her leg touching mine, rather than sitting opposite each other looking at our phones like all the other couples.

By the time Jenny arrives, I have acquired a table and drinks for both of us.

What do you think of when you think about Isla and Gregor? I ask her.

She lifts her wine glass and takes a mouthful.

Or rather, I say, what do you picture? What image comes into your mind?

While she's thinking, I notice Graham and Siobhan entering the pub, with their dog, still a puppy. Graham takes a seat across the way and settles the dog, while Siobhan goes to the bar. When he looks up, Graham sees us and lets on. I raise my hand.

I don't know, Jenny says. Their home, I suppose. That night when we were in their house after that thing.

Precisely, I say. Me too. That's what I think of.

Siobhan joins Graham and sets down their drinks and takes a seat next to him. She waves and we both wave back.

I raise my own glass to my mouth and take a sip of beer before adding, They're selling it.

Jenny turns to look at me. Isla and Gregor are selling their house? she says. Are you serious?

I'm afraid I am, I say, looking at Graham and Siobhan, who no one could deny are an extremely attractive couple. He's tall and has long hair that he wears in a ponytail and he has glasses with a fashionably thick, dark frame. All the time in here I see women looking at him, using the puppy as an excuse to start a conversation. The puppy certainly doesn't hurt. Siobhan, like Jenny, is never without lipstick, and, also like Jenny, would never reapply it without going to the ladies'. She'll often wear a leather jacket and jeans and her hair is dyed a deep Rothko red.

That's bad news, Jenny says. You were going to work with Isla.

I was, I say. I was hoping to. We had plans.

This is what happens when you make new friends, she says, and you imagine this friendship or collaboration or whatever extending into the future and then they go and ruin it by moving. Where does that leave your plans? Where are they moving to anyway? I mean, if it's just down the road...

Cornwall, I say.

It shouldn't be allowed, she jokes. It should have serious consequences.

Another dog makes an appearance and Graham and Siobhan's puppy lets out a piercing yelp. Graham tries to settle her down again. He looks across at me and Jenny and pulls a face. We pull appropriate faces back.

We should get to know Graham and Siobhan better, I say.

Yes, Jenny says.

Do you know what the worst is? I ask her.

What? she says, having a look to see how much of her wine is left.

How do you think I found out? I say.

Isla texted you? She sent you a long and apologetic email? She rang you and suggested you meet for a coffee and that's where you went this morning and she told you all about it?

You'd think, wouldn't you? I say. No, she posted it on social media.

THE THING with Isla and Gregor is the opening of an exhibition in a converted mill that is so cold within its thick stone walls that this is to be the last show of the year, in September, before it will close for the winter and not reopen until April. It is a group show and both Isla and Gregor are showing, along with a number of other artists from the Calder Valley and the wider north-west. The theme is trans-formation and it is Isla's first chance to exhibit some of her stuffed animals—a crow and a grass snake. I watch people circling both pieces on their plinths puzzledly looking for some ironic twist on the tradition. When they don't see one, they assume nevertheless that there is one and they smile knowingly as they heap praise on Isla, who accepts it with characteristic good grace and modesty.

Gregor fields compliments relating to his series of abstract paintings with his trademark half-smile.

The biting cold in the mill would be bearable if it helped keep the wine chilled, but the wine has not been cold since it left the off licence in the middle of the afternoon. As soon as Isla shyly suggests that people might want to come back to the house, everyone starts shuffling towards the door. There's no need to put coats on, for obvious reasons. I cast a last look around the space. With its dimensions, the unironic-ironic nature of the work and the uniform appearance of the gallery-goers among whom, for example, Graham and Siobhan would not have looked out of place, the mill reminds me of a New York loft. A short time later, we climb out of taxis at the bottom of Isla and Gregor's winding drive and the first glimpse of the house makes me think, as it did before, of Frank Lloyd Wright's Fallingwater. I say something to this effect to the man with heavy-framed glasses and a pale-blue Tootal scarf who happens to be walking up the drive next to me and he snorts with laughter.

But I mean it, I say. I love this house.

You've been to Isla and Gregor's before? he asks me.

Only once, I admit, but I fell in love with it.

By the time we enter the house, the Arco lamp, the Sputnik chandelier and, my favourite, the PH5 pendant lamp are all glowing, casting spots and pools of light that pick out artworks and monographs and women with angular haircuts holding out glasses to be filled as Gregor goes around with bottles of champagne. He has already stuck some crowd-pleasing but undeniably lush Harold Budd on the stereo. I think I recognise the shimmering textures of 'Balthus Bemused By Colour' from *The White Arcades* as they slither off the various shiny surfaces in the open-plan living/dining room. The man from the drive with the pale blue Tootal scarf has somehow commandeered the Robin Day reclining chair and has taken out his phone and is scrolling.

I catch Isla in the kitchen where she is talking to Jenny, who has somehow got here ahead of me, and Jenny says, Talk of the devil, and Isla hands me a drink and we all clink glasses.

I was just telling Jenny about our project, Isla says.

I thought it was more of a vague plan, I say. But I'll drink to a project.

Isla grins and we clink glasses again.

I love this house, I say.

Isla smiles. We got lucky, she says.

I feel like I've been coming here for years, I say, but I've only been here once before. I was telling someone, as we were walking up the drive. I can hardly believe it.

Isla smiles at Jenny, whose glass is empty, I notice, and Isla sees me noticing and reaches for another bottle of champagne out of the ice bucket, which is literally a bucket with some ice in it.

So what is our plan exactly? I ask.

I want to do something with taxidermy, Isla says.

But you already are doing, I say.

Thank you, says Jenny as Isla pops the cork and fills her glass.

Something more ambitious, Isla says. Wouldn't you like to learn how to do it?

Taxidermy? I say.

Yes, I'll teach you, she says. And then we'll make something together. My animals are fine, but I want to see what we might do together. Something with—I don't know—more narrative. Something immersive. Site specific.

It's very difficult, isn't it? I say.

Taxidermy? she says.

Yes, I say.

It's difficult to get right, perhaps. Easy to get wrong. Hair lines can be tricky. You have to somehow convey the idea of life. Because it is life, in a way. A form of life.

She smiles. You'll be good at it, she says. You're good with your hands. And you've got a good eye. That's all you really need—and some knives. I'll show you.

MISE EN ABYME

MIA XUAN

Originally published in *Speculative City #14: Megacity*.

Mia Xuan is a writer from New Jersey. Her other facets include artist, thesaurus enthusiast, bad pun merchant, notebook hoarder, and collector of miscellaneous trivia of questionable use. In addition to *Speculative City*, her work has been previously featured in *Apparition Lit*, *Archive of the Odd*, and *The Skull & Laurel*.

THE POPULATION of Droste is one and not one. One, because the only person who lives among the endless glass windows and clear curtain walls is Miss Misset. Not one, because there are so very many Miss Missets.

She exists in the same way the words "sheep" or "fish" exist, in both the singular and the plural. Each reflection as she passes by the mural-sized shop windows of the downtown thoroughfare emerges as yet another Miss Misset in the throng, smoothing down her dark hair, though sometimes it is gray with age, or white from stress, or blonde from bleach. On rainy mornings in Droste, when Miss Misset's visage catches in the droplets that ripple into gutters and lash against the parapets, a cavalcade of more Miss Missets spill from the upper stories and fire escapes. Some Miss Missets remember their umbrellas and dress in smart beige coats against the downpour. Other Miss Missets sprint down the street in sopping shoes, cursing at their snoozed alarms and the weather report, delivered by, of course, another Miss Misset, with her hair snipped in a neat bob.

Despite being peopled entirely by one person, Droste is not a harmonious city, for Miss Misset presents a new facet in each windowpane or compact or rear-view mirror she passes. Her multitudes share a predilection for clutter and collecting, a height of approximately five foot eight depending on nutritional intake, and a competitive streak kept well-hidden by a smile well-trained for congratulations. Outside of these commonalities, the Miss Missets have speciated in the manner of island finches. This Miss Misset kept to her dogged belief in hard work, punching into the office every day at seven with rigid punctuality; this Miss Misset surrendered to her sentimentality and bought nine cats, one for each life. This Miss Misset never managed to leave her summer job as a waitress and continues to glare at customers and take too long on smoke breaks; this Miss Misset pursued her lofty dreams of grants and galleries, and of course the other Miss Missets find much to admire in her work, as it is proof of the potential they always suspected lay dormant in themselves. Some of the Miss Missets truly achieve greatness and get their faces plastered over monolithic billboards and digital screens, further additions to the array of Miss Missets comprising the city. The other Miss Missets look upon a bright smile so much like their own, beaming down at them from such lofty heights, and they wonder if they could be the next Miss Misset to make it, even as they all drink the same coffees from the same cafes and buy the same blouses from the same boutiques, posting the same photos to the same sites, in another sprawl of Miss Missets that tangles in the greater overgrowth.

It is inevitable, with so many Miss Missets occupying the same space, that there cannot be room enough for all of them. The traditional Miss Misset has a taste for seafood and an affinity for art and architecture, but the lines for the freshest cuts at the trendy bistro are truly terrible, stretching for blocks and blocks, and there are only so many exhibitions and blueprints to go around. Only the finest of Miss Missets confirm their place in rooftop penthouses with skyline views, while the rest are left to scrabble in their wake. Countless Miss Missets spring from the sleek tinted windows of the office buildings and find their way inside, sharing cubicles and break rooms with equally bold, equally ambitious Miss Missets, each wearing crisp dress shirts and blazers to leave a good impression. Thresholds to studios erode from countless Miss Missets who haul in their sketchbooks to labor away at life drawings that double as self-portraits. And each kind remark and encouraging note they give to each other scrapes past with friction.

Like does not always suit like, after all, and Miss Misset is unlike the gridded avenues and crosswalks she navigates—she has the wrong edges to fit neatly against herself. When she goes out to the new cafes to meet other Miss Missets, she is understood, and terribly so, as she realizes her thoughts are well-trod, her dreams pedestrian. She sees what makes the select few Miss Missets succeed, which only serves to discourage her when she cannot commit to those same habits, like waking up before sunrise to exercise before work or setting aside time to meditate. There always appears to be a Miss Misset who is doing better than she, even though they start from the same template. A mirror is held up to Miss Misset every day, and it always finds her wanting.

Observing the Miss Missets who are worse off brings no comfort, either, as it is difficult to learn that one is difficult to like. Miss Misset is not oblivious to the twinge of superiority she feels when she sees another Miss Misset shivering in a threadbare coat or easing her feet from too-small shoes, and who is to say that the Miss Misset at work, who has alligator skin handbags and a nicer car with leather seats, does not feel the same way when she sees her practical windbreaker and worn briefcase. How can anyone distinguish between compassion and contempt when every Miss Misset has the same sympathetic smile? And though she sometimes musters enough magnanimity to spare some change or sound advice to an unfortunate Miss Misset, she would rather not witness how poorly she handles adversity. The Miss Missets who have upscale apartments in the nice blocks avoid the Miss Missets who snip coupons and count change out of necessity instead of frugality, because they do not want to know how easily they lapse into cursing others for their circumstances, how quickly they resign themselves to their fate, when they write in their resumes about being diligent, proactive problem solvers.

One notorious Miss Misset is said to have surfaced from the sheen of a knife, or the shards of cracked glass in a dark alley, though it is far more likely that she came from a changing room mirror or car window. Whatever the case, the ramshackle walk-up she used to call home has been abandoned, and the rumors say that she is now living as another Miss Misset. Worse than hearing that a Miss Misset is missing is the thought that nobody is quite sure who has been replaced. The new Miss Misset can be agreeable, gracious, and very endearing, and might even be more industrious than the former Miss Misset, after learning to appreciate functional heating and well-stocked fridges. And the other Miss Missets gather together to mourn their fallen friend as they encounter each other at park benches or coffee shops, chattering on about how awful, how selfish, how greedy that Miss Misset must be, instead of how frightened they are, because none of them wants to admit to suspecting everyone.

The population of Droste is one and not one. Not one, because the city is teeming with Miss Missets, who duck into vestibules to escape the autumn storms, who fidget in long lines for oyster dinners, who look over the city from balconies dotted with string lights that match the traffic patterns, who speak more in canned responses than candid ones, who commute between home and work in subways packed with identical passengers in identical seats and identical slacks, who start and spend and end the day staring into mirrors. One, because no matter how many reflections she passes by, each Miss Misset is still on her own.

THE LAST LUCID DAY

DOMINIQUE DICKEY

Originally published in *Lightspeed Magazine* #170.

Dominique Dickey is a speculative fiction writer and game designer. As the creative director of Sly Robot Games, they've created *Plant Girl Game* and *Tomorrow on Revelation III*. They contributed to the Nebula Award-winning *Thirsty Sword Lesbians,* and the ENNIE Award-winning *Journeys Through the Radiant Citadel.* Their novella *Redundancies & Potentials* was published by Neon Hemlock in 2025. Their short fiction has appeared in venues including *Fantasy Magazine, Lightspeed Magazine,* and *Nightmare Magazine.* They live in the DC area, where they're always on the hunt for their next idea. You can find their work at dominiquedickey.com.

YOU'RE asleep in dreams of your father holding your head underwater, so the call from Magnolia Assisted Living goes to voicemail.

"I didn't raise a son of mine to count on his fingers," your father says in the dream—because ah, yes, it's all of your worst moments rolled into a single nightmare.

You hear the beeping of your alarm and you know you're dreaming, but you can't wake up any more than you can pull yourself free of your father's hands. He holds you down and tells you to count the seconds, show him how long you can hold your breath, but the only way to make sense of the numbers is to tally them on your fingers. He pushes you down deeper. He walks away.

It always ends with him walking away.

It always ends with you splashing in the deep end, alone.

WHEN YOU AWAKE, sweat outlines your body in the bed like a policeman's chalk drawing. Your alarm has been going off for…how long? Too long. You're running late for work, and today already feels awful.

You call in sick. That's sorted. What's next? The voicemail.

The voice of the message is automated. You knew this was coming, but there was no way of knowing when. You figure that's the purpose of the service—to tell you exactly *when*.

Well, another hour in bed won't hurt. You want the feeling of waking up right, from a good dream or even from no dream at all. You set your alarm again and close your eyes but you can't get back to sleep. You catch yourself thinking about your father's favorite belt—thick black leather, buckle scratched to hell. You're a grown man and it still makes you feel wobbly with fear.

You haul yourself out of your sweat-damp bed. You shower. Magnolia Assisted Living is an hour away in traffic. You stop at an ATM on the way and get there just before eleven.

You were six when your parents called it quits. Mom got Christmas, Thanksgiving, and birthdays. They alternated Easters, a holiday neither of them especially cared about. Dad got every other weekend.

Every other Friday, you'd haul your overnight bag to school and stash it behind the receptionist's desk. Every other Friday, your father would show up in the pickup line in his red sports car.

His bachelor apartment was two hours out of the city. At the halfway point, he'd pull off the highway and circle on the surface streets for a bit, eventually pulling into the parking lot of a mini-mart or a gas station. You'd stretch your legs and then he'd hand you a couple of tens and set you loose on the aisles of junk food. You'd eat together in silence.

That was when you felt closest to him. Not in his apartment, a beautiful place that never felt like home, but in the car in a nondescript parking lot, surrounded by overpriced snacks, his coffee black and gritty as tar steaming in the cupholder between you.

At Magnolia, the receptionist tells you your father is in the garden. You pick through the trees and rosebushes until you find him sitting at a wrought iron table with a composition book and a ballpoint pen, scribbling. There's a long moment before he looks up and sees you. You wish time could stop, could give you space to think about the meaning behind the words he's writing—or maybe they're numbers, or diagrams.

Whatever it is, it makes sense to someone smarter than you. Someone with the specialized knowledge required to understand it. Lucid, your father is a genius. He's the most brilliant man you know.

And then he looks at you. There's a flash of surprise on his face before he pushes himself to his feet and comes close, his arms held out as if to hug you. "It's a Thursday, isn't it? What have I done to deserve this?"

You smile. Even now, he doesn't know you well enough to know you're forcing it. "I thought we'd go for a drive."

YOUR FATHER, a theoretical mathematician renowned in his field, stood over your shoulder as you did your homework. You were a child. You were counting on your fingers. He took off his belt and laid it on the table. He wasn't actually going to beat you with it, but you didn't know that—how could you possibly know that? It would take a few more years of this before you saw straight to the bottom of his empty threats.

He never hit you. The threat of violence kept you in line, and that was violent in a quiet sort of way.

Every other weekend you eclipsed yourself. You sat at the kitchen table with his belt beside you and you let your mind go somewhere else. You hid in plain sight. You spoke only when spoken to, in non-answers and with a heavy tongue. No, he never hit you, but sometimes he took you by the shoulders and shook you, as if it would bring you back.

You learned addition and subtraction by rote. You learned to swim. You learned to disappear. You learned other things, too, that you were happy to forget.

If he had hit you with the belt, if he had made you count the lashes, you would not have used your hands to find the numbers.

YOU DRIVE FOR AN HOUR, alternately talking about nothing and humming along to smooth jazz classics on the radio. You pull off the highway, circle for a bit, find a gas station with an attached market.

You give him two crisp twenty-dollar bills. Inflation, you think. That ought to cover it.

You follow him inside. He doesn't look nearly as old as he is, and he wears his excitement like a little kid. He has the cash crushed in one fist, the index finger of the other hand tapping his lips as he paces the aisles. The store's small, but he takes his choices seriously, and you let him.

After a few minutes of witnessing his indecision, you wander away to figure out your own haul. Potato chips. A bottle of ginger ale, weeping condensation. A styrofoam cup of black coffee that's somehow burnt even though it's freshly regurgitated from the machine.

You're at the register when he slides up to you, impatient —somehow he's already made his picks and purchased them —and asks for the car keys. You hand them over. You watch through the window as he folds himself into the passenger seat of your practical SUV and begins to eat. The pimply attendant takes your credit card, swipes it, and hands it back.

YOU TURNED EIGHTEEN. You stopped answering his calls and, eventually, he stopped calling. Part of you felt like he was giving up on you, but the bigger part of you felt relieved. You thought of him whenever you went to a gas station or mini-mart—all the time, at first.

The memories faded, as memories tend to do, and you thought of him less and less.

Twenty years passed. You hardly thought of him at all. It was peaceful. It was good. You had the quiet kind of happiness that's damn near impossible to capture in words. You didn't think about him, you lived your life, and you were happy.

HE CALLED after your mom died. He had a new number, but so did you, and you never asked how he got yours. He wanted to come to the funeral, wanted to know if it was okay with you, didn't want to just show up and surprise you. The thoughtfulness was unexpected—it was easier to see him as the man who would do the blatantly inconsiderate thing.

"Sure," you said.

"I'll see you there," he said.

The funeral was on a hot day. He sat in the back and left as soon as the service was over. You barely saw him, but he looked just the same as you remembered. You wondered if he was wearing the same belt: tarnished silver buckle, black leather gone limp with the years.

Two weeks after the funeral—you spent a week waffling, and another week working up the nerve—you called him. "Come over for coffee," you said. You couldn't tell if the offer was for him or for you. You couldn't tell what you hoped to gain, but you had very little to lose. Your impossible, wordless happiness had already shattered. What could he do to you that had not already been done? What more could he take?

He came to your house on a Saturday afternoon. He was a familiar stranger. He hugged you tightly and came away crying, embarrassing you both. His memory had already gone fuzzy around the edges, the past bleeding into the present, but he still knew you. He missed you. You were right on time.

___

You sit in the car and you eat. You don't speak—you don't even look at each other—but you feel close to him.

Maybe this is enough. Maybe this is all you needed.

___

Two years after you got your dad back—two years of awkward biweekly coffee visits, talking around all the things you wanted to talk about—came the fire.

He seemed to slip through time, confusing you with people he used to know, forgetting how old you were, forgetting which stories he'd already told you. He showed you proofs that made no sense, though you blamed your lack of mathematical knowledge for this. He got lost around the corner from his house, once, but his neighbors walked him home and he laughed when he recounted the incident to you.

He forgot he was cooking in the middle of frying an egg. He left a burner on and wandered out of the room. He was at his desk puzzling over an equation, a hand-drawn diagram that only he could understand, when a kitchen towel caught fire. From there it spread to the curtains. He would've been fine if he'd fled when the smoke alarm started to beep, but he tried to put the flames out himself.

You brought him gas station coffee when you visited him in the hospital. He had bandages around both his arms and he looked like he'd aged ten years in the time it took you to arrive.

"I'm not going to be stubborn about this," he said. "I'm not going to do that to you—make you get a court order or else make you watch me die the hard way. I know I shouldn't live alone anymore."

In the silence, you wondered if he meant for you to make him an offer—you did have plenty of space, after all, in your mom's old house. But you didn't offer, and he didn't ask.

"I'll send you a link," he said. "I already picked out a place. Magnolia Assisted Living. Forty minutes out of the city, specialized in memory care. Just...say you'll come visit me."

"I'll come visit you," you said.

Awkward Saturday coffee had a new location. He wore long sleeves to cover the burn scars. He worked day and night on theorems that you began to see for the nonsense they were. Time and memories flowed around him like choppy water. He was adrift. He was drowning.

You couldn't save him—you weren't even sure if you wanted to—but you visited every week.

"THERE'S THIS THING," he told you, though by then you'd already done your own research. "A service they offer. An implant. It can tell you when your last good day—your last *really* good day—will be. The catch is that if the patient

knows their time is up, then the white coats say it leads to…
negative treatment outcomes. It's a double blind, I guess. The
doctors don't even know. It's better if they just notify the
family." He scratched his arm through his sleeve. You imagined the way his burned skin went puckered and thin. "I gave
them your number. I hope that's all right."

There he was: the man who would do the blatantly inconsiderate thing, tossing you into a responsibility that you never
wanted, didn't know how to bear. Reality closed over your
head like chlorinated water.

"That's fine with me," you said.

AT THE BOTTOM of his bag of chips he licks the dust off his
fingers, then looks at you for a long time. "It's my last day,
isn't it?"

You make a concerted effort not to tense up. "What do
you mean?"

"Oh, come on. My last lucid day."

You shrug. He doesn't know you well enough to know
your tells. "I thought you didn't sign up for that."

"Don't give me that. They did all the tests. All the
implants—even the ones that are still in trials. Compre-
hensive."

You shrug again. "You sure you remember your intake
that well?"

"*Yes* I remember my fucking intake—"

"Really? Because sometimes you misremember stuff. It
comes with the whole terrain."

He doesn't say anything, but his expression is nuclear in
its rage. The anger makes you feel small, makes you think of
his belt on the kitchen table in the apartment you never felt
safe in.

And then the anger goes away all at once, his face slack as
he gropes in the footwell for something else to eat. There's an
unguarded moment where he looks hurt, and he looks sad,
and he looks very old.

The petty satisfaction you feel at having hurt him is undercut only by your own guilt. You feel like a monster, like you're no better than him. But what you want from him—it can't be a deathbed confession. The conversation will lose its value if he knows he's out of time, if he's only saying the words because it's his last chance to do so. You need it to feel organic. You need it to feel real.

You ask the question you have always been afraid to ask: "When you look back at my childhood, do you ever regret anything?"

"No." He answers so quickly he can't have possibly thought about it.

"Really?"

"No. Nothing."

"Wow."

"Does that surprise you?"

"I just think—"

"The way I see it, I did my best. I provided. And I didn't have a dad at all, so it's not like I had a blueprint in that regard. I did my best."

"But what about..." You're trying to think of a concrete example, one that doesn't hurt too much to talk about. "What about when you taught me to swim?"

"You learned."

"You could have drowned me."

"Eh," he says.

You think about him tossing you into the water, him pinching your nose and holding your head down so you'd learn to hold your breath, him walking away and leaving you flailing in the deep end. You can feel the fear as if it's happening right now. You can smell the chlorine and the sunscreen as if it's on your skin—memory is strange, that way. Funny that you thought you could bring up this story without feeling that familiar unhappy ache in your chest, your gut.

This is why you went so many years without thinking of him at all. This is what you were avoiding.

You don't know what you want. You want him to admit

he hurt you. You want to hear him say that he was wrong. You keep pushing.

"I could have *died*," you tell him.

"You didn't. You learned to swim, didn't you?"

"It's not just that. I was a *kid*."

"You turned out okay."

"Did I?"

"You did," he says, with perfect confidence, like he has no idea how wrong he is.

He barely knows you—because you haven't let him, because there is so much you haven't told him. He doesn't know about the trail of wrecked relationships, all entirely your fault, which you blame on your attachment issues, which you blame on him. Your mother is the only relationship you couldn't entirely destroy, and goddammit you tried. He doesn't know about the nightmares. Telling him how he's ruined you would constitute admitting defeat, but he can't apologize for the pain if you don't show him the wounds.

You aren't going to show him the wounds.

He's never going to apologize.

Why did you even bother? Why did you even hope? He's going to forget you and he will never, ever be sorry.

Time is kind and memory is cruel. Someday you'll forget him too.

You were in college the first time you lost your father.

"My mom's an architect," you said, when the subject of family came up in a conversation with your freshman year roommate.

"What about your dad?"

"I don't have a dad," you said. You didn't even hesitate, and you felt no guilt for the smoothness of the lie. If anything, it made you proud.

Look at me, you thought. Look at the life I'm creating without him. Look at how good that life could be.

The grief came later, when you replayed the conversation

in your narrow dorm bed—a slow blooming feeling behind your sternum, like blood spreading in water.

You realize, now, that it was practice. You've already lost him once. You know how to lose him again.

It's an hour back to Magnolia, and you make the drive in silence. He's not even angry, and maybe you aren't either. You think you're mostly sad.

He sips his shitty coffee. He turns on the radio. Saxophone trickles out of the speakers.

"Back to the garden?" you ask, once you're parked in front of Magnolia. The weather's still nice, if a bit breezy. If he wants to spend his last good day working on proofs in the sun, you won't stand in the way of that.

"Yeah." He gets his notebook and ballpoint pen out of the backseat where he stashed them. He leaves his trash in the footwell: metallic wrappers, an empty styrofoam cup. You tell the receptionist you've returned him for the day, then walk him back to his little table. He lines up his notebook along its edge, then turns to you. Waiting.

Well, what do you do?

You meet his gaze and hold it. This is your dad. He's your dad and he's old, and he's falling apart, and he's going to die. And then you'll have a dead dad, who was a shithead in life and had the audacity to kick the bucket without apologizing for any of his shitheadedness.

You miss not having a dad at all. You miss the years of easily denying his existence. The lie that felt more and more true each time you told it. The story that you know you can never slip back into, now that it's been fractured.

He will never be himself again. You hate him. You miss him already.

You hug him tightly and come away crying, embarrassing the both of you.

TOUR

ELLIOTT GISH

Originally published in *Inner Worlds #3*.

Elliott Gish wants to creep you out. A writer and librarian from Nova Scotia, her short fiction has appeared in the *New Quarterly, Vastarien, the Ex-Puritan, Dark Matter Magazine*, and many others. Her debut novel, *Grey Dog* (ECW Press 2024), was shortlisted for the Edmund White Award for Debut Fiction, and the Kobo Emerging Writer Prize for Literary Fiction. Elliott lives in Halifax with her partner and a small black cat who may or may not be her familiar.

COME FORWARD. Step into the shadow of the lane, past Mr. Akerly's white wooden fence, past the dog tied onto a stake on the lawn of the Greene house who will bark and snap as you go by, past the hopscotch grid that has not yet faded after the summer rain. Careful of that dip in the pavement there—we need to get that fixed. Cross the green grass in front of the white house with its gable windows and peeping chimneys, up the sandstone steps and onto the porch, where it is damp and dark and the air is thick with blackflies. Breathe in. Taste the smells.

This is the place that you have heard so much about. This is the house where it happened. Five dollars, please, before we start, and be careful not to touch anything. Just to be on the safe side.

Keep close behind me as I open the door, which is unlocked. It never stays locked, this door, although the real estate agent who is trying to sell the house always makes sure she turns the key at the end of the day. In front of you is the staircase, strangely grand for such an ordinary-looking house, its shining banister curling upwards. Yes, that is the staircase where she did it. You can picture it, can't you—those poor children, falling down to the ground floor? Her husband, following? To your right is an umbrella stand, and to your left is a stain on the wall. Note the colour, and the smell. If you touched it, you would find that it is sticky.

No, I'm not saying that you *should* touch it. I just thought it bore mentioning, is all.

Keep walking. In this corridor, we have the living room, the kitchen, and the door to the garage. The garage is where she put them when she was finished, as you may have heard. What a trial that must have been! If you open the door to the garage, you may note the musty smell in the air, and a kind of faint, meaty noise like a hammer repeatedly striking a side of raw beef. Don't think too much about that. Here, I'll close it again.

The kitchen, you may note, is still a mess, its counter crowded with dirty dishes, its sink half-full of cold and scummy water. The real estate agent has tried to clean it, but every time she attempts to enter the room, she feels as though someone has taken hold of her shoulders and started screaming in her ear. She once hired a cleaning crew to come in and do the deed for her, but the only one that managed to enter the room suffered a perforated ear drum and a shattered clavicle. So the kitchen stays as it is. They say that this is where she first got the idea, that something conjured itself up out of thin air and began to pour suggestions into her ear while she was washing the supper-dishes, not long after the baby was born. They say that, but it might not be true. Here, try to go inside.

All right, all right. There's no sense crying about it. Come along, let's go to the living room. We can enter that one, although you may notice a cold spot in the middle of the floor. That is always there, even on the warmest days. That curio cabinet used to be full of porcelain collectibles, little boys playing tuba and little girls feeding geese and similar, and they were, apparently, the most valuable things in the house. A distant relative appeared soon after it happened and took them all away, presumably to sell. His ears were bleeding when he left. We think he might have tried to go into the kitchen. Someone should have stopped him, of course, but who wants that kind of trouble?

Over the mantle here, you'll see a lovely photograph of the family in happier times, all five of them. Doesn't she look lovely, standing there behind her husband in his chair? Doesn't she seem content, holding her little baby, with the twins on either side of her? It just goes to show, you never can tell about some folks. You never know who will do what to who, or why, or how. They do say that if you stare at it long enough, the children will seem to weep, and their father's smile will waver and fade into a grimace of pain, but I have never experienced that myself.

Did you hear a sound, just now? A kind of whispering noise, like folds of taffeta rubbing against itself?

Never mind.

Let's go up the stairs to the second floor, where there is less light to lift the gloom. Hang on tight to the banister, so that you don't fall before you get to the landing. There is a hole in the floor, just here, in front of the bathroom. Its origins are unknown, but if you look, you will see that it appears to be quite bottomless. I dropped a pencil into it the other day, and never heard it land. You may be tempted to put a foot into it, or a hand, just to see what happens, but I strongly advise against it. Apparently, the family cat wandered up here one night and fell into this hole. It has not been seen since, although sometimes you can hear it crying.

The bathroom itself is inaccessible. These vines that curl around the outside of the door are even thicker behind it, scabbed with perfect and poisonous flowers. If you went inside, you would be dead in minutes. They say she drowned the baby in there, though I personally do not believe it. The autopsy report said nothing about drowning.

Open the first door on the right. This is the twins' room—you can tell from the bunk beds, and from the two matching dressers tucked against the wall. The light overhead, you may note, is huge and round like a crystal ball, and cracked down the middle. That happened one day, with a sound like a gunshot, and everyone on the lane heard it, although we shouldn't have. There is nothing else much of interest here, although if you look at the plush dog on the ground, you will note that it is pulling itself towards you, slowly but surely, by one arm. There is no need to panic. It is very slow and will not reach you in time.

Open the second door on the right. This is the nursery, although it has not been that for very long. It used to be a tiny office, shared by both parents, with a desk for each of them and a little shelf full of books related to their respective careers. They had not intended to have more children when they moved in, as I understand it—the baby was a surprise. Not a welcome one, either, if you listen to rumours. Now, as you can see, the desks and bookshelf are long gone. Instead there is a crib with a blanket patterned with elephants, and a rocking chair painted green, and a chest of drawers stencilled with butterflies, and a small window with white curtains that ought to look out onto the house next door. Of course, if you step close to it and peek through the glass, you will see instead that it looks onto another house entirely. A white one, with gables and a porch. Look through the small window on the side of the house that faces you. Who is that person staring back? Don't they look an awful lot like you?

No, it's not a trick. Calm down. I am sure that, whoever

they are, they mean you no harm. If they did, you wouldn't be standing here.

Back into the hall, now, and watch your step. We are going to the final door, the one on the left at the end of the hall. Touch the doorknob—don't turn, just touch. Notice the cracks that radiate from it into the wood. Notice that as soon as your fingertips kiss the metal the knob begins to turn, slowly and with a terrible creak. Watch as the door swings open, inch by terrible inch, onto...

Well, onto not much. It is a bedroom, certainly, but not one of any real interest. The bed with its purple comforter is usual, the night tables are ordinary, the carpet nothing of note. The only thing in this room that might raise an eyebrow is the mirror hanging over the dresser, where words have been written in red lipstick. (Or is it paint?) The mirror was washed after the events occurred, but the next morning the words appeared again, swimming out of the depths of the reflection to the surface of the glass. No matter how often the mirror is cleaned, the words return. I have tried washing it myself, with vinegar and water, and they always come back.

You will see that many of the words are backwards, as though someone standing on the other side of the glass has written them. This could be so. Mr. Akerley claims that on the night it happened she was screaming about mirrors, although he did not hear precisely what she said. You may see also that a sign has been scratched into the glass, as though with the tip of a knife. You are free to examine that further, but I doubt you will make sense of it. They had a man up here, a man whose job it is to read symbols and interpret sigils, and he could not make head nor tail of it when he looked, although he did begin to complain of debilitating headaches, and a soft, persistent noise in his left ear at all times. Like someone speaking at a low volume in another room. He died last week, I hear. A stroke. There was blood in his eyes when they found him.

Let's go, finally, through this door and into the ensuite. His and hers sinks, his filled with pebbles, hers heaped with dirt. There is a worm in the heart of it there, squirming

ELLIOTT GISH

happily through the muck. All her perfumes and facial products are still lined up against the wall. She was very particular
about her skin, they say, and became even more so as things
in the house began to unravel. A family friend who visited
days before everything ended claims that during that visit,
she did nothing but slather handfuls of moisturizing lotion
onto her face and arms and belly, coating herself in a thin and
slippery film. She talked all the while, the friend says, loudly
and nervously, her gaze moving from one spot in the air to
another, following something invisible to all eyes but hers.
The baby lay in its crib upstairs, screaming ceaselessly, and
strange thumps came from the twins' room, as though a large
object were being tossed from one wall to the other.

The night that it happened, the husband came home to a
cold, dark house and found his wife sitting at the kitchen
table, still rubbing lotion into her skin. They found traces of it,
after, on the walls and on the bodies. It hadn't quite been
absorbed into the skin when she did it.

The toilet is simply a toilet. We needn't pay much attention to *that*.

Here is the shower, with its curtain pulled all the way
across. That is where she cleaned herself after it was all over,
washing away the blood and hair. And this, the reports say, is
where the trail ends. She came up the stairs, through the
bedroom, into the ensuite, took off her clothes—they are gone
now, but you can see the sticky patch on the tile where she
put them—and got into the shower to wash. She did not get
out again. When the police brought in dogs to chase down
her scent, they all ended up crowded into the ensuite, sniffing
at the shower curtain, whining like puppies. It is as though
she melted in the water like a sugar cube. Or got sucked
down the drain, washed away along with the gore and the
mess. Were you afraid of that as a child—of going down the
drain when the stopper was pulled? I know I was.

No, there's been no trace of her since that day. They put a
watch on the house for a while, in case she came back, but it's
been months now and no sign of her. No activity on any

cards, no logins on any of her accounts. She really does seem to have vanished.

Yes, that shower curtain does look like it is moving slightly, doesn't it? Just the air from the vent. There's one right over the bathtub.

That's it. That's the tour. Not much of an ending, I'm afraid, but that is the way of such things, isn't it? We always want these places to force something into light, to make sense of a senseless thing. But the house where it happened is just that: a house. It is the site of the thing, not the cause. The stage and not the play. To understand what happened, we would need to see what she saw, to hear what she heard. I—

The curtain is definitely moving.

Time to go. Let's step backwards, now, nice and easy, into the master bedroom. Do not look at the mirror. Do not touch the door as we tiptoe into the hall. Do not peek into the nursery, or the twins' room. Step over the hole on the landing. Take the stairs carefully but quickly, two at a time, and if you feel anything underfoot, if anything reaches out to grasp your shoulder, if you hear someone speaking at a low volume in another room, don't stop. Past the living room and the kitchen, ignoring the sound coming from the garage—that meaty thump, over and over—ignoring the stain on the wall, ignoring the cold wind that blows from somewhere behind you, ignoring all of it. Open the door. Step over the threshold. Close your eyes as you cross and gratefully await the thick dark of the porch, the taste of cool, fresh air.

Open your eyes.

In front of you is the staircase. Behind you the front door shuts and locks.

This is the house where it happened.

THE RUINS WITH A SPECTATOR

KAARON WARREN

Originally published in *The Mad Butterfly's Ball*.

Shirley Jackson award-winner **Kaaron Warren** published her first short story in 1993 and has had fiction in print every year since. She has published six multi-award winning novels: *Slights, Walking the Tree, Mistification, The Grief Hole, Tide of Stone* and *The Underhistory* and seven short story collections, her most recent being *Spirit Level*, an artbook with Monica Carroll. Her stories have been shortlisted for the World Fantasy Award and the Stoker, and appeared in both Ellen Datlow's and Paula Guran's *Year's Best* anthologies. Her writing podcast *Let the Cat In* showcases ideas, objects, and inspirations. Her latest novel *The Underhistory*, from Viper Books, was described in the Guardian as 'a beautifully constructed, suspenseful gothic tale.'

AFTER THE FIRES, all that remained of Mollison's property was his barn. He'd been dealing antiques for years, buying cheap, pretending he was selling family heirlooms, asking high prices. I loved the guy; he was one of my favourite people, with his cranky demeanour, his dusty clothes, the way he smelled of caramel. If I ever had to play a cantankerous old man, he'd be my role model.

I had always found Mollison good to deal with. He was too old to be bothered with niceties, but he was truthful, something I very much appreciated. I wasn't much good at either telling lies myself, or about catching others out in lies. You'd think an actor would be good at deception, but I'm not a very good actor. My girlfriend Gloria couldn't stand the sight of him, although she liked the quirkiness of the items he sold, especially the stopped clocks and the wristwatches with damaged faces. She was obsessed with the concept of time, and how it passes, and fame, and how that passes as well. I was devastated to hear about the fires. There was stuff we'd had our eyes on, waiting for him to budge on price, and now it was all gone. He had the barn, though, and I knew he had some big pieces in there. He'd be happy to sell, surely. Gloria didn't want to come with me to look, said she couldn't bear to see the destruction and that was typical of her. She was very good at putting on the blinders, narrowing her world to a single plate of fruit, one song playing, one short movie to watch, ignoring all else around her.

It was one of the things I loved most about her.

The destruction of Mollison's 200-year-old farmhouse was complete. It was nothing but a smouldering pile. I could see metal legs poking out of the debris—the remains of his old wood fire stove—and melted glass discs that were once bottles. He'd stacked books in one area, all of them burnt through, some with the covers still intact, most slowly disintegrating as the wind rose and fell. There were insects everywhere.

"They'll eat it to the ground before long. They're always like this after a fire."

He actually seemed happy, relieved of the burden of ownership.

The door to the barn stuck and he had to push hard, shaking loose a dry wasps' nest and tearing aside many months' worth of spiderwebs. Inside it was light and surprisingly airy.

"I've held this for you," Mollison said. It was a table Gloria and I had been looking at for a while, big enough to seat ten, solid oak with Art Deco legs and a suitably "lived in" surface. There were small scratches here and there, and one large gouge in one corner. He named a price that was very fair. Neither of us mentioned the fact he'd brought it down; I didn't want to remind him of that and perhaps he didn't want to be reminded.

"We're not really in the market for a dining table." I was, but, unlike him, I wasn't too old and tired to bargain. We came to a happy agreement.

"Anything else you want? Fifty bucks, fill your truck."

I took a plough, a heap of rusted metal and three barrels. They'd go great in the garden. Or I'd make a dining set out of them.

I called a couple of mates to come help with the table and they scored as well; tool boxes good as new, wrought-iron fence pieces, an antique something or other and more. He wanted to sell the barn and the land to us. "It'll be cheap," he said, but greed took over and he refused to budge from the ridiculous figure he named.

"Come back for more," he said, a catch of something in his voice. Loneliness, perhaps? Wishing he was young, one of us, coming with us? We left him with a six-pack of beer and fistfull of cash, and I don't think I've ever seen him looking happier.

He'd said, "Heat'll wake the critters up. Hotter the air, happier they are. They'll be cleaning up our mess once we've all gone," and in the rear view mirror the rising heat of the day made it seem as if a cloud of insects was descending upon him.

GLORIA and I cleared out the dining area (mostly moving

boxes we hadn't yet unpacked) and somehow manoeuvred the large table in.

"The fact we did that without killing each other means we'll do okay," she said.

"Did you doubt that?" I'd been feeling settled up until then, secure that she wouldn't leave me.

She distracted me by pulling out the vodka, and we ordered Thai food for our first meal at the dinner table, inviting a few friends over. It was good the surface of the table was already damaged; it meant we didn't have to worry about it.

A FEW NIGHTS LATER, I got home late after drinks with a couple of producers and a casting director. I'd crashed the party, so I'd been on my best behaviour and looking like a star. I overheard the casting director say, "How old is he again?" but I didn't know if that was a good thing or a bad thing. Bad, surely. Every wrinkle, every lump, the sag under my chin; all duly noted. On the way home I Googled "Botox. Face. Treatment. Regenerate". *It's never too late!* all the advertising said.

It was hot, the kind of heat that still burns even when the sun has set. Gloria was already in bed. She was usually up late but she'd had a hard day at work, the Christmas rush meaning she was run off her feet. She'd left me a plate of salad to eat but I was full of beer and chips, also still full of energy, so I flopped in front of the TV. I was asleep within a few minutes, I think, our retro '70s floor lamp not keeping me awake.

Our TV turns itself off automatically when it senses no movement in the room. Deep in my sleep, I heard a scratching sound, a biting. The sound woke me, freaked me out. The TV was blank, just the flicker of the red standby button.

The noise was coming from the old table. I didn't dare move. I could hear chewing, the sound of wood splintering in the still night.

In the lamp's low light I thought I saw movement around the table's legs. I crept close and held my phone out, torch on, angled away.

I watched as a pair of insect legs emerged from the wood. Then a head the size of my thumbnail, with visible fangs, and then the whole thing pulled out of the wood and dropped to the floor.

Thinking fast, I emptied my water glass (beauty tip: always hydrate before bed) and upended it onto the creature before it could scuttle away.

The sound increased. More were emerging. I raced to grab more glasses and call Gloria, "You-Have-Got-To-See-This!!! Bring-Your-phone. You wanna film it."

A light sleeper, she was there in seconds, fully professional as she captured more of them emerging, then writhing under glass as I caught them.

"This is going to be brilliant for my documentary," she said, and I loved her dearly enough not to say I knew that.

GLORIA POSTED short clips all over her social media, trying to create a buzz. Hashtag *It's about Time documentary*. Hashtag *working title*. Hashtag *Deathwatch beetles*. Hashtag *hearing the passage of time*. She got a heap of feedback but no sponsorship offers, sadly. She pushed it, talking about her themes. "It's called Fishtime/Birdtime/insect time. Things happen faster when the life cycle is so much quicker. It's about extinction, and the cycles of time. It's about survival. It's about we will die, and we are all killers. It's in our nature."

All people wanted to talk about was that we should get our money back on the table. Gloria wanted me to call Mollison's to see if we could replace it (now she had her footage, she wanted the table out of the house) so I called the care home he'd ended up in. I'd tell Gloria I mentioned the table but what was the point? He had no room for it there. We chatted, but I could tell the oomph had gone out of him. He was full of nonsense, buzzing like a dying fly.

———

WHEN A PRODUCER finally returned her call, he wouldn't even let her speak. "You've got too much going on in this. Viewers want one train of thought to follow; you've got like fifty."

"Not fifty," she said. "But there are SOME. There are complex issues I'm exploring here. A swarm of ideas, if you will."

He wouldn't. "Time's passed on this one. Find your next idea. This one is dead in the water. You need some kind of clear gimmick."

"The gimmick is that everything changes," she said to the dead line. It didn't matter. She was going to keep at the documentary, with or without studio backing. She did get a couple of interesting invitations, though. One was for a small museum where they made war dioramas out of insects "And yours will be a most welcome addition to our Austerlitz 1805 scene. This way they will live forever!" There was no way I was letting the bugs get stuffed or varnished or whatever they'd do. So, it was the second invitation we followed up.

———

WE DROVE THROUGH A BATTERED LANDSCAPE. Floods had destroyed the road edges, which meant we all drove closer to the centre line, causing me more anxiousness than I normally felt. I had to keep the windscreen wipers on the whole time; the gnats and other bugs seemed to constantly die against the glass. We stopped along the way at a roadside café, where I took the chance to rinse all the tiny bodies off. Gloria grabbed us both coffees and a sausage roll, and we sat in the car, watching the other travellers for a while.

"We're nearly there," she said. She'd been secretive about the destination, filming me along the way, wanting my reactions. "I don't want you to ACT. I want you to be."

"I can be, whenever I want to," I said. She kissed me, filmed my reaction, then checked her phone. "Nearly there."

It looked like a failed attempt at a castle. Grey brick, three or four storeys high depending on if you counted the turrets, it was festooned with colourful flags and, strangely, looked inviting. The lawns were covered with flowers and, as I turned off the car, I could hear the glorious buzz of bees.

We were met by a well-dressed woman who opened her eyes wide at me. People do that, sometimes out of pure attraction, sometimes because they want you to think they're attracted. I wasn't sure with her.

"Welcome! I'm Melitta," she said.

"Isn't that a coffee?" I whispered to Gloria, but she didn't even acknowledge me. She held up the wooden box with our table insects skittering inside it.

"Wonderful. We promise not to hurt them. They'll go into our breeding programme, at the start at least."

I still didn't know what the place was. Gloria did and I couldn't figure out why she wouldn't tell me.

"And we have this specimen too," the woman said, turning her gaze back at me. "We won't hurt you, either!"

Gloria said, "I haven't quite filled him in yet." The woman gave her the stoniest glare I've ever seen.

"In that case, we better spend some time together. We're in the beauty and health business, Kane. We don't want to put too fine a point on it, but a healthy body is a healthy mind, a gorgeous body, and a healthy sex life. Not that Gloria says there are any problems there."

Gloria had wandered off, but she was clearly filming from afar.

"We are great admirers here of insects. Of how they live and die, how they heal. Their adaptability, their self-protection and just, well, everything about them."

We'd reached a garden atrium. Gloria had joined us and the three of us sat at a rusty outdoor setting. A young man in a very impressive insect embroidered shirt brought us drinks that turned out to be gin slings. I'd have killed for a beer but you take what you can get. The woman handed me a menu.

"I'm not sure we're planning to stay for lunch," I said.

"Keep reading."

With Gloria looking over my shoulder, I read.

HERE AT METAMORPHOSIS we not only admire the insect world, we replicate it to facilitate healing, weight loss, reinvigoration and more. We offer five services here at Metamorphosis.

The Silverfish Swim for skin tone, facial purity, and all over glow.

The honey dew Blood Cleanser, for you guessed it.

The Beautiful Cup Moth Caterpillar Connection, for a better sex life.

Surprise Feast, designed to speed metabolism, for sluggishness and weight loss.

Comforting Cocoon, for full regeneration.

GLORIA LOOKED AT ME, and at the list, and at me. She ran her fingers over the symptoms, her fingers running over the words, her face registering each one.

"You know what?" she said. I cringed inwardly. Usually when she said that there was trouble for me; some kind of long walk, or a diet, or meeting some old school friend of hers she'd never admit was an old boyfriend but of course he bloody was.

I did it all to appease her, to keep her, because she was too good for me and everyone knew it, including me.

"You know what?" she said, and, "Listen. This is so perfect for the documentary. Because what's all this health and healing stuff if not about stopping time and decay and aging and death? We film you doing all the things, before and after! It'll take six weeks, but only parts of it are residential."

I hated the idea.

She said, "There will need to be some re-enactments, some acting involved, so good for your CV and whatever."

I knew she was manipulating me; of course I knew. She already had this in place. But still. Could I call this a job? Seriously put it on my head shot, "such films as"?

"You'll get some good shots of me?"

"My darling, you are so photogenic no one could take a bad shot of you. It'll be great."

What I heard was, "I'll love you more."

THE SILVERFISH SWIM FOR SKIN TONE, FACIAL PURITY, AND ALL OVER GLOW

Silverfish are so gross. But also amazing. They've adapted over millions of years or maybe thousands; their spare legs have become jaws. They have three pairs of jaws! And you can see even more legs on their gross little underbellies. Like humans—we have a bit of a tail left, they reckon. I had the chance to see them up close. These things always gave me the creeps, anyway, with their shiny bodies, finding small nests of them amongst destroyed clothing. And the awful, dusty residue they left behind.

"That's what we're harvesting," Melitta said. "We sweep it up into little containers, mix it with lanolin, and use it for wrinkles and blemishes, especially sun spots on the face. You'll dab it on."

She sent me into the silverfish enclosure where the whole room was writhing with them, feeding on rags. She had me lie down and let them crawl all over me; they wanted to collect the residue right off my skin. I was naked, of course.

The silverfish weren't interested in my tears.

"Brilliant, brilliant stuff," Gloria was saying as I emerged after all the silverfish dust had been scraped off me, a soft white robe wrapped around me. But she wasn't talking to me. I could hear the producer's loud voice.

"Yep, that's the gimmick we are looking for. Making your boyfriend suffer for your art; love it."

She didn't say, "He's not my boyfriend." The relief of that made me forgive her the rest of it.

THE HONEY DEW BLOOD CLEANSER, FOR YOU GUESSED IT

This place was called 'The Room of Symbiosis', they said. They told me the silverfish would have prepared me for this but honestly nothing would have. There are a whole set of insects that live on what they call "honey dew", which is a very disgusting name once you know what it describes. It's the waste product of other insects which for humans is, apparently, sweat.

"We aren't going to let them eat your waste products, but they will eat your sweat and any mites on your skin," they said. They fed me sweet sweet tea, lemonade, they made me eat so many jelly beans I wanted to leap around like a five-year-old, all with the intention of turning my sweat from salt to sweet.

Naked again (and stupidly I didn't mind, knowing how it would look on my show reel) they gave me something to make me sleep, because they said they wanted the night sweats.

———

I FELT A TICKLING sensation but from far away, as if a memory. My tongue was thick in my mouth like the morning after a big night on the vodka. Whatever they gave me kept me frozen in place; there were so many thousands of insects all over me, creeping, sucking, tickling. I felt a strange sense of calm, though, even though it was disgusting. I would tell Gloria this was it; I didn't want to do the rest. Going through that conversation (and imagining the sex we'd have afterwards, when I forgave her for putting me through this) kept me quiet.

THE BEAUTIFUL CUP MOTH CATERPILLAR CONNECTION, FOR A BETTER SEX LIFE

I didn't get the chance to talk to Gloria. She was editing, they said. I was to stay overnight and go straight into the next treatment. They fed me pretty good food and set me up with computer games and a bottle of wine.

Another man came and sat in the room, in the corner on a chair that frankly looked prickly and uncomfortable. He winced, cupped his cheek with his hand.

"Toothache?"

"It'll be better soon." He opened his mouth, although I didn't want to look, and pointed. "Can you see them?" He told me to use my phone magnifier and why did I listen? Why did I look at it? Because up close I could see tiny insects in a hole in his tooth, scurrying, wriggling. I could smell the decay.

"Once they've cleaned it up the dentist will fill it," he said. "And these fat little chappies will go back to dead bodies." He asked me what week I was up to and I said three.

He nodded. "Those hairy mother-fuckers," he said, and then the bastard left the room.

TURNS out we were looking at a form of acupuncture via cup-moth caterpillar. Its defences are that its hairs will break off on entering your skin, and sit in there, painful and almost invisible. It made me anxious, the idea of invisible pain. Not that pain is visible, but the cause, that you can usually see.

Gloria came along to encourage me. She told me I was

doing brilliantly, that the producer was already talking wide release, that this would even help me, not just her career or whatever.

The practitioner didn't need me to strip off. It was only the soles of my feet he was interested in. The caterpillars were in a large glass case. They were actually beautiful; brightly coloured and weird, with those spikes ready to poke me. "They are utterly cram-packed with curatives," the practitioner said. "Anti-bacterial, anti-parasitical, the works. All of that is stuff that can affect your systems, especially the blood, and if we can purify it, you are just gonna glow from the inside. It does hurt, though," he said.

There have been points in my life where I know I'm making a bad choice, but I don't have the energy or strength to back out. He was so sure this was right, and okay, then I just let it happen.

I've never, ever felt anything more painful and I once had my foot run over by a car. It was sharp, sudden, and literally took over my entire body. I tried to pull my feet out but the practitioner patted me. "Take it slow," he said. "If you frighten them they'll drop more spines, and that's the dose that can kill you." Using gloves, he flicked them all off my feet then helped me lift myself out of there. I lay my feet on another chair, feeling feverish. Gloria entered and took close-up footage of the soles of my feet.

"Incredible stuff. Just incredible. You are so hot right now," she said. It took about three hours for the pain to subside but we'd started so early, there was plenty of time for a drive to the fancy hotel Gloria had booked us, and room service, and a cheesy car race movie, and good, good sex.

SURPRISE FEAST, DESIGNED TO SPEED UP THE METABOLISM, FOR SLUGGISHNESS AND WEIGHT LOSS

Admittedly, I felt great. I'm not sure which part of it all helped, but I felt healthier than I have in a long while and more confident. My agent had me take new headshots; he said I was looking younger.

So, when the message came that we'd gather for a special dinner before the next phase began, I decided to go. I'd previously decided NOT to go, NOT to move forward, because it hadn't been enjoyable. Not the treatment part, anyway. But the peripherals were good; the meals in between, the conversations, the house itself and the beautiful yards.

It was a free-for all, pot-luck dinner, all invited. They recommended bringing loved ones along; I didn't even have to ask Gloria, she was already picking out her outfit, a gossamer-like skirt which looked like it was made of moths' wings, and a dark purple vest, almost a corset, that was very sexy. "You don't mind if we film?" she asked me. She already had approval from the clinic.

I called Mollison on a whim, thinking he might enjoy something like that. Shockingly, the whole care home had shut down. The security guard who answered me said there'd been an insect infestation which rendered the place uninhabitable. "Was anyone a relative?" he asked, before telling me that close to half the inhabitants had died.

This threw me. I thought of that old man, confident in himself, but lonely. I wish I'd seen him again, told him about his table bugs, what they'd led to. I wish we had him on film, an interview about his life.

"He's not your dad," Gloria said. She thought that might cheer me up.

———

THERE WAS a big crowd for the dinner. The table was laden with food, from "wood-laced vegetables", apparently from some insect's fungus garden. There were fried crickets and chocolate-covered ants. There were bowls of fried rice and lobster and flaky pastries and just a wild array of food. Gloria filmed the whole thing.

Afterwards, Melitta said, "Interestingly, you've all just been poisoned! Goethe said, 'There's no such thing as poison, it all depends on the dose.' Poison can cure or kill. It's always been so. And so many of our insects can kill or cure us."

I felt a bit ill. Gloria looked quite pale; she'd had second helpings and that probably wasn't a good idea.

Melitta said, "Now I've mentioned it, you'll feel your skin flush, you might have trouble breathing, and your pulse will race. All of that is normal. If we'd given you any more, we might be looking at jail sentences. But this is just enough to make a tingle, give you a buzz. Make you feel alive."

GLORIA WAS TOO ill to film that night and I tried to care for her. We had to keep the light off, though; so many moths were in the building now, they'd flutter into the light at a constant rate.

COMFORTING COCOON, FOR FULL REGENERATION

I got cocooned on the fifth visit. I'd been having nightmares about suffocating, in dozens of different ways. Melitta said, "That's normal. It's a normal fear. It's part of the trans-formation."

I asked Gloria to let Mollison know and she looked at me as she often did; you pathetic little man. I wouldn't ask her to contact my parents because she hated them after how they treated her (I can't even remember now, to be honest, about it all) but Mollison and my father knew each other way back. I wasn't about to tell my mates what I was doing. They'd take it upon themselves to come rescue me, for sure.

I was complicating things. Melitta said, "Let things go, now. I can see your mind going a hundred miles an hour! The calm you'll feel soon will be wonderful."

She'd told me I would not be conscious in the cocoon. That my mind would be at rest for that short time. She emphasised short. And that I would emerge a new man.

THEY HAD ME "VOID MY BOWELS", and I had nothing to eat or drink for twenty-four hours. I wouldn't need anything. And if I woke up and wanted to get out, I could pull the strands of the cocoon apart, they told me. Use my fingernails to get myself out. But they didn't think I'd want to.

I was fully aware of my surroundings as I was wrapped. It felt sticky and soft. It smelt a bit like ants, a bit like my table insects. A chemical smell that wasn't harsh. I'd never felt so comforted in all my life. So safe. All I had to do was stay still, not making any strange moves.

GLORIA SAT by her cocooned boyfriend, filming, for ninety minutes. She set up a camera to film twenty-four hours a day while he was in the cocoon. Outside, in what should have been bright sunlight, she turned her personal camera on herself. "When I embarked on this documentary, I thought I'd be analysing how time works for insects. Instead, I ended up here. I'll never be the same." She said, "I thought I could help save the world." She shivered. The sun was blocked again and the chill was really setting in. "There are dark skies today, as time passes over us."

TIME DID PASS. It was a week, then two. They assured her there was no health risk, that he was receiving nutrients, that he would be utterly transformed, a new man, the best ever made.

She said to her camera, "There are millions of creatures sleeping right now. One day they will awaken and there is nothing we can do about that." Her footage showed that dark sky, thick with wings, filled with locusts beyond number, then she said, "Today we can only—

HE WAS AWAKENED BY LIGHT. Threadbare now, the cocoon let in light. Instinctively, he poked a finger in the thinnest part. His nail was long and sharp, meaning he could easily tear a hole, reaching around with his other hand to rip it apart. He was weak but this didn't take any strength.

HIS COCOON WAS on the ground and he crawled out. The floor was overrun with insects, as was every surface, and the walls, what were left of them. Something had happened; a bomb had gone off, something, because one wall was gone, and part of the roof. He sucked in a lungful of air and it hurt, seared him, after whatever he'd been breathing in his cocoon.

Through the shattered floor-length window he saw and he heard the locusts. He dragged himself there and outside, ignoring, not feeling, the broken glass. There were mounds of dead insects everywhere, and bones. There was the smell of nectar and of honey. He was suddenly ravenous but his teeth ached, and when he lifted a finger to touch them they were soft, like candy, and they crumbled in his mouth.

He tried to stand. Some part of him thought he should be able to fly but he could barely walk, and he stumbled onwards as the insects swarmed over him, looking for honey dew and finding it, sucking up his sweat and wanting more.

His bones turned to jelly, his lungs to dust, but he glimpsed the sun in his last moments and that, at least, gave him comfort.

HE DANCES ALONE

JOANNE ANDERTON

Originally published in *Shadowplays*.

Joanne Anderton is an Australian author of speculative fiction, creative nonfiction, and children's books. Her speculative fiction includes *Pixerina*, a haunted house novella set in the Australian suburbs (coming in 2026 from Bad Hand Books), the novels in the *Veiled Worlds* series—*Debris, Suited,* and *Guardian*—and the short story collections *The Art of Broken Things, Inanimates: Tales of Everyday Fear,* and *The Bone Chime Song and Other Stories.* She has won multiple awards for her speculative fiction, including the Australian Shadows Award, Ditmar and Aurealis Awards. Joanne has a PhD in Creative Writing, and worked for many years in book publishing, sales, marketing and distribution. You can find her online at Joanneanderton.com.

OUR STORY BEGINS on a mild autumn morning, before the first of the leaves had started to golden, somewhere in those in-between weeks when heat still weighed on the air. It was late in the year to be so warm. There were whispers of drought, because without the cold there would be no snow and the rivers that relied on its runoff were thirsty. Such things were almost unheard of.

On this morning our protagonist was walking through her adopted hometown in rural Japan to the senior high school where she was employed as an English language teacher. She did this trip five days a week and knew the path well, had made friends with local cats and old women, and was even starting to feel like she belonged.

An astute reader might stop here and think, ah, she allowed herself to feel a sense of belonging, did she? That had to be her first mistake.

It's a fair enough assumption to make, but they'd be wrong.

So what was it, then? the same astute reader might ask.

Her first mistake? Believing this was her story at all.

THE SCHOOL WAS five minutes from our protagonist's home, down a narrow road made for pedestrians and cyclists. Houses backed onto the path, providing her a view of neat gardens that had become an unexpected highlight. Never before had she seen so many flowers in so many shapes and colours. Tiny bells, bright red. Little sunbursts, vibrant purple. They grew in every available inch, some tended, some wild.

She doesn't know it yet, but even in the depths of winter, when the trees are bare and the grass dead, there will be hardy pink flowers riding out the chill. And when spring arrives, dragged kicking and screaming, it feels to an Australian unused to winters that ache the way this winter will ache her, the bare limbs of a large bonsai will bud, and she'll realise it's a plum tree.

There was a point in her short walk where she passed the school tennis courts, before ducking through the back gate near the carpark and canteen. And that is where our story really begins, because that is where she saw *him.*

His white sneakers scuffed and squeaked on the hardcourt as he weaved a slow waltz in the early sun. Arms raised, hands gently cupped as though cradling invisible fingers, swaying to no music she could hear. A slow smooth step, without hint of age or stiffness, though what little she could see of him looked quite ancient. Loose tracksuit pants a size too big, black sweat-slicking material with white zippers up the side. The jacket to match. Wispy grey hair peeked out from the lip of a rust-coloured beanie. His face was hidden behind a surgical mask and large sunglasses.

Our protagonist spared the old man a quick glance, no longer surprised by his presence. The first time she saw him she was certainly taken aback, so much that she paused to stare. Then, feeling rude and trying to ingratiate herself with the locals, her new neighbours, she lifted a hand and gave a little wave, called good morning—"*Ohaiyo gozaimasu!*" That first time, and on all subsequent attempts, she was ignored, so gave up.

But that didn't stop her looking for him, every morning. The old man dancing in the tennis courts, alone.

Usually alone.

Maybe she was a little early that day, because for once the courts weren't empty. A group of second-year girls were practicing serves all around him, chattering like birds, slamming balls into nets and giggling.

One of them noticed our protagonist as she stood there, watching. "Hello sensei!" the girl cried out, waving her racket. "Good morning!" Fifteen or sixteen years old, dressed in the school sports uniform of blue shorts and white polo shirt.

That was heartening. Our protagonist encouraged her students to practice English at every available opportunity, tried to get them feeling less self-conscious about the whole thing. She had been teaching these girls for two months now, and while their faces were familiar she did not know their names. This early on in her short-lived teaching career she still believed that she would, with time, be able to learn them all.

"Good morning!" she called in reply, waved back, and was rewarded with a cascade of nervous laughter. "How are you?"

Enthusiastic. That's what her Japanese colleagues call her. You, Protagonist-sensei, are very enthusiastic. She has not yet learned that this is code, or what it stands for.

"I am fine," the same girl replied. She was tall, hair tied back in a high ponytail, voice deep. Athletic and confident.

"Have fun playing tennis." There was a scent in the air, something sweet. Almost sickly. It seemed to drift in from the surrounding streets. Our protagonist turned to continue into the school grounds, then paused. "Be careful... Don't hit... You know. He's old ... just, careful."

Growing steadily more confused with every stuttered word, the girls gaped at her. Our protagonist opened her mouth, frowned, closed it. Don't hit the old man with your tennis ball suddenly seemed too complicated a sentence.

And now we come to the point of this scene. The crux.

Because the old man, he was still dancing. The whole time he just kept going. Weaving between the students and their teacher, crossing their lines of sight. Straying close to the girls, then drifting away.

Isn't that a bit odd, our protagonist thought to herself.

"Um." She pointed in his general direction even though that seemed impolite. How else was she supposed to make herself understood? "You need to be careful. When you're practicing serve. Make sure ... you know ... you don't hit..." Why was she tripping over her words like that?

Smiles slipped off the nameless faces staring back at her. Even as the old man danced around them, seemingly danced through them, their blank expressions were more unsettled by her words, her presence, everything about her, than him.

Music crackled out of a loudspeaker, perched high on a pole at the end of the walkway. The town council's morning tune. Distorted and sharp, it made her wince. Whatever music the old man was dancing to, it wasn't this. His feet scuffed slow and steady, utterly out of time.

AH, you think, I get what's happening now. The old man's a ghost or something, because those girls, they didn't see him. Guess that means he's really the main character, and we're about to learn whatever tragedy trapped him on this plane.

Sorry, not this time.

The old man, he has even less ownership of this story. He's a prompt, that's all, one that startled our protagonist's imagination and got her wondering *who, or what, is that old man dancing with?*

And that, dear astute reader, is what started the whole thing.

SPEAKING OF GHOSTS, did you know our protagonist feels like one, sometimes? She's got a desk in the staffroom—the *shokuinshitsu*—and when she's not in front of a class teaching that's where she can be found.

There are days where she can sit there, alone at that desk, and not speak a word to anyone at all.

But not all her days are like that—don't feel too sorry for her. She teaches first, second and third years, and there are eight classes in each year, so some days she's run off her feet, rushing from lesson to lesson, bouncing between languages, no time to even stop for lunch.

The day in question was one such day. Fourth period and she was teaching 2-8, a group of second years the Japanese teachers called "demons". The kids in 2-8 were creative, energetic, maybe a little troubled, though she couldn't be sure about their mental states. Definitely louder than most. Despite their reputation they quickly became her favourite because they'd take whatever challenge she threw at them and run with it, caring less about perfection, feeling less the weight of expectation, more willing to make mistakes, which is, of course, the only way to learn.

She yearned to take a page out of their collective book. Still does.

On that day she began class with a simple vocab exercise then moved to something more interesting. "Too complicated," according to one of the Japanese teachers of English she was working with. But unusually for our protagonist, who was constantly worried about making a good impression, she dismissed his misgivings and forged ahead.

She'd found a pack of cards in the drawer of her desk, left over from a predecessor. On each was printed a word in English, along with a picture of that thing. Dog, for instance. King. Flowers. Coffee.

"Let's play a game," she said, showing off her ability to shuffle. "And make up a story."

She split the class into groups of four, and had every child pick a card. For the next ten minutes, in their groups, they used the words on the cards to invent a tale. It could be anything, she tried to explain, no matter how short, no matter how silly or strange.

She wrote an example on the board. "Once upon a time there was a *king*. He drinks *coffee* in the morning. The king owns a *dog*. The dog eats *flowers*."

At this point the other classes had hesitated. They were used to memorising and repeating, didn't have much experience with creativity. But not the "demonic" 2-8.

Excited conversation filled the room, so loud at times it disturbed their neighbours. Protagonist-sensei and her teacher wandered around the room, offering assistance and clarifying definitions. At the end of the lesson each group elected a speaker to stand and read out their story.

"Once upon a time, there is a *man* who has *scissors*. His name was scissor-man. He was good at playing sports, especially baseball and *soccer*. His hobby was to cut *banana* into pieces with scissors."

"There was a *cat* which can play *violin*. The cat was hungry so she ate a *bird* and a *strawberry*."

Protagonist-sensei couldn't have been prouder of her experimental lesson and was feeling just a little smug at how well it had gone.

At this point I'll pause to say I know what you're thinking —pride comes before a fall—because this time you're right.

The final group, sitting up the back, was the only quiet one in the room. Four awkward students who rarely engaged in class and had somehow ended up together. When it came to their turn and—with a sinking feeling in her stomach— Protagonist-sensei asked them to read their story, they said nothing.

She could have let it slide. It was almost the end of the lesson and she didn't want to make their lives any harder than they already were. But her colleague would not. He strode to their table, snapped at them in Japanese, picked up the empty paper they were supposed to have written on, and waved it in their faces.

The poor kids sunk into their seats and said nothing. Protagonist-sensei, feeling like she needed to save the situation, hurried over to scoop up their cards. "Let me help you!" she cried.

So enthusiastic.

"Ghost. Ring. Girl. Music." She wrote their words on the board with a red marker. "Those are hard words," she said, looking over her shoulder, trying to catch the eye of at least one of them. "What if I get us started?"

She made a show of thinking. "Hmm…" Finger to chin, eliciting a few giggles from the other students. "Once upon a time there was a *girl*." She wrote as neatly and quickly as she could. "A boy gave her a pretty *ring*." The image of the old man, dancing alone, was rattling around in her head still. "They danced to *music*." It inserted itself into this simple narrative, this lesson for children. "But then—" And started to take over. "—he—" The story wasn't hers anymore. "— killed her—" She couldn't control it, couldn't stop it. "—and now she's a *ghost*."

A hush had fallen over the boisterous students. Even the teacher looked shocked.

"Err… And now they dance together. Forever. The end."

Our protagonist, suddenly feeling chilled, tried to cover this vastly inappropriate mistake with a laugh. She wiped the words from the board with the edge of her hand, smearing fragrant red ink into her skin.

The electronic bell chimed, made discordant by the tension in the room. As one the students stood, pushing chairs back, to bow at their teachers. Their eyes followed our protagonist as she left.

And what she'd written on that board—whoever's story she'd opened a door onto—followed.

WE ARE each the protagonists of our own stories. But some of us have to fight for ownership.

There's a girl now who didn't exist until the moment someone made her up. The man who killed her has been dancing with her ghost for decades. Trapped in his embrace, she struggles to be more than his object of desire, his possession.

The ring he placed on her finger, when they were both young and she was hopeful, chains her to him. To this place. It was in these damned tennis courts where she spent her final moments, so here she remains.

"Never more beautiful," he whispered in her ear, and smeared blood on her lips and held her upright and forced her to waltz as the life slid out of her, warm and wet.

Except she knows none of it is true.

If she thinks hard enough, she remembers that she was never alive to begin with. Less even than an object of desire, she's nothing but a figment of someone else's imagination.

And that's not fair.

Rage bubbles within her and she clings to it, draws strength from it, determined to fight for her own story. And find a way to be real.

IF ONLY OUR protagonist had been paying attention when she left school that afternoon she could have been looking at the tennis courts. At the man, still dancing there. She might have seen the way the line between path and court, concrete to hard green, had grown wobbly around the edges. Even he looked different, mirrored by some ghostly shadow, like a poorly exposed photograph.

But she saw none of this, because a voice called from the darkening carpark and distracted her. "Protagonist-sensei!"

She turned to see a teacher half-jogging towards her, arm raised and waving. This man was not one of the English-language teachers she worked with but a maths teacher she had smiled at and spoken to a couple of times. His attention was a surprise.

"Home now, Protagonist-sensei?" he asked. A young man and fit, in charge of the soccer club, he wasn't out of breath.

"*Hai*, sensei." She'd been introduced to him on her first day but couldn't remember his name. "You?" Embarrassed by her poor Japanese she tended to speak in English, which meant they'd not shared many words at all.

"Soon." He reached up to rub the back of his head, a self-conscious gesture that gave him a school-boy vibe. Very anime.

The woman who'd had this job before her, our protagonist's *senpai*, had a particular fondness for this teacher. His boyish good looks, aware though he was of them, his fumbling attempts at English. Protagonist-sensei had recently discovered a particular fondness for an entirely different teacher. She wasn't yet sure what to make of those feelings.

But that's not what this story is about.

"Protagonist-sensei, you like drink at *izakaya*? At a bar?"

You can see why, then, our protagonist wasn't paying enough attention that evening. Such a surprise invitation was enough to distract anyone from an old man on a tennis court, still dancing.

But no longer alone.

THE STORIES WE TELL OURSELVES, the silent ones in our heads that we never put to paper, or breath, do they know they are imagined?

So there's this girl, right? Late teens, sporty, quiet at school except around her friends when she's loud and passionate and bossy, even. Boys make her nervous, but there's this one young man from town she feels comfortable with. Older than she is, already in college, but he went to the same high school and volunteers at the tennis club.

He's helping with her serve. She likes the way he smells, the hint of sweat beneath deodorant. She likes his patience. His skill.

Serve by serve, game by game, they get closer. He sneaks her into clubs so they can dance through the night, walks her home in the predawn. Does nothing without her invitation, her express permission; she sets the pace and loves it. But she wasn't ready for the consequences. And while he might have been an honourable man and done the honourable thing, her father, her mother, her friends, they all drop her like a stone as soon as she's too far gone to hide.

He's the one who finds her, the night she spills her own blood across the service line. He gathers her up, calls to her to come back to him, to dance with him.

Swaying in his arms, then and for the rest of his days, she turns her vacant face on a limp neck. Looks beyond the gate, pins her gaze on the woman standing there, staring in, daring to invent her.

And smiles.

AS IT TURNED OUT, the *izakaya* was in a building our protagonist had walked past many times, but unable to read the hand-written *kanji* sign she had never opened the door. Once inside she could feel eyes on her, wary, but not unfriendly.

"Protagonist-sensei!"

She plastered on a smile and approached the small collection of teachers.

The *izakaya* was tiny, cramped and cigarette-smoke heavy. Small wooden tables with mismatched chairs congregated at random intervals. There was a bar with fresh fish, octopuses, and prawns on ice, behind a curved glass cabinet. Black and white family photos on the walls, a faded poster advertising Hawaii.

"*Konbanwa*," she said, good evening, giving a small bow to the group. Half a beer in, they gushed at how good her Japanese was even though this was an obvious lie. Along with the young teacher who'd invited her (Hatakeyama-sensei—she'd looked up his name while waiting) was an older male English teacher (Terazono-sensei), one of the rare female teachers, whose voice was throaty friendly (Suzuki-sensei), and a tall man with a bowl haircut (Chiba-sensei).

"You drink, Protagonist-sensei?" Hatakeyama pulled out a chair for her, between him and Terazono. Suzuki and Chiba hovered at the edges, glasses raised.

Japanese beer comes in enormous jugs with thick handles and is drunk quickly, each gulp followed by an appreciative thirst-quenched gasp. Our protagonist had considerable practice at this. The teachers watched her down the glass with a cheer, and quickly followed suit.

On the other side of the bar an ancient-looking woman in a white apron and floral headscarf gestured and commented and laughed. The teachers joined in, and even though our protagonist had no idea what they were saying she assumed it was probably about the Australian girl and the amount of beer she could put away.

Terazono ordered food and *nihonshu*, Japanese wine. The old woman's equally wizened husband appeared, began slicing thin slivers of *sashimi*. Where she was smiling he wore no expression. Deep bags beneath his eyes made his gaze seem smaller, sharper. Heavy lines around his mouth gave him a wooden look, like a marionette.

"You like?" Chiba asked our protagonist as the food was placed in front of her.

The fish was so fresh it dissolved on her tongue, and she couldn't stop making a small sound of appreciation.

"She likes!" Chiba cried. "Fish. Raw fish. Wasabi?"

"*Oiishi!*" Our protagonist looked the old man in the eye as she spoke. Delicious. His wooden-doll face didn't crack, even as the others whooped and cackled. But he nodded and she took that as approval.

For two hours Protagonist-sensei and her colleagues snacked on delicacies she'd have paid top dollar for back in Australia, and drank unlimited beer and *nihonshu*. A lot of what was said she couldn't follow, particularly as the teachers got drunker and found it harder to stay in English. But it didn't matter to her.

Most people would have said it was the beer, or the *nihonshu*, or a combination of both, because at some point in the night our protagonist started to feel a little fuzzy around the edges. But they wouldn't be right because while she was more than willing to acknowledge the effects of alcohol and an airless, smoky room, she didn't think it was that kind of fuzzy.

It was, instead, a tenuous happiness. A belief, a hope, that maybe she'd made the right choice in uprooting her already rootless life and moving across hemispheres and cultures in search of something that might be called home. That might be *hers*.

There is a world in every story. But the story our protagonist was telling herself—which, as I have mentioned, is not the point of this particular tale—created a world so thin it was already being undone.

LINES BETWEEN PROTAGONISTS can be just as thin as the worlds they create. One moment, we can be drinking with co-workers and the next, while in the same room, we're in a different reality entirely.

No TV on the wall playing a garish gameshow about dogs. The Hawaii poster is fresh and unfaded. The young woman behind the bar has only just married the young man beside her. Music crackles in through a radio on the bench. The *nihonshu*, the *sashimi*, the heavy layer of cigarette smoke … they are unchanged.

A protagonist enters the *izakaya*. Thin and pale, she is, perhaps, far older than she looks. A man has been waiting, holds out a seat for her at the bar. Pours *umeshu*, plum wine, and buys fresh *sashimi* and watches it slither between her teeth.

Her lipstick is dark red. She wears modern western-style clothing that the old men in the bar do not approve of. Yet they can't take their eyes off her. They are jealous of her companion now but won't be, by morning.

After she disappears, the town hunts him down, questions him. Where is she? What did he do to her? But he has no memory of her fate. The last thing he remembers is dancing under the light of the stars, in the open field beside the school, and how cold her hands were in his. How warm her lips. How powerless, how weak, he felt beneath them.

Of course, no one believed him. When they finally set him free, many decades after their first and final dance, he returns to the spot. And despite how much it has changed, it's still that field he sees, still that girl he dances with.

Little does he know, she's not there. She doesn't need him. Not anymore.

PROTAGONIST-SENSEI WASN'T FEELING like her usual self. Head spinning, jaw tight, no matter what she did she couldn't get enough oxygen. A hand on her chest seemed to be pushing down, squeezing more than air from her. The life she was building—in this town, this country, this *izakaya*—forced from her lungs. For someone else to breathe.

Later that night, walking home, she wouldn't remember how the drinks ended. Her story of that evening was of smoke and beer and the burst of wasabi up her nose. It was laughing and smiling even when breathlessness clutched at her insides. Drowning in words that meant nothing to her. Bathed in a warm cosy light. And then she was outside, and the air was crisp. And Hatakeyama was asking her something, and it could have been an offer of company—actually it might have been an invitation to lunch the next day. Whichever it was, she talked her way out of it and then she was walking alone.

The quickest route home took her down the poorly lit path beside the school tennis courts. A breeze had begun to roll down from the mountains and brought a hint of colder weather to come. Her light jacket wasn't warm enough.

This time she noticed him. No lights on the path but he was easy to see, as though bathed in the radiance of some invisible moon. As he danced his sneakers and his face mask seemed to glow.

She paused there, at the edge of the wavering threshold. The faintest of songs trickled through. Not the town chime, not the school bell. Something warbling and crackling, a dusty record on a stale machine. His feet, for once, followed the tune.

She took a half-step forward. And suddenly, he wasn't alone.

The girl in his arms was living and dead, weak and waifish, ancient and terrible, ghostly for a moment, but gradually becoming solid. Becoming real.

And those corporeal fingers let go of his, those physical legs stepped away. Left footprints. Over to the edge of the tennis court they walked, stood opposite our protagonist, and held out a hand. Unable to stop herself, she lifted her own in reply. Mirrored across the baseline, the imagined, the creator, trapped by the silent music, the old man weaving slow and oblivious.

And the girl in his arms was her.

As our protagonist danced she looked over her shoulder to the path, the flowers twinkling like stars along its edge. A woman was looking back at her, face obscured, body out of focus.

Our protagonist knew she didn't belong on the tennis

courts but she wasn't sure she belonged out there, either. The grip on her hand was too tight and the threshold too far. As she danced to slow music the woman who had become her—or, perhaps, had always been her—turned and walked away.

Taking any chance of a new life, a new home, a new family, with her.

WHY DO we believe that stories have a beginning? Is it because we need them to end?

To create a satisfying story with a sense of closure and even a little denouement I would need to explain exactly what happened to our protagonist. But I told you, this isn't her story. Whether she's trapped on the tennis court for eternity, or whether she wakes up the next morning on her futon, feeling oddly cold and bereft for no reason, like she's somehow missing a part of her—or many little parts, bite by bite slowly eaten away—is irrelevant. What really matters here, in *this* version of the story, is what happens to all those girls she so blithely invented.

They, at least, get a happy ending. The imagined creatures, the nameless ghosts, from our protagonist they found form. They took as much of her as they could, used it to escape the tennis court, and are now loose in the world. Enjoying lives of their own.

And the old man? He keeps dancing. Always, and for eternity, alone.

MEDIAN

KELLY ROBSON

Originally published in *Reactor Magazine*, March
2024.

Kelly Robson is a Nebula Award winning writer of
Science Fiction, Fantasy, and Horror. She's been a finalist
for many of the major SFF awards, including the
Astounding Award for Best New Writer. Her first short
fiction collection *Alias Space and Other Stories* was
published by Subterranean Press, and she has two books
from Tordotcom Publishing, *Gods, Monsters and the
Lucky Peach* and *High Times in the Low Parliament*.
Kelly consults as a creative futurist for national and
international organizations. She lives in downtown
Toronto with her wife, writer A.M. Dellamonica.

WHEN CARLA'S little car broke down on the highway, she
was in the fast lane, and instead of pulling over to the far side
of the road, she had to stop on the median.

She sat there, jiggling the wheel with one hand and

fiddling the ignition with the other, a hot, low sun glaring through the hatchback's rear glass. Only a few years back, a turn of a key would make an engine cough, and if it didn't, it meant the battery was dead. Or the alternator—something electrical. Now, cars were all electric, even more of a mystery than ever, and she had zero chance of figuring out the problem.

But it didn't matter, really. Dead was dead. She could press the start button all she liked. Nothing happened.

"Now what?" she asked. "Who do I call?"

Carla typed "roadside assistance" into her phone and hit enter. Trucks blasted past, so close the car shook as if grabbed by a fist. She stared at the Google logo until it disappeared, leaving a blank screen, white on white.

It had happened before. Her discount mobile provider was prone to denial of service attacks. But she still had phone service. She texted her sister Francisca in Montreal: *Can you send me the roadside assistance number for the 401?* When no reply came, she tried phoning both her sisters, then her supervisor. All three calls rang straight through to voicemail.

She would have sat there forever, alternating between pressing the button and working through her contact list, but a semi skinned by and clipped off her side mirror. A popping sound. The car pitched back and forth, bouncing on its wheels like a carnival ride. Then another truck took off her door handle.

The rear wheels of her car parted from the asphalt. It bucked once, canting into the oncoming lane. A cement truck hit the edge of the bumper. The whole rear end crunched. The car spun onto the median and slammed into the low concrete barrier.

Carla pulled herself out of the car and fell onto the gravel. She sat there, brushing dirt from her scrubs. It was her Easter pair, festooned with daffodils and tulips.

Someone will stop, she thought. *Someone will come. Someone has already dialed 911.* But nobody stopped. Certainly not the cement truck, which had long since disappeared beyond the highway's distant curve.

She climbed to her feet and waved at an oncoming car. One of its headlights glinted in the sun. The driver turned his head as he passed, mirrored sunglasses square on her, but he didn't slow. The other drivers didn't even look at her. The truck drivers stared straight over her head.

"I'm right here," Carla said, waving her arms.

Gravel and grime studded the skin of her palms and forearms, blood seeping from the abraded skin. She picked a piece of gravel out of her flesh and chucked it at her car. Such a little thing, there on the median; the rear end looked like something had taken a bite out of it. A rear wheel dangled like a broken tooth.

Hands shaking, she dialed 911. Three tries to hit the green button. She turned up the volume and listened to the ringtone, holding the phone to her head with both hands, as if praying.

"911. What is the nature of your emergency?"

"Car accident. I had a car accident. On the 401. West of Milton."

"Please stay on the line."

They put her on hold. Carla leaned her whole weight on her car, digging her elbows into the rusty roof panel. Not a good car, but the best she could afford. A 1995 hatchback with a pair of retrofitted drive trains installed by a guy in Oshawa who Frankensteined cheap cars in his backyard. She'd drained her savings account to buy it, and in two years, its charge range had gone down by half. To get enough juice to do her evening appointments, she had to stop and charge it halfway through her shift, and then charge it again to get home.

"You're a write-off, aren't you?" she asked the car.

When she laid her forehead on her arms, the phone went dead. Maybe she canceled the call by accident, or maybe they hung up on her. In any case, she dialed 911 again and waited.

"911. What is the nature of"

Dead again. The screen protector was cracked, so maybe it was shorting out the screen? She peeled off the pieces and dropped them to the median. Dialed again.

"911. What"

"Hello?" she yelled. "Hello?"

No answer, though service was fine, three of the four bars glowing white. She dialed work.

"This is the office of Care Point Care Services. Our office hours are eight am to four pm, Monday to Friday. Please leave a detailed message including patient name, address, and phone number, and your call will be returned within one business day."

"This is Carla. I've had a car accident. I'm not going to make the rest of my appointments. That's, uh…hang on." Carla fished the printout from her pocket of her scrubs. "Deborah Anders, Karen Gagnon, and David Chan. Can you let them know I won't be there? And I won't be able to do my appointments tomorrow, either. My car is dead. Okay. Thanks."

Because of the staffing shortage, the office was barely covered on weekends. Probably nobody would pick up Carla's message until tomorrow morning, and in the meantime her clients would wait. Deb needed her dinnertime feeding. Her G-tube site was getting painful, the skin around the external bumper pink and swelling. Carla had been treating it for a week with anti-inflammatories and ice. Karen had a colostomy bag that needed emptying before her bath, and Dave was waiting for meds and a toilet transfer. All three needed to be moved from chair to bed. If Carla didn't show up, nobody would get washed, medicated, fed, or toileted. They'd wait, abandoned, wondering if anyone was ever going to come.

Carla tried again to wave down a car, flinging her arms around semaphore-wild. Nobody stopped. Nobody even slowed.

She crawled into the back seat of the hatchback and rooted around. Her coffee was splashed across the dashboard, the red Tim Hortons cup rolling on the gritty floor mat. She carried a big bottle of distilled water in case her patients ran out, but now it was smashed.

Her black Care Point backpack was fine, though.

Bandages, scissors, and sterile swabs. The pair of tweezers she used to pick lint out of Deb's G-tube site. A box of latex gloves and a pack of N95 masks, size small. A blood pressure cuff, finger oximeter, and stethoscope. Plastic bottles of acetaminophen, ibuprofen, and aspirin. Anti-inflammatory gel, antiseptic cream, hand sanitizer. In the outer pocket were her wallet, keys, charge cords, and the bag of cappuccino candies she'd bought on a whim, hoping the caffeine would perk her up between visits.

Carla popped a candy into her mouth and crunched down hard. It splintered and melted into a hunk between her molars. She worried at the candy with her tongue as she pulled up the map on her phone and zoomed in on her location.

Not much detail available, not with the connection problems, but some of the map was preloaded. The highway a double yellow line on a gray background, with a sliver of blue zigzagging across it—a creek or something. Satellite view showed trees and fields. Cars and trucks frozen into specks on the dark gray highway, caught in time by the overhead camera. The median a light gray strip between the eastbound and westbound lanes, like meat in an old sandwich.

If she could cross the highway, she could walk...walk where? To the east was Campbellville, which looked like nothing more than warehouses and parking lots. They'd be empty on a Sunday. Probably wouldn't even have security guards, just rotating cameras behind which might or might not be a pair of human eyes. To the west were residential acreages, but they looked like the kind of places where nobody actually lived—second or third homes for rich people, their empty blue pools pocking the green satellite expanse. But to the northeast was a casino. People would be there, and help.

Her phone rang. Carla nearly dropped it in her eagerness to answer.

"Hello?" she yelled.

"It's my mother." A woman's voice, faint against the roar

of traffic. "She's by herself and she's on the floor. She can't get herself up."

Carla wasn't allowed to exchange phone numbers with clients. Care Point claimed it protected carers' privacy, but really, it kept clients from trying to arrange discount services under the table. A firing offense, so Carla had never broken the rule. How had this one gotten her number?

"Is it Deb Anders?" she asked. "Or Karen Gagnon?"

"Nina Sandhu. She lives at 454 Frobisher Boulevard in Milton."

"I'm sorry but she's not my client. Even if she was, I can't go anywhere right now."

"You're supposed to—" The woman gasped. A horn sounded.

"Are you driving?" Carla asked.

"Yes, I'm trying to get to my mom. But I'm caught in traffic. It'll be an hour and a half, at least. That's why I need you to go there, right now."

"Me? I can't help anyone," said Carla. "I can't even help myself."

"But who else can I ask?"

"Call 911," Carla said. "Tell them she needs a lift assist." She hung up.

North. The casino was on the north side of the highway. She'd have to cross the westbound lanes. Carla swung her legs over the concrete barrier and stood at the edge of the fast lane, trying to judge the speed and distance of the oncoming cars. At this angle, it all looked impossible, the traffic not slowing one bit. Which was strange. Anything a little odd on the highway caused a slowdown—everyone lifting their foot from the accelerator and gawking. She was right there. The hatchback was right there. Why wasn't anyone slowing?

Maybe because their feet weren't on the accelerator. Maybe everyone was using smart cruise control, the cars continually adjusting for optimal speed and distance to keep the traffic flowing.

But if one of the cars pasted her as she tried to run across the highway, then they'd stop. They'd have to.

Problem was, Carla wasn't built for speed, never had been. She could deadlift clients out of bed six times a day, but running? She couldn't remember the last time she'd tried. She didn't have to get across all three lanes at once, though. She could cross the first lane, and stand on the divider line waiting for a gap so she could run across the next. The cars wouldn't hit her if she stood still. Not unless one of them was changing lanes.

She tightened the straps on her backpack and hooked her thumbs in tight, making herself into the smallest possible human bundle. She dug her toes into the gravel, and leaned in, and watched for a gap. There. And there. And there. If she picked the right moment, she'd get across fine. Or maybe the car that hit her would be small, and she would survive.

Her phone rang.

"Hello," she yelled.

A kid's voice: "They're fighting. He's hurting my mom. Again."

"Diego?" she asked. It had to be her nephew—no other kid would call her. But it didn't make sense. Her older sister's family was on vacation in Tulum. Carla was supposed to water their plants tomorrow. "Diego, is that you? This is Tía Carla."

"Can you come?"

It wasn't Diego. "Who is this?" she asked.

"Liam. He's hitting her head."

"Liam," she said. "Get as far away as you can and hide." No idea who this kid was or why he was calling her, but it didn't matter because there was only one answer. "There's nothing you can do. Hide. And call 911." She hung up.

Trying to run across the highway was just stupid. She'd be roadkill a hundred times over. A smear on the asphalt. A human stain.

Maybe she could walk along the median. When the highway curved, the traffic would have to slow down, wouldn't it? Even just a bit, enough to make a difference.

Gravel crunched under her sneakers as she trudged east. Dust and dirt flew in her face, microscopic bits of oil and tar and rubber, aerosolized by the wheels. She reached into her backpack and retrieved an N95 mask.

Mask in place, she protected her eyes with her hand, keeping her gaze low to avoid the worst of the dust. One of her sneakers had blood on the toe—where had that come from? Her arms, she guessed, the road rash. She picked another bit of gravel out of her forearm. Blood fell on her foot, her knee, her thigh. Three drops, then stopped.

She wasn't shocky anymore, at least. Her hands weren't shaking, but she was exhausted. Every step felt like she was going uphill, and the sun on her back was fierce. A long evening shadow stretched in front of her, cool blue against the orange-tinted gravel. Magic hour, that's what photographers called it. When the sun went down, it'd get cold.

Her phone rang.

"Hello?"

A wheezing voice made itself heard over the roar of traffic.

"It feels like I've broken my arm, but I didn't."

"Dave, is that you? David Chan?"

"No. I'm sweating like crazy just sitting here. And my back hurts."

"That sounds like you're having a heart attack," she said.

"Okay, what do I do?"

"You need to go to the hospital. Don't try to drive, it's too dangerous."

"I can call an Uber."

"Good. While you're waiting, get an aspirin. Chew it up and swallow it." She hung up.

As the highway slid into the curve, the median widened into a grassy strip of wasteland. Fresh green sprouted under the mat of last year's growth, coated with salty grime from a season of snowplows.

The curve. She'd thought the traffic might slow around it, but no. If anything, the stream was faster, the cars packed tighter as the evening commute thickened. None of the drivers turned to look at her as they passed. Many were glued to their phones, just passengers in self-driving cars.

Which gave her an idea. If a self-driving car registered her as an obstacle, it would have to stop. And then everyone would have to slow down. It only took one car to make a traffic jam.

She stepped onto the white lane divider, as if on a tightrope. Widened her stance and held her arms out from her sides to make her silhouette more recognizable. *Here is a human person. See?*

The cars aimed themselves in her direction. Side mirrors blitzed past her hip, her shoulder, her head. A truck flashed its lights. It skimmed past, and the suction from eighteen whirling wheels yanked at her flowered scrubs.

She gave it a good long try, standing square to the oncoming sensors, squinting to protect her eyes from the flying grime, but it was no good. She stepped back onto the median.

As Carla trudged east through the curve, a structure appeared in the distance, stained red by the last dregs of sunset. A bridge for an overpass, flanked by the arms of a cloverleaf. This was the intersection on the map, with the Campbellville warehouses to the south and the casino to the north. Good. She couldn't get across the highway, but maybe she could climb off it.

One central bridge column parted the median, weeds growing thick at its base. She ran her hands up and down the concrete. It was smooth. No handholds. And even if she could shinny up—which she couldn't—she'd never be able to haul her ass over the concrete overhang of the bridge deck. An extreme athlete could do it, maybe, but not her.

She called 911 again. This time it didn't even ring. Dead air.

The sun set fast. Headlights turned the world into flashing intersections of night and bright, like the nightclubs she'd gone to with her sisters, back when they were all so young. On the dance floor, she'd lose herself in sensory overload, throwing herself into a bounded world of risk. A curated encounter with the unknown, where she could decide for herself from moment to moment how much danger she wanted to find.

Beyond the overpass, the median widened and dipped. Scrubby bushes grew in the ditch, and a stand of trees forced the two arms of the highway apart.

Her phone rang.

"Hello?" she said.

"Someone just smashed the window of a bank. Queen and Spadina."

"I don't care," said Carla. She hung up.

Far ahead, a long, lithe shadow darted into the glare of headlights. It slid across all three lanes and turned to look at her, pointy ears sticking up from its head like horns. Then it vanished into the trees of the median.

A dog wouldn't attack her, not unless it was rabid. A coyote wouldn't either. All the same, a chill coursed through her, starting at her toes and shivering up her torso to her throat.

Carla hugged herself, and when her phone rang, she dropped it, cracking the screen.

"Hello," she said.

"Is that all you have to say?" An elderly voice. Genderless. Crotchety.

"Hello," she repeated. "What?"

"Aren't you supposed to ask me what the problem is?"

"Okay. What's your problem?" she asked. "Tell me everything."

"When there's a fire alarm I'm supposed to wheel myself into the stairwell and wait on the landing. It's the refuge area, they said. So that's what I did. I've been sitting here for hours now, waiting for someone to come. I can't go up or down, and I can't get back into the hallway. The door's too heavy."

"Did you try calling someone?"

"Why? Are you telling me to call someone who cares?"

"I mean, is there someone in your building who can help?"

"No. You're not supposed to use the elevators during a fire alarm, but next time, you bet that's what I'm going to do. Either that or just sit in my apartment. It's not like there's actually a fire."

"What about your neighbors? Do you have the number of anyone in your building?"

"Aren't you supposed to ask for my address?"

"Why? I can't help you."

"What's that supposed to mean?"

"Did you try banging on the door? Use something hard."

"So you're not sending someone?"

Carla shifted the phone to her other ear and leaned in as if it would help her understand.

"Who do you think you're talking to?" she asked.

"911. Aren't you 911?"

"No. I'm not."

"I guess I got the wrong number. Fine."

"Wait," Carla yelled. "When you get through to 911, can you tell them I'm stranded on the median of the 401 by the Campbellville overpass?"

"Tell them yourself," they said, and hung up.

Ahead, near the trees, headlights caught on something shiny. It flashed in the beams, and the longer Carla watched it, the more it seemed like the flashes were coming in a pattern. Short-short-short. Long-long-long.

She walked toward it, why not? She had to keep moving anyway. It was getting cold, and the last thing she needed was to flirt with hypothermia.

Walking in the bottom of the ditch, the low beams of the headlights pointed straight at her, painful in their brilliance. She had to keep her eyes on her toes to keep from being dazzled. So she didn't notice the wreck until she saw blood pooling on the median.

A four-door sedan, upside down, wheels spinning. A man in the driver's seat, his body pillowed by the airbag. A woman in the other seat, her face plunged through the windshield. Carla got on her knees and shrugged off her backpack. She pulled out the stethoscope and fitted the earpieces tight in her ears. Easy to reach the driver's back, with him collapsed forward. No breath, no heartbeat. She didn't need to check the passenger to know she was gone, too, with her neck twisted, jaw pointing at the sky.

Still on her knees, she dialed 911, hugging herself, chin tucked in tight. The call connected, rang once, and went dead. Carla swiped the phone on the thigh of her scrubs and tried again. When the call didn't connect, she crawled over to look in the back of the car.

Two empty baby seats hung from the back seat. No children anywhere, not lying on the ceiling of the car, not in the dirt and weeds and gravel of the median. Obviously, that meant no kids had been in the car when it crashed. But not far away, under a bush, was a plastic sippy cup. The milk inside smelled cool and fresh, and it wouldn't have if it'd been sitting in the car even for a little while, not when the day had been so hot. Carla stood and looked around, shading her eyes against the glare.

There, at the edge of the median, were two small forms, raccoon-sized and crawling on all fours toward the fast lane. Carla dropped the sippy cup and ran across the ditch, up the slope, and into the dazzle of headlights.

No doubt now, those crawling bundles were children, their cushy diapered bottoms in terry-cloth onesies lit by the flashing lights. Their tiny hands slapped the asphalt, cloth-bootied feet propelling them in a four-point monkey-walk, knees not even hitting the ground.

A truck blasted its horn. Carla screamed and plunged into traffic, reaching for the children with both arms, as if she could envelop the whole highway and scoop them to safety. Cars buffeted her as she dodged across the lanes, grazing her hip, her elbow. Horns bellowed. She stopped on a dashed lane divider, breath rasping, hands clawing at her jaw as the traffic swirled past. Ahead, in the brief spaces between cars, the children humped over the slow lane and onto the shoulder. Their bald heads gleamed in the headlights.

One child turned and smiled at Carla before it disappeared off the far side of the road. A truck bore down on her. Its side-view mirror struck her head, and she fell backward into traffic.

WHEN CARLA CLAWED HERSELF AWAKE, she was at the bottom of the ditch with a new crack in the glass of her phone, three missed calls from unknown numbers, and a text from Francisca in Montreal.

I just got off a double. Gotta get some sleep. Call me tomorrow, ok?

The time stamp showed the text was only ten minutes old. Maybe her sister was still awake.

I'm in trouble, Carla typed. *Been stuck in the middle of the 401 for hours now. No way to get off it. Can't get through to 911.*

She waited. No response.

When you get this, call 911. Tell them there's a fatal car accident on the median of the 401, near the Campbellville overpass.

Then she tried 911 again, just in case. The call didn't connect. But there would be at least one phone in the wreck, likely two, and one of them would work.

She walked back to the sedan and got on her knees. Reaching around the driver, she shone her phone light into the depths of the interior, but couldn't see much, not with the airbag in the way. No way to reach around the driver, either— her arms weren't long enough. But she could try to wrench the door open, pull the driver out.

It wasn't the first time she'd touched a dead person, not even the first time that week. One of her clients was a late-stage cancer patient with no mobility. He should have been in the hospital but was refusing to go. She'd arrived for his evening appointment to find him mouth open like a baby bird, staring at the ceiling and gasping his final breaths.

No matter how hard Carla pulled, she couldn't get the dead man out of the driver's seat—the airbag was trapping his thighs. Carla got the scissors from her backpack, tried to cut through the tough reinforced plastic, but they wouldn't bite. So she got in close, leaning over the dead man, pressing the bloody bag tight. With the scissors in her fist like a dagger, she slammed the point down on the plastic over and over until it deflated with a hiss. Then she dragged the man out of his seat and lay him on the median with his hands crossed over his chest.

On the underside of the dashboard lay an iPhone, a photo of two bald, grinning toddlers on the lock screen. She swiped at it until the emergency call screen surfaced.

"911?" said a woman. Carla was too relieved to notice the interrogative tone.

"I'm on the median of the 401 by the Campbellville overpass. Two people are dead. And there were two children. I can't find the children."

"No," said the woman. "That's not it. There's been an accident at the Bombay Grill. 370 Pearson Street. In Mississauga. One of the cars came through my window."

"Is anyone hurt?" Carla asked.

"The driver is bleeding from her head. She's walking around, though. Yelling at the guy who wrecked her car."

"Tell her to sit before she falls down."

"Okay." Voices in the background. *Come in and sit down,* said the woman. *911 says you have to sit down. No, you have to sit. Sit. Radha, get her a towel and a cup of chai.* "Yes, she's sitting now."

"Are you calling from the restaurant?"

"Yes, the Bombay Grill is my business."

"Do you have a pen?"

"I do."

"I need you to call 911 and report a car accident on the 401, on the median by the Campbellville overpass. Two fatalities and two missing children. Would you do that for me?"

"But aren't you 911?"

"No, I'm really not. I need your help."

"Of course. I'll call right away."

"Thanks." Carla clung to the dead man's phone with both hands, reluctant to hang up. Sirens sounded in the background.

"There's the fire truck," said the woman. "Will you be okay?"

"I'm not sure," said Carla. "I really don't know."

When she hung up, the night seemed darker than before, the headlights dimmer. The wheels of the upended car were still spinning, slowly.

If she could find the dead woman's phone, she could use it to try 911 again, but it wouldn't work. Nobody would come. Nobody would help. She was alone. One faint point on the map of chaos.

Carla sat beside the dead man and brushed the hair off his forehead with gentle fingers. His eyes stared. She could close his eyes, but without something to weigh down the eyelids, they'd keep sliding open. When people placed coins over the eyes of the dead, it wasn't to pay the ferryman, they did it to keep their illusions. A dead person with closed eyes seemed to be sleeping peacefully, even if their jaw was gaping. A dead person with open eyes wasn't a person. It was a thing.

She found two pebbles, cold and smooth. She closed the man's eyes and gently placed them on his eyelids.

A shadow moved through the trees. The dog was back, likely attracted by the scent of blood. Carla climbed to her feet, stiff and awkward, and put her body between the dog and the car. She clapped her hands.

"Go away," she yelled. "Get out of here."

She threw a rock at the dog. Bad aim. Its head swiveled on a long neck, then another head, and another. Not one dog, but three, though only one body was visible. And not like any kind of animal she'd ever seen. Flat heads, eyes nearly level with their noses. Wide grinning mouths and impossibly sharp ears.

Carla put the dead man's phone in her pocket. She raked both hands though the gravel. Then her phone rang. She flung the gravel at the dogs and snatched at the phone.

"Hello," she yelled.

"Is this 911?" An elderly man.

"No." All these people thought she could help them; she could almost laugh. "What's your problem?"

"I seem to be trapped. In my apartment. It's been days and days and nobody's come. I've been waiting."

His voice had the light, childish cadence of dementia. Carla had heard it many times. It could be frustrating to deal with, but Carla always made an effort to be patient. And right now, it felt good to talk to someone.

"That sounds really awful," she said. "What are you waiting for?"

"To go. I'm waiting to go."

"Go where?"

"The place you're supposed to go, when you're dead."

"Oh," she said. She expected him to say he was waiting for his mother to pick him up from school, or for some long-dead spouse to take him home. Dementia patients were usually anxious to go somewhere, desperate for someone to deliver them from disorder. But he didn't sound disordered. He sounded nice.

"I was hoping you'd tell me what I'm supposed to do," he said.

The dog walked toward her, heads low, crouching as if stalking her. It still looked like one dog with three heads. But that couldn't be, could it?

"I'm sorry," Carla said. "I'm not sure how I can help."

"If you can't, who will?"

Family, usually. It almost always fell to family members. Even if a client got three home care visits per day, it was never enough. Family had to pick up the slack. Who else?

"You haven't been living alone, have you?" she asked. "Do you have someone caring for you?"

"Oh, yes, I did, until I died. And now there's nobody. What do you think I should do?"

Call 911, Carla thought. The ultimate answer, the last-ditch option—call 911 and beg for help. Wasn't that what she'd been trying to do for hours, find someone, anyone to help her? Someone who couldn't deny her, put her off. And everyone she'd talked to, they wanted the same.

"If you're dead," Carla said slowly, "I think you should get into bed, cover yourself up warm and cozy, and remember all the good things in your life. Try to go to sleep."

The dog was belly-crawling toward her now. Snaky necks extending from one thick-muscled torso, tongues lolling.

"I can do that," he said. "Thank you."

"You're welcome."

Carla slid the phone into her pocket and reached out to

pet the dog. Those protrusions on either side of the heads weren't ears after all, but horns, sharp enough to draw blood.

"Good boy," she said. "Good dog."

She sat in the dirt and weeds of the median with the dog's heads in her lap. Its ears were wizened carbuncles, tortured masses of scar tissue. Carla caressed them gently with both hands and the dog's eyes narrowed. It kicked up one hind foot to show her its belly.

Her phone rang. She kept one hand on the dog as she answered it.

"911," she said. "How can I help you?"

GHOST STORY

ZACHARIAH CLAYPOLE WHITE

Originally published in *Sand Hills Literary Magazine* *#48*.

Zachariah Claypole White is a Philadelphia-based writer and educator, originally from North Carolina. He holds a BA from Oberlin College and an MFA from Sarah Lawrence College, where he was a Jane Cooper Poetry Fellow. His poetry and fiction have appeared in, or are forthcoming from, **Bourbon Penn, Prairie Schooner, Strange Horizons,** and **The Rumpus,** amongst others. Zachariah has received support from the *Kenyon Review* Writers Workshop, *Writer's Digest,* and Disquiet International. His awards include *Flying South's* poetry prize as well as two nominations for the Best of the Net and one for a Pushcart Prize. Zachariah teaches at the Community College of Philadelphia, Saint Joseph's University, and the Writing Institute at Sarah Lawrence College. You can find more of his work at zachariahclaypolewhite.com.

IN THE GHOST STORY, a boy will vanish.

As the story spreads and is repeated, first by those who searched for the boy and then by their neighbors, and then by neighbors of the neighbors, the circumstances will change. The boy will disappear from the forest, from a pharmacy, from the front steps of his house. He will have been playing unsupervised; he will have been holding his mother's hand moments earlier.

SOME THINGS WILL NOT CHANGE, or at least, in no way that is substantial to the ghost story.

The boy will vanish in winter. His footprints in the snow will lead search parties away from the town and into the trees.

It will be a Sunday morning. The neighbors will cling to this fact above all others: question why the boy and his mother were not in church. They will mention this again, with knowing glances, later in the ghost story.

The boy will not be found. Or at least not in a manner which satisfies the ghost story.

THE BOY'S name will be Henry, Percy, or Dylan.

Once the alarm is raised, and it becomes apparent that Henry/Percy/Dylan has not simply wandered off (as young boys do), search parties will form. Most will be directed by the sheriff and mayor. They will comb through the wilderness surrounding the town in orderly lines, calling Henry/Percy/Dylan's name.

The town's children will also search. They will traipse through the old playground; visit treehouses long abandoned to black widows. They will hunt through their parents' basements, attics, and closets. They will discover vintage

Playboy magazines, barely-worn work boots, and unlocked gun safes.

The children will find the first clue: a Nike/Adidas/Chuck Taylor sneaker, half submerged in the town's single creek. Police dogs, followed by cadaver dogs, will sniff through the surrounding forest. Neighbors will walk up and down the banks. There will be talk of divers, but the creek is shallow, more ice and gravel than water. Divers will not be needed.

The search will continue for five days. More articles of clothing will be found: a blue sweater with the right sleeve ripped away; a second Nike/Adidas/Chuck Taylor sneaker. On the third day, blood will be found at the foot of a pine. And a tooth will be unearthed. And then another.

And then another.

DNA testing will prove inconclusive.

As the search continues, men will become lost in the woods. They will claim that the trees began to change, to grow and contort into impossible shapes. Each will say that they found themselves in a vine-wrapped clearing. And they will remember that, in the center of the glade, they saw a pillar of blackest stone, so dark—they will say—it was as if a starless night had dripped down and calcified into rock.

When these men find their way back, they will swear that it took days to escape the forest. Though, in the ghost story, they will have only been missing for a matter of hours. They will hyperventilate as they speak, grasp Styrofoam cups in shaking hands.

"The pillar reached up past the trees," they will say. "Past the sky itself. It grew down too. Oh, yes. Into the earth." They will pause, struggling against their own words and memories. "Its roots squirmed like rats' tails across our boots."

The men will maintain, despite questioning from friends, spouses, and detectives, that they were perfectly sober. That they know these woods like the hands of their wives, and that they have never seen the clearing before.

Of course, in the ghost story, no such place will ever be found.

Dogs too will act strangely in the forest: clawing at trees and rocks, charging into thickets with rage in their eyes and foam on their teeth. One dog will, without warning, attack its handler. The officer will require eighteen stitches in his right hand and forearm. He will ultimately lose his ring/index finger/thumb. He will not rejoin the search.

THERE ARE three endings to the ghost story. Any of them could be true.

In the first ending, a man will claim to have seen the boy in a clearing that cannot exist. Black roots grew into his ears and nose, through the gaps that were his eyes. The would-be-rescuer will say that he heard Henry/Percy/Dylan calling out for help but when he approached, the boy began to laugh. The man will say that it was not the Henry/Percy/Dylan laughing, but rather the bloody flowers sprouting through his lips.

In this ending the search will eventually be called off. Police will ignore the impossible accounts; dismiss them as tweaker fantasies or the last attempts at infamy from a dying southern town. The TV crews will leave, the reporters will move on to other towns with other missing boys.

Slowly, perhaps unconsciously, this town will gather cans of gasoline. Neighbors will stare at their calendars; mark the days till summer and its droughts. Then, with matches in hand, they will turn to their windows and look at the forest.

"Has it always been so close?"

IN THE SECOND ENDING, the boy will return. He will reappear barefoot on the front steps of his mother's house. At first, she and the town will celebrate. The TV crews will leave, the reporters will move on to other towns. But then the neighbors will notice—each morning—a boy's footprints leading to their windows. Some will claim to find muddy tracks leading to their beds, to their children's beds. Though, in the ghost story, this will never be confirmed.

The mother will venture into town less and less. When she does, she will ask if anyone has seen Henry/Percy/Dylan. She will say—again and again—how her boy went missing all those weeks ago. The neighbors will remind her, not unkindly, that her son is safe. That he is at home. The mother will only shake her head.

Then she will stop leaving the house. Some of the neighbors will recall, with knowing glances, how she and Henry/Percy/Dylan never went to church.

In this ending, the mother and the boy will be glimpsed each night through their dining room window. They will stand there, unmoving and unblinking, until the sun rises and sends shadows like black roots, writhing across their skin.

In the third ending, the children will find Henry/Percy/Dylan. Or rather they will find his blood in the basement of an uncle/family friend/beloved teacher. Testing will be conducted and unlike the evidence in the woods, DNA will match this to the missing boy.

The uncle/family friend/beloved teacher will be arrested but released soon after. He will never be charged. It's only blood, after all. No body will be found. The TV crews will leave, the reporters will move on to other towns with other missing boys.

In this ending the ghost story will not truly be a ghost story.

But the mother will remember. Every night she will sit on her porch and stare into the forest. She will call to its impossible clearings and black roots, beckoning them closer, towards the town that consumed her son.

NOTABLE STORIES

- *The Sea, Like Glass,* by Ainsley Hawthorn. *Off Topic*
- *Caesura,* by Alice Hatcher. *Reed's Magazine*
- *Hair of the World,* by Aliya Whiteley. *Green Ink Sponsored Write 2024*
- *Their Wings as Powdery As Bones,* by Avra Margariti. *Apex Magazine #147*
- *The Beautiful Thing You Once Were,* by J. Ashley-Smith. *Bourbon Penn #34*
- *The Coalface,* by Jack Klausner. *Fictionable*
- *Way Up in De Middle of De Air,* by Jamie Roballo. *FIYAH #31.*
- *Plunged in the Years,* by Jeffrey Ford. *Conjunctions: 83 / Revenants, The Ghost Issue*
- *Absent Below the Lip,* by Charles Wilkinson. *Unquiet Slumbers*
- *Wayback,* by Leslie What. *khōréō 4.2*
- *The Ferryman,* by Lynda E. Rucker. *All the Haunts Be Ours: A Folk Horror Storybook*
- *The Dying Chorus,* by Max D. Stanton. *Cosmic Horror Monthly #46*
- *After We Kill Our Father and Before We Reach the*

Mainland, by Max Franciscovich. *Beneath Ceaseless Skies #416*

- *Brick City, Stick City, Straw City*, by Nika Murphy. *Seize the Press #10*
- *Not All Your Bones Are Yours*, by Plangdi Neple. *FIYAH #30*
- *Warmth*, by Seán Padraic Birnie. *Interzone #299*
- *Shepherd Not Sheep*, by Simon Strantzas. *Bourbon Penn #32*
- *The Limner Wrings His Hands*, by Vajra Chandrasekera. *Deep Dream: Science Fiction Exploring the Future of Art*
- *Dissection of a Mermaid*, by Wailana Kalama. *Flash Fiction Online*
- *Paraffin*, by Will VanDenBerg. *hex literary*

COPYRIGHT ACKNOWLEDGEMENTS

"Alabama Circus Punk" by Thomas Ha. Copyright © 2024 Thomas Ha. First published in *ergot*. Reprinted by permission of the author.

"Our Best Selves" by Hiron Ennes. Copyright © 2024 Hiron Ennes. First published in *Weird Horror #9*. Reprinted by permission of the author.

"Black Water" by Seán Padraic Birnie. Copyright © 2024 Seán Padraic Birnie. First published in *Weird Horror #9*. Reprinted by permission of the author.

"A Woman's Place is in The Haunted Home" by Charlotte Tierney. Copyright © 2024 Charlotte Tierney. First published in *Conjunctions: 83 / Revenants, The Ghost Issue*. Reprinted by permission of the author.

"Ruminants" by Kay Chronister. Copyright © 2024 Kay Chronister. First published in *The Dark #113* Reprinted by permission of the author.

"The Last Lucid Day" by Dominique Dickey. Copyright ©

ABOUT THE EDITOR

Michael Kelly is the former Series Editor for the *Year's Best Weird Fiction*. He's a World Fantasy Award, Shirley Jackson Award, and British Fantasy Award-winning editor. His fiction has appeared in a number of journals and anthologies, including *Best New Horror, Black Static, Nightmare Magazine, The Dark,* and *The Year's Best Dark Fantasy & Horror;* and has been previously collected in *Scratching the Surface, Undertow & Other Laments,* and *All the Things We Never See.* He is the owner and Editor-in-Chief of Undertow Publications, and editor of *Weird Horror* magazine.

www.ingramcontent.com/pod-product-compliance
Lightning Source LLC
Chambersburg PA
CBHW030639020726
47493CB00006B/1786